Black Sun

Fury of the Phoenix

I0639375

Daniel Crux

INKWELL BOOKS

Writing-Publishing-Printing

ISBN   978-0-578-70836-2
Library of Congress 2020949256

Published by Inkwell Books LLC
10632 North Scottsdale Road, Unit 695
Scottsdale, AZ 85254
Tel. 480-315-3781
E-mail info@inkwellbooksllc.com
Website www.inkwellbooksllc.com

INKWELL BOOKS
Writing-Publishing-Printing

Acknowledgments

My loving family, who continue to support my dreams even in the most trying of times.

Contents

Upon the twilight of the First Age of Terra, the Age of Progression, a series of great and cataclysmic wars would erupt between its human inhabitance and a mysterious race of invaders from the stars. The consequences of such devastating conflicts were far-reaching. The invaders were eventually defeated and repelled, but in the aftermath of these End Wars, governments would collapse, and humanity would face widespread starvation and extinction.

Thus would begin Terra's Second Age, the Age of Desolation, or, as it is more commonly known, the Thousand Year Darkness.

For seeming eternity, the human race would endure a dark age of utter chaos, a period of everlasting ruin and strife in which only the strongest and most capable survived. Through this desolation, a lone warrior would rise from the shadows. Seeking to reestablish order, this warrior would utilize a combination of hopeful words, what military power he held at his disposal, and most importantly, lessons learned from civilizations past to bring humanity's remnants under his banner.

Though this warrior's crusade would last many lifetimes, the human race, for the first time since its birth, would, at last, become united under a single cause and purpose. From this, order and culture would be revitalized across the ravaged earth, giving rise to a power that would rule over all, the Terran Empire.

With the Empire's birth and the warrior's coronation as the first Emperor, human civilization had officially been reborn, thus beginning the Third Age, the Age of Ascension.

But even with this Rebirth of Humanity, Terra remained broken and devastated, possessing few remaining resources to sustain its inhabitance. For humanity's continued survival, the Empire would turn its attention toward the final conquest, Space.

The foundations of this new age are marked solely by humanity's intent of settling its star system. Once space was reached, the Empire's first act was to establish space colonies in geosynchronous orbits around its homeworld. After vast expenditures of funds and manpower, the colonies *would become the agricultural centers of this newborn nation, ending all lingering traces of the Darkness virtually overnight.*

Even so, humanity continued to look to the stars, and soon lunar colonies were also developed for industry. Additional colonization and space exploration would continue unabated, with new settlements established on nearly all planetary bodies in the Sol System, from Mercury to the moons of Neptune.

Mining adventures, agricultural experiments, terraforming projects, and other endeavors were developed upon these colonies. Technologies that would also come to be used upon Terra itself, transforming the planet from a dark wasteland into a reborn blue and fertile world. New natural resources would also be discovered throughout, further nourishing humanity's growing empire as it began to transcend the borders of the Sol System.

Not long after the establishment of these colonies did Terran scientists finally make the discovery of faster than light travel in the form of the Arc Engine. With this breakthrough, humanity became further enamored with exploring the universe around them and expanding their reach throughout, establishing their beloved Empire's rule to the very borders of the galaxy. Seemingly, their only hindrance would be the various "alien" civilizations, which would inevitably seek to impede their progress, perhaps even attempt to subjugate them as those invaders had so long ago.

With that in mind, the Emperor would declare the formation of the Imperial Starfleet, the military arm that would defend humanity from its future enemies. It would not be long before the Imperial fleets and armies became as countless as the stars themselves.

Well into the Age of Ascension's third century, humanity would make first contact with an alien civilization in the further reaches of space. Unexpectedly, this civilization and many following it would turn out to be far more primitive than humanity had come to believe, varying from cave-dwelling races akin to the ancient Neanderthals to some relatively advanced races that were equal to humanity's development in the midst of its First Age.

Even so, fearing the potential threat of these races, the Empire fell upon these worlds with great fervor, conquering in the name of humanity's progress while adapting whatever technology and advancement they found along the way. Not even the more advanced societies were capable of defending themselves against the mighty warships and combat-ready men and women under the Emperor's service. Thus, humanity's dominion would spread vastly and rapidly throughout the Milky Way, challenged only by twelve others of similar power.

And yet even with the rebirth and growth of human civilization, the freedom offered by space also led to the establishment of much darker enterprises. As humanity expanded further into the darkness without end, its ability to maintain order throughout its colonies continued to wane. The equally continued usage of merchant lines to resupply settlements with whatever necessary resources made attractive targets to those who operated outside civilization's law.

Piracy had at last emerged.

Despite every effort to prevent its growth, piracy would soon become abundant throughout the galaxy. Men and women of all races and backgrounds would commit themselves to the dream of vast power and wealth, utilizing knowledge of the space around them to exploit shipping lines and plunder and pillage in reflection of the ancient Terran buccaneers. Amongst that number, the most successful in these endeavors would come to form the infamous Pirate Clans, establishing their dominions over the stars. All while retaining no mercy for those who may oppose them.

It is now the ninth century of humanity's Third Age. The galaxy progresses on as Terra, and the other twelve Galactic Powers struggle and conflict amongst themselves, each vying for complete domination. Throughout, piracy retains its sway, innumerable renegades sailing under the Jolly Roger's shadow.

This is a tale set upon one such band...

Prologue: Flames of Ire

Red Phoenix *Yunnan*-class battleship *Zhang He* Qingdao System

Passively, he observed the destruction, the final destruction of his latest enemy, from the bridge monitor. And indeed, there was much destruction to be had. What had once been a relatively powerful battle fleet – or at least a bold enough one – was now reduced to variously shattered forms of ships and smallcraft, some still noticeably burning. There was no comm chatter now, no calls of defiance as when the fighting had started, and certainly, no desperate offers of surrender as the fighting continued. Only the ubiquitous silence of the void, coupled with the lifeless remainders of a once boisterous armada. All under the observance of another, far more intact fleet of ships, which bore the emblem of a crimson, flame trailing bird upon their black and red hulls.

And so, he reflected, was the ultimate fate of the so-called Free Qingdao Starfleet. No, he corrected himself. So was the ultimate fate of any and all who dared defy his clan. Especially those who dared attempt to remove themselves from its protection and authority altogether.

Admittedly it wasn't the most pleasant assignment he had been given, butchering a vastly inferior force of would-be revolutionaries. Still, it had to be done, and it was his to do regardless. He was, among other things, an executioner. His responsibility was to dispense with all threats both without and within the clan, and that included non-compliant star systems and their agitators. After all, too many ancient civilizations had fallen due to internal strife, namely when one part of the whole decided it did not wish to be part of the whole anymore. He had no desire to see his clan become one such civilization, and though it was presently in no real danger of fragmenting, even the most minor of infections, if left unattended, could become the most grievous and festering of ailments. And that was more or less what he had done there, burning out the infection before it could spread through the whole before it could truly damage his nation from the inside.

"Shall we commence the second phase of the operation, sir?" the Zhang He's captain inquired to his superior, his voice monotone and entirely focused on carrying out whatever orders were given.

To that, he turned away from the devastation just off his flagship's bow and gazed further ahead, toward the one inhabited planet in the Qingdao System. Though it appeared innocuous enough from his perspective, he had a feeling that, on the surface of Qingdao, the entirety of its populace was now staring up at the sky and stars beyond. Watching and waiting to see what their defiance, as well as their defenders and liberators' inability to stand the tide, would truly cost them.

After a moment of consideration, however, he shook his head minutely. "There is no need," he answered, causing more than one held breath to be let out around the bridge. "They understand their folly."

The captain merely nodded. "As you wish, sire," he answered, standing by to await his liege's following orders.

"Receiving new signal," the communications officer reported, causing both his and the captain's eyes to shift. "It's from Penglai."

Frowning somewhat, he did not need to hear who was the source of that signal. He already knew. In fact, he had been waiting for it.

"I'll take it myself," he said as he rose from his chair. "Have the fleet remain on standby until then."

"Yes, sir," the captain answered, retaking the center chair.

Without another word, he made his way into the turbolift, the doors closing behind him, already anticipating what he was about to hear from his homeworld.

Within minutes he had reached his private quarters aboard the *Zhang He*, the doors shifting open to allow him inside. Without wasting any time or unnecessary movement, he came to a specific area of the main space, then kneeled. No sooner had he assumed this position did the holographic generator flicker active, projecting a single image. That of a long, dark-haired woman dressed in an ornate, flowing black and red gown, her exterior calm yet her gaze of unquestioned authority and equal intensity. As usual, he bit back the temptation to look up, even as he felt the power of her eyes fall upon him.

"My Lady," he started. "It is done. Qingdao is pacified."

"I trust you ensured they understood the price of brazenness," she remarked.

"Yes," he said succinctly, reneging from the fact he had not carried out the second part of the task given unto him. Not that he needed to.

"Very well," she stated, resolving that it was of no concern. So long as the inhabitants of Qingdao *truly* understood and made no further attempts at secession, she need not waste any additional thought on the matter. Instead, she moved straight to the point.

"I have a new task for you," she indirectly commanded. "You are to carry out their sentence. Immediately, and with finality."

Somehow managing not to frown, lest the one before him detect such action, he simply inquired. "Then the deliberations are over..."

"No," she responded with clear dissatisfaction. "Unfortunately, the deliberations are ongoing, but unilateral action shall be taken regardless."

He only felt her eyes focus further upon him, searching for any sign of hesitance.

"I trust you will see this through?" she challenged as though to probe even deeper.

Only then did he look up to meet his lady's gaze. His own as cold and resolved as it had been when he had seen the Qingdao fleet's destruction. And many, many others before.

"Yes, my Lady," he answered with complete resolution. "Your judgment shall be carried out."

Nodding in apparent satisfaction, her gaze softened somewhat. Fully assured that her executioner would indeed fulfill his new task. "Return to Penglai," she commanded further. "For this, you will need as many forces as can be provided. And I will wish to hear of your strategy, of course."

"Of course," he acknowledged, bowing his head once more. "I shall return immediately."

With one final nod, the holographic image disseminated, the space returning to its prior tranquility. And though he stood, the cold resoluteness within his eyes remained. He had been given his newest task, and he would see it through. As he had many, many others.

——————————— ———————————

Turbolift doors opening once more, he reentered the *Zhang He's* bridge with the force of a meteor. Instantly did the captain all but leap out of his chair, already knowing that his liege had been given his latest mission.

"Your orders, sir?"

Retaking his chair, he paused for only a small moment as though in lingering consideration. "Take us home, Captain," he commanded. "There is much work to be done."

Though visibly unsure, the captain nonetheless carried out the given command. "Set course for Penglai," he ordered, the helmsman already bringing the ship about. "Maximum arc."

As the fleet turned away from Qingdao, he continued to muse silently to himself. Once more, the work would be less than pleasant. Compared to the assignment he had just completed, this one would be far more difficult, to say the absolute least. The enemy he would soon fight was not to be taken lightly at any point, even if one discounted their most recent accomplishments. He understood that with absolution.

Regardless, his task was given, and his path was set. One way or another, he would see it through to its end. Morganna Flint's legacy would be left unclaimed, the final remnants of the Gold Dragon eliminated. Jonathan and Alexander Flint would die by his hand.

The hand, the *talon*, of the Red Phoenix.

"So shall it be," he declared as the *Zhang He* entered arcspace, his mind already formulating plans against the Golden Queen's heirs.

Black Sun
Fury of the Phoenix

Chapter I: In Tempore Pacis

Clymene Beach
Calydon, Atalanta

It was nearing evening as the local sun set toward the east and the second moon began to rise as though to replace it. The corresponding tide was also shifting, Jon noticed, the waves coming in faster and with a greater reach onto the shore. Not that it was a concern to him, as he was seated well away from the shoreline and otherwise in no danger of being drawn out into the Calydon Sea. And even then, he likely wouldn't be out there for much longer anyway.

He had been going out to that part of the beach, which for some reason had remained unnoticed to the present since he and the other Flint Pirates had arrived on Atalanta just over three weeks prior. With the Dreyfus affair all but ancient history and the crews' pockets still filled with their latest acquisitions, it hadn't taken much effort for them to gain their much needed respite, as well as live their downtime to the fullest simultaneously. Jon certainly partook in this with the rest, but now and then, he found himself in need of some brief solitude and contemplation, which was why he was where he was now. With nothing but the crashing of waves and the ever darkening sky before him, though he knew that wouldn't last for very long.

Within moments, his ears picked up the sounds of movements, specifically bare feet against the sand and the gentle swaying of cloth against the wind. Naturally, he didn't need to look up to see who was approaching him; there were only a select number of people that he allowed to do so without getting defensive, and this one had remained with him since their arrival. After all, she was his woman, as many had since recognized.

Continuing to move slowly and serenely as not to disturb the overall tranquility, Lorelei couldn't help but allow a bemused smile to come over her lips as she came up to her captain. Dressed in a dark blue bathing suit with an accompanying sarong around her waist, she fit the beachside setting as well as Jon, who was adorned with a simple white shirt and loose trousers. As she stopped and slowly sat next to him, Jon did not look up. Not that Lorelei minded as she turned to gaze out toward the sunset.

"It still bothers you, doesn't it?" she queried without turning away from the horizon. "All that has occurred, all that you have gone through, since Aurora."

"In a way," Jon admitted with a slight nod, his voice as distant as his eye. "As well as how much further we still have to go." It was only then that he looked down a little, his gaze glancing over the sweeping waves. "It's nearing two years since then, and we've come so far. And yet…" His frown deepened. "And yet it feels as though the journey is still just beginning."

"But it is," Lorelei assuaged, intertwining her hand with his as her smile took on a warmer, reassuring note. "There are still five Babels to reach before Arcadia, and you've only just begun your efforts toward reviving the Gold Dragon."

"Yes," Jon responded, once again allowing some of his inner turmoil to show through his usual impassiveness. Once upon a time, he would have only done such around his brother. Now, however, he was doing it around her more and more, and he still wasn't quite sure how he felt about that.

"Five more Babels," he found himself repeating. "And the legacy of the most powerful woman in the universe." A wry smile came over his lips then. "We may really have all of eternity before us with either."

Lorelei laughed a little at the description. "All great labors feel that way at the start, Captain," she continued to assure, now leaning against him. "If they could be completed so quickly and so easily, then anyone would be able to do as such."

"I suppose," Jon responded, wrapping his arm around her waist, drawing her closer to him. He felt some additional uncertainty from the act, but he didn't concentrate on it. Instead, he chose to enjoy the moment, having the woman that meant so much to him by his side.

"We will both gain what we seek, Captain," she now spoke in a near murmur, all but directly into Jon's ear. "We will reach Arcadia, and the Gold Dragon will be revived, in time." Once again, did she feel her captain relax. Both with her words and her touch, much to her satisfaction. "Until then, however, you need only enjoy the journey. And all else we find along the way."

This time it was Jon who smiled knowingly. "Somehow, I don't think you would have felt that way if Nathanial North were your captain," he posited, mentioning her original choice to command the *U-7501*.

"Heh," Lorelei exclaimed, again bemusedly. Mentioning another man, especially the one that had betrayed her, would have potentially ruined the moment in another setting, but she knew what the elder

Flint meant. Alongside, he seemed to misunderstand.

"Nathanial North would have been many things to me," Lorelei replied with minor correction. "An associate, a partner-in-crime, a benefactor, perhaps even a friend on some level." Her smile grew even further as she continued. "However, he would never have been my captain, as I never intended that for myself, once again, until I met you."

Jon, despite everything, found himself matching her smile. Indeed he had heard that line from her much as of late. How Lorelei had intended none of this, and so much more, until Jonathan Flint had entered in with that single beam pistol shot. How the captain and crew she would have helmed the *U-7501* would have been assets and a means to an end, and little else to her.

Not that he had been much different from North, he admitted to himself. In the not so distant beginning, he had only intended to fulfill his accord with her and bring her to Arcadia while using the *Black Sun* as his and Alex's means for greater fortune. He had never intended to rebuild the Gold Dragon or otherwise live up to the great Morganna Flint's image, as he had long thought of those as beyond him, and he certainly hadn't intended to find such deep and meaningful companionship along the way. To face the evils of the galaxy with another standing alongside. Another that was not his younger brother.

Yet, despite his intentions, and hers, it had all fallen into place somehow. Such that they were where they were, enjoying being beside one another in that exact moment, watching the sun and twilight both gradually recede. All while the universe, and especially their fellows, continued elsewhere.

Hotel Clymene
Calydon, Atalanta

Brown eyes hazily opening in a few blinks, the first thing Alex realized was that he was *not* in the same position when he had originally fallen asleep. More specifically, his head was no longer resting against the cushion of the couch in his suite. Rather, it was now resting in the lap that belonged to an all too certain woman, whose blue eyes were the first things Alex found himself staring into upon reawakening. Feeling that same woman slowly stroke his hair with her fingers, Alex could only grin before closing his eyes again.

"Somehow, I don't recall you being here before."

"Sumimasen," Kaguya responded with a small smile, feeling Alex relax that much more as she continued running her fingers through his brilliant red hair. "I came and found you here. Everything simply transpired thereafter."

Alex laughed a little at the facetiousness behind her tone. "Checking to see if I was still breathing? That some local goon squad hadn't taken me out in my sleep?"

That description brought to mind a certain possible outcome in Kaguya's mission with the Flints, but she chose not to dwell on it. As much as that troubled her well into the present, she doubted she would be called upon for that now. Besides, she would rather not ruin the harmony of the moment, among other things.

"Something like that," Kaguya responded before reaching down to stroke Alex's cheek, to which the younger Flint reached up and momentarily pressed his hand against hers.

"What time is it?" he asked, not wanting to open his eyes again, at least just yet.

"Almost nightfall," Kaguya answered, taking on a knowing expression. "You've clearly been asleep for some time."

"I was out most of the morning with Jon and a few others. Apparently, I overextended myself," Alex responded. "You?"

"Same, only with Anna and other female members of the crew," Kaguya acknowledged.

Alex paused for a moment. "Lorelei?"

For once, Kaguya did not inwardly flinch at the mention of that name. "No psionic episodes this time," she answered, again doing her best not to ruin the mood.

Once more, Alex smiled, this time in amusement. "That's always a good thing. And I suppose no Pisceans have shown up either."

"Indeed," Kaguya allowed herself a light laugh. "It still feels so strange."

"Indeed," Alex repeated in agreement. Not that they hadn't had any prior downtime between raids and galaxy-ending events, but such breaks were becoming too few and far between. Even after the last few weeks there on Atalanta, such peace and ease still felt so foreign.

Alex couldn't complain too much, and he knew Kaguya couldn't either. They may not have moments like these as often as either of them would have liked, but they still managed to have them all the same.

"It's nearing *bangohan*," Kaguya spoke softly, having returned to stroking Alex's hair and face with her serene touch. "I'm sure the others will want us to join them."

"They can wait," Alex countered, taking her hand. Somewhat daringly, he brought it to his lips and placed a light kiss on her pulse point. The already present red tinge on Kaguya's face deepened.

"If we show up, we show up," Alex continued, unable to keep from smirking at his handiwork, as well as their current state of affairs. "Otherwise, it's not like the universe is going to implode without us there."

Again Kaguya let out a light, quiet laugh as she discreetly slipped her hand behind Alex's head.

"You never know," she responded in a lighthearted whisper. "Especially with our present record."

Nonetheless, she lifted Alex's head, planting her kiss on a more traditional area. Alex's eyes widen a fraction in response, which remained so even as she drew away. It hadn't been a very deep kiss, but it was undeniably a daring move on the Dragon Princess's part, especially had others been there to witness it. Fortunately, there weren't.

"Heh," Alex blew out a small breath in comprehension, both at her quip and her responding act. Though still admittedly slow, they moved more and more down their shared path – whatever it truly was – with each passing day, regardless of all that would otherwise stand against them. He could ask no more, and again he had a feeling it was much the same for her.

Thus the pair remained where they were for the foreseeable future. All while night gradually fell upon Atalanta.

The Parthenopeus Club
Calydon, Atalanta

"Here we are, ladies and gentlemen," the very well proportioned, bikini topped Lyran waitress announced as she brought over a hover tray of exquisite appearing food for the waiting party. "Two fish and chips, one po'boy, one cubano…"

She then flashed a hinting smile toward her final customer. "And conch chowder for you, sir," her smile turned into a full grin as she deliberately leaned over for that customer to gain a good view of her cleavage.

"Thank you," Davis replied with an anticipating smile of his own as the waitress moved back up again, all the while ignoring the eye rolls from three of the other table guests. He also did well to note the additional slip of parchment under his dish, which had a specific time, "the usual place" and a heart drawn around the message. "I've been dying for this all day."

The waitress's smile only deepened. "I'm sure you have, sir," she responded rather slyly before turning toward another table.

As with Anna and Boss, Cheney looked all too ready to gag. "Would it be poor table etiquette for me to throw up? Or should I wait until dessert?"

"Seriously, what do you do to these women?" Boss couldn't help but exclaim in exasperation.

"Wouldn't you like to know," Davis responded all too sweetly before taking a spoonful of conch chowder and bringing it to his mouth, visibly and purposely savoring it. Again the rest of the table, save for Braun, who was more interested in his Cubano, looked nauseated.

Somehow managing not to shake her head, Anna took a bite of her po'boy and concentrated on keeping the bile down while chewing the bread and shrimp, or whatever appropriately fried species of crustacean had been used for the sandwich's filling. She should have been long used to it by now, but it still irritated her to no end. How could a sleazy bastard such as Howell Davis be so popular?

Well, maybe not that sleazy... Anna once again found herself admitting, as she had off and on since their arrival to Atalanta. For all of her disdain toward the *Sun's* helmsman, she could not stop recalling that one place and time on Orpheus. When, in what had been her most desperate hour to the present, that same man put aside his usual bravado and Lady Killer image and came to her side with helpful words and reassurance. Pulling her back from the brink and keeping her focused, both in regard to herself and toward what she had set out to do.

Even now, she remembered the sheer force behind his gaze during that time. As though she were looking into the eyes of another...

"Anyway," Boss spoke up, effectively and inadvertently snapping Anna out of her recollection. "I have to say this has been a pretty good rest. Makes you almost not want to go back out there again."

"I'll say," Davis agreed sweetly before taking another mouthful of chowder. This time the others ignored him, albeit with some visible effort.

"Eh, it's all well and good, but eventually it's back to work," Cheney commented, crunching his local deep-fried fish audibly as he thought out loud. "Wouldn't do well for us to settle down on a planet like this anyway. Just farmland and vacation spots."

Boss grimaced at that idea. "I joined Starfleet just to get away from the former," she espoused. "Of course, that was a long time ago."

"A lot of things are like that, yes," Braun, at last, entered into the discussion, as though to reemphasize his position among the "young'uns". "Myself, while I certainly enjoyed my time here, there's still much of the galaxy out there to explore."

Davis laughed. "Ah yes, our resident saucerhead," the helmsman lightly chided, using the slang term for the modern age explorer. "Going where no one has been prior and all that."

Braun merely shrugged. "As I said, there's still much of the galaxy that remains uncharted, Mister Davis," he responded without offense. "And there's still our main mission..."

"Yes," Anna nodded, the group easily recalling Arcadia. "I don't suppose, by any chance, the third Babel has been identified yet."

"Not yet, no," Braun admitted. "Though I imagine it won't be too far out in the future. Not that the Circumgressus functions on any identifiable timetable."

15

"Yeah, funny that," Davis responded lightly. Sometimes he wondered if the Circumgressus was drawing out the Babel locations on purpose. If so, he had no idea what it was, though the Flints had plenty else to do in the meantime. "We'll just have to 'settle' for more pillage and plunder and having our downtime in places like this."

"Here here," Boss agreed for the rest. "Of course, that assumes nothing else will happen to us along the way."

A general sigh passed around the table, recalling all too recent events. First was Ephesus, of course, and then the whole ordeal with the Black Moon, and now most recently the Dreyfus-Baranov War and all the conspiracy around Nyx and the Tartarus Nebula. And it was only nearing two years since the Flint Pirates had reformed in the first place.

"It will be alright," Anna assured before anyone could dwell too much on their not so distant history. "So long as we have a tall ship and a star to steer her by, we'll make it through as we have already."

"Heh, you sound like the Captain," Boss chuckled, once more finding herself unable to disagree. She raised her tankard, causing the rest to do the same. "To the wheel's kick, the wind's song, the white sail's shaking…"

"The grey mist on the sea's face and the grey dawn breaking," Davis finished the recitation, causing Anna and Cheney to look on him with raised eyebrows. "What? Hasn't everyone read that poem?"

Suppressing a grin, Boss at last declared. "Let all those things be before us, no matter where we may sail!"

"Cheers!" the other four responded before each taking a swig.

Hotel Clymene
Calydon, Atalanta

"By the Gold Face, this boy must weigh a whole metric ton!" Apache let out as he and Gran lugged a very disheveled Kaiser into the designated hotel room. The strain on the Aquilan healer very much apparent. "How much grog did he have in this 'contest' anyway!?"

"I wouldn't know," Gran managed to force out through her efforts. "But it was enough to outdo the entire tavern."

"Figures," Apache responded as he and the Lyran communications officer drug their Herculean charge to a nearby couch. Without even considering whether or not it would support said charge, the pair struggled to place Kaiser, who may or may not have been conscious, onto it, just managing to lay him out comfortably. "On the plus side, he's sure to have one galaxy-sized hangover this coming morning."

"Eh, I wouldn't be too sure," Gran uttered as she knelt beside the Herculean, running a hand across his face. Between that and what her auditory senses were picking up, she could "see" that Kaiser had already fallen to sleep, seemingly at relative peace. She couldn't help but smile. "His alcohol tolerance *almost* rivals Anna's, and you know how much she can drink."

"Yeah, well, not surprising considering her background," Apache spoke with a grimace, easily recalling the deranged parody of a home and family that their operations officer had come from. He had known other sentients that had turned to grog, and piracy, over much less than what the woman formerly known as Camille Dreyfus had had to deal with back on Orpheus.

"Indeed," Gran nodded in agreement, still running a finger across Kaiser's finely textured face. The latter noticeably relaxing with the act.

Apache shook his head, somehow not being surprised. "If you'd like, I can leave you two alone."

Though it was partly a jest, Gran took it in stride. "No need to be so jealous, Apache," she resounded in a more chiding tone. "I'm sure there are plenty of Aquilan females out there."

"More than enough, and I'm well past that stage of my existence," Apache rejoined, though he was appreciative of what he saw. Gold Face only knew how much the lug had suffered since Lady Flint's passing. If Gran brought him some amount of peace and happiness, then Apache could think of no better medicine. "How long have you two...?"

"Since Ephesus," Gran answered before getting up and moving to sit down in a nearby chair, notably the one directly beside the couch. "Though if you're only seeing it now, I can safely assume no one's noticed."

"More like some have been hoping and praying for it not to happen," Apache spoke out of bemusement now, his eye shifting over Gran's form. Presently dressed in a turquoise and silver print swimsuit and sarong, the Lyran's picturesque figure was very much apparent. "You're quite popular around the ship, you know."

The Lyran laughed rather proudly over that comment. "Yes, well, sorry to all my admirers out there, but some dreams are just not meant to come true."

She faced the sleeping Kaiser, a small but quite warm smile emerging from her lips. "And I don't think I would be any happier with any other man."

"Heh," Apache espoused, a far less noticeable smile extending from the corner of his beak. Even he could not help but feel appreciative toward what he saw between the Lyran woman and the near-snoring lummox.

Good for you, Kaiser, he found himself congratulating his comrade, whom he had known since Jon and Alex had been in diapers. Since the days their illustrious mother, the Lady that they had both loyally served, had held the galaxy in the palm of her hand. *You, out of everyone, have truly earned this.*

Kaiser, naturally, remained in blissful slumber, all while Gran once more reached out and softly stroked his cheek.

———————————————————

Admittedly the view from his hotel suite was still quite spectacular, even though he had been on Atalanta for several weeks alongside the rest of the crew. Not just the small pinpricks of light that made up the city of Calydon, but also the shoreline and ocean beyond, which, thanks to his felinoid eyes, he could depict through the darkness. A beautiful world, to be sure, as well as peaceful and well away from the usual conflict. An ideal respite, even for one such as him.

Sighing, Barbarossa spent a few more minutes looking out over the world outside before turning back into his domain off the *Sun*. It probably wasn't as large or as fancy as other parts of the hotel, but it suited his needs just fine, allowing him to rest and rehabilitate following the strenuous episode with Dreyfus and Baranov. A much-needed vacation, he again was forced to admit, given all that he had endured with the rest of the Flint Pirates. Surely Aslan would not begrudge him of that, even if he was technically spending his leisure time on a world that did not fall under His domain, whose populace had yet to embrace His light. Just as the Giver of Honor had not struck him down for actually going outside his room to enjoy the other sights and forms of hospitality that Atalanta had to offer, which Barbarossa had done more often than initially planned since coming there.

In actuality, Barbarossa knew, or at least felt, that Aslan did not hold it against him in the least. After all, even the Tevret, His most holy book, proclaimed the need of rest and respite for even the most driven of prophets and believers. Instead, the uncertainty that Barbarossa felt within now came from a source on the mortal plain.

One whose mortality, as Barbarossa had learned not long ago, was quite apparent. Indeed, it was quickly becoming a year since his meeting with Yusuf and whole decades since the end of the Third Jihad. Though Barbarossa remained cut off from his homeworld and the Caliphate proper, he doubted very much had changed; that its downward spiral into the waiting arms of Dajjal was continuing even now. All the while, he remained far away, on this godless yet comfortable world, daring to enjoy himself.

The renegade Kapta – one of the refusers to his Caliph's command to return to Leo following the Third Jihad's end – could not help but feel more than a simple pang of guilt. Though he found it doubtful, even in his present melancholy, that his return would affect any positive change whatsoever, the fact was he was comfortable while his people were suffering. His Caliph was increasingly moving toward Aslan's side with each passing day. The rightful Crown Prince was nowhere to be found, itself contrasted with the bastard, degenerate whelp being next in line to take the throne. Instability plagued the Consei, its assemblers and legislatures repeatedly turning upon each other for promises of power, if not salvation. Even the Cihat, the ultimate expression of Aslan's might and will against the evils of the universe, had become stagnant and impotent following the jihad, unable to do much more than ensure that Leo and its possessions remained untainted by its outside enemies. All while the Aslan fearing citizenry could only watch helplessly as their nation gradually crumbled around them.

Taking to a nearby chair, Barbarossa leaned forward to rest his chin over his folded hands in further thought and reflection. Yes, all of Leo was breaking at its foundations. Yes, Prince Ismal remained missing, while his less than desirable brother Prince Mamluk was set to take the throne when Caliph Salman breathed his last. Yes, the turmoil from the Third Jihad's abrupt end had yet to dissipate; in fact, it seemed to have only grown stronger. Yes, Barbarossa was outside all of it, playing pirate under a Terran captain and an

infidel crew, gradually rebuilding the honor he had lost when he had originally refused his Caliph's direct command. And yes, he also admitted, he had since grown accustomed to the latter, such that he was enjoying the "pirate's life," as it were. By the psalms of the Amirs, he was having *fun* with it!

Even so, it still didn't sit right with him, even if there was no real sin to be had, at least in this particular instance. At the same time, Barbarossa remembered that he had his chances to return to Leo. The first had been offered by Captain Flint upon the *U-7501*'s capture, and the second had been provided by Yusuf during their meeting on Nassau. Both times Barbarossa had refused; he would not return to his home until the debt to his Caliph – whether he remained on the mortal plain or since joined Aslan when it happened – was fulfilled, and Barbarossa's honor regained. And, of course, there was his claim to Yusuf that he may be of better service to Leo and Aslan on the outside, away from the internal strife and instability. Had he been wrong in assuming such?

Shaking his head, Barbarossa ultimately decided that it was of no real matter. Once again, there was no sin here, only a selection of choices. No matter what state Leo was in now, the fact remained he was where he was by his own will and that he had come too far for regret or remorse. He was "Beast King" Barbarossa, Tactical Officer of the *Black Sun* and third in command of the Flint Pirates. Any second thoughts toward that, as well as all he had gained through said pirate's life, would serve no purpose. And surely, if this were all somehow an affront to His will, then Aslan would have righted his path, yes?

That was not the first time Barbarossa had considered that last thought, and as so many times before, he had no definitive answer. Only that he was where he remained, as did his faith. There was no need for further contemplation on those things.

Thus deciding he had had enough activities for the day, Barbarossa rose from his chair and began to clean up for greatly-needed slumber. It would not be much longer before the Flints resumed business as usual, so, again keeping to the pirate's life, he intended to enjoy whatever days of leisure remained to him on Atalanta. Beyond that, only Aslan could tell.

<u>Chapter II: Lazy Afternoons</u>

Saffron Inn
Calydon, Atalanta

Dazedly did Howell Davis' eyes open, taking in the soft light that now filled his hotel room. As was becoming more and more standard with his awakenings as time went on, it took him a moment or two to remember where he was and how he got there, especially when he realized he was not in the hotel room he had taken upon first arriving at Atalanta. This one was much simpler in comparison, smaller in size and facing beachside, such that it only required Davis to look over slightly to see the open sky and swaying sea just beyond. It took him a moment to recall that he had not entered this room alone the previous night, to which he glanced over to his opposite side. Sure enough, there was the waitress from the Parthenopeus Club – whose name he couldn't remember at the moment – still asleep with an arm over his chest, holding him quite comfortably to herself. If Davis recalled right, she had been more than satisfied with the previous evening, as she had those before.

Feeling her arm tighten around his chest somewhat, a soft, near unde-
tectable sigh escaping her lips, Davis couldn't help but smile, both
toward his handiwork and the present sentient. Indeed, he could not
have asked for more than this. As reluctant as he had been to be a
Flint Pirate, at least at the beginning, he could not deny the perks
of his position were quickly outweighing the shortcomings. Yes, the
near-death situations were practically continuous, and half the galaxy
was probably out for him – assuming that half of the galaxy wasn't
already made up of any lovers he may or may not have wronged or
the opposite numbers he may have stolen them from – for his association to the Flint name alone. But at the same time, he would never
have found himself where he was now, lying in a seaside room with a
beautiful woman by his side, enjoying a still somewhat foreign peace
and tranquility that would not have otherwise been available to him.
All with the great wealth he had amassed from the Flints' plunders
and the security and opportunities that it provided. Truly he could ask
for no more, at least for the moment.

In the middle of that thought, his bed partner subconsciously cuddled
tighter, again sighing into his ear. Responding in kind, Davis drew
his arm around her, reveling in the warmth her body provided, all the
while his eyes began to drift closed once more.

This really is Heaven...

"HAH!" his bed partner suddenly called out, her knee launching
straight into the most favored part of Davis's body.

With the force of a thundercrack, the peaceful serenity came to an
abrupt end, replaced with instant agonizing, mind-searing pain.
Despite his best efforts, Davis could not keep from deeply wincing.
He struggled with wanting to leap out of bed and make an emergency
medical call to Apache, but moving was not in his immediate future.

This...really...is...Hell...! Davis gratingly managed to think through
the torture, the world now wholly white and blaring around him.
He could only hope that he was not irrevocably damaged. At the

moment, he couldn't quite feel anything but throbbing, stinging torment.

Once more, letting out an airy sigh, a small grin soon emerged over the waitress's lips as she continued her deep, uninterrupted slumber.

Hotel Clymene
Calydon, Atalanta

Though still somewhat blurry-eyed from sleeping in, it didn't take Alex long to find his elder brother. Sitting at a table in the hotel tavern, sipping what was undoubtedly Old Caribbean, with a second tankard noticeably placed and waiting, Jon appeared at ease but otherwise thoughtful. Eyepatch and body scarring aside, wearing a simple blue shirt with light brown trousers and generally keeping to himself, he also seemed to be little different from the rest of the tavern occupants, who may or may not have been other pirates and criminals on holiday. Naturally, Alex took note that several nearby women, and one or two men, took discreetly interested glances toward his elder brother, as well as himself when he moved to join him, but Jon pretended not to notice. For obvious reasons, he just wasn't interested, and neither was Alex for that matter.

"I take it you didn't sleep much last night?" Alex began with a small but quite wry grin, taking note of Jon's eased composure. It was something only he would detect from his older brother, who was otherwise quite skilled at concealing his emotions and state of mind. And, of course, there was the fact Lorelei wasn't with him now.

"The responsibilities of the captaincy," Jon mused nonchalantly, though allowing a small corner of his lips to upturn toward his younger brother. "And you?"

A slight frown entered Alex's face. "Work in progress," he admitted, taking the first sip of his tankard. "It's all there, but…" he momentarily trailed off, lest he somehow say something regretful. "It just hasn't happened yet."

Jon nodded in understanding. His brother's feelings for the Dragon Princess had been obvious for a long time, and it hadn't taken much longer for him to confirm her feelings for him. For whatever reason, however, they had both chosen the slower route, taking their time and letting things develop naturally. Admirable and perhaps warranted given Kaguya's character, but most certainly not without its own set of frustrations, which Alex was clearly feeling now. Even with ideology on the matter aside, the physical body retained its wants and needs.

That being said, however, Jon could tell that it wasn't entirely frustrating for Alex. Though certainly aggravated on some level, he could depict a fair measure of satisfaction in his younger brother's expression; clearly, whatever was between him and Kaguya was already substantial. Jon would have smirked at this but didn't want to show Alex that he had taken notice.

"So," Alex moved on, deciding to address the matters at hand. "Only three more days, and it's back to work we go, yes?"

Jon nodded. "Rather fitting if you think about it," he posited knowingly. "We will be returning to 'work' on Ash Wednesday."

"Heh, more like ironic," Alex responded, now letting off a full grin at the prospect. "If memory serves, Lent is a period in which one purifies the body and soul of sin."

"Yes, in spite of the fact that the Messiah had already done so upon His great sacrifice," Jon responded while taking a casual sip. "Still, it's six weeks until Easter, and idle hands remain the Devil's workshop, as the ancient saying goes."

"And it helps that neither of us nor any of the crew, for that matter, are particularly religious," Alex smirked again. "Godfearing certainly, but it's not like anyone wants to take marching orders from Basilica."

"Indeed," Jon replied, again knowingly. Basilica was the world in which the modern Catholic Church – one of the very few institutions that had survived through the First Age's abrupt end and the Thousand Year Darkness that followed – was headquartered, a world akin to the long-lost Vatican City. And just like it had been on Ancient Terra, the Pope and his entourage commanded much in the way of power and influence, even though freedom of religion and tolerance of individual faith remained fixtures throughout humanity.

"In the meantime, however," Alex smiled even more now. "There's all the fun to be had *before* Lent."

"Yes," Jon confirmed with a nod, this time allowing a smirk of his own. "The crew would mutiny otherwise."

"Could you blame them?" Alex now spoke with visible anticipation. "Carnival, just like Christmas, only comes once a year, and we're on an ideal world to celebrate it."

"I suppose," Jon acknowledged, thinking aloud. "Two days in which sin is rapidly accumulated and all of humanity's vices are brought to bear."

"To say nothing of grog consumption," Alex added, relishing the event. "Though, to be honest, two days of sin as compared to six weeks of repentance seems rather lopsided to me."

"That is the intention," Jon retorted. "According to tradition, sin, whether physical or spiritual, is much easier to gain than it is to get rid of. Thus the extra time and required energy."

He again took a swig as though to make the point. "But again, this conveniently discounts the Messiah having already made the ultimate sacrifice beforehand."

"Yeah, funny that," Alex remarked. "Well, whatever. We still get two whole days of lights, color, and meat and drink to go around. Can't complain."

"Agreed," Jon responded with another nod, then looking on musingly. "The ideal finale to our respite, as well as the grand prelude to our return."

"Hallelujah," Alex fittingly concluded before taking another swig.

――――――――――――― ―――――――――――――

"It comes down to duty when you think about it. Our squabble with Baranov left many of these colonies and outposts in ruin, their populations destitute, if not worse. Thus it is not only the Dreyfus Company's obligation but its duty to rebuild and rehabilitate these affected worlds. To return them to the glory and prominence they held before Marzanna Baranov took up arms…"

"And to the victor belong the spoils," Anna mused while lounging poolside as she continued listening to her elder sister's live interview. Had she been a lesser, or vindictive, woman, she may have been put off with how, even weeks later, Delphine was taking the credit for effectively rebuilding the Company and merging the remaining Baranov assets overnight, when in reality that had only been through the efforts of one Camille Dreyfus. Even the program, no, the mere inclination, to address those worlds and populaces devastated by the war had been made through her directions. Delphine had not even known where to begin with the relief efforts, much like with anything else following the cessation of hostilities.

Yet now, the new President of the Dreyfus Company was basking in the limelight, a skill at which Delphine excelled. Taking in all the glory and tribute for "her" tireless endeavors in ending the Baranov "squabble", restoring her family business to its former providence, if not beyond, and otherwise working to right the wrongs that Marzanna Baranov and the previous President, who remained unmentioned, had inflicted upon the Outer Rim. All while the real mind behind all of it was laying swimsuit-clad on a lounge chair countless lightyears away, listening to her elder sister make herself out like the Second Coming, taking full credit for the younger's actions and achievements. Irony, much like death, taxes, and stupidity, remained a constant, it seemed.

Fortunately, Anna could not have cared less. She soon disengaged her wristcom and went back to her relaxation, taking a swig from the drink next to her, something the locals referred to as a Pan-Galactic Starburst or "Paga Star" for shorthand. Rather than being offended by Delphine taking the credit, at least entirely, Anna was rather grateful for it, as well as keeping her former name 'Camille Dreyfus' out of the news. Despite the loud and quite numerous demands for Camille to take leadership of the Company toward the end, the middle daughter of Vincent and Dominique Dreyfus had no wish to return to that life. She was more than happy for her elder sister to advance to Corporate President. If that meant Delphine got all the praise for Anna's hard work following the Dreyfus-Baranov War's end, then so be it. It only took one sip of her cool, refreshing drink to assure the former company executive turned pirate that it was so much for the better.

As irritating as it may have been otherwise, not helped by the sound of Delphine's voice, Anna only hoped the best for her elder sister and the family business. With Baranov out of the way and the issues with the Tartarus Nebula wholly resolved, the Dreyfus Company had a bright future ahead of it, one that Delphine could bring about if she kept her head in the game while staying away from old habits. Previously, Anna's younger sister Lisette's horrible behavior had drawn almost all the attention; nobody outside the family had paid heed to Delphine when she had been experimenting with every form of alcohol and narcotics on that side of the galaxy. Now, however, all eyes were firmly on Delphine, which meant that the moment she spoke idiotically out of turn, snubbed the wrong VIP, or otherwise acted in the way that Anna remembered her best, the news bulletins would be all over the cortex less than a solar day later. And that only precluded the possible damage Delphine could do from her newfound position of power.

Well, not my concern, Anna again resolved while taking another sip of her Paga Star. It no longer mattered to her whether the Dreyfus Company rose from the ashes or returned to its previous state as a smoking crater. Nor did it matter to her if Delphine shot her mouth off to the wrong sentient, if Lisette was due for another month at rehab or if their mother needed to be institutionalized now that their father was out of the picture. Camille Dreyfus had officially exited the universe, leaving Anna Reed where she was now. Relaxing under a bright yet soothing sun, a cool drink in hand, with much more available if she wished, and all the problems of the universe far and away from her. For the next three days anyway.

Anna raised her glass to the sun admiring the light as it shone through the bright yellow, red, and purple swirled slush. "The *real* spoils," she mused as she smiled before taking a much deeper drink.

"This concludes my report," Kaguya finished, once again seated before the hologram of her father on distant Ryugu.

"Very well," Lord Fuma took it all in with a single nod. Not much had happened with the Flints since the Tartarus War's conclusion, but the Lord of the Blue Dragon knew better than to discount his daughter's observations. "How are they doing now?"

"They've more or less recovered," Kaguya responded diligently enough. "Such that we will be able to resume normal activities upon our return."

"Yes," Lord Fuma considered, suddenly looking away.

Kaguya, naturally, was quick to notice. "Has this truly caused so much concern, *Otou-sama*?"

"More than it should," Lord Fuma responded, allowing some measure of weariness to grow. "They should have known and anticipated all of this from the beginning, and yet..." He closed his eyes in open despondence. "Have there been any particular movements around Atalanta?"

"Not that I've seen," Kaguya rejoined, frowning. "Of course, that doesn't mean there are no others out there."

"Indeed," Lord Fuma concurred, knowing how many of those 'others' were skilled at concealment. As well as how several of them were also Wielders.

"Perhaps it would be wise to depart this world earlier somewhat," Kaguya mildly suggested.

To that, Lord Fuma shook his head. "No, there is no need to cause undue alarm," he indirectly commanded his daughter and agent. "And it would only serve to forewarn those who may be watching."

Kaguya nodded in confirmation, seeing that herself. "I understand," she responded. "What are your orders?"

Settling back on his throne, Lord Fuma commanded. "Continue as you are now, Kaguya, short of any disturbances in the coming three days, allow their respite."

The lord's eyes then narrowed as he added. "However, stay wary. Though deliberations remain ongoing, there can be little doubt that some may take the initiative regardless."

Kaguya frowned again. "Do you believe an attack may be imminent?"

"That is quite possible," Lord Fuma acknowledged. "Heightened movements among the other clans have been reported."

The Dragon Princess's frown deepened. Though Atalanta was placed well within Imperial space, that did not stop the clans from mounting a direct attack before. And again, considering their collective subjects of interest, the clans could launch such an assault regardless of Imperial reprisal. The Golden Queen's legacy, and the possible resurgence of her clan, were expressly dreaded, especially now.

"Once more, remain on heightened guard, my daughter," Lord Fuma commanded. "The enemy may be within their midst, and yours, already."

"Hai Otou-sama," Kaguya recited, the hologram dissipating not long after. Slowly, the ninja rose to her feet, her expression neutral. Underneath, however, her disturbance remained well in place. And well in force.

Pastoral Square
Calydon, Atalanta

Slipping out the appropriately summed payment, Cheney took the curious beverage, what the stand owner referred to as a "Tortuga", and sipped it as he began to wander again. As had been claimed, the drink was quite sweet; some local brand of tea mixed with an equally local brand of brown sugar and cinnamon with a lime wedge at the top. Fortunately, there were few things in life that Cheney enjoyed more than sweets, so he found the drink quite refreshing and to his liking. The perfect companion to have as he moved aimlessly through the square, past the other wanderers and apprising shoppers and the stand keepers that called out to them, advertising their wares to anyone even remotely interested.

Taking it all in, Cheney could not help but feel that familiar measure of melancholy. Once again, in three days, he would be leaving all of this behind to return to the stars and the pillage and plunder that awaited. Not that he was complaining; after all, he was having the time of his pirate's life, but admittedly he would miss Atalanta and all peace and serenity it had to offer. It was no wonder that so many in his *former* profession, including him at certain times, had proclaimed their desire to retire to some beachside property somewhere when their time fighting for the Emperor was done. There was just something easing about waking up under a bright sun and next to a great blob of water, especially when you did not have to worry about a beam or a projectile landing on top of you at any point. And, of course, scantily clad female folk walking around in the open certainly helped that image, three of which passed Cheney as he continued to wander. At least one of them turned to make a corner glance at him.

Laughing and shaking his head a little, Cheney again felt melancholy, albeit concerning another source. Unfortunately, even if that girl, who was likely half his age, gave a blatant invitation, he could not and would not follow up on it. He was thinking of another woman altogether, one that he had long ago sworn to the Lord Almighty to be true to in good times and in bad, in sickness and in health. In many ways, he wished she were here with him now; she certainly would have been having as much fun as he. Unfortunately, she had her reasons for remaining behind, up to and including covering for his "sorry posterior" when the powers that be on Terra learned that the Dread Soldier had since transitioned into the Dread Pirate. Still, that didn't make him miss her any less.

It was then that another sentient began to pass by him, one that was far less attractive to Cheney, both in gender and in appearance. Though obviously Terran and otherwise dressed no differently from the rest of the locale, the sentient's build was notably more muscular than average. Simultaneously, the expression in his slanted eyes and emphasized grin were unseemlier and more off-putting than jovial. The newcomer triggered Cheney's instincts, but he didn't respond, even as they crossed by each other in their respective paths. Though Atalanta was nominally an Imperial world, it was very much open to anyone and everyone, including those of the criminal element, so the former Imperial Marine wasn't surprised to see anyone so shifty, for lack of better description, there. So long as the miscreant didn't bother him, he...

And then, all at once, Cheney felt that being's eyes shift as they passed, along with a surge of malevolence.

Twisting around in a flash, Cheney's hand immediately reached for his Grenada. But before he completed his draw, the raider found only an open space. The interloper had disappeared into thin air.

After blinking a few times to make sure that he was, in fact, alone, Cheney paused to 'sense' the surrounding area. Whatever had just happened, his instincts told him there was no danger now. The bastard's presence was gone. Thus moving his hand away from his gun, he turned and continued on his way to wherever he may yet end up, noting to mention the incident to his commander when next they met.

Chapter III: Carnival

Saint Anaud's
Calydon, Atalanta

With much in the way of flash and thunder, the hotly awaited celebration had at last begun. Lights and streamers adorned virtually every sector, as was the night sky through the near-constant fireworks. Costumed partygoers, their ensembles as varied as the modern and ancient eras they were meant to represent, moved and laughed throughout the respective streets. Music of all forms, once again both ancient and contemporary, cascaded across the open air, enjoyed and oft danced to by the young and old alike. Local establishments, from the brothels and taverns to the dance halls and narcotics dens, teemed with widely anticipated business, while planetary law enforcement – who may or may not have been among the partakers – only stepped in when and where necessary. Politics were mocked, formalities ignored, and sin and wickedness were welcomed and brazenly displayed. A virtual orgy of color, decadence, and vividness, an antithesis to all things moral and sanctified given rampant form. And it was now making its unbridled charge through all of Atalanta.

Even now, well after his prior conversation with his brother, Jon found the whole concept, as well as the execution, of Carnival to be wholly ironic. From what he understood of the occasion, it had originally begun in the First Age as a last supper of sorts; the final point of the year in which food and drink could be consumed in abundance before the supplies ended and the fasting, which was for practical purposes as well as faithful, began. Somehow that had transitioned along the way to embracing the other six sins as well as *gula*, with but common sense – as much remained of it when alcohol was firmly involved at least – and law otherwise keeping the celebrators in check. As though, for all of humanity's emphasis and belief on morality, especially that which has been passed down from on high, there remained an ever-present desire to break if not outright violate the rules. Even the most "holy" of men – men who would go through their entire lives without missing a Bible study – could not but give in to temptation, albeit only at certain times of the year. Funny that.

"Jon?" Alex called out to him from across the table, indirectly alerting his elder brother that he was staring off again. To emphasize, the younger Flint reached out and made a knocking motion against the side of his sibling's head. "Anybody?"

Inwardly sighing, Jon ultimately decided it was of very little matter then and there. Though he liked to think of himself, as well as Alex, Lorelei, and Kaguya – the latter two seated with them on the restaurant's second level – and the rest of the Flint Pirates as well above the average rabble, the fact remained they were all as far from holy, pious men and women as was otherwise permissible. But then, even Christ had been a known oenophiliac, enough to turn water into wine when *that* supply hadn't been readily available. And He certainly wouldn't have skimped on the alcohol.

"Just enjoying the view," he claimed to his brother and their respective dates, which was more or less truthful. Outside the fireworks and the streets being packed with revelers, there was the parade that was marching down the center of the main thoroughfare. As with the rest of the occasion, the procession was full of life and color, made up of various floats and men and women in costume, each as uniquely designed and adorned as the last. All very spectacular, and all very captivating.

"Hopefully not too much," Lorelei put mildly, noting that several of the female revelers, both in and out of the parade, had little in the way of clothing. She was joking, of course. Of all things that could be questioned about Captain Jonathan Flint, his loyalties were not among that line. Something the siren knew and understood more than most, though that didn't mean she couldn't have fun.

Knowing and understanding from the opposite end, Jonathan simply passed off a wry grin as he took a sip from his wineglass. As if *that* would ever happen. Especially when the most exceptional, most fascinating woman in the galaxy was already by his side.

"Well, it is a sight to behold, I'll say that much," Alex admitted as he watched one particular dessert-themed float, the essential parts of the men and women up top strategically censored with fruit, sweets, and cream, glided by. For a moment, he wondered if the act would elicit a similar response from Kaguya or at least a dirty look of some kind. To his mild disappointment, his date didn't seem to mind in the least, though the younger Flint supposed she knew where his loyalties were. "Not to mention one real hell of a sendoff for us."

Lorelei chuckled a little. "As if the populace of Atalanta put this on for *our* exclusive benefit," she spoke before sipping her wine. "Though the timing could not have been better admittedly."

"Do we have any particular heading at this time?" Kaguya posited to Jon since they were technically moving toward that subject matter.

Jon shrugged. "There are a few points of interest," he answered, knowing that whatever he said would be in Kaguya's next correspondence with her father. "The Graaff System, in particular, stands out. From what I've learned, there's a fair-sized smuggler base on the moon of the third planet."

"Heh, haven't done a lunar raid in a while," Alex said, now rather intrigued. "They have anything of particular value?"

Again the Captain shrugged. "The usual objects of gleam and sparkle," he answered casually while taking a sip. "As well as a few pieces of stolen artwork, Terran and otherwise."

He then smirked knowingly at his younger brother before he continued. "At least one is reportedly dated back to the Italian Renaissance."

"Shiny," Alex smirked with emphasized interest, quoting another random Ancient Terran term in the process. While the arts were nominally Jon's area of interest, there had been many scientific breakthroughs in that era, much of which had been made into picture form on well preserved paper. "You think it's the *Vitruvian Man*?"

Jon tipped his head at the idea. "Only one way to find out," he responded, right as he caught sight of their waiter moving toward their table, their entrees on a hover tray beside him. "In the meantime, however, the night, and our sendoff, remain well in motion."

The waiter completed his trek, the four already looking on in anticipation as he placed and described their respective dishes.

———————————————

"It's alright, dear, really," Gran assured for what had to be the third time to a near incredulous Kaiser. The Herculean, while appearing outwardly calm, was seething and about to charge the middle of the parade for a literal clash of titans. "No, he wasn't ogling my chest. His eyes never narrowed that far in."

Boss was *still* laughing. "The fact you could hear that one point in all of this din makes you a true clairaudient, Gran," she let out through the overabundant cheering surrounding them. "And honestly, Kaiser, who *wouldn't* look over your girl?"

Kaiser's brow furrowed deeply, to which Gran had no choice but translate. "'This particular *who* will become as lost as the genuine article if he doesn't keep his 'marble' eyeballs to himself,'" the communications officer could only speak in exasperation. "'This time Goliath's going to win!'"

Even Braun could not help but laugh. "Now *that* would make an interesting float!" he declared before drinking from his beer cup.

The subject in question was on one of the passing floats, apparently themed to the legendary *David*. As one would have otherwise expected, this *David* was a very nude Herculean, standing upon an overelaborate pedestal and frozen well within an articulated pose, such that the only noticeable change was that the more specific parts of "David's" anatomy were shielded from view, even as the float hovered on down the street in uninterrupted motion. However, this particular *David*'s eyes' had shifted to peruse an equally exquisite Lyran woman. Much to Kaiser's ire.

"Look, he's moving away now," Gran gestured while tugging on Kaiser's arm, as much as she could anyway. "I doubt we're going to see him again. We're leaving soon, remember?"

Though still visibly bristling after the "sculpture", the knowledge that they would shortly be offworld calmed Kaiser down enough to let it slide. Though, now he wished the Flints were leaving Atalanta that night. Maybe he could get the Captain and First Officer to do him a favor in the meantime…

"Seriously!?" Boss sputtered, nearly gagging on her drink. Wiping her mouth with the back of her hand, her outcry managed to carry over the cheering, though hardly anyone paid attention. It was then the group turned to another, entirely different kind of float.

A float that showed a certain woman pilot in the open cockpit of a shortened, cartoonish depiction of a Mustang fighter. Not only was the "plane" in question a noteworthy shade of blue, but the pilot happened to be blonde with a *marginally* familiar face, her arms raised up and outward in dual 'V for Victory' signs, as though she were literally flying with "no hands". The base of the float spelling out "BLUE COMET" in bold, electrically illuminated lettering only finalized the image.

Even Kaiser could not help but silently laugh alongside Gran and Braun. All the while, Boss looked on with as much incredulousness as had been previously displayed.

"Who in the Sixth Circle authorized *that*!?" the ace nearly stammered as the exaggerated image of her younger self moved by as passively as the *David*.

"Well, you are quite renowned," Braun spoke through his chuckling. "My guess is Snoopy and the Red Baron were used in last year's parade."

"Think of it as a compliment, Boss," Gran assured, smiling in approval as the float continued down the thoroughfare. Though she couldn't actually see the image in question, there was enough sound around it for her to depict the shape of the open cockpit starfighter with the deliberately proportioned pilot therein. In fact, she could even "read" the "BLUE COMET" bannering from the arrangement, and power generation, of the lights therein. "Your legend lives on."

Boss folded her arms across her chest. *Not much of a legend,* she thought, certain memories beginning to enter into her consciousness. Fortunately, she was able to force them back, just as she always did.

"At the very least, they could have gotten my nose right. My plane, if it can even be called that, might as well have *three* wings."

Right hand stroking his chin as though its owner were in deep thought, Braun gave his usual bloated smile. "That would certainly allow for stabler flight within an atmosphere," he mused, then finishing the remainder of his drink. "Regardless, I think the resemblance is fair enough."

"Yes, well, speaking of resemblance," Boss spoke up again, this time smirking herself. "Look what's coming our way now."

Upon seeing the next float, Braun felt his smile drain away into an unamused frown, all while the other three enjoyed yet one more round of laughter. No, this float wasn't made in a deliberate image of his younger self, but that ultimately meant very little. As though the scene took actual place in the middle of some cliched castle laboratory, a *highly* exaggerated caricature of a scientist, one with wild hair and maddened grin, eyes covered with oversized goggles and hands covered with equally oversized gloves, stood "proudly" with two vials of vibrantly colored green and purple liquids in hand, the latter tipped over with one drop about to land in the former. Along the sides, multicolored letters spelled out "WHAT COULD GO WRONG?"

"'I think the resemblance is more than 'fair enough' with this one,'" Gran recited while Kaiser nearly doubled over in silent laughter. Beside them, Boss, apparently having finished her drink, was now in the process of lighting her pipe, the smuggest of grins across her face as she began to puff smoke.

"Hmph," Braun let out while clasping onto his right arm, which, having already crushed and thrown away the emptied grog cup, was in the process of transforming into its beam gun mode. All the while the cheering, and the laughter, continued around him and his "comrades".

———————— ————————

"Refresh my memory," Anna inquired as she strolled down the street and through the revelers with a certain lady killer pirate. The latter, unless she saw it incorrectly, was walking rather strangely. "Why couldn't you get a date for this?"

Davis somehow managed not to wince as he moved wrong, causing a highly specific form of pain to run through that part of his body once more.

"She couldn't get the night off," he managed to respond, thanking God that Anna hadn't yet noticed his predicament. "And it was too short notice for me to find someone else."

I'm sure, Anna thought dubiously. Well, no matter. At the very least, she had an excuse to get out and enjoy the fun rather than make final inventory checks to the *Sun* as she had originally planned. "Where are we going anyway?"

Choosing not to answer verbally, Davis grinned as he gestured toward a venue that they had just come upon, one whose overhead sign read "THE BOBBALOO" with a short line of music notes underneath. If the name and icon weren't any indication, even to someone as culturally inclined as Anna, then the type of music that reached out to her from the interior certainly provided clues.

A jazz club? Anna thought curiously, once again assuming she wasn't interrupting the sounds incorrectly. Jazz wasn't a rarity in the galaxy. It was within the first items rediscovered from Alexandria, and rumor claimed Emperor Tiberius himself had held a liking to it. Still, she hadn't expected to discover such a venue on Atalanta, but again decided it was no matter, especially as she found the resultant music to be rather catchy.

Once again, managing not to wince through his movements, Davis extended his arm for Anna to enter first. As with everything else on Atalanta at that time, the Bobbaloo was effectively packed with patrons, both in the dining area and on the dance floor, the latter set before a rather elaborate band. Smooth yet quite "hot" as the lingo went, the "swing" was in full display between the band and the dancers, appearing more as a scene from a viso, one that would have depicted the early twentieth century of the First Age, than an actual dance venue.

"I confess, I intended to take my original date here, for reasons that should be obvious," Davis explained, as though he had to remind Anna that he had been dining, dancing, and sleeping with a Lyran up to this point. "But I thought you would like it as well, considering your own…background."

Though an admittedly clumsy explanation, Anna had to give the helmsman a plus for effort. Having taken into account her tastes before deciding to come here or not.

"I like it," Anna spoke approvingly as a hostess led them to a nearby table. A waiter took their respective drink orders then continued away just as quickly.

I suppose I could do a lot worse tonight, Anna mused. Though she had very much *not* intended to spend her second to last night on Atalanta with the insufferable Lady Killer, she admitted it wasn't as bad as she thought. Of course, this only precluded any bedding attempts on his part.

"Is this the kind of place you take your dates usually? Or was that waitress just special?"

Davis grinned; the game was on. "Quite the contrary, Miss Reed, I do not have a 'usual' place for my dates," he proclaimed. "An evening with a beautiful woman is no different than any other form of diplomacy. You have to *know* what you are dealing with."

"I never quite heard it *that* way before," Anna laughed a little. "Not that one *usually* engages in the bedroom when negotiations have concluded."

Again Davis took it in stride. "That's simply one of the primary objects of said negotiations," he responded. "You want to make the other side feel good enough that they're willing to make that particular concession."

The Duchess flashed a wry grin. "Admittedly, I have heard of the other side 'taking it up the ass' off and on," she mused, this time remembering her activities following the Tartarus War rather fondly. "Though whether or not they felt 'good' enough to make such concessions is a matter of debate."

The Lady Killer immediately knew what she was referring to. "Once more to the contrary, you did make them feel good, or at least worthwhile," he pointed out. "Despite possessing the advantage of position and power, you still made Anatoli Baranov, or whoever it was you exchanged with, feel that, despite everything, they were still worthy of dignity and being seen as an equal. Alongside, you made a point of sparing any further aggression to innocents, even those within the Conglomerate. That lessened the tension to the opposite part, who obviously was tired of war by then, as well as made it a point that you just wanted to end the fighting, not to stand atop of Marzanna Baranov's corpse."

This time it was Davis that held a wry grin as he saw it sink in with Anna. "Once again, an evening with a beautiful woman is no different. You want to make them feel that they are not simply worthwhile, but that they are the most beautiful, most perfect woman in the universe, even if only in their consciousness," he spoke assuredly. "Likewise, you want to make yourself out to be the most perfect man for them to have…"

"If only in *your* consciousness," Anna couldn't help but rib as the waiter came back with their drinks.

Taking a sip from his rum swizzle, Davis shook his head. "No, not quite," he corrected. "It doesn't matter what one thinks of themselves as opposed to what the other side views them as."

"Touché," Anna conceded. Indeed, that was a standard essentiality to negotiation. To influence the other side into seeing what you wanted them to see, even if it was not actually there.

Davis nodded approvingly, noting that Anna truly understood. "It's all just another form of diplomacy," he repeated. "Perhaps not so much over territory or resources, but still a form of negotiation between two very separate yet otherwise interested parties."

"Sure, sure," Anna responded, taking another sip, once more seeing the similarities. "I suppose that makes you an accomplished negotiator then?"

"More than you will ever know," Davis resounded quite proudly. "My accomplishments, and gains, speak for themselves."

Somehow not rolling her eyes as she usually did, Anna decided to concede the point to the helmsman. Like it or not, he knew his "trade", as it were. Much as it unsettled her stomach.

Fortunately, it didn't take long for her to move beyond the subject, her eyes drifting to the dance floor. "I don't suppose you perform all of your negotiations at the table or in the bedroom."

Suddenly feeling a coming resurgence from his lower parts, Davis, this time cringed. "Uh," he almost stammered. "Maybe not toni…"

"My apologies, Mr. Davis," Anna smiled sweetly as she got up. "But I'm afraid this is one concession you will just have to make," she finished, holding out her hand in a more traditional manner.

Discreetly gritting his teeth, Davis, while trying not to think of the fast and ferocious dancing style that the present form of music employed, could only hope he would heal overnight. Otherwise, knowing better than to try and dodge the inevitable, he took her hand and rose. Smiling brightly, Anna led him to the dance floor, Davis biting back the responding "ow ow ows" along the way.

All the while, unnoticed in the background, one strangely interested patron watched as the two pirates began their own "swing".

Saint Anaud's
Calydon, Atalanta

"All in all, it sounds like we're going to have our hands full for a while," Alex observed after taking another bite of his jambalaya, which went down his throat smoothly yet warmly. In his opinion, every civilization with some level of culinary inclination had that type of dish; assorted meats, vegetables, and spices mixed in with some form of grain. Despite that, however, he had yet to find a dish that truly outdid the Terran version, which he enjoyed whenever the opportunity presented itself. The name was also pretty cool too.

"And if the Circumgressus were to present us the third Babel?"

Jon shrugged while swallowing. As with Alex's, it was a local take on an Ancient Terran entrée, this one an Atalantan rendition of a crab cake. As opposed to the original, however, this one was flatter and larger, as big as Jon's plate, while the meat inside was firmer yet more succulent. More akin to a crab *steak* than anything else.

"Then we drop everything and head for it," the pirate captain responded while taking another sip of wine, as though it were obvious. "It shouldn't be much of a detour."

"That's what you said about Smyrna," Alex reminded, somewhat pointedly.

Again Jon shrugged. "If the local inhabitants take issue to our presence, then we deal with them accordingly," he stated wisely. "Better such than an Imperial fleet."

"Indeed," Kaguya agreed, memories of the Second Battle of Ephesus starting to emerge as they did periodically. To forestall the unwanted recollections, she concentrated on her meal. It was some kind of local fish originally sealed in a paper envelope with assorted crustacean meat and a sort of white wine sauce. It was a strange-sounding entre, Pompano en Papillote if Kaguya had read and heard right, but she couldn't deny the rich flavor of the combined ingredients, which had melded deliciously within the warmed parchment.

"Though it would still be preferable if this next world were deserted of any hostile life."

Lorelei chuckled a little at that, as well as the memories she picked up from the ninja concerning Smyrna. It was hard to fault her, Jon, and Alex, as the fighting at Smyrna had been an unnecessary frustration for them. Still, since she had been as far removed from the battle as possible and would be wherever they found the remaining Babels, she simply took a sip of her wine and then another bite of her food, which as opposed to the other three, was based around a land-based creature. Specifically, the Atalantan rendition of Steak Delmonico, fileted and covered with a kind of blue fat that somehow made the meat even more tender.

"As said," Jon repeated as he lifted his wine glass. "We will deal with any opposition as it comes along. And that includes where we stage our raids."

Both Alex and Kaguya nodded and focused on enjoying their meals. Jon appreciated their acceptance. While the first two Babels, especially the first, had proven more troublesome than anyone would have wished, their course remained set regardless. As much as they were pirates, and as much as he was dedicated to restoring the Gold Dragon, the central focus of their voyage remained Arcadia, and they would not deviate from it. No matter what they ended up facing, around the Babels or in between.

It was with that last thought that Jon experienced an all too familiar feeling. One that nearly caused him to drop his wine glass to the floor.

"Jon?" Alex looked up in alarm, as did the two women. They had all seen that expression on their captain one time or another, and it had never indicated anything good.

His eye suddenly taking on a much darker glower, Jon did not answer his brother. Rather, he turned to face the ground below, moving his gaze toward a specific part of the city and its celebration. There, positioned a little away from the crowd, the silhouette of another sentient

47

being stood. Clearly observing him and the others.

His expression became a full glare as he found that intruder. Jon downed the rest of his wine and placed the emptied glass on the table before signaling their waiter.

"I'm afraid we'll have to depart a little earlier than expected," he informed both their attendant as well as the other three. "I trust this will not be an issue?" he inquired as he placed a few extra aurics on the table.

Though confused, the waiter assured him. "No sir, this will not be a problem," he said, already eying the aurics more eagerly than he should. "I trust you will have a pleasant evening regardless."

You have no idea, Jon thought as he, Alex, Lorelei, and Kaguya all rose and made their immediate exit. The silhouette had vanished from where it previously stood.

He was being tracked, and not just by one. Moving through the crowd of drunken hedonists, who admittedly knew how to celebrate their collective debauchery quite thoroughly, Barbarossa kept his senses focused for far more specific sights and sounds within the abundance of noise. For once, very few were bothered by the Leo's presence, either too focused on the still moving parade or otherwise being so drunk and deluded that they likely believed him to be another costumed partygoer. It was all too easy for Barbarossa to move through the horde without confrontation. Before, he had used that to his advantage, if only to get out of his hotel room to have one last night on the stroll, as his Captain had insisted. Now though, he was using it to keep ahead of his apparent stalkers, which he also kept appropriately accounted and numbered.

Already he could tell his pursuers were not simple muggers or would-be thieves that saw him as an easy mark. No, these were *professionals* of a military grade. Not Imperial Starfleet, but certainly of the warrior class. They knew the danger he represented, and so kept their distance and discretion. But at the same time, he, and perhaps more like him, remained their objective, and they would not allow him to shake them off. So far, they had kept up with him, slipping through the masses of proud and vocal "sinners" as efficiently and as unnoticed as he had. Remaining distant enough to stay out of harm's reach, but close enough that when the time came…

Having said that, Barbarossa was still a little perplexed at the identity of their faction. Again they were not Imperials, that much he could ascertain, but that hardly narrowed it down. Even if they were all Terrans, which he did not quite discount yet, there were more than enough military organizations in the galaxy for them to align with, some of which were quite formidable. However, Barbarossa had a distinct feeling that this was not some random PMC or mercenary force. No, for them to pursue him specifically, they would have to be willing to fight the whole of the Flint Pirates, which in itself not only further indicated their organization and fighting capability but also who their *true* target was.

Of course, that still didn't narrow down the answer much. The Flints had their share of enemies, with the Empire simply being the first in a very long line. Until now, only the bravest and most foolish had attempted to challenge them and always straightforward, oft to their unlamented demise. This force, once again, remained discreet, doing well not to engage unless either commanded to or an opportunity presented itself, which Barbarossa had taken much effort in avoiding. Just as he was also aware of how spread out they were, both to conceal their numbers and attack from different vectors when the time came. Venerable opponents, to be sure, which made him wonder at the one, and there was always just one, commanding them, to say nothing of the banner under which they fought.

It didn't matter though, Barbarossa knew all too well. This force was methodical and intent on pursuing him; it was quite clear they intended to attack and soon. Not even the crowds of otherwise inno-cents seemed to dissuade them; the Leo could tell that if they had to shoot and cut through the revelers to get to him, they would. Whoever or whatever was after him, and the rest of the Flints, clearly wanted them all dead, yet were not so foolhardy to believe they could do it by running and gunning. No, this was an elaborate operation, one meant to fulfill an objective or multiple objectives as opposed to simply gain personal glory or vengeance. This was a *military* opera-tion, and these men and women were soldiers. Not unlike those that the Flints had fought on Ephesus, which to date had been their hard-est-fought battle.

Barbarossa saw that it was only a matter of time before the prover-bial refuse hit the spinning blade. Undoubtedly this force was spread across the whole of Calydon and beyond, ready to strike at any Flint within their reach. And though the Leo could only wonder why they hadn't attacked just yet, he had more than a few possible answers. Chief among them involved whatever his captain was doing now or was about to do...

——————————— ———————————

Now garbed in his "uniform" as it were, Jon stood atop a nearby roof, staring out as the fireworks continued to ascend and burst around him. From an outside viewpoint, he undoubtedly appeared very focused, apparently not paying attention to his surroundings. Obvi-ously, this was far from the truth. Jon knew that only the less inclined would believe he had let his guard down. Which, again obviously, could not be said about the one who soon leaped up and landed just behind him on said roof.

Not quite ready to turn around, Jon surmised the sentient's appear-ance. As with the rest of the city, the being appeared dressed in a reveler's costume of sorts; a kind of elaborate dark red and white robe, topped with a conical red hat and face concealed behind a blank white mask that was little different from what the other carnival participants were wearing. He had seen no weapons visible upon the form, though that meant nothing. The way the entity held his arms together, such that it appeared the widened sleeves were physically connected, certainly could have hidden a blade or firearm of some kind. And of course, there was the method, and the weapon, that Jon, and Alex, were all too familiar with.

"Before we begin," Jon stated, once more without turning around. "I wish to know exactly what, or *whom*, I am dealing with."

That appeared acceptable to the intruder as, after a moment, its form began to visibly fluctuate. Shifting, his shroud gradually rescinded, revealing his true form. A man that, of all that he could have encountered short of a returned Raphael Drake, Jon had wished never to see. Especially there.

Now adorned in black and red with fair amounts of embroidery, it was quite clear the Terran man was, even dismissing his being a Wielder, not some random bystander. Underneath a very upscale, modestly embellished long coat, this man wore a tunic of a rather particular styling, itself indicative of the civilization, the culture, that the wearer hailed from. Beyond that, he wore the standard trousers, accompanying boots of similar styling to the tunic, and a pair of gloves over his hands. Again there were no visible weapons upon his person, but it was quite evident by that point he was not unarmed.

And then there was the man himself, which the clothes merely complimented as opposed to having made. Being of a slender yet relatively muscular build, the man could easily be depicted as a fighter, again even if one discounted his possessing a Devilblade. Though not quite as large as Jon, he still presented an intimidating, undaunting appearance. The face underneath short black hair only reinforced the image. Just as well-structured and handsome in its own right, the face's most noteworthy trait was the cold, unflinching eyes that looked upon Jon's back with dispassionate indifference. Not simple aloofness; the eyes projected nothing, as did the perpetual frown worn across the rest of the face. No emotions, no fervor or sentiment of any kind. Only an apparent nothingness with which he seemed to regard the pirate captain.

Closing his eye, Jon muttered the man's name in understanding. "Ching Shun."

Once more, no emotion of any kind was presented. Not even when the intruder responded to his quarry in kind.

"Jonathan Flint."

Chapter IV: Night of Fate

Making their way through the crowd with as much energy as they could muster *without* appearing anxious, Alex and Kaguya continued to move past the revelers and pedestrians, acknowledging that the party was effectively over for them. Though Jon, however he had detected the apparent interlopers, had not quite identified their newfound enemies, it had been clear enough that they were hostile and that at least four were targeting their group. For that, they had split up in three different directions, with Jon, suspecting the leader of the opposition would pursue him specifically, moving to one part of Calydon, Lorelei to another, and Alex and Kaguya to yet another. All while the city continued celebrating around them, blissfully unaware.

As lights, fireworks and merriment continued to flicker all around, the two pirates kept to the crowd, knowing full well that they were being followed throughout. For a time, they had hoped to shake off the two pursuers, both of whom were dressed not much differently from the rest of the planet, save for the somewhat out of place conical hats atop their heads, through said crowds, but that was clearly not about to happen. Whoever these two were, both the younger Flint and Lord Fuma's daughter could tell that they would not be so easily dissuaded. That, no matter how many pedestrians were placed between them and the two pirates, the pursuers would remain fixed upon their objectives. And neither Alex nor Kaguya had any doubt toward how their opponents would regard such innocents if they decided to attack.

It was with that knowledge, as much as it galled either of them, that the pair came to a sudden halt in the middle of the street. They knew there was no point in trying to evade them further. Not even with the prospect of alerting the surrounding innocents toward the coming fight, much less preventing their being affected by it.

"At last," a belligerent sounding voice let out from behind as its owner and the other pursuer came to an equal stop, regarding the two Flints through their respective carnival masks. "I almost believed we would go through this all night."

"At least until we started removing the garbage," the other pointed out, his voice similarly full of virulence, leaving little doubt he and his partner would have indeed done as such.

Wearing similar expressions of disgust, Alex and Kaguya both stood by as Forneus' energy flashed around them. Within little more than a second, Alex's regular attire and Kaguya's tactical armor, complete with ninjato across her back, reformed. The duo ready for what was to come.

It was then that the other two dropped their shrouds, revealing their full forms to the Flints. Adorned in identifiable black and red attire, two men of roughly similar muscular build, with dark brown eyes and black hair now stood before the Flint pirates. The first wore his hair in a taper cut while the second's hung down to his midback, secured with a black cord. Minute details, however, when compared to the violently anticipating expressions with which they regarded their adversaries.

Through these transformations, the surrounding pedestrians were quick to realize the danger in their midst. Panic and self-preservation immediately took precedence. The revelers dispersed in varied but otherwise standard noise and motion, clearing the whole of the street while the warriors simply stood by, never looking away from their opponents. In a few short minutes, only the combatants were present.

Alex immediately took note of the coloring and unique embroidery of their enemies' attire. "Red Phoenix?"

"Shì," the long-haired one confirmed, seemingly pleased that it had been deciphered so quickly. "We are here to kill you, Alexander Flint, Fuma Kaguya."

"Is that so?" Kaguya responded disdainfully, already focused and ready.

"Shì," the other added, grin enfolding. "You and the rest of your *jīn hundan* crew. Tonight, you die."

Alex sniffed contemptuously. "Far better than you have tried," he spat as Forneus formed in his hand while Kaguya drew her ninjato, both assuming fighting stances.

Immediately, the Red Phoenix fighters formed their own weapons and took their own stances. One held a large ornate white, grey, and red guandao, while the other grasped an obviously smaller, but no less opulent, blue and silver piandao. Both weapons bore sigils on their blades.

The enemies immediately charged at their respective opponents. Raising their own armaments, Alex and Kaguya met the attacks with equally powerful counterattacks. A far greater display of light and energy quickly engulfed that section of Calydon.

――――――――――― ――――――――――

With some effort, Lorelei managed to move through the revelers on her side of the city, doing well to remain ensconced within their numbers. Naturally, there were more than a few of them around her, which was most preferable at that time, although there was only one that she needed to track. And unfortunately, that one was just as apt at shielding him or herself within the crowd, such that Lorelei was having some difficulty pinpointing that exact psyche. But then, as she kept wading her way through the surrounding pedestrians, she had a feeling that it wouldn't be too long before...

Sure enough, a hand suddenly grasped her throat, holding her in place. While another began to run over her left hip and thigh.

"My, aren't you a lovely one," the molester claimed through his carnival mask, itself partially shrouded by a conical hat that no one else appeared to wear. Taking a deliberate sniff of his apparent victim's scent, the aggressor gleamed. "I just may take my time with you."

Lorelei only frowned. "Somehow, I doubt you possess the requisite capability."

The interloper opened his mouth to respond, as well as attempt something more physical, only for the woman to blur and disappear from his grasp. Immediately realizing what had just happened and what was about to occur, the intruder abandoned his shroud and leaped forward, narrowly evading Lorelei impaling him through the back. Alighting a short distance away, the intruder could only glower as the White Siren, having shed her evening attire for the familiar black and gold of the Flint Pirates, levitated forward a few more paces before coming to an opposing position. Only then did the carnival celebrators, and whatever else made up the collective psionic projection, rapidly vanish, leaving only the two fighters standing in the middle of the street.

"Yǒuqù," the spikey-haired fighter in black and red exclaimed. "It appears you're going to be even more fun than expected."

"Much more so," Lorelei responded, amethyst energy flickering from her hands. "Though I suspect you will have a different outlook by the end."

The assassin laughed all too sinisterly as energy flickered and formed from his own hands, then shaping into a pair of characteristic silver, yellow and black hook swords, both of which bore an ubiquitous sigil. Crossing them together in a fighting stance, the entity wasted no further time and launched forward to attack. Lorelei surged to engage the antagonist; violet and yellow lightning soon thundering between them.

"May I inquire as to why?" Jon posited as he turned to face his opponent for the first time. He already had a feeling what the answer would be, much to his newly emerging apprehension.

"The 'why' is quite simple," Shun responded, retaining his monotone and detachment. "By the will of my Lady, the Flint Pirates have been marked for extermination."

"Before the Gold Dragon can be resurrected," Jon surmised. "Is that it?"

"As well as Morganna Flint's legacy realized, yes," Shun confirmed. "Though I harbor doubts toward your abilities to accomplish either."

"Heh," Jon bitterly let out, not at all surprised by any of it. He should have known this would eventually happen. That at least one, if not all of the clans outside the Blue Dragon, would see the danger of a resurrected Gold Dragon in the making. The Flints' recent successes would have only emphasized that potential threat.

"And so you intend to wipe us out, here and now."

"You and as much of your followers as possible, yes," Shun admitted. "Once again, from my standpoint, however, it would only take the removal of a mere four to finalize such destruction."

Jon arched an eyebrow. "Four?" he repeated out loud. Obviously, he and Alex were among that number, but...

Shun was quick to sense his adversary's inquiry. "Though you and your brother are the rightful heirs to both the Gold Dragon and Morganna Flint's testament, it is clear that you would not have made it thus far without the powers and intrigues of another."

It didn't take much for Jon to realize. "Lorelei."

"Without her behind your apparent throne, your capabilities would be rendered mute," Shun again confirmed. "A truth you have undoubtedly surmised for yourself."

The first vestiges of ire began to take root. Jon kept such growing animosity restrained and controlled while allowing but a fraction to enter his eye. "And the fourth is Kaguya?"

Red Phoenix warrior confirmed once more. "Even if one were to disregard her present association with you, Fuma Kaguya has long been a thorn that refuses to be removed," he stated, forwardly and dispassionately. "Alongside, my Lady cannot and will not risk her taking up Morganna Flint's will for herself, should she feel inclined."

Against the elder Flint's baleful glare, Shun remained nonplussed regardless. "Once you four have been destroyed, there can be no others to follow in Morganna Flint's footsteps, even if the rest of your band were to survive," he concluded. "The last remnant of the Gold Dragon will effectively cease to exist, its name and power never to be reclaimed."

The ire within only compounded as Jon heard the diatribe. It was indeed an extermination. Not just for the brothers, but any and all possibilities of his mother's name and legend being reborn. The mere suggestion of such was enough to elicit further rage from within, but as before, Jon held it all in place. He would need it for what was about to transpire but could not allow it to run rampant as had happened once before. No matter how much it churned and writhed from within, alongside the evoked memory of his mother.

A burst of flame then emerged in Shun's right hand, taking the form of an ornate dark red and black jian, a characteristic sigil placed at the base of the blade.

"Shall we begin, Jonathan?"

Sneering as Astaroth formed within his own hand, Jon readied himself. "By all means," the eldest son of Morganna Flint responded, composed fury facing off against cold heartlessness. "Let's see how this concludes, Shun!"

At that, the two fighters charged, their respective black and red blades clashing almost instantly. Darkness and fire roaring as the scions of the Gold Dragon and the Red Phoenix engaged in their fated bout.

———————

Leaping back as the guandao's blade struck the ground, Alex immediately created a fire wave. His opponent spun his weapon against the onslaught, effectively dispelling the flame. The latter then countered with a white energy pulse, which Alex noted had a distinct sound akin to a thundercrack. The younger Flint dodged it regardless, dropping his body beneath his opponent's attack. As the energy pulse heaved past, he surged forward and attempted to stab his adversary in the torso. Startled but not caught unaware, his enemy pivoted and turned again to parry the follow-on attack and then reversed to strike with his pole weapon. Vaulting away, Alex landed on the sidewalk in front of a now deserted eatery. The Red Phoenix warrior pursued, thrusting his Devilblade repeatedly to attempt to impale Alex, but the Flint Pirate was able to evade and parry regardless, eventually executing another, more lateral fire whirl that forced his adversary to dodge back. The smell of burnt cloth drifted in the breeze.

Unrelenting, Alex rushed his opponent to gain the offensive. Before he could draw in, however, the Red Phoenix fighter spun and slammed his blade onto the ground, causing what could only have been a Devilblade energy-infused sonic boom, once more sounding akin to thunder. Upon recognizing the oncoming attack, only the timely rise of a fire shield diluted the force somewhat, but it was still enough to knock Alex backward, slamming him against the wall of a nearby building. He barely had time to recover from the blow when the attacker performed a burst strike with his guandao, effectively surging back upon the younger Flint to impale. Twisting to the side, Alex dodged this as well, the large blade striking deep into the vacated wall. Immediately, Alex unleashed a scattershot from his left hand, catching the Red Phoenix warrior on the flank; a timely move with his guandao and a hasty withdrawal minimized the damage. Sneering after him, the younger Flint wasted no time pursuing the combatant, Forneus and the still unknown Devilblade clashing once more.

Not far from the younger Flint's position, Kaguya performed several flips as she withdrew from her opponent, narrowly eluding a deep blue, fluidic wave. She retaliated with a shuriken, but her opponent was able to sidestep at the precise moment, then strike back with a second wave and then a third that forced the kunoichi to dodge and spin. Upon the latter, Kaguya slashed her ninjato about, effectively cleaving the on-coming wave down the middle just as it would have reached her. Undaunted, she proceeded to draw forward against her adversary. As the enemy Devilblade's piandao form was little different in shape from a Blue Dragon katana, the Dragon Princess had no trouble striking it with her ninjato, then executing slashes and parries in tandem. Unfortunately, however, her opponent was just as adept at evading and deflecting her strikes as well as attacking in turn, such that Kaguya was unable to find an opening to exploit.

Amid one such attempted attack, she was just able to depict energy, which looked even more like water up close, building across the curved edge. Immediately recognizing the danger, she leaped back as her adversary again slashed, generating an elongated blade that would have bifurcated her at the waist had she remained. Pressing his offensive, the enemy Wielder raised his hand, causing energy "rain" to fall from above, each drop striking the ground with meteor-like force. Yet again, Kaguya was forced to dodge, somehow managing to keep away despite the sheer abundance, all the while drawing and launching two kunais that were deflected just as quickly. The Red Phoenix chased after her, again bringing his blade against her ninjato with full force.

Sneer deepening against her enemy's smug gleam, Kaguya repelled the piandao while drawing a kunai. Utilizing the force of the weapons' impact for momentum, she spun and moved to impale the smaller blade into her opponent's throat. Again, the Red Phoenix fighter was more than quick enough to evade, jerking his head back while grabbing her left arm, his contemptuous scorn apparent.

Wrath evident in every move, Kaguya ripped her arm away, the speed and force of the action startling her opponent. Taking full advantage, she executed a snap spin kick, striking well into her adversary's previously grinning face, causing the *kuso yarō* to stumble backward into a destroyed Carnival effigy, with what appeared to be a broken nose. Upon her follow-up slash to the neckline, the Red Phoenix fighter managed to bring his piandao back up and deflect the blow.

As more slashes and parries were exchanged between the two fighters, Alex reentered the area, sliding back several meters after being struck by another thunderclap. His Red Phoenix opponent, scornful of his target, pulled his Devilblade back and spun the polearm to strike a hammer blow. Undaunted, Alex raised Forneus, intercepting the attack, thankfully preventing another thunder burst, right before redirecting the blade away and executing a fiery slash aimed at beheading his opponent. Another evasion, another counterattack, and the assault continued.

Lightning fell and struck around her in rapid bursts, compelling Lorelei to focus on weaving between them while simultaneously engaging her opponent. The Red Phoenix fighter was relentless, pressing the offensive and attacking with his hook swords, such that the psion continued to parry and defend with her psi blades while maneuvering. Even with her telepathy in play, elaborating on her opponent's movements just before they were made, this fight was still taking more in the way of effort than she would have wanted.

The White Siren fought with thought to the innocents in the combat area, whereas the Red Phoenix warrior, disdainful of all sentients but his clan, thought nothing of collateral damage. Regardless, Lorelei held her ground through the surge, dodging or deflecting both the lightning bursts and the twin curved blades with stylized movement, right before catching an opening and launching a rapid-fire energy burst of her own directly into the fighter's torso. The enemy warrior withdrew, leaping back, and left to dodge the oncoming violet bolts, with Lorelei following up with equally violet lightning. This, too, was circumvented, but not without difficulty and stumbling.

Surging after the apparent Phoenician, for lack of better description, the psion slashed with her blades once more, executing three strikes and then a spin attack. The first hit, the enemy fighter parried, then lunged back, evading the remainder of the offensive. While retreating, he directed twin lightning waves at Lorelei, who raised a barrier to deflect. Another barrage of violet energy shots quickly followed, with the opposing fighter 'dancing' to elude, executing several emphasized movements in the process. He rapidly countered, a singular swell of yellow lightning coursed outward from his location; Lorelei ascended up and over the bolt before diving back down, psi blades reextended as she drew close. It was all the Red Phoenix fighter could do to cross his hook swords together to intercept, from which the two reengaged in an elaborate fast-paced ballet of slash and parry. The encircling structures bore the full brunt of the energy volleys; destruction was immense and all-encompassing.

In the midst of their melee, more yellow lightning bursts struck from overhead, once more forcing Lorelei to withdraw and weave around each bolt. The Red Phoenix warrior took immediate advantage, launching further lateral energy breakers that swept across the area to augment the bursts falling from above. Even so, the White Siren evaded or deflected all of it, alternating between flitting in midair to forming barriers at different angles, ensuring that she remained untouched. Only when another opening presented itself did she create a crescent formation of violet bolts, which launched as one after the Red Phoenix, who was forced to raise his own barrier in defense. Without hesitation, Lorelei flanked him, moving to strike from his left side and quite nearly splitting him at the waistline. Again the brigand dodged, flipping sideways as she swept her psi blades across; however, dual thin streams of blood running down his hips attested to the incomplete success of his maneuver.

Insensed, the wounded fighter spawned another lightning wave from midair, forcing Lorelei to withdraw once more. Then bringing down both hook swords in a battering motion, the Red Phoenix generated a grand column of lightning, which fell with the force of a downburst. Even though she dodged this blast successfully, the resultant shock-wave was still enough to fling Lorelei well off her vector, causing her to fly through the front window of a nearby gift shop, shattering glass and displays. Grinning in triumph, the brigand once more hurled dual lightning waves, which surged straight into the building, obliterating it in a reverberating explosion. Not satisfied, he generated additional lightning strikes from above, lancing in repetition into the burning ruin, one after the other. All the while displaying an expression of sheer ecstasy with each strike.

And then, right before another blast of yellow lightning could fall, a violet-shaded burst launched from the fire. The brigand barely eluded the strike. From the burning ruin, Lorelei reemerged, still relatively untouched, psi blades reextending as she swept in like a proverbial tempest. Far from aggravated by his enemy's survival, the Red Phoenix warrior gleamed in further ecstasy as the White Siren slammed her psi blades against his hook swords, less endearing thoughts shifting through his consciousness as the dual blade sets locked at that moment. Glaring down in visible disgust at the wretch, Lorelei's psi blades began to glow and vibrate, the movement breaking apart the locked blades and simultaneously flinging her adversary backward. He countered with a near point-blank energy enhanced sweep. Still, Lorelei advanced, continuing to ignore the sheer euphoria that all but erupted from her opponent's consciousness, overcoming his rapid, brute force-based form with her far more refined, elegant strides.

With another ringing metallic clang, the black and red blades crossed, their respective Wielders moving to overpower the other. Several more such knells sounded in rapid succession, as well as one darkness-infused slash in which Jon attempted to catch Shun from the flank, but this "merely" caused the enemy Wielder to vault away before any damage could be realized. The elder Flint rapidly followed with a full black groundswell, but the Red Phoenix scion was just as quick to generate a blood-red fire shield that effectively dispelled the attack, then transformed into a fire blast that surged toward Jon. Blackhole forming in front of his position, Jon simultaneously moved through and disappeared, the shot decimating the tree behind Jon's previous location. The pirate captain reappeared through a black hole that materialized above Shun, moving to strike his adversary from overhead. Unfortunately, Shun was just as fast at defense, raising his blade to parry the strike, thereby forcing Jon to flip away.

As he withdrew, Jon couldn't help but remark somewhat on the difference between Shun's Devilblade Haborym and Forneus. Both were fire-based blades, obviously, but whereas Forneus' flames were brilliant, perhaps even radiant like that of a sun, Haborym's, by contrast, were dark, malignant, and strangely spectral, more akin to a funeral pyre or the flames of Purgatory. Not that it truly mattered, as Haborym's fire remained destructive; Jon was taking great pains to defend himself against them. He created a black hole to absorb one such burst of dark fire, only to form an additional number around the originator, redirecting the flames back at their maker. However, Shun remained alert, leaping away right as the fires converged, with Jon in pursuit. Black and red blades again clashed in midair as the two Wielders flew, soon landing on the rooftop of another nearby building, where they continued their duel. Neither even close to relenting to the other.

Launching a vertical fire wave from Haborym, which his adversary did well to move around, Shun followed up with a diagonal wave and then another, ensuring that Jon remained on the defensive. Upon evading the last, Jon retaliated; multiple black whirlwinds spun across the roof at random trajectories, rapidly closing in on the Red Phoenix's position. Shun was forced to pivot quickly and generate numerous shields while performing multiple energy slashes to dispel the twisters right before driving after his opponent with a beheading attack. Jon easily parried by inverting Astaroth, keeping Haborym's blade from even coming close to his neck, then throwing it aside entirely to slash back at its Wielder. Concurrently, miniscule black needles flew from the Flint pirate's left hand. Again, Shun leaped back to dodge, but three needles struck the fighter on the side. Small wounds appeared and slowly started to grow.

Insensed that the "mongrel" drew first blood Shun vaulted away to momentarily assess the damage. Undaunted, the captain of the Flint Pirates drove against him, pressing the offensive with attack after attack, both physical and energy-based. Unfortunately, Shun defended against all of it, not even dodging, instead quickly and precisely maneuvering Haborym about to either deflect or dispel, right before launching another fire surge. Only then was Jon's offensive broken.

Landing back some meters, Jon detected the attack had indeed left a mark, though only on his clothing, his vest and shirt visibly burned. He had just enough time to repair the damage before Shun rushed upon him once more, Haborym positioned to skewer. Jon moved to knock the dark red blade off course with Astaroth before it could reach its target while also bringing up his left hand, darkness forming within the palm. Sensing the attack immediately, Shun whirled Haborym about, dispelling the energy as well as eliciting a wound in Jon's open hand before spinning and kicking the opposing pirate away. Again as he slid back, managing to remain on his feet despite, Jon was just able to repair the damage to his glove, but not his hand, right as Shun struck again. A large black hole appeared between the fighters. One immediately stopped his forward movement, and one moved through, disappearing from sight.

Ignoring the burning pain in his left palm, Jon reappeared, rising up through the floor at his opponent's back and performing two energy slashes that caught his opponent on the thigh and kept Shun on the defensive.

Fire and abyss emerging that much more as, once again, the scions of the Gold Dragon and the Red Phoenix refused to relent. Their struggle only having just begun.

Chapter V: Ignis Aurum Probat

The Bobbaloo
Calydon, Atalanta

Several beam shots clipped the wine cellar that Davis and Anna had managed to dive behind, causing an assortment of debris, along with large quantities of rare vino, to spray the area. With the next opening, they both lunged up and returned fire, managing to strike down at least one of their black and red adorned attackers before the counterfire was renewed, forcing them to drop back to their cover, but not before Anna availed herself to a mouthful of the spurting alcohol. So far, they were doing well keeping the enemy from advancing on them, but both knew that they could not remain in the club for much longer. They needed to get outside, and soon, otherwise they would be overrun.

I should have known this would happen! Davis fumed as additional beam shots struck their cover, which was rapidly being torn apart. He moved to the left and fired a head shot into the nearest bad guy, darting back before his or her buddies could get a bead on him. *We just can't get a break in this damned galaxy!*

"Move!" Anna yelled as a grenade fell in their midst, forcing the duo to scramble. The device exploded seconds later, destroying what little remained of their barricade, but fortunately, they managed to vacate the blast zone.

"That wine was vintage, Neanderthals!" Anna seethed as she eliminated additional attackers while running. Davis wasn't totally sure her wrath was for the assault or the negligent destruction of alcohol.

They dashed to another hiding place, one that was closer to the back exit, all the while dodging rounds from the Red Phoenix raiders. Again Davis and Anna returned their fire, this time more to dissuade than to actually hit anything as they ran across the dance floor to the end of the disco club and fell behind the remnants of a dessert display. More beam shots soon followed, both at them and from them, as the pair fought to keep the aggressors back for that much longer.

"You really know how to show a girl a good time, don't you?" Anna huffed dryly before she leaned out from the cover and fired two shots, having to duck back immediately. Though she and Davis both had their Braun-enhanced pistols, neither she nor the helmsman was adorned in tactical armor, much less possessed personal shielding. Thus they had to take extra care. "Drinks, music, and beam fire to go around!"

"Don't look at me, I didn't invite them!" Davis yelled back before taking a few shots of his own, managing to nail one more Red Phoenix raider in the torso. He didn't know if that was enough to kill the bastard, but it at least knocked him off his feet, though his buddies ensured the Lady Killer wouldn't be able to add more injury. "I know I was hoping for some action later tonight, but this is decidedly *not* what I meant!"

"What in the Second Circle did you do anyway!? Sleep with one of Lady Ching's daughters!?" Anna hollered as she took her turn, firing at the nearest enemy raider. Unfortunately, the latter anticipated her attack and managed to move behind a mound of overturned musical equipment and backdrop, toppled and discarded in the band's haste to escape the battlezone. "Or maybe one of her *sons*!?"

"Hah hah, as if," Davis actually grimaced at the idea as he swapped another power cell into his Antilles. "I'm an old-fashioned, one-gender kind of guy," he retorted before firing on the same raider that Anna had been shooting at, dropping him the moment said raider peered out. "And it's pretty well established *which* gender!"

"Your 'friend' from Gallia would say otherwise!" Anna shouted, clipping the shoulder of one more raider that was attempting to close in but not much else. Not that she would have expected otherwise, but the Red Phoenix soldiers were proving to be quite challenging. These were not normal combatants, Anna surmised, much to her discomfort.

Davis shared the sentiment, even as he daringly forced himself up and fired his pistol in rapid suppression fire. That caused more than one enemy raider to take cover, thereby allowing the Flints to sprint from their position to the cooking area and that much closer to the exit. Unfortunately, it wasn't long before the clansmen regained the initiative and started their attacks anew, forcing the helmsman and the operations officer to move behind another set of obstructions. Responding in kind, the Flint pirates kept the enemy pinned, though Anna and Davis were not idealistic about how much longer they could hold out. They weren't dealing with Pisceans or corporate mercenaries this time around.

"I don't care for the aftershow!" Anna spat as she and Davis inched toward the exit, continuing to fire and forcing the raiders' to duck back. The pair moved closer to their intended salvation, the outlying street and open-air beyond, only to be pinned down again mere feet from the door. Additional beam fire, as well as quipping, soon following.

While paying mind to the fleeing revelers, the four Flint Pirates held their ground, moving as one through the mayhem as black and red armored attackers seemingly came out from every direction. It had all happened so abruptly that Boss, and likely Kaiser, Gran, and Braun with her, was still reeling from the initial ambush. It was sheer luck she had seen it coming before the first shot was taken. One shot rapidly became multiple, and the four soon found themselves running down the street with the screaming horde, moving to whatever cover they could find, returning fire before moving again, all while the enemy continued its pursuit. Unlike the Flints, the Red Phoenix troops cared little for collateral damage, a fair number of civilians having already been cut down as they fled. One such casualty, a man with the majority of his head missing, fell across Boss's path, causing her to leap, then turn and glare.

"Húndàn!" she shouted out the appropriate word, assuming her memory served, as she fired a shot straight into the enemy raider's head. As usual, the enemy's shielding and armor were of little hindrance to the Flints' weapons; the raider dropped as quickly as his last victim. *Eye for an eye,* she thought as she turned and bolted.

Of course, there were more than enough of his friends to stand in for him, and sure enough, two more raiders aimed at the ace, forcing her to all but dive behind a now ruined party float. She fired three more shots but, this time was unable to strike anything substantial.

Not far away, the distinct booming of Kaiser's Blunderbuss B-60 sounded, eliciting a massive hole in another raider's torso. Two more soon fell in similar fashion, the centers of their respective bodies blasted out entirely, before the Herculean was forced to seek cover. In his place, Gran, along with Braun, rose from behind a nearby food stand and added firepower. Her own Virago VF-300 snapped into the exchange, and though her firearm lacked the sheer power of the Blunderbuss, the Lyran more than made up for it with extreme accuracy, quickly taking down multiple raiders, one with a shot through the eye camera. That was more than enough of an opening for Kaiser to fire again, blasting more Red Phoenix raiders in the process, while Braun, also not to be outdone, fired from his right arm simultaneously.

Taking that moment to duck back behind the float and eject the spent energy cartridge from her smoking pistol, Boss quickly reached into her jacket, withdrew another, and slapped it into place. Off her left shoulder, she saw a shadow move dangerously near; she instinctively lunged out of the way as an enemy raider struck at where she had been crouching. The pilot was just able to turn to face the attacker, bringing her pistol to bear, only for the raider to slap the Marianas out of her hand with his polearm. She recognized the weapon as a qiang. Having but a brief second, she dove to the right and rolled out of the way as the raider twirled the spear around and thrust it at her repeatedly, the end blade continually striking the ground. Boss evaded, all the while moving to recover her firearm, doing all she could to keep ahead of that barb.

At last, retaking her pistol, she rolled onto her back and took aim; both Boss and the Red Phoenix raider looked on in dazed surprise as a set of very familiar claws suddenly protruded through the latter's chest armor. The deceased attacker was lifted off his feet and thrown aside, landing on the street corner in a metallic heap. An armored Barbarossa stood before the fighter ace, his baneclaws receding as he reached out to help her up. Smirking at his intervention, Boss wasted no time taking his hand and moving behind another damaged float.

"How in the Fifth Circle did you get *that* out here?" she couldn't help but ask, looking over the Leo's cherished armor almost incredulously.

Barbarossa only grinned. "It seemed to fit the occasion," he retorted casually, right before both war veterans reared back up and fired. The enemy continued their onslaught while gradually advancing upon the five. Grossly outnumbered, they knew they could only resist a little longer. All the while, other such battles between the Flints and their newfound opponents took place across the whole of the city, fire and fury shifting about.

Another blaze of energy swept after him, forcing Jon to power leap to his right; a black gale soon surged at his adversary. Anticipating the attack, Shun raised a dissipative barrier as the gale reached his position. Still, Jon continued moving, circling, and coming in at the Red Phoenix warrior's left, slashing Astaroth in a decapitation strike. Shun deflected this as well, knocking the obsidian blade away with a well-placed parry, then thrusting at the elder Flint, forcing him to defend. The attacks and deflections continued as both pirates soared into the air and onto another rooftop, each unable to overcome the other as they fought and then fell back onto solid ground. Only upon their brief landing did their blades separate, with Jon touching down a few meters from Shun; the Red Phoenix warrior wasted no time in rushing forward once more. A feign, spin, and another timely parry on Jon's part kept his throat from being pierced, after which the two adversaries resumed their duel.

Defending against another attack from the Flint captain, Shun diagonally side-stepped and kicked into Jon's torso, forcing him back a short distance. The elder Flint stabbed Astaroth into the roadway to halt his recession; all the while Shun leaped back into the air, Haborym raised overhead for a downward strike. Jon naturally formed a black hole and moved through. Evasion imperative, Shun immediately changed his vector and landed on the balcony of a nearby building, his dark red blade slamming against the surface with enough force to shatter the edifice considerably, thereby allowing the elder Flint to launch another black bolt through the evasion and directly at his opponent's chest. Shun raised his left hand and, generating another fire barrier, deflected the attack. He immediately retaliated with a spray of fireballs, which Jon absorbed with a spontaneously generated black hole. Shun was quite aware of that technique now, and so power jumped away as more black holes emerged, the fire shooting out and converging where he had just been positioned.

Landing on another neon-lit building, Shun was just able to jump back as Jon, having anticipated the warrior's defensive move, charged, slashing a darkness indued Asteroth at the Red Phoenix fighter's abdomen. Corresponding flames emerged from Haborym, canceling out the attack with the Devilblade's own energy.

Undeterred, Jon concentrated further on the offensive, implementing several more slashes and generating whirling tornados of black energy that danced all around his opponent, forcing Shun to block or maneuver but preventing him from power jumping away lest he land in a black vortex. Thus constrained to face his adversary, Shun turned as the elder Flint executed a corkscrew attack, flinging himself and twisting in midair to perform multiple slashes. Dodging and weaving, Shun was taxed to maintain his deflections.

The sweeping of a lateral fire wave forced Jon to abandon his assault and dodge left. Two more waves soon followed, all running across the rooftop. Jon dove off the building's side, simultaneously reaching out with his left hand, he formed a shadow at Shun's feet. A set of black claws immediately emerged to ensnare. Shun barely evaded in time, leaping away while still avoiding the twisters.

Sneering after the Red Phoenix fighter, Jon turned midfall and lunged after him. Shun retaliated with an even larger volley of fire at the elder Flint's approach. Not having enough time to form a black hole, Jon focused more on speed and drove himself through the fire as it fell around him, soon closing the distance on his opponent and leaping upward for an overhead strike. Again, Shun was able to knock away the strike, and Jon with it, before executing a point-blank lateral fire wave that swelled over the pirate captain and sent him flying back. Only by concentrating Astaroth's power around him did Jon manage to diminish the wave, as well as keep from being incinerated.

Landing yet remaining in a kneeling position, the Flint captain brought Astaroth up to defend as Shun attacked again. However, just before it would have intercepted Haborym's next strike, Jon ducked under the attack with a drop onto his free hand, rolled to the left, and deliver a counter strike catching the Red Phoenix warrior on the back of the knees. Incensed, Shun reached out with a power blow with his left palm, again knocking Jon away. This time the pirate captain utilized the energy to separate from his opponent, eventually landing against a distant sidewall.

Jon had a moment to catch his breath before Shun launched an even greater firestorm for his finisher. Opening another black hole, Jon let lose the previous wave into this one in another canceling attack, which among other effects, resulted in the rooftop becoming ablaze with the corresponding flame. Through that conflagration, Shun charged again, the dark flames casting him in a spectral quality, in turn further emphasizing his reticent visage as he advanced. Despite that, Jon met him head-on, bringing Astaroth's obsidian blade against Haborym's almandine, both edges clashing together in darkness and fire. The scions of the Gold Dragon and the Red Phoenix keeping to their bout, progressing ever so gradually to the anticipated outcome.

———————————   ———————————

Quickly deflecting the next white beam with a single swipe, Alex was just as fast in launching a scattershot from his left hand, which the opposing Wielder again blocked by spinning his guandao-formed blade. The younger Flint attempted to advance on his opponent, only for the Red Phoenix warrior to slam the pommel of his weapon into the ground once more, generating a sonic boom that shattered windows, destroyed carnival kiosks, and knocked Alex well across the avenue. Fortunately, it took only a brief moment for him to reorient himself mid-flight. Landing on his feet, he skidded across the street as his adversary vaulted into the air, guandao extended. Rather than deflect again, Alex simply jumped back and allowed the Wielder to fall; another thunderclap boomed upon impact. Learning his opponent's fighting style, the younger Flint was prepared. Though he felt as though his skin would tear off his body from the reverberation, the younger son of Morganna Flint drove forward regardless, the still unknown enemy fighter only managing to raise his polearm and block the fire-indued attack at the last second. Blocking Forneus, the Red Phoenix fighter attempted to counterattack, only for Alex to respond in kind, fire and thunder flickering and reverberating between their clashing blades.

Not far away, Kaguya also fought, three shurikens flying out of her hand while additional blue energy "droplets" fell over her. As her opponent raised another water-like barrier to deflect the weapons, the kunoichi landed on a nearby staircase; her feet balancing and moving, she continued her onslaught, throwing more shurikens as she dashed along the balustrade. These too were blocked, but it allowed her to position herself for a running strike, which the enemy Wielder was only able to evade by bending his head back, down, and away from the sweeping blade. Out of position, he raised a point-blank barrier to defend from the following slash. But Kaguya, having anticipated the move, easily cut the shield in a diagonal slash with her ninjato. Undeterred, she drove to slice at the Wielder's stomach. This time her opponent employed his piandao to deflect, effectively preventing her attack from so much as grazing his abdomen. Kaguya was not about to let up and executed three more slashes, only for each to be deflected, with the last locking with her blade momentarily.

"Not bad *gōng zhǔ*," the Red Phoenix fighter proclaimed, all but gleaming into Kaguya's glaring blue eyes. "But still lacking."

Choosing not to respond verbally, Kaguya simply twisted violently, forcing her opponent's blade upward, and then executed a spin kick into his sternum, knocking the air from his lungs and driving him back several meters. Redoubling the ferocity of her attack, she charged again. Despite the power behind her strike, however, the Red Phoenix Wielder recovered and propelled a torrent that literally cut through the ground as it swelled, forcing Kaguya to dodge left and behind a mobile café. Her opponent followed up with a horizontal wave and then another that spun as it flew. Kaguya lept over the first and, while still airborne, turned and cut down the second straight on. The now split wave crashed into two separate buildings behind her, obliterating the facades and flooding the structures. The mobile café bobbed in the water-like energy and floated away.

The Flint ninja, alighting on an overturned float, pivoted and hurled a kunai at her target's head, only for him to raise another barrier before the throwing blade could come close. Once again, however, that was enough of a distraction for her to move in and slash at the same appendage. Yet the Wielder was just as fast in parrying her kill strike, and then the next, and the following. His face retaining the smug assurance that, no matter what Kaguya attempted, her "normal" blade would never reach him.

His partner, who was several meters away, held a similar expression as he raised a white energy barrier to cancel out the oncoming fire-infused attack right before slashing his blade about to launch a pressurized pulse. Once more, Alex evaded by jumping aside, feeling as though his eardrums would explode as the pressure wave passed and blasted through another nearby building. It disheveled him, but not enough that he failed to detect his opponent rushing upon him, guandao blade raised up to deliver a hammer blow. Alex intercepted the strike by deceptively altering the attack line, passing Forneus under the adversary's point, then, stepping past the still moving warrior, he raised his sword with both hands and swung down and back around, catching his opponent in the back and executing a fire indued slash that would have bifurcated his adversary at the waistline, had he not power jumped away. The smell of charred flesh mixed with the odor of burnt structures.

Pursuing, Alex generated a wall of flame directly in front of the Red Phoenix fighter and moved to catch his opponent in the flank. Another timely deflection thwarted the attempt as the warrior angled his polearm, simultaneously vaulting over the flames while intercepting the blow. Alex charged through the blaze and caught the fighter just as he landed. Pivoting, the Red Phoenix combatant threw up an energy shield to evade being impaled right before slamming his sword pommel into Alex's chest, creating another thunder blast in the process.

Flying through the air even faster than before, Alex fell through a nearby window, which naturally shattered upon impact, and into the middle of a deserted tavern. Falling in a heap against a set of tables and chairs, the younger Flint then let out a bloodied cough. Prepared for the pulse, Alex had protected his ears with energy shields; his chest, however, bore the brunt of the strike. Rapidly, he ascertained his injuries; nothing vital was damaged. It was not long before another thunderclap sounded, causing the entire wall to explode as his enemy charged through, still unidentified Devilblade raised to finish the battle. Glowering at the oncoming Red Phoenix, Alex sprang back to his feet, quickly renewing the attack, fire encompassing his form as the Red Devil kept up the fight.

Again her opponent stormed after her, lightning indued hook swords slicing in an effort to overpower. Maintaining her barrier as she retreated, Lorelei observed the display as the attacker hacked and hewed through the charge. Only at a precise moment did she eventually drop her defense and move against his exposed back, executing a cross slash with her psi blades. Her assailant barely evaded critical injury by leaping forward. Rebounding off a nearby wall, the Red Phoenix surged after her again, this time meeting her straight on, forcing another exchange of psi blades and hook swords as the fighters continued the bout. The mania even more apparent now in the clansman's expression and psyche, much to Lorelei's ever-increasing disdain.

Flipping back and airborne, Lorelei launched four energy orbs, which flew out and burst as one around the enemy fighter, compelling him to raise a spherical barrier to keep from being overtaken. Immediately the White Siren shifted to the right, firing violet lightning that struck and shattered the barrier, once again forcing her opponent to abandon his defense and withdraw. He countered with his own yellow lightning, which fell from above to hinder the psion, but Lorelei moved through it undaunted, performing a buzzsaw-like attack with her blades as she closed in on her quarry. Evading by dodging left, the enemy fighter performed another power leap when Lorelei added a spin attack at the last second. Another yellow lightning wave soon broke across the space. Irritated but wary, Lorelei sidestepped the roller and retaliated with a barrage of violet barbs that inundated her enemy's position, again forcing her opponent to cross his blades and reform his barrier.

Taking a subtle cue from her captain, Lorelei formed several more shots from overhead and had them fire down from different vectors, once more shattering her opponent's defense. Unfortunately, what the Red Phoenix lacked in defensive power he more than made up for in evasiveness, the fiend flipping out of the way before the bolts could converge upon him. More yellow lightning shots followed, Lorelei weaving around each one before striking back with violet blasts, which kept her adversary running. And then he was on her again, moving in close and slashing at her right side with his hook swords. Ascending to avoid his weapons, she spun, inverted, and soared downward, psi blades clashing against said hook swords. Once again, the frenzied nature of her adversary was palpable as they attacked, deflected, and evaded with their respective weapons, his movements even more erratic as a result. Fortunately, she was more than able to match him through her own balletic motions without incurring any damage.

And then the Red Phoenix moved to strike from overhead, bringing down his dual formed Devilblade to pummel, energy flashing and flowing around the knife-edges. Lorelei crossed her blades together and blocked the blow. Lightning surged and flickered around the curved weapons as the Wielder increased his force; the psion was again confronted by her opponent's ebullience and sheer euphoria in fighting one such as her. Or, more specifically, sheer ecstasy in being able to *destroy* one such as her. All but sniffing contemptuously at the literal thought, she responded by forcing the Devilblade back with telekinetic force, just enough that she could uncross her blades in a sudden forking attack. Once more, however, the Red Phoenix warrior

leaped back and evaded the amethyst blades, immediately responding
with dual lightning bolts, both forming into a yellow 'X' as they flew
at her. This time she chose not to dodge.

Apparently, struck directly by the yellow lightning, Lorelei appeared
to lose all bearing as she was flung through the air, slamming into
an unidentifiable structure. Such was the force behind that attack
she looked dazed and unaware. Within moments her enemy was
upon her again, hook swords raised to finish her, yet the Wielder
paused for the briefest of seconds to seemingly relish the victory. A
simple but no less powerful telekinetic "push" kept that killing stroke
from connecting, followed by twin bursts of violet lightning from
the White Siren's hand, which, although deflected and evaded, still
rendered the warrior breathless and injured. Lorelei rose from her
position, a new gleam of understanding in her eyes. She reenergized
her psi blades and swooped back in, bringing down both against her
opponent's Devilblade once more, forcibly ignoring the noxiously
euphoric thoughts of her opponent, which remained centered upon
her violent and utterly vivid destruction.

Struck with a fierce, fire-enhanced blow, Jon fell to the rooftop,
managing to orient himself so that he would land on his feet. Shun
did not relent in his attack, slamming Haborym down against
Astaroth the moment the elder Flint's bootheels touched down. A
black hole appeared below Jon's feet, allowing him to drop through
the roof and into the dwelling below, throwing his adversary off
balance. Shun pursued, but Jon was ready. Multiple black holes
appeared throughout the room. The Flint captain shifted into one
and emerged through another with no pattern to his movements.
With each appearance, he slashed at various parts of his opponent with Astaroth and then disappeared through another black
hole. Shun deflected each strike then spun, trying to anticipate his
adversary's next materialization. Energy rushed from a black hole
directly in front of Shun. As the warrior evaded the deathly cold

flow, Jon emerged at his opponent's right and slashing at his flank, only to withdraw back through the black hole to avoid Shun's counterattack.

Through defensive actions, the Red Phoenix heir sent a fire wave into one black hole, only for it to reappear directly behind him. A timely evasion prevented Shun from being burnt from his own attack. To this, Shun executed another fire wave, one even larger than those previous. A torrent of fire spewed from multiple holes. This time, the warrior stood his ground and deflected all incoming flames. The structure was consumed in seconds.

Powerleaping away to escape the inferno, Jon immediately found himself among civilians, some of which had, in typical fashion, stopped their flight to see what was the source of the destruction and commotion. Shun descended, landing several meters away from Jon, Haborym remaining in hand. Raising Astaroth back up, Jon readied himself to continue only, to see his opponent tilt his head in speculation, specifically to look past Jon's shoulder. Only then did Jon detect the lone child running toward their position, well in front of the crowd and well out of reach of her pursuing parents. A doll lay on the ground at Shun's feet.

Not even having time to curse the Red Phoenix, much less form another black hole or any kind of elaborate defense, the elder Flint did the only thing he could in those seconds. Turning and moving fast, he captured the child and threw her toward her parents. A short moment later, Haborym's almandine blade pierced his back and exited his chest, Jon's teeth gritting together against the resultant agony.

"Predictable," Shun exclaimed from behind, dispassionately and disdainfully. "To the end, your honor remains your weakness, Jonathan."

No sooner than those words were uttered did the hellfire emerge, sweeping across the area and encompassing all within, from the child and her parents in front of Jon to the very last bystander in proximity. The blaze was only overpowered by the screams of its victims, all collapsing into ash around him.

"NO!" Jon cried as it all occurred, the accumulated screams causing him far more torment than the impalement. In renewed fury, he focused all of his energy into raising Astaroth back up. Black energy swirled around his form as he yanked himself free of the still aglow blade and turned to face his adversary. Wrath and condemnation emanating.

Right before the continuance however, the Red Phoenix warrior abruptly looked up and away, listening as a signal came through his comlink from the *Zhang He*. Though he remained as cold and impassive as he had been since the beginning, a slight frown crossed his expression.

"It appears you have a stay of execution," Shun informed the elder Flint. "An Imperial warship is en route."

Through his rage and wavering consciousness, Jon stood firm yet understood. If the Red Phoenix's presence on Atalanta had not drawn the Imps' attention, then the battle they had just had would have done it. And both he and Shun knew better than to continue with the possibility of drawing the Empire into their conflict.

"A setback, but a very short one. My Lady's will shall be carried out. You and your followers will be destroyed, and the Flint name will vanish for all time," Shun continued as he stepped back. "I suggest you make use of your remaining time accordingly."

Seemingly without further thought, Shun turned his back upon his adversary, and power leaped away to another part of the city, disappearing from Jon's view entirely. Leaving the elder Flint to glower in his own fury.

"We will," Jon managed to growl, using the last of his reserves. "You and your Lady can be assured of that."

Cringing against the pain and the scorching heat, Jon raised his left arm up and activated his wristcom's distress function before allowing himself to crumble to the ground, consciousness fading entirely now. He would not die here. He knew his crew; with their assailants now withdrawing, Alex or Barbarossa was already directing the rest of the Flint pirates to return to the *Sun* for immediate departure. They would find him and bring him back as well.

It was safe to say that the peaceful days that they had all enjoyed were now over. All the while, darker, more turbulent days lay ahead as a new enemy now surfaced. One whose emergence Jon, and Alex with him, had long anticipated. And feared.

Such realization served as Jon's last conscious thought before he slipped away into the emptiness, not knowing when he would wake up again.

Chapter VI: Uncertain Tides

Ryugu Castle
Kyoto, Ryugu

It was with concealed weariness that Lord Fuma Kotaro sat upon his throne, waiting for the inevitable communique. By now, the events on Atalanta had come to pass, and a fair portion of the galaxy, up to and including his opposite numbers, was all too certainly deliberating upon them. He had anticipated such an advent, as he had spoken to Kaguya about not too long ago. Still, at the same time, even he could hardly believe the brazenness, the sheer audacity of their execution. To attack so openly upon a world held by one of the Powers, and without any care toward collateral damage or casualties. He couldn't fathom what the one he was waiting on now had truly been thinking, even if she had not personally carried out the attack.

Soon enough, a holographic image took shape and form in front of his throne. Somehow the Blue Dragon Lord managed not to furrow his brows as he greeted it.

"Lady Ching."

"Lord Fuma," Ching Shih, Lady of the Red Phoenix, acknowledged before tilting her head with interest. "I see you have anticipated this conference."

"I have," Fuma confirmed, gazing upon the enlarged image of his opposite with a muted expression. "Not that it was difficult to anticipate, any more than its intended purpose."

"Good, then I need not waste my breath on a formal ultimatum," the Red Phoenix Lady spoke. "Instead, I will simply ask. Will you, or won't you stay out of the way?"

Fuma slowly exhaled. "For the sake of inquiry, what should occur upon my giving the latter response?"

"I would think the answer obvious," Ching retorted, matching Fuma's confrontation with her own. "Our clans would go to war, and the Treaty of Libertalia would be nullified for it."

Again Fuma could only marvel at the audacity. "You would threaten the agreement that, for three hundred years, has kept peace among us as well as the Powers?"

Ching sniffed contemptuously. "Only if you were to do as you so brazenly suggest," the Lady retorted. "As long as you and the others remain casual observers, full war can and will be avoided."

The Red Phoenix Lady then fixed the Blue Dragon Lord with a heavy gaze. "You would do well to keep this in mind, Lord Fuma," she continued. "As well as that even the slightest act can lead to provocation."

Fuma easily depicted the veiled threat therein. "I do keep such in mind, Lady Ching," he rejoined, turning it back around toward the originator. "Though I hope you are doing the same on your side, up to and including your own words."

He then looked upon the Red Phoenix Lady with accusation. "After all, was it not the 'slightest act' that provoked Qingdao toward succession?"

"Qingdao is none of your concern," Ching easily countered. "As Lady of the Red Phoenix, I will address my territory and my subjects as I see fit."

She then glared down with an indictment of her own. "And with that same power and authority, I will address the ailment you and the others refuse to acknowledge, much less cure," her eyes flashed as she prevailed. "The same ailment you failed to remove long ago, even when its originator was well within your reach."

Fuma refused to rise to the deliberate provocation. He also noted his lack of response seemed to fuel the Lady's barely suppressed anger.

"This will not be another War of the Dragons. Nor will I repeat Drake's failures at Ephesus," Ching spat. "This time, nothing of that pretender, not even the last vile drop of her blood, will remain."

Once more did Lord Fuma's nostrils flare. "And what of the others? Surely Lord Pargo and Lady Levasseur have not been so silent, especially over your more recent actions."

Ching momentarily grimaced. "Unfortunately, it is as you state," the Pirate Lady admitted with some agitation. "In fact, I fear I still have not heard the end of their ramblings."

Fuma couldn't help but allow a small grin at the Red Phoenix Lady's irritation. Ching forced herself to ignore it.

"Despite that, neither Lord Pargo nor Lady Levasseur holds any real care or concern," Ching continued, unabated. "Their ire is of Atalanta and my circumventing their council, not my actions toward the pretender's children."

Discreetly did the Blue Dragon Lord keep those words to mind. Such knowledge may prove vital, especially in the near future.

"Which is where I come to this final admonishment," the Lady proclaimed. "Remain neutral, and know any attempt at intervention will not be tolerated."

Fuma folded his arms in response. "Not even for my daughter's benefit?"

Ching made her contempt even more apparent. "You knew what her taking on the pretender's colors would entail. She will share in their destruction, and you will allow it."

Her glare deepened in challenge. "That is unless you do indeed wish to initiate the Fifth Clan War."

This time Fuma did visibly frown, but neither spoke nor revealed anything else. The Red Phoenix Lady took that as a sign of compliance, not that the opposite Lord had any choice in the matter. Not if he wanted three hundred years of peace to remain.

"A wise decision Lord Fuma," Ching concluded. "I expect you to hold to it."

The hologram then vanished. Leaving the Blue Dragon Lord to further pursue his thoughts and the possibilities therein.

Flint Pirates umbra *Black Sun* Deep Space

Slowly but surely, Jon returned to the realm of consciousness, his eye opening and attempting to focus. It took a few moments to recognize that he was in the *Black Sun*'s sickbay, as well as to identify the music playing from his left as *These Are the Days of Our Lives*. Smirking over the melancholic rhythm of the song, he closed his eye again as he realized who was also there, sitting next to his bed.

"How long?"

"A little over twenty-four hours," Lorelei confirmed without looking up from her book. Like the music, it was one of his, specifically a somewhat worn copy of *Out of the Silent Planet*. "Despite the relative severity of your chest wound, we were able to find you fast enough."

Hearing that, Jon pulled back the blanket and looked over his bare chest. Indeed, there was a new scar among his "collection".

"No abnormalities?"

"None outside of some rather high-level burning, which Apache actually had difficulty with," Lorelei answered, at last closing the book and looking toward her captain. Not at all bothering to hide her concern. "But that was expected, considering your opponent."

Jon frowned as he leaned up, now recalling the prior battle. "Shun…" he spoke the name out loud, feeling the vestiges of rage begin to reemerge. He forced it all down, however, having much more to worry about now.

"This was not an unanticipated outcome," Lorelei assured, reaching her hand over to cover his. "In fact, it was only a matter of when and where."

"Yes," Jon agreed as he intertwined his fingers through hers, visibly taking her consolation at some measure. "Alex and I had long feared this would happen."

He then looked up into the air, allowing a little bit of his uncertainty to show. "And now that it has happened, I don't know…"

"That will be discussed soon enough," Lorelei interrupted, stopping the elder Flint before he depleted his strength.

Jon nodded in turn. As overwhelming as it all was, he would deliberate their next course of action with his crew. For the moment, he needed only the present bearings. "Where are we now?"

"Under cloak within an uncharted star system," Lorelei reported. "The Psi Disruptor is also online."

Jon nodded again, clenching her hand a little more in assuagement. Though Lorelei never showed it outwardly, Jon knew the Psi Disruptor affected her power as well. Not enough to cancel it out as it would lesser psions, but at the same time, he doubted it was a pleasant sensation to her.

"Were there any others on Atalanta?"

Again Lorelei understood. "No," she replied, taking in her captain's visible relief. "Only the Red Phoenix."

Jon actually let out a breath he didn't know he had been holding. *At least there's that,* he thought, though he also admitted that didn't quite rule out the other clans just yet. It only indicated that the Red Phoenix was the only one actively hunting them for the moment.

"Anything else?"

Lorelei flashed a smaller version of her usual knowing smile. "Just the usual apprehensiveness that occurs with events such as this," she informed Jon. "Despite everything we've gone through to the present, the crew is rather anxious over this one."

"They would be fools not to be," Jon acknowledged. Fighting Drake on Ephesus, sailing the Sognare, and even fighting the Baranovs had all been trials unto themselves, each of which the Flints had emerged beaten and battered, yet much stronger as well. Compared to those, however, there was something different about being set against a Pirate Clan. Not because it would be a more difficult adversary to contend with, but rather an unfamiliar one. Only once in the last three hundred years had there been a major shooting war within or without the Clans, and as a result, very few could attest to ever fighting one. And as far as Jon or anyone else knew or heard, there had been no claims of success in that area.

Alongside, it was a pretty fair guess that this would be an all-out war in which the Red Phoenix would employ the bulk of its military and logistical assets. Not simply because they had made enemies of the children and followers of the Golden Queen, nor even because of said children and followers' prior achievements. Rather, it would be because the Red Phoenix was set to prevent the Gold Dragon's rebirth, as well as ensure the very name of Morganna Flint was truly forgotten. Lady Ching's eldest and heir apparent had spoken such to him, and Jon was well aware of how the "original" Pirate Lords had viewed his mother and her "pretend" clan and dynasty. That knowledge by itself affirmed that the Red Phoenix would stop at nothing to see them all exterminated, to the point of the Flint line being irreversibly broken. Again Jon didn't bother concealing his discomfiture, such that Lorelei leaned over to kiss him on the cheek.

"It won't happen," she again reassured. "Just as your mother once made a name for herself contesting one of the four, so shall you." Her smile deepened, this time in faith. "And we will emerge better for it."

"Heh," Jon responded, smiling. Yes, his mother had done precisely that long ago. Not only in accomplishing what had long been claimed impossible and establishing a fifth clan but also in triumphing over the original four when one of their number, a very particular one, challenged her founding. Indeed it was only fitting that he do the same, given how much he was already following in those footsteps.

"Well, either way," he said, slowly pulling himself up and off the bed, his clothes reforming as he stood up. "It appears our vacation is officially over."

Lorelei nodded in affirmation as she rose to stand by her captain's side.

——————————— ———————————

"We really can't catch a break, can we?" Davis griped as Lloyd passed he and Alex their respective drinks at the counter, the helmsman gazing sullenly into his as he took it. "It's only been a few weeks or so after Dreyfus and Baranov, and now we're in yet another damned war!"

"If only this one were as simple," Alex responded sullenly, taking a quick drink. "I'd rather fight Marzanna Baranov all over again than face what we're about to."

Knowing how much of an ordeal that had been for the Brothers Flint, especially when the opponent in question had transformed herself into the eldritch "goddess" Nyx, Anna, Davis, and Gran all felt a simultaneous chill run down their spines. Were they really that deep in the waste matter?

"I know we're not up against any single fleet or a 'mere' conglomerate this time," Gran spoke evenly toward the younger Flint. "But that shouldn't mean we're outmatched either."

Alex flashed a wry smirk. "I didn't say we were. Just that we're in for the *real* fight for our lives," he stated, taking another drink before continuing. "Have any of you heard of the Treaty of Libertalia?"

Anna was quick to answer. "The non-aggression pact signed between the Clans and the Thirteen. In exchange for each recognizing the Clans' respective sovereignties, both the Powers and the Clans would not pursue further acts of war against all parties involved."

"Yes," Alex nodded in confirmation. "A little known fact is that the clans had existed at least a century or two before Libertalia," he paused to ensure that he had his audience's complete attention. "They weren't anything like they are now, but they were still a cut above the average pirate territory, enough to warrant attention from any one of the Powers or each other."

He took another sip of his Old Caribbean. "Many a war, including the four titular Clan Wars, had been fought during that period, with immense destruction all around."

"Enough to warrant such a treaty," Anna surmised, frowning at the implications.

Alex nodded again. "It reached the point where the Powers could stamp out the Clans, or the Clans could stamp out each other, but it would expend far too much in the way of effort and resources for all involved. So, while the Clans are still *de jure* unrecognized states…"

"Nobody wants to have another fight over it," Davis deduced before taking a more serious expression. "Outside of events not too long ago."

Again Alex smirked wryly, knowing what Davis was referring to and that Anna and Gran also understood. "The War of the Dragons only lasted one year," he stated sagely. "You can imagine how much of a fight that was."

"I'd rather not," Anna exclaimed, taking her own drink. Many stories had been told of the newly founded Gold Dragon Clan and its stand against the "original" four, namely the one that challenged its formation in full. "Even so, Gran has a point. We've already fought Drake, the Pisceans, the Baranovs, and several eldritch abominations in between..."

Alex let out a small laugh, seeing that the others still didn't yet understand. "Let me put it to you this way then," the younger Flint explained further. "Of the first two, we only fought segments of the whole. Drake only had a portion of the Thirteenth Fleet with him at Ephesus, while at Timas, we only fought one dag and a minor one at that. For the third, the Baranov fleet was a mercenary force..."

"A mercenary force with nuclear weapons," Anna was quick to remind.

"Granted, but still not a true military," Alex resounded. "And yes, Kraft and the family Baranov were terrifying, but they had their respective weaknesses."

He down the rest of his tankard before delivering the ultimatum. "What we're about to face is a sovereign state. One that controls much in the way of territory and resources, with a military that has fought in conflicts that none of us can ever imagine, well before any of us were born."

The younger Flint spoke with uncharacteristic somberness now. "Instead of one fleet, we face legion. Instead of one battleground, we may very well fight across the galaxy proper. And rather than one

Devilblade Wielder or one or two unstable psions, we're now against at least four of the former."

An even larger chill ran down the three as their First Officer faced them unflinchingly. "I'm sorry to say nothing we've fought until now can compare to what's ahead of us. Before, we were just one ship facing down a fleet here, a ragtag band there, a megalomaniac further on," he stated with utmost seriousness. "Now, we face the entirety of an *empire*."

With that single word did Alex get his point across. "One that is very much set against the name of Flint," he emphasized further, much to the even greater cold swell over his audience. "And any and all who dare bear it."

It was only then he passed his tankard back to Lloyd, who took it and moved to refill it. All the while, the other three at the counter, all of whom fought under the late Golden Queen's banner and Death Mark, could only ponder their future.

——————————— ———————————

As with the rest of the ship, Fuma Kaguya could not help but feel apprehensive, even if she was better at shrouding her emotions than most. Indeed she had anticipated such an advent, but only now, after it had taken place, did she realize how truly unprepared she had been to face it. And not simply because of her prior showing on Atalanta.

Within the solitude of her quarters, she meditated, both to gain some measure of calm as well as to dwell upon what she, and the rest of the Flint Pirates, faced. War was upon them, there was no doubt. Nothing as great or as destructive as those past, but war it remained, for it would not be centered upon one battle or confrontation as it had upon Ephesus. And though they had fought one war just prior, the petty brawl between Dreyfus and Baranov had been but an amateur production, a fight between neophytes and their corporate masters. It would hardly compare to what the Flints would soon confront, especially when they had been supporting participants in the preceding conflict. In this war, they would be the primary belligerents whose enemy grossly overpowered and outnumbered them.

In many ways, this would be a first for her as well, she could only admit. Though she had taken part in many clandestine operations of her clan, as well as several actual battles against innumerable adversaries, she could not say she had ever been involved in war at its fullest. Once again, Ephesus had been a battle unto its own, as had Ianessa and Mayak Prime thereafter. By comparison, what lay ahead of her was a multitude of battles, in which the Flints either fought on the defensive end or, as she suspected, they fought offensively on multiple fields. Each of which would play a role in the war's overall conclusion but would not gain complete victory by themselves. While by contrast, any severe enough loss could entail the Flint Pirates' wholesale destruction.

Kaguya would have been lying if she claimed not to be disconcerted, especially at the notion that victory and triumph would not be obtained so easily nor so quickly. She was a ninja; by her very nature, she fulfilled her objectives swiftly and without waste of time or movement in such ways that her enemies were defeated as soon as the fighting began. By contrast, war such as this was fought by attrition and endurance, in which the side that lasted the longest won overall. Not that she lacked endurance, far from it, but it was still not the way she preferred to fight. Especially when the enemy had far more firepower than the Flints.

The opening salvo on Atalanta only added to her discomfort, namely her own battle against that enemy Wielder. She had fought and fought hard, to the point that her opponent never struck her with a critical blow, and yet neither had she in return.

"Not bad gōng zhǔ, *but still lacking."* The *konoyarô* had claimed in the middle of the fighting, and unfortunately, he had not exaggerated. For all of Kaguya's efforts in making a quick and decisive kill, her sword never truly reached him.

The same sword that now rested in its usual place sheathed and appearing innocuous enough. Kaguya knew better, of course, much to her concealed disdain. She, more than anyone else, knew that her sword was a cursed blade, even as it appeared otherwise dormant and motionless. There had been far too many nights in which she had been rendered sleepless, haunted by familiar dreams. Just as there had been too many battles in which she had been tempted to release it in full, to make her killing stroke as overwhelming as it was swift and precise.

Such dreams and temptations, such promises and assurances of unfathomable power and might, she had long ignored. And she would ignore them forever on. For she possessed her sword for that precise reason.

And yet, as her mind continued to reel from the last battle and her inability to kill her enemy, Kaguya felt such enticement even more, and not from her chosen weapon this time. This time the allurement for further power came from a far simpler yet far more damning source. Once more, her knowledge, her fear, of the future. And all that it would entail.

Even so, she held strong and would continue. The Flints would claim victory, that much she was certain. It would be a difficult fight, much more demanding than those previous, but they would win all the same. And she would contribute to that winning without having to give in to the allurement. As she had always done and would do to the end of her days.

So she had vowed long before.

Chapter VII: The Inevitable War

Flint Pirates umbra *Black Sun*
Deep Space

It was a grim company that entered the briefing room and took their usual seats, anticipating what would soon be discussed. Not since the prelude to Ephesus did the core membership of the Flint Pirates feel such apprehension, such dread concerning their recent experience, and much more considering what would soon transpire. Though exact details had yet to be given, they all had a good idea of what they were up against, and not simply because of their fighting on Atalanta. They all knew what they were facing was unlike anything they had encountered before and that it would be a most brutal affair. Just as it was questionable *how* they would fight such an opponent, with more than one of their number looking toward the Captain and First Officer for answers. If any of them had any idea how they would challenge this new enemy, it would surely be the Flint brothers.

Jon was well aware of the group's trepidation as he took his seat, eye sweeping across both ends of the table. Some were glancing toward him already, while others simply sat, either looking upon the tabletop or, in such cases as Braun attempting to rein his right arm back in, were otherwise concentrating on some side task. All of them held the same unspoken questions, and all of them were waiting for him, and Alex, to provide those answers. Only Lorelei and Kaguya had some idea of what those answers would be, yet they did not appear any more hopeful than the rest. Needless to say, it was not going to be a pleasant meeting, but it was necessary all the same.

"I will move straight to the point," Jon began, causing all eyes to look toward him with that opening statement. "We are now at war with the Red Phoenix Clan."

With those words, Jon wholly affirmed the Flint Pirates' position, earning a small line of acknowledging nods from around the table. Though each of them remained apprehensive, there was no questioning it was exactly as their captain spoke.

Running his gloved hand across his coat sleeve, Jon continued. "Both Alex and I have long anticipated this, as you have probably guessed. For all of our mother's legend, there is no denying she made more than a fair number of enemies throughout her lifetime, some of whom are still set against her and her legacy."

His eye narrowed as he stated. "As you have witnessed just a day before, the Red Phoenix is among that number. And quite possibly all but one other clan with them."

"If I may, Captain," Gran inquired. "What exactly did Morganna Flint do to incite the ire of the other clans?"

Jon nodded in understanding. Though it was likely every sentient being in the galaxy had at least heard the name Morganna Flint, not all of them knew the exact history behind that name. The eldest son of the Golden Queen answered thusly.

"The most unforgivable, and at one time believed impossible, offense: the formation of a fifth clan, when it was held that only four would be."

It was then Alex stepped in. "You have to think in terms of *vieux riche* to *nouveau riche*. Though they were made through and by piracy, the original four clans are dynasties that have existed for centuries, all having accumulated much in the way of power and influence. Through the efforts of their forebearers, they have all contended with the Thirteen and additional enemies in one way or the other and have gained not only their right to exist, but to *rule*."

The elder brother then reentered. "During the same period, some had voiced the possibility of a fifth clan, but between the unique set of circumstances that birthed the original four as well as the sheer arduousness of the task, it was long thought to be an impossibility," he clasped his hands together as he spoke. "That has long since come to pass, as we all know."

Another line of nods, from which Jon went on. "None of the other clans took well to the Gold Dragon's initiation, though only one actually challenged it."

Kaguya nodded in confirmation; Jon moved further along. "And while the enmity with Lord Fuma has long been established, it's safe to say the other Lords were not very fond of our mother during her time. Only the War of the Dragons' conclusion, and the set of circumstances therein, kept another Clan War from taking place."

It was then that Braun spoke up. "Forgive me, Captain, but for those of us not fully knowledgeable on this kind of thing. What is this 'War of the Dragons'?"

Jon again nodded in understanding. "The War of the Dragons was the first and only shooting war between the Gold Dragon and the Blue Dragon," the Captain turned to Kaguya. "To date, the closest iteration to a Fifth Clan War."

Kaguya took her cue. "It is as stated. Though all four Lords were set against this fifth clan, only one actually challenged its formation," she explained. "My father, who had only succeeded my late grandfather by one month, was affronted more so than the others."

The daughter of the Blue Dragon Lord frowned at her knowledge. "What followed was a year of brutal fighting, in which, against all presumption, the newborn Gold Dragon held its own against the older and better established Blue Dragon. A war, whose conclusion was brought about specifically to prevent escalation."

Jon returned to the matter at hand. "It was from the War of the Dragons that, among other outcomes, the Gold Dragon was wholly recognized and therefore established as a beneficiary to the Treaty of Libertalia."

"I see," Braun nodded, now having gained the answers he needed.

Again Jon elaborated. "In spite of that, however, the other Lords had long held my mother as an upstart and pretender among them. That she would 'dare' establish her dynasty virtually overnight to theirs, whose foundations existed for centuries, was considered the ultimate form of hubris."

He then closed his eye as he said. "As you can imagine, not many of them were broken over the First Battle of Ephesus."

That earned a solemn note from all around the table, as well as more than a bit of disdain for the subjects in question. After a short moment, however, Davis spoke the obvious question. "So why now?" he put forward. "Why is Lady Ching coming after us now specifically?"

Once more did Jon turn toward Kaguya, who gave the following explanation. "Following the second turn at Ephesus, there have been...*deliberations* between the Lords regarding the Flint pirates," she stated, now earning the complete attention of the other twelve. "Deliberations as to the rebirth of the Gold Dragon."

Before anyone could inquire, the Blue Dragon scion continued. "Though the possibility has been held since the Captain and First Officer's survival of the First Battle of Ephesus, it was not until the second that Lord Pargo, Lady Levasseur, and Lady Ching came to the same realization as my father," she stared back toward the brothers.

"That Lady Flint's spirit is still among us, and with her the Gold Dragon's inevitable return."

Kaguya again frowned. "These deliberations are still ongoing. While my father and Lady Ching's positions are quite clear, Lord Pargo and Lady Levasseur are otherwise undecided."

"And as a result, Lady Ching has chosen to take matters into her own hands," Anna surmised, also turning toward the brothers.

"Indeed," Jon answered, tapping his keypad. "Which brings us to our precise opposition."

At that, the room monitor flashed active, displaying Shun's profile and data.

"Ching Shun. Heir apparent to the Red Phoenix, Wielder of the Devilblade Haborym," Jon introduced, ensuring that all present memorized that name and its face. "And Lady Ching's chief executioner."

Davis visibly swallowed as he took in the Red Phoenix's face, especially his eyes. Those were eyes he had rarely seen in the galaxy, and only among the most soulless, most coldhearted of killers and villains. Eyes he had long made a point of avoiding at any cost.

"Alex and I have had our run-ins against him, but we never truly faced him head-on until now. Suffice to say, he is exactly as you see him. Cold, ruthless, highly intelligent, and as skilled a fighter as they come."

Jon elaborated. "Shun will not rest until we are laid out in the company of the Red Phoenix's enemies, much of whom he made a point of eliminating *completely*," again, the Captain let that settle in. "Obviously, he has the bulk of the Red Armada under his command, as well as the ability to act in his mother's place. Alongside, he has these three…"

The monitor flashed again, displaying the visage of the other three

Wielders fought at Atalanta. "The Sanxing, or Three Stars. The Red Phoenix's highest cadre of warriors, all of whom are also Wielders."

Again the table occupants took the time to memorize the faces and the names associated with them. Lei Fu, Meng Lu, and Dian Shou. Wielders of the Devilblades Amdusias, Crocell, and Furfur.

"Altogether, we have four Wielders set against us," Jon surmised, right as the monitor flashed again, this time displaying a starmap of the Red Phoenix's accumulated territory. "As well as an untold number of capital ships, smallcraft, ground troops, and armor. All spread over a great span of space and countless star systems."

"God be merciful," Davis murmured as he took in the sheer scale of the opposition. Drake's forces at Ephesus felt much insignificant compared to this, not to mention the fact the Admiral had been but one Wielder. "We really are up against an empire."

"In more ways than one, Davis," Alex concurred, for once taking no pleasure in the helmsman's despondence. Such was felt all around the table, as the occupants could only fathom the fight they would soon be in.

"So, how do we go about this?" Boss spoke up, at last, having fished out her pipe and lit it if only to calm her nerves. "Hiding is no more an option than it was before."

"But at the same time, we're only one ship against all of that," Cheney added in as well, folding his arms with a frown. "This one's a real tall order, even for me."

"I unfortunately concur, Captain," Barbarossa solemnly stated, recollections of his own unsanctioned jihad against Terra coming to the forefront. "Our position alone…"

"On the contrary, we could not be in a better position," Jon interrupted, now taking on a visage of assurance. "For we hold both the advantage and the means to achieve victory."

Again did the captain of the Flint Pirates tap his keypad, marking several points across the starmap.

"Have any of you heard of Ancient Terra's Second Punic War?" Jon posited. "Or of a man named Hannibal Barca?"

Red Phoenix *Yunnan*-class battleship *Zhang He* Deep Space

With thunder and fury did Lei Fu lunge at his superior, Devilblade poised to strike. Having anticipated the attack, Shun easily leaped back and countered with a fire wave, which his subordinate dodged. Meng Lu and Dian Shou rushed him simultaneously, torrents of water and lightning launching out. The heir apparent to the Red Phoenix avoided these attacks all too deftly before sending an even larger fire blitz at the pair, forcing them to evade in turn and then augmenting the offensive with an overhead fireball shower that kept all three ducking and maneuvering. None of the Sanxing disappointed their leader in their proficiencies, moving around the fiery hail with speed and precision.

Shun closed in upon one of them, in this case, Shou. The opposing Wielder quickly raised Furfur to deflect the expected attack from Haborym, only for Shun to execute a power kick to the sternum, the force actually causing Shou to cough up blood as he flew across the sparring ground. He landed some distance away, all the while his two comrades charged after Shun from either side, Amdusias and Crocell both poised for swift vengeance.

Far from receding, Shun met the two assailants head-on, blocking both adversarial swords with a fire shield and Haborym's physical blade. Fu was the first to overcome the defensive move, generating a sonic pulse to penetrate the fire shield. Shun remained firm, absorbing the pseudo-soundwave before countering with a blast of fire just before parrying Lu's attempt to strike him from the right side. Another sidekick, this time to the head, easily knocked down that Wielder temporarily, right as Fu lunged forward with Amdusias prepared to strike at his master's seemingly exposed back. Though Amdusias' guandao form granted it superior reach, the blade failed to connect as Shun leaped upward and over, executing a flaming slash at Fu. A fiery gash instantly emerged on Fu's chest as he too was knocked away, though, to his credit, he managed to land on his feet, skidding back a fair distance in the process. Shun would have pursued, but Shou, already recovered, attacked again, followed by Lu. As before, Shun blocked both sets of blades simultaneously, weaving fire against water and lightning as he deflected and parried.

It wasn't long before Fu stirred, rose, and rushed to join his three comrades in the assault. Leaping into the air and landing with Amdusias in a hammer blow, Fu added thunder to the other elements, releasing a white pulse of sound and fury. Rather than absorb this foray, Shun, right as he knocked away Shou's attempted strike, slashed Haborym about, using his fire to meet and cancel out the incoming energy and then countering with another flaming blast of his own. Repeating his master's technique, Fu knocked away the fire wave as he charged on, set to impale simultaneously alongside his other Sanxing, who swung the piandao and hook sword-styled blades for their own respective strikes. Again Shun had none of it, leaping away at the precise moment to cause the three blades to reach and clang against one another, right over his previous position.

While still in midair, the Red Phoenix scion launched a tremendous whirlwind of fire. One far too fast for the Sanxing to dodge and too powerful for them to deflect or absorb. In fact, all three barely registered the attack as it struck them straight on, the dark fire washing over them in a great and hellish baptism.

Landing some distance away, Shun looked on passively as the fire dissipated, the Sanxing all laid out across the ground before him. Scarred and burned to a considerable level, the three attempted to stand up to continue the spar yet could not draw enough strength to do so. Only Fu managed to some degree, using Amdusias' pole to bring himself up to a kneeling position. Without word or warning, Shun executed another fire outburst that struck the crippled Wielder head-on, sending him soaring backward to the opposite end of the hall. He slammed violently against the back wall. This time Fu, now burned over most of his body, did not attempt to rise again. In fact, he had been rendered wholly unconscious from both the flames and the resultant impact.

For a brief moment, Lu and Shou wondered if they would be next; as had just been demonstrated, their master was not one to show mercy in any form. To their meager respite, however, Shun turned and abruptly exited the fighting hall. Effectively leaving the two remaining Sanxing to summon medical assistance for themselves, as well as Fu.

Strange, Shun wondered as he gained the outside deck, gradually moving toward his quarters. *I do not usually become so agitated.*

Indeed, agitation was what he felt now and had been feeling since Atalanta. Not so much because he had failed to fulfill his mission then and there; there was still much time for that. Rather, it was because of the image of Jonathan Flint, which remained a fixture in his memory despite his best efforts. The visage of the Golden Queen's eldest, especially in the moment of his intended sacrifice, would not leave Shun's mind. Nor could Shun force away his adversary's condemnation, his defiance.

Yes, that was the source of his uncharacteristic irritation, Shun felt. Jonathan Flint, and by extension his brother and the rest of their mongrels, did not know his rightful place. That he, and again the rest of the Flint Pirates, were *inferior*, mere rabble chasing the false legacy of the most arrogant pretender. How dare he look down upon one such as Ching Shun, who was the eldest and rightful heir to a *true* dynasty.

Well, no matter, Shun ultimately surmised. Jonathan would realize his place in time, alongside his inevitable demise. The only downside to this, a temporary setback at best, was the next move lay squarely with the rabble, as Shun had no way of tracking the *Black Sun* under cloak.

Somehow and someway, however, the Flints would reemerge; whether to attempt a strike against the Red Phoenix or simply to find another safe haven, they would reemerge. When they did, Shun would be upon them once again, and this time he would not let them slip away.

Thus Shun reentered his quarters and began preparing for the evening's rest, knowing that he would need his full energy for the coming days and the fulfillment of his tasks. All the while, the image of the pretender's eldest remained prevalent, much to his lingering vexation.

Flint Pirates umbra *Black Sun*
Deep Space

Both feeling as though they were walking to waiting gallows, Jon and Alex nonetheless followed Kaguya as she led them into her quarters, not even pausing as the door slid open. For the first time in two years, both brothers knew they were about to tread on highly precarious ground; even the prelude to Ephesus, when Jon had made their *second* outreach just before the battle, seemed far less shaky by comparison. Unfortunately, however, both he and Alex knew that there was no other choice. Not if they were indeed going to wage war against a clan.

After a few more moments in which the proper channels of communication were established, the Flints and Kaguya, who remained off to the side, watched as the holographic image of Lord Fuma appeared before them. The Lord of the Blue Dragon stared upon his former students, the sons of his one-time adversary.

"Sensei," Jon opened, both he and Alex bowing. "We come before you, as heirs of the Gold Dragon, to make this request."

Easily recalling two years ago, when the two brothers made their original request *without* invoking their lineage, the Blue Dragon Lord looked on with interest.

Resisting the urge to swallow, Jon spoke the awaited words calmly, keeping the hesitance in check. "We beseech you, and the Blue Dragon, for your support. As we wage war against the Red Phoenix."

"Because the scope of such a task is beyond any one ship, no matter how powerful," Lord Fuma summarized. "Is that it?"

"Hai, sensei," Alex confirmed alongside his brother, also managing to keep his apprehension at bay.

For a brief moment, the Lord seemed to study the two brothers intently. However, before long, Lord Fuma began to speak with them. "You both realize that the Treaty of Libertalia forbids the Clans from raising arms against another."

"Yes, we are aware," Jon respectfully answered. "And yet, that is what has happened."

Despite the weight of Lord Fuma's gaze, Jon persisted. "The Gold Dragon was also a signatory of that treaty, yet the Red Phoenix has chosen to strike against we the rightful heirs."

Lord Fuma could not help but feel some amusement toward this. "Lady Ching would claim that the Gold Dragon no longer exists," he responded rather obviously. "That, despite your right to Morganna Flint's name and legacy, the Treaty of Libertalia does not apply to the 'likes of you'."

"We do not ask you to go to war with the Red Phoenix on our behalf, *sensei*," Alex quickly rejoined. "We request, with utmost respect and understanding, any support we can gather."

Again Lord Fuma seemed to study the two brothers for a moment, shifting his gaze from brother to brother. He could see that both had resolved to accept any answer they were given, regardless of their desperation. Just as they also knew that they were indeed overstepping their bounds, at least potentially. Though Lady Ching had made it clear the lengths she would go to hunt down and destroy Morganna's children, including instigating an all-out clan war, Lord Fuma was a man of honor and dedication. He was not so forward in violating the document that had brokered peace between the Blue Dragon and its contemporaries for *centuries*. That left very few options in regard to the brothers' request, something that both Flints and Fumas understood all too well.

And yet, after another long moment of silence, Lord Fuma answered with a simple nod. "I can send you one ship."

At first, Jon and Alex felt as though the galaxy had fallen out from under them at that precise moment. One ship? One other ship to compliment the *Sun*? What good would such a thing do for them? Instead of one, they would only be *two* ships against the whole of the Red Phoenix!

Despite that momentary despair, however, the Flints could not help but feel something underneath their teacher's tone of voice. That, while Lord Fuma's hands remained tied by Libertalia, that one other ship could perhaps make all the difference for them. And if nothing else, it meant they would not be fighting this one alone, as they had so many previous battles.

Thus as both bowed in gratitude, Jon answered, respectively. "We accept, *sensei*."

Nodding in approval, Lord Fuma gave the final instruction. "The Sentok System, twenty-four hours," he outlined. "Do not be late."

Once more, the two students bowed, the hologram disengaging soon after. With one final nod to Kaguya as they exited her quarters, Jon tapped his wristcom.

"Flint to bridge."

"Barbarossa here."

"Set a course for the Sentok System, maximum arc," Jon commanded as he and Alex entered the waiting turbolift.

Upon that command, the *Black Sun* came about and sped into arcspace. Both ship and crew preparing for and anticipating whatever allies they would soon meet.

Chapter VIII: Two Shadows

Flint Pirates umbra *Black Sun*
Sentok System
Twenty-Four Hours Later

Though it was far from the first time anxiousness had dwelled upon the *Sun*'s bridge, Jon knew this time was different. Even more than previous events, neither he, Alex, nor Kaguya, who was standing just off from Alex's station, nor the rest of the bridge crew, knew what they would soon encounter. Thus, doing their best to keep their collective uncertainty in check, the Flint Pirates could only standby and wait for their Blue Dragon "allies" to arrive.

More than once in the last twenty-four hours, Jon had wondered about the arriving "help". Though he knew his *sensei* to be a man of honor, and just as importantly, he had taken an interest in the Flint Pirates' development and given them any support he could from his position, Jon still questioned his intent in this instance. How could one other ship help them? Even if the one were a battleship or a carrier, Jon knew that would only amount to so much against the whole of the Red Armada. Especially when the ship in question would not possess the advanced defensive power that the *Sun* held. Really, what was his *sensei* thinking?

Sighing, Jon ultimately resorted to his better logic before his apprehension rambled too much further. Though there remained only one being in the universe he fully trusted, he knew Lord Fuma, and he knew that the Blue Dragon Lord would not have granted them such reinforcement if he believed it would be insufficient. The fact he was doing so at the risk of violating the Treaty of Libertalia only emphasized such intent that much more. No, Jon suspected whatever was being sent their way, it would make all the difference.

"Anything yet?"

Barbarossa shook his head. "Not even an oncoming arc signature," he espoused, trying and failing to hide his own frustration. Like his Captain, the Leo could only wonder how one more ship would really help them. "Perhaps this was all for jest."

"*Sensei* would never do such a thing," Alex almost snarled toward the Leo.

"My Lord's word is beyond question," Kaguya spoke her own subdued warning. "If we are to meet our reinforcements here, then they will be here in time."

Barbarossa only sniffed at both exclamations as he leaned back in his chair, still waiting. Indeed, he suspected no reason why the Blue Dragon Lord would deceive them in such a manner. And yet, his sensors remained clean of outside contacts all the same.

Again sighing, Jon turned to Lorelei to inquire if she felt anything, only to stop as he saw something rather peculiar. Rather than looking toward her station, the psion was staring straight ahead, seemingly past the monitor, her eyes fixed with apparent interest. He watched as her lips folded into a smile, amusement claiming her expression.

Only then did Jon realize what exactly Lord Fuma had sent their way.

"Umbra decloaking ahead!" Barbarossa let out in warning as the sensors alarmed.

"Imps!?" Davis questioned as the bridge crew went to full alert, barely keeping from going to battlestations as Jon had yet to order them. It was fortunate that they hadn't done so. Just as it was soon apparent the newcomer was *not* an Imperial starship.

Reforming back into open space in her entirety, the first thing one realized of the opposing umbra was its remarkable similarities toward the *Black Sun*. She too possessed a jet black hull, as well as a similar design and structure, though with minor alterations to seemingly differentiate the pair. Namely, whereas the *Sun* held golden lines across her hull, this umbra held blue. And most importantly, whereas the Golden Roger was prominently displayed upon the *Sun*'s bridge tower, this one bore an all too familiar serpentine dragon, also of blue. Thereby establishing the Pirate Clan of its belonging.

Even Kaguya could not help but gape at the opposite umbra. Despite her prior exclamation, even she had not known, much less expected, her father would be sending *that* ship to meet them. Much less her captain.

"We're being hailed," Gran announced, inadvertently breaking the shock that had replaced the prior uncertainty.

Jon nodded. "On the monitor."

At that, a vidwindow opened up, revealing a new face. A young man, clearly of Blue Dragon origin, that, much like his ship toward the *Sun*, held much in the way of similarity to the present Clan Lord. As well as to Kaguya.

"Oniisama," Kaguya greeted, causing further realization through the rest of the bridge, save for Jon, Alex and Lorelei, of course.

"It's good to see you as well, Kaguya," Fuma Kazama, heir apparent to the Blue Dragon, nodded in warm acknowledgment toward his younger sister. He then turned to Jon. "And greetings to you, Captain Flint and the total Flint Pirates. I apologize for our abrupt entrance, but I wanted to see how my ship's cloaking system faired against your sensors."

Even Jon could not keep a grin off his face, though he tried hard to conceal it. It was just like Kazama to make an 'abrupt' entrance. "I trust she is completed then?" he questioned, his prior doubts now laid to rest.

"She is," Kazama nodded in confirmation. "It took some time and much more in the way of effort, but she is now fully operational."

Kazama then grinned predatorily as he added. "The *Tsushima* is ready for battle."

Renewed hope swelled through the *Sun*'s bridge at that exclamation, burning away their own prior doubts and apprehension. Indeed, that one ship would make all the difference for them, even against the forces of another clan.

"We can discuss the particulars here if you're so inclined," Kazama offered.

"That would be acceptable," the elder Flint answered, not having to turn to Alex and Kaguya to see their agreement as well. Nor Lorelei, for that matter, who Jon knew would be joining them. If Kazama was present aboard the *Tsushima*, then *she* would be right next to him.

Jon smiled, allowing a glimpse of his joy to be revealed. "Circumstances aside, it's been quite a while, Kazama."

Mirroring the elder Flint's smile, the elder Fuma again tilted his head in acknowledgment. "It has Jon, but we'll make it right with everything else," he responded. "See you when you get here."

With that, Jon looked toward the expecting Barbarossa. "Second Officer has the conn," he said as he, Alex, Kaguya, and Lorelei all moved toward the turbolift. Only a few minutes later would their shuttle exit the *Sun*'s hold and enter the *Tsushima*'s.

Blue Dragon umbra *Tsushima*
Sentok System

For once exiting the shuttle before the others, Jon was not at all surprised to see the *Tsushima*'s Captain and one other there to meet him and his entourage. Adorned in a black and blue intricately embroidered longcoat over a dress shirt, vest, trousers, and corresponding boots and gloves, the heir apparent of the Blue Dragon appeared young and able. He smiled at his Gold Dragon counterpart and old friend. As Lord Fuma's eldest son and the next Lord of the Blue Dragon, Jon had known Kazama from childhood, though this would be the first time either of them had met in a long span.

Such was confirmed from the images that ran through Lorelei's mind as she also exited the shuttle. The first set showed Jon and Kazama as children, running and playing through the wilderness of a planet unknown to her, simultaneously as Alex and Kaguya wandered about exploring the surrounding nature, all under the watchful eyes of Kaiser and another certain woman. The next set of images was much later in time, specifically the days Jon and Alex had spent on Ryugu under Lord Fuma's tutelage. Just as Kaguya helped train Alex, so did her brother aid Jonathan, from practicing swordsmanship and other martial arts to various forms of exercise, all toward honing the future captain's body to better control his Devilblade. Though she could see that her captain's character was much different from the young boy he had been long before, the camaraderie between him and Kazama appeared to remain the same.

And then there was another image that emerged, which seemingly stood out over the rest. That of Jon, Kazama, Alex, and Kaguya walking through the streets of Kyoto during an apparent festival, speaking among themselves as they moved from one part to the other.

The familial bond, which Lorelei had sensed in the previous images, most apparent in that scene. Lorelei felt rather intrigued before she shifted back to the present, where Kazama brought his hand out to shake Jon's.

"Welcome aboard the *Tsushima*, Captain Flint," Kazama began with, quite apparently delighted to see the elder Flint once more. "Though I admit I wish it were under better circumstances."

"The feeling is mutual, Captain Fuma," Jon responded as Alex and Kaguya joined him. The latter visibly beaming at the sight of her elder brother.

Kaguya suddenly returned to her usual formality. *"Oniisama,"* Kaguya greeted with the standard bow. Somehow managing not to roll his eyes, Kazama responded by embracing his sibling. Formalities be damned between the two of them.

"I'm glad you're well, Kaguya," he said as he released her, then turning toward Alex. "I trust you've been taking care of her?"

"More the opposite," Alex shrugged, smiling as he bowed, albeit more out of jest, to the future Blue Dragon Lord. "Fuma-*sama*."

That earned a small laugh from Kazama. It was nice to see how few things had changed with the children of his father's one-time enemy. Then, he turned toward Lorelei. "And I assume you are the White Siren that I've heard so much about."

"You assume correctly, Captain Fuma," Lorelei espoused, not quite sure how to refer to Kazama since she wasn't as familiar as the others. She was respectful regardless. "I only hope the stories have been flattering."

"Quite a few have actually," the woman that had stood next to Kazama responded, speaking up for the first time. There was no need for introductions as Jon, Alex, and Kaguya were already quite familiar with her. And though Lorelei had only just met her, much had already been spoken and exchanged between them. *Lorelei*-san.

Heh, Lorelei telepathically replied to the woman, bowing in standard form. Following in the image of her husband, Fuma Izuna was young, regal, and beautiful. Dressed in simpler garb, she wore a black and blue lined *kosobe* with complimenting *hakama,* her hair tied by an equally simple blue ribbon, otherwise possessing no further adornments. Though the coloring was much different, it was clear that Izuna was clothed in the manner of a *miko,* a priestess of the Blue Dragon's Shinto religion.

Turning toward her, Jon and Alex both bowed respectfully. "It is good to see you as well, Izuna," Jon smiled.

"Likewise Jonathan, Alexander," the future Lady of the Blue Dragon acknowledged the brothers with a nod and then repeated it to her sister-in-law.

"I take it you and Lorelei have been communicating behind our backs?" Alex inquired with a grin, now understanding why their own psion had not alerted them to the *Tsushima*'s presence beforehand.

Izuna shrugged in the manner of a mischievous troublemaker pretending to be innocent. "I have no idea what you are talking about, Alex," she threw in for equal measure. "If the *Sun* was unable to detect the *Tsushima* as we approached, then the fault lays entirely on her and you."

"Tsushima," Jon repeated, turning back to Kazama. "You didn't invoke the Captain's Right?"

In pirate tradition, the Captain's Right denoted that captains could change the name of their ship as they saw fit, even if they had inherited their ship from another captain. Though they were far larger and tremendously more organized than the standard band, the Clans had retained that tradition, though there was something of a bureaucracy to weed through to invoke the Right. After all, it would not do well to give one's new ship a name that poorly reflected on their clan at large.

"I thought about it but decided it was unnecessary," Kazama responded knowingly. "I'm sure you can understand why."

It was then that another image flashed through Lorelei's mind, that of Kazama showing his friend a specific book during the latter's time on Ryugu. Written in Blue Dragon script, Lorelei identified the title as *Tsushima no Yūrei*.

Kazama then clasped his hands together. "Now that greetings have been exchanged, we have much ground to cover, to say nothing of a war to fight," he said, the newcomers turning serious. "May I suggest we move on to current business?"

Flint Pirates umbra *Black Sun*
Sentok System

"Got to hand it to those bastards in Kure. They really made her well," Cheney observed as he and Boss both stood on the observation deck, looking toward the still visible *Tsushima* in the relative distance. "The bigwigs back on Terra will really soil themselves if they ever find out about her."

Boss shrugged as she lit her pipe. "More than likely," she admitted. "Though if anyone else besides Terra is going to have umbras, better it be the Blue Dragon."

Cheney turned to her with an arched eyebrow. "Are you sure?" he questioned, as though having to remind the fighter ace about a more sensitive subject. Specifically that the Blue Dragon hadn't built her simply to safeguard their territory.

Boss closed her eyes as she recalled. "For the time being," she again admitted. "They've been our allies from the start, and they will continue to be our allies through the foreseeable future…"

"I know," Cheney responded, though that didn't assuage him too much. Today's allies were not necessarily tomorrow's; he understood that concept all too well. And again, he doubted the Blue Dragon made the *Tsushima* to fight their nominal opponents, as opposed to the one. "I'd hate to see that day, however."

"As would I," Boss agreed, almost shivering at the idea. Fighting the Blue Dragon on its own would have been excruciating, even if the clan had not possessed its own umbra fleet. And going by the *Tsushima*'s outward appearance, one could tell she had borrowed much from the *Sun*.

Ultimately, however, both pilot and raider decided that it was of little concern. Once again, the Blue Dragon Clan was their ally today, and they would be their allies for the foreseeable future. Against the might and power of the Red Phoenix, the Flint Pirates could not ask for a better supporter, especially when it came in the form of another umbra.

Tomorrow would simply bring what it would. Preferably after their immediate enemy had been vanquished.

Blue Dragon umbra *Tsushima*
Sentok System

"Kure took as much from the *Sun* as they could possibly reverse engineer," Kazama briefed the three before him in his main cabin, a schematic of the *Tsushima* projected on the central monitor. Lorelei and Izuna were noticeably absent, but that hardly mattered. The four "mundanes" knew the women were listening in from another part of the ship. "As you can see, they were successful to a fair degree, even if they could not completely replicate the whole."

"Indeed," Alex said, scanning the schematic with interest. Quite a few systems were present aboard the *Tsushima*, though he could understand why not the entirety. The *Sun* was, after all, centuries more advanced than anything in existence. "Will we see any more like her?"

Kazama smiled sadly. "That was the original plan, but no," he clari-fied with newfound solemnity. "It took the bulk of Kure's knowledge and resources just to produce this one prototype. And though there were several attempts to further refine the *Tsushima*-class, it was still projected to cost more than otherwise feasible. And that was with the parts and systems that could, in fact, be comprehended, as well as manufactured."

Leaning back in his chair, Kazama's regret was very apparent. "Suffice to say the *Tsushima* will be the only one of her class," he concluded. "Kure has since moved on to the *Wakasa*-class."

Both Jon and Alex nodded in understanding. As opposed to the *Tsushima* being based on the *Black Sun*, the *Wakasa*-class umbra was a direct reverse engineering of the Imperial Type VI umbra. Nowhere near as advanced as the Type VII, but given the Blue Dragon's current level of resources and technology, easily the better for larger scale production.

"And before either of you say anything, I will admit it now. She is *not* the *Sun*," Kazama spoke directly, as though Jon or Alex really would bring it up at some point. Following that, he smiled as he added. "But she can damn well give her a good run for her money."

"I'm sure she can," Jon nodded in acknowledgment, doing well to keep the obviousness to himself. It was clear to all of them *why* Lord Fuma commissioned the *Tsushima* in the first place, but that was a non-issue in the present. "Your father could not have sent us anything better."

Alex and Kaguya nodded in affirmation, already anticipating how much hell they were sure to inflict on the Red Phoenix. If the *Black Sun* could do immense damage on her own, one could imagine how much she could wreak alongside another umbra of similar capability.

Kazama nodded in turn, out of appreciation. "My crew and I are glad to be here, Jon," he declared, the camaraderie once again apparent between them. "As it was meant to be."

The monitor then flashed to display the star map of the Red Phoenix Clan in its entirety. Key points already marked.

"Now then, since you're the one Shun picked the fight with," Kazama continued. "Where do you want to start?"

Smiling, Jon gestured toward a particular system. Kazama arched an eyebrow and then grinned once more in a predatory fashion.

And with that, we march to war, Izuna telepathically communicated to her guest as they both picked up on the designated target. Sitting in the captain's personal mess, the two women waited, sipping their respective teas, as the men made their plans. *Though the circumstances do admittedly warrant such a course of action.*

Yes, Lorelei concurred as she poured more tea into her waiting cup. *Lady Ching has made it quite clear what she intends for us and anyone else who stands in her way.*

Quite, Izuna sipped her own glass, having already sifted through the psionic imagery that her guest had provided. She then smiled conspiringly as she added. *Not that either of us is unfamiliar with fighting.*

As she had done with her host, Lorelei also beheld as Izuna projected the associated memories. Much of which had centered around combat in one form or the other.

I might not be as powerful as you, Lorelei-san, but I've fought my own share of battles, Izuna spoke with assurance. *I am, after all, the Lady of the Blue Dragon in waiting.*

Lorelei laughed a little, both physically and telepathically, at that proud exclamation. *I did not know it was an actual requirement for the Lady to be as much a warrior as the Lord.*

More to stand beside the Lord in battle than to be an actual warrior, Izuna admitted. *Kaede-sama was renowned for doing so with Lord Fuma, as were many who came before.*

Izuna took a sip from her cup as she emphasized. *Who am I to break tradition?*

Even though your upbringing was more religious in nature? Lorelei casually observed, picking up on images of a younger Izuna dressed in more traditional white and red, attending to various duties around her family's shrine.

Izuna smiled toward that set of memories. *That was a long time ago,* she admitted with some melancholy. *A life I gave up so that I could marry Kazama.*

Following the initial set, Lorelei depicted young Izuna alongside an equally young Kazama, both away from the shrine. She easily discerned the shared joy and happiness between them.

And what of you? Izuna turned the question around to her guest. *I don't suppose you were brought up in a warrior household?*

Lorelei laughed at the question. *Not so much,* she admitted, then taking an apologetic expression. *Forgive me if...*

No need to apologize, Izuna disarmingly interrupted her. *Your secrets are your own.*

Lorelei nodded in gratitude, though she could not help but wonder if Izuna at least suspected *what* she truly was and *where* she truly came from. Even so, neither woman felt any need to address such matters. Much to the White Siren's appreciation.

I do, however, understand your outlook, Lorelei admitted further, being forthcoming in one particular area. *To face the universe itself, beside the one...*

Yes, Izuna concurred, detecting her guest's thoughts and feelings. No mental imagery this time, just the sheer passion and devotion she felt toward her captain, and dare she hope future Lord of his own clan.

Telekinetically taking Izuna's cup to refill it with tea, Lorelei then waited for Izuna to use her own power to recall the cup before speaking again.

It as you say, Izuna-san, Lorelei granted, using her power to gaze into the vastness of space, where their enemies lay. *We march to war so that we may stand beside our Lords, our Captains.*

The Siren's eyes focused with resolve. *No matter what may be sent against us.*

Izuna nodded as she sipped her refilled cup, her own resolve apparent. Even with the combined might of their ships and crews, the two psions knew the days ahead would be arduous, possibly more than either of them had endeared to the present. Even so, they knew who they were to fight against and who they would fight alongside. Such was enough for both.

"Kanpai!" Kazama recited, both he and Jon then downing the contents of their respective *ochoko* cups. With the planning for their first operation now completed, there remained much to catch up on between the two friends. Thus, as Alex and Kaguya followed Kazama's First Officer on a tour of the *Tsushima*, he and Jon remained in the main cabin, doing just that. With choice grog between them, of course. "So, you feeling better about your chances now, Jon?"

"Much more so than before," Jon admitted after downing his *sake* in one go, then refilling his cup. "Though technically we're still only two ships against all of *that*," he gestured back toward the monitor, which still displayed the Red Phoenix's vast territories.

"That just means we have the advantage," Kazama responded with utmost assurance. "Because we have more ways to hurt them than they do us."

Jon nodded in agreement. "True," he replied as he sipped from his *ochoko* again. "How much do you know about these deliberations between the Clans?"

"I've been keeping track, but you probably know as much as I do now," Kazama answered. "Until the Black Tortoise and White Tiger Lords make their own decisions, the talks continue."

Jon actually smiled wryly toward that. "No tie-breaker vote?"

Kazama matched his smile in full knowledge. "The downside of being even-numbered," he said, drinking from his own cup again. "To be honest, though, I think this will all be resolved by the time they come around."

"Heh," Jon let out, unable to help but wonder about that. "You have much in the way of confidence, Kazama."

"Don't I always?" Kazama rejoined with even greater assurance. "We may only be two ships as you said, but neither the Red Phoenix nor the other clans have dealt with such ships, or us, until now."

The heir to the Blue Dragon adopted a more serious expression. "And while I cannot speak entirely for my father, I can speak for myself, as well as Kaguya. Neither of us and those that would follow are about to let Morganna Flint and her legend be snuffed out without a fight."

He then took another somewhat longer sip from his cup. "You're not alone on this one, Jon," he stated in a direct promise. "However this ends, I and my ship and crew are with you all the way."

Jon smiled in gratitude. "I appreciate that, Kazama. More than you will ever know," he confessed, at last feeling the vestiges of hope as he again lifted his cup. *"Shōri!"*

"Seikatsu!" Kazama resounded with his own raised cup, both downing their respective beverages simultaneously. All while the monitor still displayed the starmap of the Red Phoenix, with one point in particular noticeably designated.

Chapter IX: Dead Man's Party

Taishan Shipyard
Taishan System

"This is our operations center," the administrator introduced all too brightly as he led his "guest" off the turbolift into the very nerve center of the shipyard he oversaw. "As you can clearly see, we remain wholly focused upon efficiency here at Tianshan. And efficiency can only begin at the top, as we all know."

"So you have made me aware," the inspector from Penglai espoused with a bland expression, marking down further information into her datapad while continuing to ignore the administrator's anxiousness. It was far from a pleasing job, but even within the Clans, somebody had to do it. To ensure that order and production remain continuous, lest chaos and sloth replace them and cause the whole of the Red Phoenix to suffer. And more importantly, it ensured the inspector collected a tidy sum to put food on her table. "I trust you observe and control the whole of the shipyard from here?"

"Indeed we do," the administrator continued confidently, aware that the inspector knew the answer to her own question but went along with it regardless. After all, it was this woman's word that reached all the way back to Lady Ching and her circle, and the administrator had no wish to suffer his Lady's wrath. The events at Qingdao were not very long ago, after all.

Leading the inspector over to one station, the administrator gestured for emphasis. "We can access literally every corner of the shipyard from here, though we rarely do so for obvious reasons," he nodded to the station operator, who acknowledged his superior before turning back to deliberately concentrate on whatever it was he was doing. "Every system and function takes care of itself for the most part, such that we need only intervene should an issue occur..."

"And what would such issues be, specifically?" the inspector inquired, remaining bland-faced even as the administrator nearly quaked from his knees. "Issues that could, perhaps, cause a shortfall in production?"

"No, not at all!" the administrator nearly blurted out. "Shortfalls never occur here at Tianshan!" *Certainly not on my watch.* "Just the usual glitches and quirks that come standard with automation..."

"Glitches and quirks can be damaging in my experience," the inspector reprimanded before tapping on her datapad. "Those who I report to, including *our* Lady herself, do not take kindly to such errors. Especially if they were to prove detrimental to the ships that are made here."

"O-of course!" the administrator affirmed. "Rest assured, Madam Inspector, that we deal with such things as they come along, and they are corrected swiftly and completely!"

"So you claim," the inspector replied before making another mark in her datapad. "And what of preventative action? So that you *wouldn't* have to deal with such things 'as they come along'?"

For a short moment, the administrator tried to peer over the inspector's datapad but quickly withdrew upon realizing that she knew what he was attempting.

"Our technical and engineering staff labor around the clock for that precise reason. Process Hazard Analysis, Risk Hazard Analysis, Single-Point Failure Identification and Elimination are just a few processes we employ on all our assemblies, along with extensive training of employees in safety and accident prevention," he nearly stammered. "Which, I dare say, is why we at Tianshan have not had a single lost-time incident in over three years!"

"Mm-hmm," the inspector responded, making yet another mark in her datapad, this time without even looking at it. She suspected the real reason Tianshan had not had an incident in that span of time, conveniently the same span in which the current administrator had held his post, was because they never reported any of those "such things" as they took place. Not that it ultimately mattered, so long as the ships continued coming off their proverbial assembly lines, of course. "And what of your defense systems?"

The administrator seemed to scoff at the idea. "With respect, Madam Inspector, we can hardly expect a raid to take place this deep in…"

"Tianshan's defenses," the inspector pushed with visible impatience. "Are they up to par, or aren't they?"

Somehow withholding the urge to sigh, the administrator opened his mouth to reply. Which was precisely when the trumpet sounded throughout the center, causing the administrator to snap his mouth shut out of shocked reflex. He stood frozen in disbelief.

As additional trumpet notes thundered throughout the complex, the inspector turned to the nearest station operator. "What's happening?" she demanded, already recognizing by the administrator's demeanor that this was *not* part of standard functions nor an unscheduled drill.

"Broad-range transmission, ma'am!" the operator reported, already working to isolate. "It's overriding all frequencies!"

"Qingwa cao de liumang!" the inspector cursed, now understanding *precisely* what was happening. No sooner were the words spoken than the first torpedo struck the shipyard, the resultant shockwave all but ripping across space and through the operations center.

"Don't just stand there, you idiot!" the inspector bellowed at the administrator. "We're under attack!"

It took the second such torpedo hit and detonation to emphasize such to the administrator.

"En..engage defenses and scramble the garrison! There can't be too many of them out...!"

"No contacts detected, sir," one of the operators reported in a high panic, as third and fourth detonations soon decimated the production areas, now only smoking ruins. "Wait, enemy fighters incoming!"

The main monitor then flickered to display the fighters in question. All black save for their respective gold and blue markings, it was quite clear to everyone, including the hapless administrator, who was attacking them. Even before one picked up on the Golden Roger or Blue Dragon sigils that adorned each fighter.

"Hen mei naixing de Fozu," the administrator breathed as he urinated into his trousers. His standing with Penglai now the very least of his concerns.

Taishan System

Grinning from behind his visor as he watched the opening torpedo salvos continue to take place, Jon couldn't help but already feel triumphant. The enemy had truly been blindsided. A fair portion of Taishan was already obliterated and set to the flame, yet none of the defense batteries were active, nor had enemy ships and fighters come about to meet them. That would change in the next few moments,

Jon knew, but all the same, it was a good feeling. To strike such an opening blow against a conceited, disdainful enemy as the Red Phoenix.

Sure enough, the shipyard's defense batteries soon went active and began firing beams and projectiles at the fifty oncoming fighters, just as Jon, and Kazama with him, signaled the rest to break formation and attack at will. As luck would have it, that was also precisely when the "background music" began to pick up, with drums and a multitude of other instruments joining the prior trumpet and guitar in a full raucous opus. Indeed as the fifty smallcraft maneuvered around the encroaching fire and attacked in their own sequence, *Dead Man's Party* seemed to emphasize such actions with jovial affirmation, perfectly matching the furiousness and alacrity of the fighting. Jon reflected he could not have picked a better medium for a jamming signal as he brought his Corsair into his own run, Kazama following in his Shiden.

The vocals to the still playing music started up again as both fighters let loose their beam cannons, striking the nearest drydock, and the *Ningxia*-class destroyer berthed there. Between the two heavy fighters' armaments, it wasn't long before the structure gave way and buckled, followed by the ship itself, which rippled and fragmented as it broke apart. Both were effectively rendered to free-floating remnants as the Flint and Blue Dragon fighters passed, both pilots feeling satisfied with their shared first kill. Naturally, more would soon follow.

"That was fast," Jon heard Kazama espouse as their sensors picked up new incoming signals. Whether someone had managed to get an alert through the comm jamming or someone outside the shipyard had noticed the attack in progress, there was now a large number of Red Phoenix fighters moving to intercept. "Any particular ideas to deal with them, Corsair Zero?"

"Just shoot them down as they come along," Jon responded as

he examined the enemy composition. Mostly light fighters – the Red Phoenix's trademark Jian – with some heavier craft mixed in. Nothing any of their own number couldn't handle. "They are *not* primary targets."

Signaling with his Shiden's right wing in acknowledgment, Kazama continued to follow his comrade's lead as both fighters came about, now advancing toward another drydock. As opposed to their first target containing a destroyer, this one held a *Gansu*-class cruiser. Naturally, it wasn't long before the defense batteries in proximity began to fire, forcing the two heavy fighters to evade the beam shots and missiles while still maintaining attack vector and velocity. Some of the *Gansu's* phalanx also went active, adding their own beam fire against the Corsair and Shiden, yet neither Jon nor Kazama broke away. All the while, the defense fire never so much as grazed the shielding of either fighter.

Jon struck first, flying straight up to the cruiser and firing his beam cannons near point blank, blasting open the upper hull as well as disintegrating the bridge tower as he passed. Shun followed up by targeting the dock itself, destroying enough of the structure that the drydock broke apart on its own. The *Gansu* seemed to retain some semblance of a crew, however, as both fighters immediately took note of its arc engine going online the moment they completed their attack run, but that hardly mattered, as one of the *Tsushima's* torpedoes found the cruiser and struck straight through the prow. The resultant detonation easily finished off the cruiser, and whatever remained of the drydock, leaving the two fighters to search out other targets.

Unfortunately, that was the precise moment that Red Phoenix fighters entered range, such that Jon and Kazama were all but buffeted by oncoming fire. Having to maneuver their fighters more defensively than when facing "mere" stationary batteries, the two fighters returned the beam fire in earnest, shooting down two Jians each as the formations passed each other. It was much the same throughout the rest of the shipyard as several of the compatriots were forced to break off their own attacks to deal with the enemy fighters first, though obviously none of the Flints or the Blue Dragons intended to be tied down for very long.

All the while, torpedo salvos continued in the background, soon complemented by missile fire from the cloaked umbras. More and more sections of the shipyard erupting in fire and debris with each unnaturally precise strike.

Flint Pirates umbra *Black Sun*
Taishan System

It really is the simple things in life you treasure, Alex thought rather smugly as he and Kaguya, who was standing just right of the command chair, watched the devastation play out with the rest of the bridge crew. Of that number, only Lorelei seemed to have attention turned away from the main monitor, her eyes closed while she faced her station. Such was part of the plan that she and Izuna had come up with regarding how Lorelei could take direct control of the *Sun* at will, with Izuna holding a similar ability with the *Tsushima*. Why not put that ability to use for the greater good, as both psion women had apparently concluded.

Thus, feeling more like a spectator to a light show as opposed to a ship commander, Alex watched with a visible gleam as Lorelei, having since taken control of the *Sun*'s helm and tactical systems through her power, turned Taishan into absolute hell. She and Izuna maneuvered and weaved their respective umbras in a near balletic pattern, ensuring that the Red Phoenix remained unable to gain even a semblance of a position on either ship while also launching and guiding the torpedoes and missiles through the same process. Neither psion need utilize their ships' targeting systems for this either. The same power that granted them control also allowed them to select their targets and coordinate with the other, ensuring that Taishan suffered the maximum damage in a short period. All very beautiful to observe and all very damning for the shipyard occupants.

Of course, as Lorelei had explained prior to the attack, this strategy had its limitations and could not be used so forwardly in the future. The main reason Lorelei had sought out a crew for the *Sun*, then the *U-7501*, in the first place, was because she was only one sentient, and even with heavy automation, it was impossible for her to guide and control the *Sun* for any prolonged periods. Likewise, while it wasn't impossible for her to perform complex movements and maneuvers with the *Sun* on her own, it was still extremely difficult and certainly nowhere near as efficient as with a crew to manage the various parts and systems. Again, Lorelei would not have gathered the Flints together from the beginning had it been otherwise.

Those limitations established, however, it was an all too simple affair for Lorelei and Izuna with her, to utilize the *Sun* and the *Tsushima* as bombardment platforms, continuously raining destruction upon a designated set of targets while maneuvering their ships gradually. Combined with the synchronization that their powers granted when working in tandem, it was truly less an attack and more like a well-choreographed dance between two master-level performers. A dance that the crews of either ship were enjoying thoroughly, especially since they need only watch and not take direct part.

"Approximately forty percent of the shipyard now destroyed," Barbarossa reported with an appreciative expression. As much as he enjoyed being the tactical officer, it was actually nice to let someone else handle his job for once. Usually, that only happened when he had to take command as Second Officer.

"Any oncoming reinforcements?" Alex inquired.

"None that I can see," Barbarossa observed from his station display. "Countdown continues at ten minutes and fifteen seconds."

"Noted," Alex nodded, doing well to keep that in mind. Though the comm jamming did well to delay reinforcements, it would not prevent such entirely. In fact, it was a sure bet that someone in Penglai or elsewhere had already found Taishan to be out of contact and so deployed a taskforce to investigate. All too likely a sizeable taskforce, considering how vital the shipyard was to the Red Phoenix.

Not that it matters, Alex reflected, watching as the *Sun*'s latest missile barrage struck its full set of targets. *At this rate, there won't be much of anything left in ten minutes regardless...*

Taishan System

Seven minutes... Boss thought as she took a quick glance toward the counter, right as another formation of Jians, supplemented by one or two heavier Daos, surged after her and Corsair Two. Both fighters coming about, they returned their vulcan fire against the would be aggressors, taking down two Jians and one of the Daos between them before the Red Phoenixes broke formation and scattered. Though tempted to pursue, Boss was well aware that she was on the clock with this one and so reangled her fighter toward a more substantial target. Corsair Two naturally followed while their attackers attempted to pursue.

Dodging or outright ignoring the attackers as she drove on, Boss angled her beam cannons and fired into another drydock space. This one didn't have a ship berthed in it, but that hardly mattered to the ace, as she was about to deny its foreseeable service to the Red Phoenix. Though shielded, as was the rest of the shipyard, the dock could never hope to hold up against her Corsair's beam cannons. Its defenses broke within the first two or three shots alone, thereby allowing Boss and her wingman to proceed in raking fire across the topside as they passed over. By the time they completed their shared attack, the dockyard was an expanding field of blazing fragments.

Shame they won't all be this easy, Boss thought solemnly as she watched the components of her target spread further and further into space, some even going so far as to impact other parts of the shipyard. A few moments later, the Red Phoenix fighters caught up to the Blue Comet and Corsair Two, forcing both to make abrupt vector changes and move to dissuade their pursuers once again. This time three more Jians fell as they passed, neither Corsair so much as blemished by enemy fire. Not that either of them expected much from a garrison unit.

Still, as Boss struck down another Jian before veering away toward her next selected target, she again felt some portion of melancholy. They were having an easy time with this, as well as a fair amount of fun along the way. Unfortunately, she knew it would not last, not with a Pirate Clan. Any additional targets the Flints pursued after Tianshan would be much harder to reach, as well as more heavily defended.

But then, Boss supposed, as she dove upon a docked *Sichuan*-class frigate, which she decimated in but one pass, that was more or less the point. If Lady Ching thought that the Flints would cower and hide from her big bad Clan following Atalanta, then what was occurring now in Tianshan would serve as the perfect rude awakening. This was all-out war of a different nature than what they previously fought under Dreyfus. This time the Flints' fight would be *personal*.

Thus continuing her line of attack on the next selection of docked ships, Boss gunned her thrusters and moved straight in. Further fire and destruction soon following across her wake, with just over five minutes to spare.

———————————————————

Vulcans blazing until the Jian in his target reticle was thoroughly shredded, Kazama grinned in triumph as he flew past the flaming remnants. He could not remember the last time he had so much fun, even in the heat of battle. Despite the fact it was a battle that he was purportedly *not* participating in whatsoever, at least as far as his father would claim to the other Clan Lords. Such only added to the young heir's vigor, however, as he again moved alongside his friend and wingman's Corsair, both firing upon the next set of enemy fighters.

Indeed, as Kazama rolled out from the oncoming beams and then twisted around to catch one of the enemy Jians across the side, the future Lord realized that Taishan was the first of many things. Not simply the first reprisal that was to be struck against the Red Phoenix for their hubris at Atalanta, but also the first true battle for the *Tsushima* and her crew. The ship had been in operation a mere three months before Atalanta, during which only function tests, system evaluations, and the occasional deep reconnaissance mission were performed. Only now was she and the crew that manned her truly being put to the test, and Kazama was quite pleased with the results. Izuna certainly seemed to be having fun with it, judging by how she was maneuvering the ship in tandem with the Siren-controlled *Sun*.

And, of course, it was also the first combat run for the Shiden. Just as the *Tsushima* borrowed much from the *Sun*, so did the Blue Dragon's latest fighter borrow from the Corsair. In fact, aside from the Shiden having straightened wings, a different canopy, four vulcans instead of six, and other minor cosmetic alterations, the Shiden was practically the same heavy fighter design as its ancestor. This included possessing wing-mounted beam cannons, which Kazama again put to use as he and Jon dove at another installation, a holding dock for multiple ships, up to and including at least three different cruiser types. The Shiden swooped over the docked ships and fired, eliciting significant damage to each vessel, if not destroying them outright, exhibiting its deadly capabilities alongside its Corsair brethren. Needless to say, as he moved away, Kazama was falling in love that much more with his new fighter.

"Three minutes, twenty-seven seconds," Jon recited to his wingman after taking a glance at the displayed counter that showed the approximate time in which the Red Phoenix relief force was sure to arrive. "Last one's on you."

Kazama was just about to respond when his instrument panel lit up, causing him to twist his fighter away out of reflex. Moments later, twin cannon-sized beams lanced through the space he and his wingman had previously occupied. Capital ship cannon-sized beams specifically.

"In that case..." Kazama smiled evilly as he found the origin of the fire. A *Guizhou*-class battlecruiser was in the process of leaving its dock and moving out to engage its enemy. Several Jians were also moving in to support the warship, driving after the two opposing fighters with a clear vengeance as the battlecruiser continued firing its main armaments.

"Banzai!"

Kazama put power to his sub-arc drives and effectively took the lead; Jon moved his Corsair back in a support position. Within seconds the Blue Dragon fighter entered into range against the Jians and open fired with its vulcans, obliterating one Red Phoenix fighter and blowing off the left side of another, with Jon scoring his own hit against a third. The Jians attempted to turn and catch the two oncoming craft as they shot by, but the Corsair and Shiden were just too fast. The few beams that connected were easily deflected by either's shielding. Thus outside a single one hundred eighty degrees turn to shoot down another Jian, and then another such turn to maintain its approach vector, both fighters advanced on the enemy warship.

Upon the two fighters' approach, the battlecruiser, seemingly not about to take any chances, immediately stepped up its rate of fire, soon adding its phalanx to support its main cannons and missiles. In a display that was almost as elaborate as the maneuvers Lorelei and Izuna were presently employing, the Corsair and the Shiden weaved around each beam and projectile, neither Kazama nor Jon willing to take a chance against the *Guizhou*. Crossing in their flightpaths to attack the battlecruiser from opposite vectors, both open fired with their beam cannons, striking multiple blows against the battlecruiser's shielding. Unfortunately, said shielding held against the onslaught as the two fighters passed overhead. Even the shots that would have otherwise hit the bridge tower were ultimately repelled.

Of course, the pilots were nonpulsed at the outcome; it was a battlecruiser after all. Undeterred, Kazama banked his fighter in another abrupt turn, effectively reversing his prior vector and recrossing the battleship, from port midships to starboard bow. Again the shields held, but the Blue Dragon pilot maintained the assault, eventually diving and encircling the battlecruiser, pouring additional beam cannon fire against its shields while doing well to keep ahead of its phalanx.

Unable to withstand the onslaught, the shields buckled, broken by the Shiden's beam cannons. With the shields gone, Kazama circled the bridge tower once again. This time his shots connected, obliterating the entirety of the structure.

Capitalizing on the brainless condition of the *Guizhou*, Kazama targeted the exposed arc engine, concentrating his shots on a single point in the stern. Once again, the ship, in this case, its main power/propulsion system, buckled from the high-powered beams, pulsating and then rupturing just as the Shiden zoomed away. By the time Kazama had gained sufficient separation distance, the listing battlecruiser detonated, annihilating more of the shipyard with it.

"Not bad," Jon observed as his Corsair leveled out to rejoin its wingman. "For one's first ship kill."

Kazama pretended to be irritated. "And what about you, Black Angel?" he retorted. "You disappeared on me for a good while."

"Just dealing with the Jians you left behind," Jon countered, not missing a beat. "I didn't think you wanted them interrupting your fun."

Waving his port wing in a "touché" motion, Kazama took a moment to consult his sensors. By now, it was clear the vast majority of the shipyard was either destroyed or otherwise beyond salvage. Likewise, it seemed the bulk of the garrison had also been decimated, as Kazama depicted only a select few Red Phoenix craft around the area. And they all appeared to be fleeing.

Obviously to wait for the relief force, Kazama thought, checking his own counter. Only forty-two seconds before the enemy force's estimated time of arrival. "I think it's best we end it here, Corsair Zero."

"Agreed, Shiden Zero," Jon acknowledged, then tapping his broad-

133

band. "Corsair Zero to all fighters. Mission accomplished. Standby for arc speed on my command."

Disengaging from their remaining attack runs, the Flints and Blue Dragons effectively turned and moved away from the shipyard as one, now proceeding toward open space. The still cloaked *Black Sun* and *Tsushima* did so as well, coming about as they both set up for arc transition.

"Corsair Zero to *Sun*," Jon continued, smirking toward the *pièce de resistance* that was to come. There in Tianshan and many future targets. "Don't forget to leave them our calling card."

Flint Pirates umbra *Black Sun*
Taishan System

"Will do Corsair Zero," Alex acknowledged, then nodding toward Barbarossa, who had since retaken control of his station from Lorelei. "Make sure they don't miss it, Barbarossa."

Grinning, Barbarossa simply tapped the appropriate key, launching one final torpedo that turned and shot back and away as the *Sun*, the *Tsushima,* and their respective fighter contingents all entered arcspace.

The torpedo penetrated the ruined and burning shipyard until at last reaching its designated point. Only then did it detonate, but not in a conventional explosion. Rather than generate a wave of destructive force, which would have been quite redundant in the current situation, the torpedo's detonation generated a great energy field. One that instantly expanded and took shape until it loomed and shone predominantly over the myriad detritus.

By the time the Red Phoenix relief forces arrived, those crews therein could only look on in cold overwhelming horror as the Golden Roger beamed across the void and well over the vestiges of the once proud Taishan Shipyard.

Chapter X: Afterparty

Ryugu Castle
Kyoto, Ryugu

"This is an outrage!" the holographic image of Lady Ching bellowed as additional projected images of Taishan, at least what remained of it, shifted between her and the other three Clan Lords. Up to and including the oversized Golden Roger that shone from the center of the ruin, which Lord Fuma, at least, found to be a clever finishing touch.

"How could any of this have been possible, even for them!?" the Lady of the Red Phoenix fumed toward her visibly bored and unsympathetic audience.

Why is it those who start such conflicts always claim victimhood upon reprisal? Lord Fuma blandly thought but did well not to speak aloud. Right then did Ching's eyes fix squarely upon him.

"And worse yet, they were not alone," Ching growled in clear accusation. "There have been reports of additional fighters, and possibly one other ship, having attacked Taishan beside them."

The Red Phoenix Lady almost spat as she added. "All marked with the styling of an azure dragon."

Fuma maintained his unmoved expression, even throwing in a sigh for additional effect. "Do you hold any proof toward this, Lady Ching?" he inquired, already knowing the answer.

"Nothing of record," Ching was forced to admit, bristling as she did. "But witnesses have…"

"Such testimony could mean anything, as we all know," Fuma interrupted all too wryly. "And even then, how could it be any of my ships? They have not even been mobilized."

Ching almost gnashed her teeth in her spite toward the Blue Dragon Lord's audacity. "Obviously, the ship in question would have been another umbra, operating under cloak," she managed through her sneer. "Or are you going to tell me you *didn't* acquire the means to make your own umbras when the Flints originally bartered with you?"

Fuma still remained unmoved. "Perhaps it was an umbra; perhaps it wasn't. The fact remains, however, that you possess no proof nor any means of validation. By contrast, I have made no aggressive action toward you, the Blue Armada remains well within its home space, and your territory remains unviolated through all of it."

Again glancing toward the still present Taishan imagery, the Blue Dragon Lord at last grinned. "Outside the obvious at least."

"Liu koushi de biaozi he houzi de ben erzi!" Ching hatefully bellowed once more. "I warned you, Fuma. I warned you what would happen…"

"That is quite enough, Lady Ching," Lord Amago Pargo interrupted. Though there was no true hierarchy within their company, the White Tiger Lord remained the oldest among them and so wielded the authority of an elder. "Regardless of whether the Flints had aid or not, you are still the one who fired the first salvo."

Now it was Pargo's eyes, old yet of iron will, that narrowed with accusation. "In spite of deliberations having been far from concluded."

Ching actually clenched her teeth but was forced to look away as the White Tiger Lord's words struck.

"It is by your own actions that Taishan now burns," Pargo continued glancing toward Lady Levasseur. Upon receiving the expected nod from the Black Tortoise Lady, Pargo turned back to Ching. "And it is by those same actions that you shall face them alone."

The Red Phoenix Lady almost gaped as she huffed. "What are you saying, Lord Pargo?"

"You understand my words well, Lady Ching," Pargo responded. "Just as Lord Fuma has already spoken for the Blue Dragon, neither the White Tiger nor the Black Tortoise will support you in this matter."

Lady Ching started to swell with righteous indignation when the Black Tortoise Lady entered into the discussion.

"It is as Lord Pargo states," Lady Olivia Levasseur confirmed, her own tone thick with condemnation. Though the youngest among their number, the Lady of the Black Tortoise yet wielded her own force of will. "This is all entirely of your own making Lady Ching. As is your choice to disregard this council altogether…"

"Nimen dou shi shagua!" Ching cursed in her clan's tongue once more, now incredulous. "Can none of you see them for what they are!? Are you truly blind to the threat they pose to us!?"

Then with even further power she thundered. "Do none of you understand that, through them, Morganna Flint walks among us still!?"

No verbal response came from the three Lords to any of these outcries. Only a collective air of firm, unchanging resolution.

Her eyes shifting between them, Ching studied her three counterparts to verify that they were, in fact, set with their decision. Upon confirmation that they were, the Lady of the Red Phoenix ultimately closed her eyes and nodded in a begrudging acceptance. She and her clan would indeed fight the Flints on their own.

"Very well, I shall eliminate this *wángbādàn* myself," Ching viciously declared, eyes spitting her resolve. "And through their destruction, we shall, at last, be free of that *yáng lājī*."

She glared one final time upon Lord Fuma. "Once and for all."

Her projection abruptly vanished.

Horai

Despite the fact it had been very few hours since the raid's conclusion, the celebration was in full swing, with the crews of both ships taking an active part. In the middle of the small encampment they had set up on that otherwise unnamed world, since christened "Horai" by Kazama who had claimed it as the first Blue Dragon colony within Red Phoenix space, the Flints and their allies ate, drank, and danced the local night away, commemorating their first victory against their newest enemy. A party remained a party, no matter the excuse, and partying remained as integral to piracy as the usual rifling and looting. Besides, in the standard fashion of war, one never knew how much time one still had, so it was always best to make the most of it as one still could.

As he made his way back to the table he shared with the Kazama and Izuna, Jon could see that his crew, as well as Kazama's, were embracing the concept. A great bonfire, courtesy of Forneus, was set within the center of the settlement with several crewmen from either ship dancing around it while the rest remained around the circumference eating, drinking, and conversing. A well-sized cooking station manned by the galley staff of either ship, who, after their initial landing, had somehow managed to come to a truce regarding who was running it, was continually producing entrees for the impressive queue of hungry pirates. Said entrees were based around a fusion cuisine of sorts, a natural product of the Flint and Blue Dragon chefs working in tandem.

And then there were the Psirens with Lorelei at her usual helm, placed at the other end of the encampment and performing in full form to everyone's collective entertainment. Their present choice was *Over the Hills and Far Away*, a tale of a man, having been wrongfully convicted, yearning for his freedom and love from within his prison cell as he served his ten-year sentence. Jon found it fitting for the present circumstances, nodding his approval to Lorelei as he passed by the stage.

Eventually, he made it to where Kazama and Izuna were seated, the Blue Dragon captain raising his tankard as the elder Flint approached.

"My compliments Captain Flint. You and your crew truly know how to have a good time."

"All part of our fair and noble profession, Kazama," Jon answered as he took his seat, tapping his own tankard against his fellow captain's to toast. He looked out toward the dancers around the bonfire, as well as the shadows they projected against the backdrop of stone and trees. "This has been a tradition since we arrived on Ryugu the first time."

"So I see," Izuna concurred, easily picking up on the associated images. She couldn't help but feel amused at Lorelei's original debut therein.

It was then that she turned her eye toward her husband. "Shame that we don't have our own band aboard the *Tsushima*," she spoke none so hintingly.

Kazama wisely took a sip from his tankard before replying. "I'll inquire of Father for one when we return," he spoke precisely and diplomatically, in all too traditional husbandly manner. Not that he would have minded one for his ship, it just hadn't been a priority, or even a consideration, during the *Tsushima*'s fitting out. Not that it assuaged Izuna, who easily picked up on his unspoken disposition.

Jon also took a sip from his tankard, if only to keep from smirking to his friend's detriment. "I want to thank you again for doing this," the elder son of Morganna Flint spoke earnestly. "I know how much you and your father are risking..."

"You've long earned the honor, Jon," Kazama waved him off, almost affronted by the insinuation. "Family helps family."

Hearing that, Jon again took a deliberate sip from his tankard. Though this time, he couldn't quite keep from smiling in his gratitude.

"Besides, Lady Ching had it coming over this one," Kazama added on, seriousness now entering the prince's expression. "Kaguya's report from Atalanta was quite...informative."

That in itself caused the memories to nearly reemerge, but Jon, while unable to stifle the resultant frown, was quick in forcing them back from his consciousness. Now was not the time to remember such senseless carnage.

The Blue Dragon psion picked up on Jon's remorse. "None of it was your doing," she assured in comforting sympathy.

"I know," Jon again responded in gratitude. "Yet it all happened regardless," he couldn't help but espouse.

Sensing his friend's lingering pain, Kazama reached out and took his shoulder. "I told you before, we'll make it right," he stated firmly as he squeezed Jon's shoulder in assurance. "Ching will pay dearly for her belligerence, as will Shun if we run into him."

Nodding, Jon clasped his hand over Kazama's and squeezed in acknowledgment. "I know," he repeated. "In their arrogance, both mother and son made the most ancient of mistakes."

Upon Kazama's curious expression, Jon's smirk emerged in wry form. "They left a live dragon out of their calculations."

Easily catching onto the reference, Kazama nodded in concurrence. "Two of them, and hungry at that," he added with a laugh, both captains then toasting once more.

"Oh yeah," Cheney sighed, watching the rest of the crowd as Kaiser downed the contents of his tankard, then slammed it back onto the table to rancorous cheering. "That five hundred is already mine..."

"Not just yet, Master Chief," Davis countered as his own bet was about to go next. As much as Kaiser's stomach was akin to chiseled stone as the rest of him, he was still no match for her, Davis knew. In fact, considering all that she had gone through in her time, the helmsman doubted anyone could match Anna Reed's alcohol tolerance.

Upon her own tankard being refilled, the operations officer tilted back and began to drink. For several more minutes the crowd watched with collectively held breath, the first vestiges of cheering beginning after but a few more moments as the spectators saw Anna had already downed the majority of her tankard. As she slammed it back on the table, the cheering restarting in abundance.

"We could be here all night, you realize," Boss exclaimed around her smoking pipe, knowing just how much grog either challenger could take. She glanced toward Braun. "How far along are they now?"

"Alcohol content is roughly three times the standard for either," the engineer reported as his built-in sensors analyzed. "Closing rapidly in on four."

"Great," Apache let out grumpily, knowing that he would be dealing with both in his sickbay when all was said and done. Even Herculeans could get hangovers, as he knew from repeated experience.

"Come on!" Gran called out in support to her significant other as he visibly struggled to raise his refilled tankard. But raise it and drink he did, with the crowd joining the cheering moments later. Again did Kaiser slam his mug back onto the table. "Don't let up! You almost have her!"

"The night's still young Gran," Anna quipped to her friend without slurring, right as her tankard was refilled. "And I didn't go through my home life to lose to Michaelangelo here."

Kaiser responded with his own sordid version of the Imperial salute. The more astute within the crowd could see the security officer sway somewhat, though the majority of the attention returned to Anna as she took her next swig. Once more, downing the contents, followed by another slam with further cheering.

"And there it goes," Braun proclaimed brightly. "Alcohol content now *four* times the standard for either."

Even Davis could not help but swallow as he felt the tension that now reverberated throughout the captive audience. It would not be much longer, they all knew, especially as Kaiser began downing his next drink. One would stand, or remain upright, and one would fall as the ancient quotation went.

Kaiser appeared to be well in line for the former as he slammed his tankard back down once again. He remained upright for a few more seconds, right before his eyes rolled backward, and his body fell in the very same direction. His impact with the ground was equivalent to a falling boulder, even generating a small rockslide.

"Damn it!" Cheney cursed as the winnings began to be collected. Having no other choice, he passed the five hundred to the helmsman's waiting hand. "Don't spend it all on one girl," he stated before getting up with the rest of the spectators.

"Oh, I won't," Davis assured as he pocketed the aurics, perhaps the easiest winnings he had ever made. It had been quite close, however, considering that Anna not only remained seated in front of him but was swaying in a wobbly manner. Sighing, the Lady Killer ultimately decided to render aid. Besides, he didn't want to break his back with Kaiser, who he noted had a whole contingent from both ships trying to drag him to wherever.

"My compliments on a fine showing, m'lady," he praised the operations officer as he managed to lift her to a passable standing position. "Though I do think you're going to feel it tomorrow."

"I think I feel it now," Anna burped as she attempted, unsuccessfully, to walk. Fortunately, Davis remained at her side to hold her up. "And if I happen to feel *you* anywhere near me in the morning…"

"Thanks for the invite, but I don't sleep with lushes, sweetheart," Davis responded as he half drug half guided her along. That much was true. For all of his admitted faults and flaws, Howell Davis wasn't the type to take wanton advantage of the inebriated.

Don't worry, though, the helmsman thought as he moved the woman beside him along, smiling in concealed assurance as he kept her upright. *There* will *be a night for us, in time.*

He felt an entirely different feeling in his stomach from that thought, one that *wasn't* a product of alcohol. The Lady Killer forced it back down, once more knowing that there was still time yet. And it wasn't like he didn't have enough to worry about along with the rest of the Flints, especially as he did well to remember what they had just pulled at Taishan. Much to his internal melancholy, especially as he couldn't help but feel the warmth of Anna's body pressed against his.

Even so, Davis concentrated on the task at hand, gradually bring his charge toward one of the nearby and seemingly few *unoccupied* tents. All while the party and the music continued around them, with Lorelei soon stepping down and a male backup taking her place. The opening tones of *Night Moves* began but a few moments later.

——————— ———————

He was a fair distance from the party now. Although he still heard the music, it was faint and melded into the background night sounds. In a strange way, Alex found it a fitting backdrop for the image in front of him. He was captivated. He had always found her to be beautiful, perhaps the most beautiful woman in the galaxy, but as she stood there now, even with her back turned to him, Alex only felt that familiar overwhelming draw toward the Dragon Princess. Much like he had upon meeting her the first time so long ago.

Seemingly oblivious to his approach, Kaguya continued to face away from him and the party, standing under the bright blue light of the local moon. Silent and alone, the kunoichi seemed so withdrawn from all around her, such that Alex, despite the beauty and majesty she projected as she was now, could not help but feel unsettled. The Dragon Princess had become more and more distant as of late, and the younger Flint did not understand why. He knew her well enough to know when something deeply bothered her, and something was indeed doing so now.

As he moved closer, Alex, for a brief moment, thought he saw the glint of her sword against the moonlight. Confusion entered his mind. Hadn't Kaguya left her ninjato back on the *Sun*? Which presently remained in orbit alongside the *Tsushima*?

And then, the glint disappeared. Just as Alex picked up on Kaguya's responding frown at his approach.

"I'm sorry," she apologized straight away, without turning to face him. "I wanted to spend some time to myself."

Smiling despite, Alex moved up to her. "You've been doing that a lot lately," the younger Flint pointed out as he came to stand beside her, both now gazing up at the full moon. "Anything you want to talk about?"

It took a moment for Kaguya to respond. "I'm...discouraged," she admitted. "With how fast our battles have been escalating."

Alex nodded in understanding. "Our enemies are getting more difficult, aren't they?" he agreed, recalling all the fights that they had been through. "First Drake, then Kraft, and then the Baranovs and their Mavkas…"

"And now we face four Wielders," Kaguya finished for him.

Again Alex nodded. "With any luck, this will all be over before we have to fight them again," he tried to assure her.

"Possibly," Kaguya replied, looking down at her clenched hands, obviously disturbed. "And yet…"

Again Alex smiled as understanding dawned. "You're not holding us back, Kaguya," he spoke reassuringly. "That's what you're discouraged about, isn't it? That you're not able to fight like Jon and I?"

Exhaling through her nostrils, Kaguya nodded in admission. With a flick of her hand, a kunai appeared therein.

"I've fought and killed my share," Kaguya continued, staring down at the throwing blade, which partially reflected her visage. "But I can only do so much, against so much."

With another flick of her hand, the kunai disappeared from whence it came. "How much further can I go on, Alex?" she questioned, at last turning toward the younger Flint. "Before…before I become a liability…?"

Exhaling, Alex turned to face her, all the while the glove over his right hand receded in Forneus' flames. Slowly, he brought his uncovered hand up to stroke Kaguya's cheek.

"You will *never* be a liability, *anata*," he stated, watching as the Dragon Princess closed her eyes, visibly drawing comfort and reassurance from his touch. As well as his words. "More than anyone, or anything else, you and I will *always* fight as one."

Reaching her hand up to cover his, a small tear slipped down Kaguya's cheek. All the while, her opposite hand slipped unseen around Alex, drawing him to her.

"We will *always* be one," Alex avowed as he wrapped both arms around her, pulling her close. Holding her tightly, he could feel her heartbeat, her breathing, the soothing warmth of her body but also her uncertainty, her apprehension – her *fear*. Yet, as they stood together in the moonlight, little by little, uncertainty, apprehension, and *fear* gave way. Reassurance and reaffirmation began to emerge within Fuma Kaguya once more.

"Tsuneni?" she questioned one more time, if only to hear him confirm as such again. Especially in the face of her uncertainty, which lingered for just a little bit more. *Always?*

Breathing in the scent of her hair, Alex smiled as he kissed the top of her head. *"Hai, tsuneni."* Yes, always.

Sniffing somewhat as more tears fell, Kaguya raised on her tiptoes, speared Alex's hair with her hands, and nudged his head down, closing the distance between their lips and intensifying their embrace.

"Tsuki ga kirei," she breathed before kissing him, losing herself in the emotions only he evoked. Alex quickly took the kiss deeper, intent on affirming their devotion to each other, their shared love.

It did not completely dispel the darkness she felt, especially from what was now back aboard the *Sun*, but it distanced her from it for the time being. And likewise, it assured her that she and Alexander Flint would remain as one, against whatever evil the galaxy would throw at them. No matter how much harder the fighting would become.

The music continued in the background as the two younger children of one-time enemies remained as they were, in each other's arms, bathed in moonlight. And love.

Chapter XI: The Fire Rises

Red Phoenix *Yunnan*-class battleship *Zhang He*
Deep Space

The rage radiated off of him, even hotter and more apparent than the surrounding blaze. Standing in the middle of his self-generated inferno, breathing in rapid bouts, Shun looked at the destruction he had caused to his quarters, toward the wavering but still otherwise active projections across from him. All of which displayed their own images of destruction, though rather than from the interior of a starship, this one was of a very specific space station with derelicts of numerous Red Phoenix ships afloat around the devastation. Too recently set to ruin.

Again feeling his rage, which for perhaps the first time in his existence was firmly beyond his control, erupt from within, the surrounding fires turned hotter and wilder, flickering through the whole of his quarters. Datong Station was simply the latest of Red Phoenix outposts destroyed; it was not the first since Taishan, Shun knew all too well, and the way all was progressing, it would not be the last. The latest part of his clan's territory to be sundered by the Flints and their Blue Dragon allies, whose participation Shun was not fooled toward in the least. All well within what should have been secured space, and all in complete defiance of the Red Armada, who were very well chasing after shadows now.

Indeed the Flints were as methodical as they were audacious while they carried through their insurrection. Not only were they striking deep within Red Phoenix space, far deeper than any previous would have dared, they were hitting and decimating targets one after the other that should have been well defended. Each time Shun or another commander would anticipate an attack, only for Jonathan Flint to circumvent them completely and attack where his band of rabble *hadn't* been expected. Each time Shun and his taskforce would arrive all too late, only to behold the burning remnants of a once-proud fleet or installation. And each and every time, the destruction was left with a Golden Roger emblazed across, just as the gutted husk of Datong now held upon its form. A flaunting reminder of what the Flints had done there, would continue to do elsewhere, and insinuating Shun and the rest of the clan were powerless to stop them.

Swinging Haborym about, Shun launched a dark fire wave into the holographic projector, obliterating it and causing the vidwindows to abruptly vanish. How could the pretender's sons be capable of such destruction? Against a *Clan,* no less? None of it should have been, no matter their prior victories against Drake, the Pisceans, and the Baranovs. The Red Phoenix was above all of them! Beyond all of them!

Finally managing to gain some hold over his rage, such that the fires all extinguished as Haborym vanished from his grip, Shun sat back on his now charred but structurally functioning chair, calming himself. Eventually, he was able to force the fury back down, regaining the cold passivity he was known for, at least on the exterior. Well within, however, his rage remained, burning even more than his quarters had previously. He could not allow the Flints to continue any longer. He needed to end all of them, not just the brothers and their respective women. Now the entirety of the Flint Pirates would be put to his torch, as would that Blue Dragon umbra and her own crew. They would all burn, cleansed away from the Red Phoenix forevermore.

Yet, the question remained. How could he track them down? Even the Red Phoenix's most powerful diviners (psions) had been unable to accurately anticipate where and when the Flints would strike next, and the Red Armada was as far from breaking their cloaking systems as everyone else in the galaxy seemingly. If he could locate them, Shun knew he could smash the *Black Sun* and her partner with over-whelming force, but first, he needed to find them. But he didn't even know where to start...

"Bridge to Lord Shun," Shun suddenly heard from overhead.

Exhaling through his nostrils, Shun tapped the comm switch. "Yes."

"My liege, we're receiving a new signal from Penglai," the *Zhang He*'s captain reported, barely managing to keep his nervousness at bay. Shun picked up on it but ignored it. "Priority one."

Exhaling once more, Shun simply disengaged the bridge comm. and switched over to the Penglai one. What could his Lady want of him now?

Instead of a holographic projection of the Red Phoenix Lady, a simple holographic window appeared in front of him. One that was marked "SOUND ONLY".

Flint Pirates umbra *Black Sun*
Deep Space

"And then there were seven," Davis beamed quite proudly as the images of Datong Station, or what remained of it, shifted across the monitor. Beginning with Taishan, Datong had been the seventh Red Phoenix basin that the Flints had struck, as well as the seventh they had successfully raided. "Considering we haven't even been at this for three weeks, I'd say we're doing pretty well."

"So far," Barbarossa commented. Though he understood the helmsman's feeling of accomplishment, Datong had also been the most difficult raid for them to date, the station having been better defended than anticipated. Their enemy was clearly learning from their mistakes and acting accordingly. "If the battle had lasted any longer than it had..."

"Yes," Jon concluded, clasping his hands upon the briefing room table, looking at the images and recalling just how much energy it had taken to pull off that raid. The remnant of a *Liaoning*-class battleship floated across the window, further emphasizing that what they had just faced at Datong had been much more than expected. "They may be unable to track us, but they can still reinforce their defenses. And they have more than enough ships and support forces to do so."

"What about striking lesser targets then?" Anna offered. "It might not hurt them as badly, but it could possibly divert some of those defenses..."

"Not nearly enough, and the damage would be negligible as you said," Kazama, who had been invited to the meeting, answered. "Remember, we want to end this all as quickly and efficiently as possible. Otherwise, we enter a war of attrition."

"Which we would obviously never win," Jon nodded in agreement. "For that, we have to continue bloodying them until Lady Ching at last capitulates."

"Unfortunately, she does not seem the least bit interested in capitulation, brother," Alex said, sighing audibly. As much as he was having fun with all of this, as well as seeing the Red Phoenix twist in the proverbial wind from said bloodying, the fact was they were still at it. And would remain so for the foreseeable future if they kept going as they were now.

"Agreed," Jon responded to his brother, taking on another of his wryer grins. "Which is why we must now force the issue."

Realizing their captain had another plan, the officers of the Flint Pirates all turned their attention toward him. As did Kazama, who nodded his continued assistance to Jon as the latter set to proceed.

The monitor flashed once again, now displaying a planet that the gathered did well to recognize. Much to their astonishment.

"This is where our next target is located," Jon spoke, already feeling the uncertainty from around the table. "Penglai."

Though the officers – at least those who weren't aware of the plan yet – were visibly anxious, none contested their captain on the issue. Clearly, he would have thought this out.

Still, Davis could not help but question. "We're going to stage a raid *there*, of all places?"

"Not entirely," Jon corrected, re-earning his audience's attention. "In lieu of a raid, it will be a *heist*."

With that, the monitor flickered again. This time displaying the object of their apparent interest.

"The Fengguan, otherwise known as the Phoenix Crown," Lorelei spoke up in her captain's place. "A ceremonial headdress originally worn by the inaugural Lady of the Red Phoenix, Ching Xiao."

The officers all took a moment to study the article, as did Kazama. Somewhat dome-like in shape, the titular crown was heavily ornamented, possessing much in the way of gold, rubies, pearls, and other such adornments. All taking various forms and depictions, namely of articulate phoenixes.

"Since the original wearer, it had been passed down from one Lady to the next as a symbol of her majesty and sovereignty," Lorelei went on. "For whatever reason, however, the present Lady of the Red Phoenix has chosen *not* to retain it as part of her standard wardrobe. Thus it is kept within the royal treasure vault deep inside Bayue

Palace."

"Bayue?" Cheney questioned, realizing the significance of the name along with the rest. "Not just the capital world, we're pulling this in the lady's residence as well?"

"It's possible," Boss murmured around her still smoking pipe with some consideration. "There's no way they'd see it coming."

"Precisely our main advantage," Jon spoke again. "It is the one part of the Red Phoenix where neither Lady Ching nor any of her commanders, including Shun, will anticipate an attack."

Another monitor window soon appeared, once more displaying the outlined Red Phoenix territory. Multiple red dots and lines were emphasized therein.

"With the bulk of the Red Armada out searching for us, a basic rear-guard now remains in the Penglai System," the captain of the *Black Sun* continued. "Leaving it all but completely open to infiltration."

"Okay, so why not an orbital bombardment then?" Davis suggested. "Fly in, launch a torpedo and send Ching and everyone else to Kingdom Come?"

"Bayue Palace is located well within the heart of the city of Shandong," Jon emphasized to the helmsman, effectively silencing any such debate. He knew the others concurred with him there as well. Unless it could not be helped, collateral damage was to be avoided as much as possible, and the Red Phoenix had plenty of innocent life within it.

"Besides, there would undoubtedly be a high-grade shield system in place," Alex responded knowingly.

Davis took the hint, though that didn't assuage him of their chances, especially with a heist. Especially if, given that this was indeed the Lady of the Red Phoenix's personal residence, what would keep the strike team from running into Ching herself? And her elite guard alongside?

"Obviously, we will take measures to avoid such an encounter," Lorelei answered the helmsman's unspoken question, which had been spreading around the table among the others. "Only a select number of us will land on Penglai. Specifically myself, Captain Flint and these two," she nodded to Alex and Kaguya.

That assured the table a little bit, knowing that of their number, those four were the best fit, as well as the most experienced, with thievery. Just as Lorelei and Kaguya both spoke for their own backgrounds, Jon and Alex had also performed such assignments during their "Pirates For Hire" days.

"The heist will be based around swift precision," Jon stated affirmingly. "The four of us will go ahead and utilize civilian transport to reach the planet, while the *Sun* and the *Tsushima* are to arrive later, under cloak and enter into orbit. Upon receiving the given signal, you will send the retrieval ship to extract us, and then we will all slip out once more," he surmised. "Questions?"

Davis folded his arms. "I don't suppose you're going to tell us *how* you're going to grab the fancy hat?"

"That's for us to worry about, Davis," Alex answered for his brother. "You just concentrate on keeping the ship out of sight until we need you."

"Fair enough," Davis muttered. He was likely better off not knowing anyway.

"If I may, Jon," Kazama raised his hand to inquire. "While I doubt you'll have trouble with the palace guard, much less actually run into Lady Ching and her protectors, there'll still be obstructions within the interior. Such as the Hongwu."

The rest of the table glanced back to the *Tsushima*'s captain, with more than one arched eyebrow among them.

"What's the Hongwu?" Anna asked for the rest.

Jon frowned at that mentioning. "It's the Red Phoenix's secret police," he stated with open disdain.

"Charged with protecting the Lordship and Clan from enemies within and without," Kazama added. "Through any means necessary."

The gathered could only look on even more questioningly. "A Pirate Clan that functions as a police state?" Anna let out in near astonishment as though unable to actually wrap her mind around it. "That's almost a contradiction in terms!"

Kazama merely shrugged at that exclamation. "The Clans are nations like any other, and a nation is only as strong as it is secure," he seemingly quoted from somewhere. "Even the Blue Dragon retains the Shinsengumi for that purpose."

Despite that claim, the Dragon Prince's eyes narrowed with contempt. "Having said that, the Hongwu are a little more…*extreme* on that obligation than others. And their agents will be all throughout the palace, along with other security assets."

He then looked over toward Lorelei. "Including a building-wide Psi Disruptor," he pointed out.

Lorelei merely shrugged, visibly unmoved. "If I were so over-reliant on my power, I would not have been an effective thief," she retorted assuredly. "In fact, it will work to my advantage since it also means no one will be able to *see in*."

"And as for the Hongwu," Jon supplied with equal assurance. "They will be dealt with just as summarily," he stated, emphasized as Kaguya flicked a kunai into her hand and then withdrew it just as swiftly. Alex audibly cracked his neck alongside.

Given such responses, Kazama smiled in acknowledgment. "Fair enough," he repeated Davis' reaction, ultimately deciding that, at least seemingly, the situation was well in hand. And if not so much, then the would-be thieves were certainly confident. "And once we have the Fengguan?"

Jon's eye flashed as he grinned quite viciously. "We bring it back to Ryugu," he answered. "And present it before the Lords."

Needless to say, Kazama was quick to match that grin, as were many others around the table. Not only would they be out of the Red Phoenix's reach by that point, but the resultant political and *personal* humiliation – not only for claiming such a national treasure but also successfully infiltrating their opponents' throneworld to do so – would be something that neither the Red Phoenix nor Lady Ching would ever recover from, even if the Fengguan were returned or ransomed back. Between that and the decimation of seven Red Phoenix strongholds, Lady Ching would have to acknowledge her defeat and consequently drop her vendetta against the Flints.

"A most daring strategy indeed, Captain," Barbarossa nodded in approval, feeling its similarity, if contrasting, to his own quest to restore his honor to his Caliph. That nearly brought to mind events on Leo again, which he chose not to dwell on then. "Though I cannot help but also feel that we will be risking much alongside."

"We will be at that Barbarossa," Jon admitted, a little bit more solemn now. "Perhaps even more than in the past."

He then turned to address the whole of the table. "Even so, this remains the only viable means to end this war, quickly and decisively," he assured all of them. "Otherwise, our risk rises exponentially with time, especially as our enemy gathers more and more in strength."

Again they all understood, and they all knew. Although successful to date, having struck the insufferable Phoenix with seven harsh blows, the Flints all saw they could not continue with that strategy. They would only be able to make an eighth, possibly a ninth, such attack before Lady Ching's forces at last, by one means or another, shifted to the offensive. After that, the former hunters would be hunted, and the kill would be made just as instantly.

Thus they needed to end the war, and they needed to end it soon. Not through their enemy's destruction as had been with Baranov, but rather in such a way that their enemy could no longer pursue them. And if that meant having to break into their epicenter to force the issue, then so be it…as they all came to resolve, but not without trepidation.

Tactics determined, the briefing continued on to the finer points of the operation, such as what transport service the strike team would use to reach Penglai and from what vector the *Sun* and the *Tsushima* would approach and when. All throughout, however, more than a few of the gathered remained wary. Especially as, with the displays of the Feng-guan and the territorial map since rescinded, the image of Penglai remained placed before them all.

Red Phoenix *Yunnan*-class battleship *Zhang He* Deep Space

With great abruptness, the turbolift doors open, allowing Shun to enter the *Zhang He*'s bridge. Entirely unexpecting of that entry, the crew all but unanimously jumped from their posts, those having been otherwise lax in their duties straightening out at once; the *Zhang He*'s captain drew to full military attention. Shun ignored all of them as he made his way to the center chair, promptly taking his seat. The crewmen who could see their liege's face thought they depicted some level of disturbance on it. Shun remained silent for a few moments before he spoke.

"Set course for Penglai, maximum arc," Shun commanded the helmsman, with hardened authority. The officer immediately set to work to do just that. Turning, he followed up with the communications officer. "Inform the Palace that I wish an audience with my Lady at the first opportunity."

The *Zhang He*'s bridge shifted to full activity, the captain shouting out additional orders as the various crewmen went about their individual tasks. With their attention now turned wholly away from him, petulance made its discreet return into Shun's expression. His eyes furtively staring down toward the bridge floor, seemingly, and highly uncharacteristically, distant and unsure.

All while the *Zhang He* came about and, upon reorienting itself, went to arc on the appropriate vector.

Flint Pirates umbra *Black Sun*
Deep Space

The "END RECORDING" line flashing across the screen of his terminal, Jon allowed himself to relax and take his seat. The entire project, if it could be called that, had taken much more out of him than he had anticipated, far more so than the prior meeting. He supposed it was fitting, considering the amount of energy he had put into it.

For the life of him, the Captain of the Flint Pirates hoped, almost prayed, that that message would *not* be put into play. In fact, a part of him wished that he had not made it at all and instead simply took his chances as they were. Unfortunately, if there was one thing Jon could not do, especially in his present position, it was leave *anything* to chance, at least as much as he could. His survival, and the survival of so many others, relied on his not placing his hopes and expectations on any one preferred outcome, which was why Jon, again whenever he could do so, had backup plans in place.

And though he was not very enamored with this particular plan – especially as he withdrew the associated datachip from his desk, eying it apprehensively – it would grant them a fallback if the worst outcome were to indeed occur. He only hoped that would not be. That, as he had said before, they would slip into Penglai, slip out with the Fengguan in tow, and then make their way to Ryugu before anyone realized it.

"I take it you just finished?" Lorelei spoke up as she entered his quarters, her own expression apprehensive as she regarded the dataclip.

Jon nodded. "It's ready," he confirmed, placing the clip back on his desk. "Should we require it."

Lorelei contemplated the clip for a little longer, then turned to Jon. "I'm surprised you didn't bring it up before," she stated. "Not even to Captain Fuma."

The elder Flint solemnly nodded. Outside he and Lorelei, only Alex and Kaguya knew about this. The former because he would be the one implementing it when the time came, and the latter because she would have figured it out anyway given her "profession".

"If I had, they would have all objected to it," Jon responded knowingly, returning the psion's gaze. "Penglai will be dangerous enough."

"I see," Lorelei nodded in understanding, moving to stand beside her captain's chair. "I suppose it's not much to worry about. As you said before, our enemies are so convinced of their superiority and focused on hunting us down they're far from anticipating a strike against their center."

"Yes," Jon said, reaching up and taking the Siren's hand, pulling her down to his lap and squeezing her fingers comfortingly, a gesture she returned. He smiled as he wrapped his arm around her waist. "You must be really looking forward to this, given that you're falling back on your old calling."

"Heh," Lorelei laughed, as though she had forgotten her days before the *Sun*. "I was mainly a thief because I needed to build up an under-world identity and gain the necessary reputation and contacts therein."

She then glanced aside, a little nostalgically. "That being said, I do admit it was rather fun," she chuckled. "Stealing treasures from those who could never understand their value."

Despite himself, Jon couldn't help but ask. "I don't suppose you miss any of it."

Lorelei only grinned. "Not in the least," she affirmed, her amethyst eyes staring deeper into his one sapphire. "Penglai will be a nice diversion in itself, but beyond that…"

She chose not to say any further words on that subject matter; she just lowered her head and kissed him. Indeed the original identity of the White Siren, and all that it entailed, had been a simple means to an end for her. So that she could gain everything she held presently; the *Black Sun*, a crew at her helm, and their voyage toward Arcadia. And that was before one mentioned all the other things Lorelei had gained therein, as Jon was all too aware.

Thus, a very comfortable silence soon nestled between the two, with the Captain and the Captain's Woman lost in their shared emotions. Then, remembering they had much ahead of them, Jon broke the kiss, squeezed her waist once more, and released her. She stood and waited.

"Get some rest," he advised, turning back to face his console. "We'll go over the plan again in the morning."

Smile marginally increasing and becoming coy, Lorelei slowly shook her head. Instead of leaving, she leisurely trailed one finger of her gloved hand across Jon's left shoulder. The pirate captain didn't need to look up to see the glove on that hand dissolve away as her fingertip gently progressed up his neck, along his jaw, across his cheek, and circled his mouth. The heat from her bare finger caressing his lips attested to that. Slowing, she slipped her finger into his mouth, stroked, and then retracted her hand and stepped back, assured she had her captain's attention.

Rotating his chair, Jon watched as Lorelei continued to move away, her eyes hot and intent, her smile now wicked. Her choker and the edges of her corset dissolved from her body bit by bit, the latter gradually giving way to her breasts. Then, with a flip of her hair, she turned and gracefully walked away, the rest of her clothing receding just as gradually. Her boots, the legs of her trousers, the parts of her corset over her back. All of it slowly and deliberately melted away, covering her more essential areas until the very last moment. All the while, she moved in an enticingly intentional strut.

The last of her attire – conveniently the portion that had once concealed her finely shaped posterior – vanished the moment she reached the bedroom door, which shifted open upon her approach. Lorelei turned one more time toward her captain. Her fiery glance that much more enticing.

"Don't keep me waiting," she whispered, then proceeded inside. The door shifted closed behind her.

Almost sighing as he felt the weight of responsibility, to say nothing of the weight of his own desire, upon him once again, Jon stood. He was well aware they had much ahead of them, and only a fool would choose not to hold this time dear. Besides, even as exhausted as he was, he had to answer the Siren's call or relinquish his title of "Pirate".

Thus as his own clothes dissolved away, he proceeded into the waiting bedroom with a gleam in his eye. There they would remain for the rest of the evening and well into the following morning. Embracing all their time allotted.

Chapter XII: Penglai

Mount Taizong, Penglai

The garden was thriving today, thanks largely to the rainstorm that had moved through the previous night. Despite the sky remaining cloudy, with only a little of Penglai's sun shining through, he found the scene around him to be beautiful, from the abundant, multi-colored flowers and the varying hues of the trees and bushes that he walked by to the cool wind sweeping across his face and, of course, the complimenting light rain falling from above. Each planet in the galaxy had its own unique biosphere and corresponding climate, and though each civilization that practiced colonialism labored tirelessly to terraform such worlds to their standards, very few were fit for habitation from the beginning. From what he understood, Penglai was one of those few worlds, such that it was only a small effort to change the local climate to match that of distant Terra's. He found himself strangely grateful for this, as he rather enjoyed the transference from winter to spring to summer to fall and back all over again. Just as he was enjoying it now.

Eventually, he came to the very edge of his retreat, with but a small boundary wall dividing his domain, if not the whole of the mountaintop, from the outside world beyond, namely the city of Shandong in the distance. Again he preferred it this way. Not only was the view breathtakingly spectacular, but it also removed him from the greater part of society while yet allowing him access to the universe at large whenever he required it. Though it was quite possible for him to simply slip away from his mountain and enter into the city, if not elsewhere on the planet or within clan space, it was still something of a risk he'd rather not take. Nor would anyone else for that matter, including Lady Ching, though he wasn't afraid to go around all of them if he so desired. He, and he alone in all the Red Phoenix, had that power.

For now, however, he was simply content to stand by and gaze down upon the city, which was within its local afternoon and filled with life and activity as a result. Even from his seclusion, he could depict the various sentients within the city, all going about their lives and surviving in the ever uncertain universe around them and being content to do just that. It was not that the inhabitants of Penglai, and by extension the rest of the clan, were not ignorant of current events, it was that they simply accepted they could do nothing toward it and so focused on their own rigors and strides to prosperity. Merchants and shopkeepers continued to sell their wares to their potential customers, chefs and bakers continued to create delectable foods for hungry mouths, and artists and entertainers continued to create fine works for the enjoyment of all. Everything as far removed from the rather abundant destruction that had been occurring as of late, despite the relative closeness of the latter. Once more, for any dismay they may have held, the general public could not do anything toward it and so chose to remain to their own obligations and aspirations. The present Ladyship could sort it all out herself.

Indeed it was that perceived distance that served as the key element to the citizenry's apathy. So long as the invaders kept their activities within the depths of space and did nothing to affect daily life throughout Penglai and the rest of the clan, all were otherwise content to go about their business. And for those who weren't so interested in such, there was always the Hongwu and the rest of Red Phoenix's security apparatus to keep law and order enforced. The citizenry did well to keep that in mind.

Thus he could not help but feel the irony toward it all as he continued to look out over the city, in which he knew *they* were now present. They had arrived but a day ago and were otherwise biding their time in the present, but they were there all the same. Hidden well within Shandong's streets and among its people, and the Vermillion Palace well within their sight. All the while, life continued unknowingly around them...

Chen Wu Teahouse
Shandong, Penglai

"Xiè xiè," Lorelei thanked the waitress as the teacups were placed in front of her and Kaguya. For a moment, the psion woman and the kunoichi, whose applied shrouds made them appear as well-off inhabitants, were content to simply draw in the tea's aroma and corresponding heat, the latter a welcome contrast to the cool winter afternoon. However, upon finding said aroma to be uniquely different from any that she, at least, had experienced before, Lorelei casually picked up the teacup and took the awaited sip. From that, a light warmness ran through her body, accompanied by a refreshing taste and fragrance.

So this is Penglai Cloud Tea, Lorelei thought somewhat airily, just as Kaguya also took a sip from her own cup, being visibly refreshed as well. *It's certainly... different.*

You get used to it, Kaguya responded as she put her teacup back down. Unlike her partner, this was *not* the first time she had been to

Penglai or Shandong. Nor would it be the first time she had infiltrated the palace itself, though Kaguya purposely chose not to think too much on that subject matter. *If we had more time to spend here, you would find Penglai to be a thriving universe unto its own.*

I already am, Lorelei responded, generating a small wave of telepathy over Kaguya to emphasize. She then looked outward toward the busy street beyond them. *It too is different.*

Kaguya nodded in understanding, also looking outward toward the local citizenry as they moved to and from, both in transport and on foot. As had been remarked upon even recently, the Pirate Clans were all nations unto themselves, albeit nations that had been built on piracy, and the Red Phoenix was no exception. Far from the destitution and pestilence one would have otherwise expected, Penglai, as with many others beyond, was a thriving world of abundance, one whose culture was valued and where prosperity was ever striven for. Such was emphasized by the sheer vibrancy and elegance of the city of Shandong, whose beauty was such that the two women could not help but feel captivated. Especially as Lorelei could depict from the minds of some of the sentients moving by similar settlements around Penglai and offworld, each retaining their own designs, foundations, and customs.

And, of course, there were the inhabitants of the Red Phoenix Clan themselves. Also far from destitution, at least, for the most part, the sentients largely did well for themselves, managing to prosper in a galaxy that could very well be set upon malice and bellicosity. A proud, robust people, the Red Phoenixes were all well into their traditions and modes of life, keeping to them as well as any other civilization could successfully do while also retaining enough open-mindedness to allow new ideas and practices to enter where needed. All while there remained much in the way of opportunity toward advancement within their society, despite the clan rulership. As Lorelei found, the latter was something of a mixed bag from the onset, alternating between the benevolent to the tyrannical with each knew Lord and/or Lady. Ching Shih was just the latest in the line.

Indeed, Kaguya thought as she peered over to where two particular individuals, plainclothes Hongwu specifically, were standing by, observing their surroundings before moving to another part of the street. The ninja casually took a sip of her tea while waiting for them to depart, only then withdrawing her kunai. *Very different.*

Lorelei could easily pick up on the disdain, the great indignity that emanated from the kunoichi toward the secret policeman. Kaguya wasn't simply affronted because any prestige or notoriety on the Red Phoenix's part fell back on the Blue Dragon and the other clans, at least as far as the outside galaxy was concerned. It angered her that such a proud, beautiful nation and people could be so subverted. All because of the paranoia and apprehension of those who would sit upon the Vermillion Throne.

We're not here to remove the present Lady of the Red Phoenix from power, Kaguya, Lorelei had to remind. *Just to stop her from continuing after us.*

Exhaling through her nostrils, Kaguya nodded. *I know, and I understand,* she answered, once more taking a sip from her tea. Unfortunately, it was for the best since removing the present Lady Ching would simply cause the next Lord Ching to take the throne. And Kaguya did well to remember all too recent Atalanta.

Besides, from what I've come to learn of Lady Ching, she is actually an effective ruler in her own right, Lorelei continued, sipping her tea. *Just more heavy handed than Lord Ching had been.*

Kaguya nodded to this as well. She had only met Lord Ching Heung once in her lifetime, during a summit between the Red Phoenix and Blue Dragon on Ryugu. Her impression of the late Red Phoenix Lord was that of an otherwise benevolent leader whose wisdom extended beyond his years while only wanting the best for his nation and people. How and why such a man would choose to marry a *bu huihen de pofu* like Yang Shih, as she was originally known, was beyond

Kaguya, even if the widow was otherwise as skilled and efficient – if "heavy handed" – a ruler as her late husband.

And, of course, there remained the matter of their firstborn, who was even more ruthless, as Atalanta had emphasized. Kaguya didn't want to think about the day of Shun's ascension, much less the days to follow, regarding the Red Phoenix as well as the rest of the galaxy.

If it helps, the fallout will undoubtedly have additional effects, Lorelei attempted to assure. *Neither Lady Ching nor Shun nor any of the other children will be so emboldened in the future.*

There is that, admittedly, the kunoichi responded back. Granted, they still had to steal the Fengguan, though all preparations were in place. If and when they succeeded, however, the Flint Pirates would certainly become the least of Ching's problems, then and well into the future. Though that didn't mean Kaguya would lose focus on their main reason for being on Penglai, of course.

It remains as you said, Lorelei-san, Kaguya communicated in return. *What's most important is that she halts her efforts against us.*

The ninja then gave a sly smirk. *On the other hand, if such requires her to be* firmly *put into her place, then so much...*

Lorelei was about to respond when the sound of an engine entered hearing range, followed soon by the shape of a distinctly marked transport moving in and stopping next to the teahouse. She and Kaguya immediately became defensive as uniformed Hongwu then dispersed and entered the patio, the waitstaff and customers nearly tripping over themselves not to obstruct them. As the officers moved precisely toward the shrouded pirate women, Kaguya fanned her hand out, no less than three kunais slipping between her fingers. Only Lorelei's telepathic signal to stand down stopped her.

"What in the Eighth Circle!?" Juan shouted as the officers moved up to the table that he, Ponce, and Leon had been sitting at and other-wise enjoying their own afternoon tea. The old men became even more virulent as the officers, without a single word, forced them all to their feet.

"Goddamn it, Juan, I told you not to swipe those potstickers!" Ponce shouted through his apprehension.

"Shut up, Ponce! You ate more of them than me!" Juan hollered back as the three were led away. "Let go of me! *He chusheng zajiao…!*"

"Do we have the right to remain silent?" Leon questioned the officers in his usual airy way, only to be entirely ignored.

Through the banter and abundant threats of vengeance, the Hongwu officers promptly loaded their captives in their transport and moved away. Activity at the teahouse, and the rest of the street, resuming not long after.

Letting out a breath as she withdrew her blades, Kaguya took another sip of her tea; Lorelei joined her. Newfound silence, both on the physical and telepathic levels, enveloped the pair.

Lu Xun Park
Shandong, Penglai

"Damn it to hell!" Alex cursed as Jon made his next move on the xiangqi board, removing one of his red horses from the game. "You'll pay for that!"

"You said that three moves ago," the elder smirked at the younger. "So far, I remain thoroughly unrevenged upon."

"Uh-huh. Well then…" Alex then proceeded with his next move, striking down one of Jon's black horses in turn. "Hah!"

Deliberately yawning, Jon proceeded to unleash his black cannon, decimating the offending chariot. Only after did Alex realize his blunder, much to Jon's grinning satisfaction.

"Damn it to hell!" Alex repeated, nearly throwing the board. It was bad enough that this was their second game, but now he felt like he was losing even more, and at a faster rate, than the first. Ultimately the younger decided to just quit while he was still somewhat ahead. "I fold. This is a lame game anyway."

"Heh," Jon laughed somewhat as he cleared the board, deciding to just let it be. In truth, he wasn't good at strategy games such as this either, though he wasn't about to let his younger brother know that. Somehow it was much easier to manage and implement in the openness of space or upon a wide-ranging terrestrial setting than on a confined small board with set spaces to move upon. And seldom had Jon gone into a fight or battle in which his enemies – there tended to be more than one – had precisely the same number of soldiers and cannons as he.

"So, what now?" Alex questioned as he leaned back nonchalantly in his chair. "Catch an early dinner? Meet the girls at the teahouse? Vocalize our grand conspiracy and have some fun with the Hongwu?"

Jon was keen enough to pick up on the unmentioned "more" between the "some" and "fun" of that sentence. A fair part of their morning had been spent tracking down and subduing Hongwu agents stationed in Shandong and appropriating their wristcom data. With as many defenses and security that the palace would undoubtedly possess – a fair portion of which Kaguya had explained in precise detail – the front gate would be their only way in.

"I'm fine with simply sitting for the moment," Jon answered, relaxing into his own chair. "The view is, after all, quite spectacular."

Alex nodded, though with some forlornness. The view in question was Bayue Palace just beyond the park, its red-roofed edifices standing out in the city skyline, despite the palace's lesser height to the more conventional buildings. Compared to say Baranov Tower, Alex found the palace to be far more beautiful, having been built around similar ancient architectural stylings as Ryugu Castle. Unfortunately, said beauty did not make it any less ominous, as Alex knew what, or more precisely *who*, was within that palace.

"It's funny, I don't remember Mom ever having any dealings with her," Alex continued to observe the palace exterior. "Since Lord Ching was alive then and all."

"Yes," Jon confirmed, also remembering that the Red Phoenix Lord was the one their mother usually spoke with regarding clan business. "Your point?"

The younger son of Morganna Flint merely shrugged. "I don't quite understand the Lady's vendetta against Mom and us," he explained. "I mean, I know I said *vieux riche* to *nouveau riche* before, but somehow this feels much more than that."

He turned toward Jon, staring into his brother's single left eye. "This feels personal in some way, and I'm not seeing how."

Jon nodded his concurrence. It had to be personal; Lady Ching would not be so driven to destroy them if it weren't. And yet, he could not think of any reason why. Especially when he could not remember their mother having any interaction with the Misses Ching whatsoever.

"You think she's in there now?" Alex questioned further, noting his brother's own uncertainty.

Hearing that, it was the elder's turn to shrug. "It makes no difference," he responded. "We'll deal with her if it comes down to it. Otherwise, our focus is the prize."

"Of course," Alex agreed with another nod. In the end, that was all that mattered, why they were there to begin with.

Ultimately Jon decided to take his brother's prior suggestion and rose from his chair. "Come on," he said, causing Alex to rise as well. "I want to try this 'Dragon's Beard' I've heard so much about."

The younger Flint raised an eyebrow. "Since when did you have that kind of a sweet tooth?" he couldn't help but ask.

"It's just something new," Jon stated, then looking toward his wristcom. Evening was starting to set in now, but they still had time yet. "And something to do at the moment."

"Can't argue with that," Alex rejoined, deciding he wouldn't mind trying it himself. "After you, brother."

Nodding one more time in acknowledgment, Jon moved around and away from the table, shifting through different candy store locations on his wristcom as Alex followed closely. Their backs now turned to it, Bayue Palace continued to loom in the background. As did the gradually setting sun and ever emerging night.

Chapter XIII: The Vermillion Palace

Blue Dragon umbra *Tsushima*
Penglai System

"We have entered the Penglai System."

Exhaling as his eyes took in their much awaited destination, Kazama looked upon the throneworld of the Red Phoenix Clan with a sense of foreboding. It was not the first time he had visited Penglai – having accompanied his father several times before on diplomatic functions – but it was the first time he had visited without warranted invitation, and most certainly during a state of war, even a *de facto* one. Thus he could not dispel the feeling of uncertainty, or the slight churning of his stomach, as his eyes remained upon the seemingly distant planet, whose capital city now lay turned away from its sun. Somewhere down there, he knew, Jon and the others were already beginning their mission.

"Standard orbit," he commanded simply, the helmsman following suit and nudging the cloaked *Tsushima* along, the equally cloaked *Black*

Sun following at her starboard side.

So far, it seemed everything was proceeding as anticipated, at least from Kazama's point of view. Though a system defense fleet was present, they were few in number and spread out around said system, more on watch for a possible, but not expected, enemy incursion than an entrenched defense. That suited Kazama just fine, as it meant a lot less hassle when the time for extraction came along.

"Enemy fleet status?"

"All standard patrol patterns. No indication of combat alertness," the tactical officer reported after consulting his sensor readout.

Again Kazama regarded that as a positive sign. For all accounts and purposes, the Red Phoenix had not and were not expecting them. Good. Once again, a lot less hassle.

It took a few more minutes for both umbras to reach Penglai and achieve orbit, conveniently in relative proximity to a *Fujian*-class cruiser off the *Tsushima*'s portside. The Red Phoenix ship had inadvertently drawn so close that Kazama could individually depict the elaborate red lining across her black hull, though the cruiser remained as unaware of their presence as the rest of the defense force. Still, it did well to remind the aspiring umbra captain not to take any chances that he did not need to, especially as his eyes drew over the engraved phoenix sigil on the cruiser's bridge tower.

Eventually, the Red Phoenix ship veered away and moved to another area of its own orbit, allowing Kazama to relax a little more. He looked toward his wristcom and the counter it now displayed. Approximately twenty-seven minutes before the mark, at which point he and the *Sun* would both disengage their Psi Disruptors, but not their cloaks, and await Lorelei-*san*'s telepathic signal.

On that thought, Kazama turned toward his wife, his gaze one of mild concern. He hated having the *Tsushima*'s Psi Disruptor engaged, as the effect it had on Izuna was more than a little disorienting to her.

For her part, however, Izuna seemed to be handling it well enough, indicating that she was doing fine to her husband, who nodded back before returning his gaze to the planet below them. He had a feeling this was going to be a long and just as uncomfortable wait, despite the relatively short countdown. But wait he would all the same, until the appointed time. And the much anticipated and hoped for signal for extraction.

Bayue Palace
Shandong, Penglai

So this is how the other half lives, Alex thought upon entering the palace alongside his brother, Lorelei, and Kaguya. With all four shrouded in appropriate guises and possessing Hongwu identifications and corresponding access codes, it wasn't difficult for them to move through the front gate as planned. In fact, it took only their projected Hongwu uniforms and Jon's cold stare for the palace guards to respond with compliance, the identifications and the access codes being little more than an afterthought. From that, it was but a simple walk through the gate and into the receiving courtyard, where they all stood now, taking a moment to gaze toward the location where the object of their interest remained within.

Less any singular "palace" and more a miniaturized city unto itself, the Vermillion Palace did well in living up to its name and perceived majesty. It took the form of an immense center hall, which the four now stood facing, surrounded by a multitude of smaller buildings, the latter holding designated functions that contributed to the whole. All colored in the most brilliant shades of red, though other colors such as gold, an irony that both Jon and Alex could not help but remark toward, were also present. And of course, it did well in being as defended as its reputation bespoke, both in the form of the Palace Guard as well as uniformed Hongwu, which were spread out across the complex at key points. None of them appeared to notice the

Flints' entry, much less be aware of their true identities, but all four knew that could change at any moment.

Thus with a simple nod from the Captain, the four broke away and moved onto their individual tasks. Similar to the outlying structures that contributed to the center hall, each of the four undertook a mission that would contribute to their obtaining the Fengguan. Alex moved toward one of the side buildings, which happened to be the main Hongwu station on the palace grounds, while Jon and Kaguya both went about their own specific routes. Only Lorelei moved directly forward, toward the center edifice itself.

———————————————— ————————————————

Much like it had been at the front gate, Alex's entry into the Hongwu station was of little hindrance, though, unlike the gate guard, those that allowed him entry simply regarded him as a colleague and otherwise paid him little notice. Once his identification and corresponding codes were verified, Alex proceeded into the building without pause or second thought. His "work associates" none the wiser, or so the younger Flint dared to believe.

Apparently having been constructed well before the Hongwu's formation, the station appeared to have once been a guest house of some kind and largely appeared the same on the interior despite its differing function. Far from the blandness one usually associated with secret police structures, Alex found himself surrounded by a somewhat sparse but ornately comfortable setting, with a fair amount of fine architecture and well-designed furniture placed around specific areas, but not in such a way or in sheer abundance as to obstruct the present tenets in their duties. Naturally, there were plenty of them there as well, perhaps more than there were on the outside, but once again, they paid little mind to their "colleague". Thus taking a moment to recall the route Kaguya had provided him, Alex proceeded to the main surveillance room.

Making himself appear that he was moving onto another part of the building, Alex eventually came to the hall in question, the doorway flanked by two guardsmen in black and red tactical armor and holding heavy weapons. Fortunately, he had expected that as well, no way the goon squad would leave one of the more vital parts of their station unattended, and so generated Forneus as soon as he was close enough and launched a fire wave straight ahead. Both guards were immediately vaporized and in such a way as not to even leave ash or blast outlines where they had originally stood. That part of the caper attended to, Alex then all too casually came up to the side keypad and entered his ID and associated codes. The door shifted open the moment it went through, but Alex didn't go in just yet.

Launching another far larger fire wave, those within soon joined the outlying guards in *Diyu*, or whatever the Red Phoenix's rendition of Hell was, while their own work stations and instruments were left undamaged, if not entirely unblemished despite Alex's care-fulness. Regardless, upon verifying that the room was cleared out, the younger Flint entered and promptly locked the door, only then dispensing with his shroud. As he had half-expected, the surveillance room was fairly immense, more akin to a tactical center than a simple watch post. A main monitor was situated forward, with several indi-vidual stations placed in front of it, followed by a main station at the back end. All still operating despite the fact their former attendants were now reduced to submicron level.

In any case, it all seemed simple enough to one such as Alex, who made his way to the main post. Tapping in some key commands, he soon found Jon, Kaguya, and Lorelei within their specified areas of operation, the former two already going about their tasks while the latter was now moving through the front section of the center hall. They were all unobstructed for the time being, just as Alex.

Nodding as he watched their progress, Alex slipped his hand into his coat pocket and withdrew another item. Sighing as he brought the dataclip into view, the younger Flint could only hope and pray that they succeeded here that the contents of the dataclip would remain unused. Unfortunately, he knew this was the only *alternative* course of action beyond betting everything on a successful heist. Far from the most ideal course of action, certainly, but the only one that could be accomplished should the worst possible outcome occur.

Thus, ignoring the biting in his gut, Alex reached out and placed the clip into a waiting port. It took only a few moments after that for the data to be uploaded into the Vermillion Palace's computer network, where it would remain until recalled.

———————————————— ————————————————

No sooner had the kunais impacted the skulls of the two patrolling Hongwu did Kaguya plant the two desolation charges onto each corpse, vaporizing the bodies quickly and quietly, without leaving any traceable residue. It was tedious work, she was finding, as though the killings in themselves weren't monotonous enough, but for obvious reasons she dared not leave any dead around for others to come across. Even if it meant having to come out into the open whenever she struck her targets from the shadows to ensure their impromptu "cremations". Still, no alarm had yet been raised, so she counted it as progress.

Slipping back into the nearby shadows as she detected additional guards near her position, Kaguya readied a set of shuriken while retaining her alertness. As per her Captain's plan, it was her job, and his, to clear out the interior of the palace of any guardsmen, thereby allowing easier flight when the time came. Again it was tedious work, especially when there were a fair number of guards and an equally fair amount of space around the palace to cover, but Kaguya would see the task completed regardless. Anything less would lead to unsat-isfactory results, to say the least.

Sure enough, another patrol, this time three guards instead of the usual two, came into her sight, all seemingly unaware or uncaring of her presence. Either way, as she remembered that she had been shrouded by Forneus' energies into her present form, Kaguya casually withdrew her throwing blades and moved out into the open, appearing yet again as "just another" Hongwu officer moving from one part of the complex to another. As she hoped, the three paid her little notice as she passed; in fact, they were so focused Kaguya wondered if they had seen her at all. Whatever the case, it would serve as their downfall as Kaguya quickly twisted around and launched all three blades into their backs, the precision and depth of the impact enough to strike their lungs. Outside a fairly audible gurgling sound from one, no death cry was given for any of the three. Just the dull impacts of their bodies falling forward.

Once again moving fast, as per her creed, Kaguya bent down and slapped additional charges onto the three bodies as she passed, leading to their own "cremations". That in itself led to another dilemma of hers, as she only had so many charges to utilize, and there appeared to be an infinite amount of guards, especially Hongwu, around the palace. And even if it was only Alex watching her now through the surveillance network, Kaguya would rather not resort to having to drag bodies to wherever she would find to store them. Not in such a setting as this, at least.

Fortunately, Jon had been aware of her plight and had effectively informed her to do the best she could with what she had; he would work to pick up the slack from the other end. That reassured Kaguya somewhat, knowing that Astaroth would leave absolutely nothing of the dead behind, not even free-floating particles. Even so, she wasn't about to withdraw and hide at any point, not even if she ran out of her central means of disposing of her kills. To do so was to effectively leave the others on their own, and Kaguya was too professional, not to mention loyal, to even consider such actions.

Thus she continued her hunt, moving from one part of the complex while remaining keenly aware of Jon's own position, and dispensing with one set of guards after another. More than once, she came so close to them she simply beheaded them with her ninjato, if not through some other form of execution. Tedious once again, but considering what she and Lorelei had witnessed mere hours ago at the teahouse, a likely favor to the people of Penglai and the Red Phoenix at large. That only propelled Kaguya more; her blade was soon driven through the back and out the chest of another guardsmen. His own desolation occurring but moments later, as though the unfortunate Hongwu lackey had never existed.

———————————— ————————————

It was proceeding as well as he had hoped, despite his remaining disconcertion. Not that Jon, who had just finished dispensing with another set of guards, would expect it any other way, again despite his concealed anxiousness. Everything had progressed without flaw or hindrance since they had first arrived on Penglai proper and was certainly proceeding now that they were within the palace itself. They need only continue and short of any unforeseen occurrences, which remained a universal possibility, they would all be back aboard the *Sun* and well into Blue Dragon space before Lady Ching or anyone else realized what had occurred in their midst. Such would be one more accomplishment to the Flint name, Jon knew, but first, they had to accomplish it, which was admittedly taking some effort on his part at least.

Pausing as he came across what appeared to be a barracks, Jon ducked behind the nearest corner and glanced at his wristcom. Sixteen minutes, fifty-two seconds from the mark. That was the allotted amount of time they had, namely Lorelei, before the *Sun* and the *Tsushima* were to disengage their Psi Disruptors and risk exposure to telepathic detection in order to receive the retrieval signal. The palace Psi Disruptor would have to be disabled as well, but Alex could and would do that from his present position, albeit a little earlier than the ships. Lorelei might not have been so reliant on her power, but they remained pressed for time regardless, and as far as chances went, Jon found Lorelei being able to use her telepathy and telekinesis to be much less risky than not. Especially when she came to Lady Ching's personal saferoom.

A few moments was all it took for Jon to confirm that the building before him was, in fact, a barracks, namely as two Hongwu guards exited, appearing to begin their own patrol. He didn't know how many others were inside or if they were any others on the inside at all, but it hardly mattered. From his feet a dark shadow extended and swept into the building, where, upon entry, it expanded in less than a few seconds, dispelling any and all sentients therein. With a little bit more time and much in the way of energy and concentration, Jon focused the shadow's power until all within its reach were completely drawn into the void. Only then did he allow it to dissipate, effectively leaving the barracks emptied of all sentient life. That being said, he did well to allow the non-sentient parts to remain, just in case of an impromptu return.

Taking a moment to regather himself, he had spent much on focusing his attack, Jon eventually moved away, not unlike the literal shadow. There were still many such buildings, and many such guards, for him to decimate before they were finished, but at their present rate, he was confident to have much of it cleared away before Lorelei finally reached Fengguan. Again so long as nothing unforeseen occurred toward any of them.

———————————————

Compared to the open but otherwise well-adorned exterior, the palace interior was something to behold, even for one such as Lorelei. Not unlike such edifices and structures back on Ryugu, Bayue Palace had been built around the auspices of an Ancient Terran nation, in this case, "China", and neither the original Red Phoenix Lord-ship nor their architects and designers had spared any expense in emulating such grandeur. If she had still been a thief *entirely*, Lorelei would have taken her time in seeking out the various treasures that the palace surely held, from the priceless vases and statuary to the various artwork and banners across the walls and ceiling. Now, however, she only wanted one treasure in particular, and though she could not quite detect it through the still active Psi Disruptor, she knew it was somewhere in the most heavily guarded area of the palace. Thus she proceeded carefully.

Moving through the halls, she alternated concealment and moving openly with her Hongwu guise; it took quite a bit of time before Lorelei reached the outer area of the central space. It was here things would quickly become tricky, as indicated by what lay before her now. Though the space appeared as forwardly innocuous as the rest Lorelei had moved through, she knew that it contained the first line of traps, in this case, the set of pressure plating concealed throughout the floor. One step in the wrong position would result in a shield instantly generating around her and cutting her off from escape. And again, with the Psi Disruptor in effect, she could not use her telepathy to identify in which parts of the floor the plates were located. It was like a vast field of static was now forced upon her consciousness, obscuring anything and everything around her.

That being said, she had not exaggerated to Fuma Kazama. She had never been over-reliant on her power, and she certainly wasn't going to be here. Thus, using her physical eyes to scan the flooring, she proceeded, moving about the space with her dancer's grace. Stepping around each and every plate as though they were atop the floor and openly visible, all the while also doing well to keep ahead of any possible alarm triggers. Of course, that still left the ceiling cameras and the overall surveillance net, but Lorelei, again not needing her power to verify as such, knew Alex was the one watching her throughout. She could only wonder how he would rate her "performance" as she gradually drew closer and closer to the opposite end of the room.

A few minutes in, she reached the safe area, with no force shield having been generated to keep her in place. Excellent form, she couldn't help but compliment herself, though she knew that there was much more to come. Thus moving toward the next doorway, she again inputted her stolen Hongwu access codes, the ornately engraved door promptly shifting open to allow her passage. Turning back and smiling one more time at her handiwork, the White Siren proceeded through, once again moving toward what was arguably the most secure, most inaccessible area of the palace.

Chapter XIV: Toward the Prize

Flint Pirates umbra *Black Sun*
Penglai System

Twelve more minutes, Barbarossa thought after checking the chronometer again, doing well to keep that precise number in mind. It was getting close now, such that the Leo could almost feel it against his skin, not unlike an itch that he was unable to get rid of. He wasn't too worried about dropping the Psi Disruptor, as even without such cover, the odds were they would remain unseen. For whatever number of psions that the Red Phoenix had in its employ, the sheer amount of sentient minds around Penglai would do well to mask the intruders' collective presence, and even then, said psions would have to be actively searching for the two umbras in orbit. No, as long as they remained under cloak, they would be safe.

That being said, Barbarossa was still agitated, though he could not quite understand why. Something was quite possibly amiss about their current setting, and for the life of him, he could not identify it no matter how hard he searched. Perhaps it was because everything was falling into place as otherwise anticipated, from Penglai retaining a small rearguard as the Red Armada deployed elsewhere to the apparent ease of infiltrating the planet, as well as the Vermillion Palace itself. Everything was going smoothly, almost too smoothly for Barbarossa's liking, yet he could not find any indication of deception on the part of his enemies. For all intents and purposes, the Red Phoenix really did not know that they were there, nor had they even conceived of the possibility. The Fengguan was all but in their grasp.

Exhaling through his nostrils, Barbarossa eventually settled back and decided he was overanalyzing the situation, which could be as potentially detrimental as true callousness. There were times, seldom as they were, when the situation truly was as it appeared. That seemed to be the case now. There was no deception, no turnabout waiting to be enacted. The defenders were truly ignorant of their enemy's presence, as so many had been in the past. There was but a small risk of detection once the countdown ended and the Psi Disruptors were disengaged, and even then, their enemy had to be on the lookout for them, which in itself was doubtful. And, of course, Barbarossa knew better than to question whether his Captain and the others had successfully infiltrated the palace at all. Chances were they were well on their way to gaining the object of their interest now, with the palace's guardsmen as well as Lady Ching's tamed thugs none the wiser. *Precisely* as it all appeared from Barbarossa's present perspective as well as present indications in general.

But...there remained that itch, and all the assurances Barbarossa told himself would not relieve him of it. Unfortunately, until he found something out of place, he had nothing to act or react against. And he knew better than to try and search it out now, as such action would prove to be their potential undoing. Thus, as the timer now came to the ten-minute and twenty-four-second mark, the Leo could only settle back in the command chair and continue to wait with the rest of the *Sun* and the *Tsushima*. Ignoring the itch as best he could as the count itself continued to draw downward, gradually reaching the much awaited, almost agonizingly in fact, point of execution.

Bayue Palace
Shandong, Penglai

Lorelei sighed as she came into the virtual center of the palace, where the next step to the Lady Ching's vault awaited her. She could not help but wonder as she stared blandly at the turbolift concealed behind a set of highly ornate and highly reinforced doors, with an equally concealed keypad beside it, why did her targets always have their most priceless treasures underground? Did they really think that would deter thieves such as her? She couldn't count the number of times she had broken into such troves, regardless of how deep they laid underneath a planet's crust or within an asteroid or space station. It was almost cliché to her.

Still, it was what it was, and she did well to remember that she was on the proverbial chronometer. Thus after maneuvering her way toward the turbolift, doing well to avoid any further pressure plates and traps along the way, she stared down at the seemingly innocuous security device. Knowing the value of the Fengguan, as well as the other treasures that were undoubtedly stored within the vault, it was a fair guess that the keypad and turbolift were accessible only by the Lady of the Red Phoenix and whatever family members she held in trust. In fact, it was just as fair a guess that the moment Lorelei's finger so much as grazed the pad, the entire palace would go into lockdown, and she would be trapped and isolated. Thus sighing again, she ultimately knew what she had to do.

Just as it wasn't her first time breaking into an underground vault, it also wasn't her first time forcing her way around a Psi Disruptor, even one that would have overwhelmingly incapacitated an average psion. While her telepathy remained obscured, even if it was technically still active, her telekinetic abilities were otherwise available, though it was something of a strain to employ them under the disruptor's field. It was like trying to move one's limbs under heavy gravity. However, she knew the countdown was progressing, so Lorelei closed her eyes and, with her power, reached into the keypad's internal mechanisms. Though she probably could override the lift itself that way, making the keypad grant her access via "rewiring" – once more as Terran lingo went – was both the more subtle and simpler approach. It allowed her to localize her power through the disruptor as well.

Much like in the visos, Lorelei, with her telepathy obscured, had to "feel" her way through the keypad's internals, matching her thief's instinct with her special senses. The keypad wasn't a very complex mechanism, but it was still a delicate process to "fool it" into believing she, in fact, had right of access. From making one segment generate an electrical discharge to realigning another more modular mechanism, it was not unlike how – again as so depicted in the visos – a "bank robber" on Ancient Terra attempted to access a safe by turning the access knob and reading the distinct 'clicks' through their fingertips. Just as dangerous as well, as a single misstep could alert the keypad's computer system that someone was tampering with it and cause it, and the rest of the palace, to go into lockdown. The White Siren thus treaded with utmost caution throughout.

After a few more minutes, she felt, as well as heard, the signal that access had been granted; the appropriate icon now flashed upon the keypad screen. Silently, the ornate set of double doors shifted open. Again she took a moment to appreciate her handiwork – she forgot how much fun heists like this were – before stepping into the turbolift and entering the specific command into the internal keypad. The doors closed, and the lift descended into the deepest area of the palace.

"Now we are ready to head for the Horn, weigh, hey, roll an' go! Our boots an' our clothes boys are all in the prawn! To be rollickin' randy dandy O!"

Alex could not remember the last job where he had been as bored as he was now, sitting by and watching from his little corner of the palace as the other three got to have all the fun. Though the younger Flint wasn't the type to normally give into envy, especially in a life or death situation, there was something to be said when he could only sit by as Jon and Kaguya slaughtered bad guys in increasingly creative methods, and Lorelei got to reembrace her thievery trade, the latter now descending into the vault with no sign or indication of alarm. All the while, the most excitement Alex got to have was disengaging the Psi Disruptor when his console indicated she had reached the bottom. Yay him.

"Heave a pawl, oh, heave away! Weigh, hey, roll and go! The anchor's on board an' the cable's all stored! To be rollickin' randy dandy O!"

The worst part was he couldn't even enjoy his music or at least the classical tracks that Jon thought he would enjoy. Having since learned from his brother, Alex now had a music player feature in his commlink inserts but could not access them currently due to the risk of obscuring his hearing. Thus he was forced to sing acapella, which was yet another glaring emphasis of his boredom. Far from the likes of the White Siren, Alexander Flint had never been a gifted singer. While he enjoyed taking part in chants and sing-alongs with others around him, there was just something miserable about singing alone. Especially when he didn't have an audience to sing to, much as he had with Cromwell and the crew of the *Cormorant* just before the whole Tartarus mess. Alex really wouldn't have minded subjugating Lady Ching, Shun, and their miscreants to something similar, but for the moment, this was the best he could do. At least it was keeping him awake and relatively alert.

"Oh, man the stout caps'n and heave with a will! Weigh, hey, roll and go! Soon we'll be drivin' her way up the hill! To be rollickin' randy dandy O!"

He was now on his third shanty and counting, much to his frustration. As skilled and as efficient a thief as Lorelei was, Alex wouldn't mind if she got to the Fengguan already, any more than he would mind if the *Sun* and the *Tsushima* dropped their Psi Disruptors early so they could call in the getaway ships. And not just because of his boredom and inability to set something, or someone, on fire; the longer they remained on Penglai, the likelier someone actually doing their job would figure out they were all there. They had all done well up to the present. Still, Alex knew better than to try and overstay their collective welcome well within an enemy stronghold – *the* enemy stronghold especially – and he wanted to get as far away from Penglai as soon as possible. In fact, if he had his way, they would already be en route back to Ryugu, with the Fengguan in tow and Lady Ching screeching about "those thieving bastards" or whatever. Alas, it was what it was.

"Heave away, bullies, ye parish-rigged bums! Weigh, hey, roll and go! Take yer hands from yer pockets and don't suck yer thumbs! To be rollickin' randy dandy O!"

"Finally!" Alex huffed as he completed that last verse. According to the display in front of him, the lift had reached its destination. Being the Red Phoenix Lady's personal vault and all, there were naturally no surveillance devices therein, meaning Alex could not actually see Lorelei stepping out of the lift. Even so, knowing that she had done just that, he reached out and disengaged the Psi Disruptor. With any further luck, she would snatch the fancy fez, and they would all be back aboard the *Sun* by dinner.

"To be rollickin' randy dandy O," Alex sang with emphasis, effectively completing the shanty and his own "exhilarating" part of the caper.

———————————— ————————————

At last, feeling the great weight of the Psi Disruptor recede, Lorelei felt alive again. Through her special senses, she could now see and feel the whole of the Vermillion Palace, from the front gate to the deepest chamber that she was in now, alongside the distinct sentient presences that marked her three comrades. She also felt a much larger number of Red Phoenix sentients as well, though she imagined their number had grossly dwindled through her Captain's and Kaguya's efforts. Still, it was a reminder that the enemy was present, and she needed to work fast. Especially as there were but three minutes left on the counter.

Now within what was likely the most secured space of the entire Red

Phoenix, Lorelei found herself in a circular chamber, as ornate and well-decorated as the rest of the Vermillion Palace. A line of doors was placed around the circumference, each marked with a single numerical icon. Frowning as she realized each door led to another chamber that contained a portion of the Ladyship's personal trove, Lorelei again could not help but feel melancholy. There were likely hundreds of if not thousands of treasures here, each holding high levels of historical as well as aesthetical value. Unfortunately, she could only take one at this point and so extended her senses further until she found what she sought, placed within the center of the fourth subsection.

With access since granted to her, Lorelei didn't need to rewire the section door the way she had the turbolift keypad. Thus knowing that no further hindrances were before her, she took a step toward her destination and the object of her desire. Which was precisely when she froze in place, feeling something else within. Something that began to move, as well as take shape…

Realizing quickly what was actually in front of her, Lorelei leaped clear. An instant later, a column of yellow lightning erupted, obliterating the marked door and smashing straight into the central turbolift, destroying it as well. Landing in another point of the vault as well as dropping her shroud, the psion seethed in angered dismay as Shou casually walked out of the remnants of the doorway, the hook swords of Furfur in either hand and a gleaming smile across his lips.

With a bellowing bout of sharpened laughter, the Sanxing warrior charged straight after his target, hook swords raised for the kill. Her own psi blades forming in response, Lorelei met him in the middle of the chamber, both dual weapons clashing against the other as their wielders reengaged their bout upon Atalanta.

———————————————

What in the Fourth Circle!? Alex thought as he felt the rumble that seemingly erupted throughout the palace. Before he could figure out what had just occurred, his instincts, complimented by the shifting of air against his skin, compelled him to power jump away from his space. A white energy wave soon erupted where he had been sitting, smashing its way through the entire surveillance room as Alex, dropping his shroud in the process, manifested Forneus and deflected the oncoming blast. He watched as another entered the now decimated space, his own spear-shaped Devilblade formed and aglow in white.

"Pretender's son, you die here and now," Fu raged as he faced the younger Flint right before surging onward.

Choosing not to respond verbally, Alex charged his adversary, Forneus raised to meet Amdusias head-on. From that opening clash, white and red energies flared between either Devilblade, emphasizing the contending furies of their Wielders.

Flint Pirates umbra *Black Sun*
Penglai System

"Picking up activity planetside," Anna reported as soon as the sensors readings came up. "I think they're blown."

Inwardly growling, Barbarossa all but shook his head in dismay. Whatever had happened, he had but moments to act. "Drop the Psi Disruptor, and…"

Suddenly, the *Sun*'s sensors alerted further. "Enemy ships incoming!" the tactical operator warned. "Over thirty!"

Realization once more reared its unwanted presence to Barbarossa, causing the Leo's eyes to widen in horror as his initial discomforts solidified and became validated. There could only be one reason that number of enemy ships were about to enter the Penglai System. One reason alone.

"Evade, now!" he commanded, already knowing he was too late. Within mere seconds the first wave of Red Phoenix ships dropped out of arc, their main cannons firing in precision. The still cloaked, and therefore unshielded, *Sun* and *Tsushima* were struck head-on.

Chapter XV: Vengeful Phoenix

Bayue Palace
Shandong, Penglai

No! Jon gaped as he realized precisely what was now occurring, both in orbit and inside the palace. Within a few seconds, he felt the air suddenly shift around him. Abandoning his shroud and leaping back, the ground he had been standing upon turned ablaze in a column of dark flame. No sooner had he touched ground again, Astaroth forming in hand, did a most sinister figure appear from within the column, his own Devilblade brandished as he moved into the open.

"You knew we were coming," Jon growled as Shun gazed upon the elder Flint with the same cold listlessness he had held at Atalanta. Despite that, however, Jon suspected that something more lurked underneath his opponent's exterior. Something far more malevolent. "How?"

"That is not for you to know," Shun responded, the column then dispersing as he raised Haborym so that its ethereal dark red blade was angled against his adversary. "Yours is simply to die, *zázhŏng.*"

With that, the Red Phoenix warrior swept his weapon about, generating a fire wave which Jon dispelled with a corresponding black void. Both fighters then charged forward, Astaroth's obsidian blade once again clashing against Haborym's carmine as both Jon and Shun attempted to bypass or overwhelm the other's defenses. Additional blasts of black and dark red were expelled and maneuvered around or deflected entirely as the two warriors kept up their bout until, at last, Jon executed a point-blank black shadow that forced Shun to power leap back, with the eldest son of Lady Ching again responding with a torrent of fire. Jon generated a black hole to absorb the onslaught before leaping into the air after his adversary, slashing and parrying Astaroth with Haborym before the wielders both landed in the far off distance. The fight continuing as Shun launched a lateral fire breaker that cut a great blazing line across the ground. The elder Flint evaded then countered with his own black wave and a follow-up horizontal wave, with Shun dodging both just as efficiently.

Pivoting, Shun rushed the elder Flint, attempting to crowd his opponent and return their battle into close quarters. Unfazed, Jon spun sideways and circled left, almost catching his opponent at his right flank. Shun dodged the attack, however, before countering with a fire burst that Jon absorbed then returned via spontaneously generated black holes, forcing Shun to continue his evasion as dark flame literally rained down on him from multiple vectors. The Red Phoenix heir responded upon the first opening by propelling three fireballs from his left hand, forcing Jon to vault away, the surrounding structures and ornate facades exploding in flame and debris at the moment of impact. Chasing after the Flint pirate, Shun was able to reengage in their melee, Haborym slamming against Astaroth with the force of a hundred hammers, yet Jon remained standing and unyielding. More slashes, thrusts, parries, and maneuvers flashed between the opposing pair, the clanging of their ever impacting blades resounding throughout much of the palace, affirming that neither would let the other slip away, not this time.

As Shun had so elicited, there would be no quarter for the arrogant, contemptible son of the equally arrogant and contemptible Morganna Flint. The diseased Flint bloodline, by the will of the Lady of the Red Phoenix as well as Shun himself, would at last end. Such disdainful ire was more than mutual for Jon, who even now remembered the conclusion of their fight upon Atalanta, as well as the innumerable screams of the innocents. The heir to the Gold Dragon did well to force it all back – but not entirely – instead, he channeled his wrath into energy as he drove his blade against his most despised foe, who continued to respond in kind.

Flint Pirates umbra *Black Sun*
Penglai System

Barbarossa's ears were still ringing as additional blasts struck the decloaked *Sun*'s newly engaged shields, battering the umbra's portside. The initial attack, which struck across the port quarter before the shields had come online, had been a heavy one, enough to elicit much damage from the onset; had the *Sun* been any regular ship, Barbarossa suspected she would have been obliterated then and there. Still, despite the direct hits, she had remained firm, all the while her Mobius System addressed the damage. Of course, that was the least of their problems now.

"Additional enemy ships incoming!" Anna warned as multiple Red Phoenix warships entered Penglai, exiting arc right in formation with their comrades and firing just as quickly. In but a few minutes, the enemy had almost encircled the *Sun* and the *Tsushima*, all the while maintaining their barrage as the two isolated ships returned fire as much as they could. A beam cannon blast here and a torpedo shot there took down one or two Red Phoenix ships at a time, but the enemy's numbers and formation, as well as their relentless attacks, had effectively cornered the umbras from the onset. They were doing well to keep the enemy fleet at bay. And that was before the fact that neither the *Sun* nor the *Tsushima* could stray too far out of position, as they still had to retrieve the strike team.

It had all been perfect, too perfect for the Red Phoenix, Barbarossa knew. The positioning, the sheer timing, the obvious fact that the Red Phoenix ships had waited just outside the system to be undetected yet close enough to arc straight in when called; it had all been composed and melded together to form the perfect trap for them. Thus the conclusion was as wholly evident to the Leo Kapta as the beams, missiles, and torpedoes that were still firing at them. And just as hardened in its impact.

They knew we would be here, Barbarossa thought, glowering at the realization. How in Aslan's shadow had they known? Even if there was an agent or two aboard either ship – doubtful in itself, as either Lorelei and/or Lady Fuma would have weeded them out – there was no way they could have signaled the Red Phoenix to their plan without being detected. Nor had the Flints or the Blue Dragons left a single indication, no means for Ching Shun or whoever else may have been pursuing to learn of their plans, and the enemy clansmen certainly could not have detected them while they were under cloak. So again, just how in the depths of Jahannam had they known?

Another blast of energy against the *Sun*'s increasingly dwindling shields reemphasized the Flints' plight, bringing Barbarossa back to the forefront.

"Redirect all non-essential power to shields! Do not let them collapse!"

Once more, the Flints', as well as the Blue Dragons', present state was most desperate. Forced to remain all but stationary in Penglai's upper orbit, the two umbras both turned and faced the enemy, their bow weapons firing in tandem as the Red Phoenix fleet continued their barrage. Additional enemy ships fell as a result, but this neither dissuaded the Red Phoenix nor did it seem to disempower them. The black and red warships continued to rain beams and projectiles across their equally black, yet also gold and blue, adversaries. All the while, the *Sun* and the *Tsushima* were limited in the available maneuvers as to stray too far would make recovery of the strike team impossible. And Barbarossa was not about to leave without them, any more than Captain Fuma was.

They needed an opening, Barbarossa knew; some kind of opening to send the Condor out to retrieve the ground force in one go. Once they were all aboard, there would be no further reason for either ship to remain in Penglai, but again they needed to find some means of getting the assault shuttle through. Until such an opening presented itself, they were stuck taking fire, and Barbarossa knew their shields would only last for so long, along with the ships themselves.

Bayue Palace
Shandong, Penglai

The whole of the Hongwu station exploded as Alex and his pursuer exited the control center, leaping out and away from a newly forged opening right as the building went up in towering flame. Landing a fair distance away from the freshly lit inferno, the two Wielders wasted no time in driving against the other, Forneus and Amdusias again clashing in metallic thunder. Unable to overpower Lei Fu's guandao polearm by direct contact, Alex moved right, launching a fire wave at close quarters. The Sanxing's response was swift, sweeping away the flames and then twirling Amdusias about to slam against the ground, generating a thunderous shockwave. The younger Flint, however, remembering that move from Atalanta, formed a fire barrier, redirecting the portion that would have struck him. The surrounding structures exploded with the ricocheting pressure wave. Quickly sidestepping right, Alex executed a fiery slash at Fu's hip, but the Sanxing dodged at the last moment, escaping injury. Relentless in his attack, Alex twisted around and launched a scattershot of fire from his left hand, only for Fu to again spin his polearm to dispel the flames then counter slash, forcing the opposing Flint Pirate to vault behind a nearby ruin of what used to be a portico. Fu naturally followed, intent on finishing his most despised foe once and for all.

Fu reangled Amdusias to impale from overhead as he fell on his opponent. Again knowing what would come next, Alex made a smaller leap back, right as the Sanxing dropped down and spawned a great booming wave of white that sundered the surrounding area. Still airborne, the younger Flint deflected the attack with a fire shield. Somewhere a series of bells rang out, disturbed by the reverberating pressure swells. Landing, he spun Forneous and generated three vortices of bright red flame that twisted across the area, forcing Fu to break into a defense run, dodging the first and repelling the next two. Suddenly, a wall of flame appeared in front of the Red Phoenix warrior; he slammed his pole into the ground to halt all forward movement. Surging through the inferno, Alex brandished Forneous and once more clashed with Amdusias. Right as Forneus' blade slammed against the guandao's pole, however, Alex lunged up and flipped behind, moving to catch the Sanxing's open back. But Fu was just as fast; he twisted around and parried the intended strike. The two fighters again slashed, maneuvered, and battled against the other, fire and thunder erupting between their blades. The air was now thick with smoke, particulate, the ringing of bells, and the sounds of disintegrating structures. Neither noticed or cared.

"You're nothing pretender's son!" Fu seethed as the two ended up locking blades, their eyes set against the other. "Nothing!"

"You took the words right out of my mouth," Alex chimed back as he held firm for just a few moments longer. "You're about to be nothing yourself, *gēn pì chóng. Nothing but ash!"*

In a blink, Alex broke the lock, taking advantage of Amdusias's size and knocking it to the right, then driving forward, slinging a blaze of flames against Fu's face. The Sanxing managed to duck most of the fire, but the attack still struck, and Fu screamed in pain as a fair portion of his flesh burned. Alex immediately flung another fire burst, but the Red Phoenix's reflexes remained up to par. Bringing Amdusias about, he disbursed the flames right before smashing the pommel end into the ground to generate another eruption of white thunder. Rather than remain stationary and deflect, Alex circled, erected another barrier, and launched several fireballs that dropped from overhead, pummeling the Sanxing and forcing him to stay on the defensive. The younger Flint took immediate advantage, lunging forward at full speed and slashing another burning cut across the Sanxing's back. Again it wasn't deep enough to cause overly significant damage, such as cutting Fu's spine, but it certainly hurt like hell. Which was what Alex needed it to do.

"Léi shēng dà, yǔ diǎn xiǎo!" Alex taunted. He was far from fluent in the Red Phoenix's inhouse language of Mandarin, but as with his prior insult, he still knew that one proverb and what it emphasized. *The thunder is louder than the little rain warrants.*

Fu bellowed at the insult, hurling a massive white wave at the welp. Undeterred, Alex proceeded to cleave the energy flow down the middle with Forneus' enflamed blade. The younger Flint again drove forward, bringing his crimson blade against his opponent's white polearm. The resultant cacophony of thunder and metal once more sounding throughout that increasingly devastated section of the palace.

——————————— ———————————

I was hoping we would meet again, liàng nǚ, Dian Shou deliberately thought as he generated additional bursts of lightning, forcing
Lorelei to continue weaving through each one. *We had so little time
together before...*

Ignoring the dripping vileness of the owner's voice, as well as his
highly *purposeful* thoughts toward her person, Lorelei concentrated
on closing the distance, then sweeping her dual psi blades outward
to bifurcate the Sanxing. With a lascivious snarl, Shou jumped
up and away before he could be separated from his lower torso.
Knowing he was about to land on the sidewall, the White Siren
fired a barrage of violet energy shots after the Red Phoenix fighter,
only for the warrior to break into a run at the precise moment of his
landing, effectively rounding the room. Without stopping his movements, he deployed another lightning bolt that swept across much
of the space; easily evading, Lorelei ascended as well and charged
after him, psi blades manifested and ready to slice.

Lorelei's frustration was high in times such as these as she and her
unwanted adversary danced and weaved through the vault, their
respective twin blades ever shifting and striking against the other
set. To begin with, many priceless treasures could be damaged
or destroyed in the melee. It wasn't exactly a huge priority to the
former thief, especially when compared to her livelihood, but it was
something she would have preferred to avoid. And that was before
one took into account the overall setting in itself.

As deep and as confined as they were from the surface, it would
have been relatively simple to overpower the *biàntài* then and
there, as she had long caught onto his mental impulses and fighting
style, and as skilled a wielder as he was – as opposed to what
he thought of himself – Dian Shou was nothing compared to the
likes of Laurentius Kraft or the Mavkas. Yet, also as deep and as
confined as they were from the surface, Lorelei could not guarantee

that, through her own overpowering attack, she did not bring the whole of the vault down on top of her as well, effectively slaying herself as well as the Sanxing. Thus she again had to narrow if not outright pull her punches, confining her power to that relatively meager span while also remaining well aware of the mounting damage. All the while, her adversary showed no more concern than he had the first time.

Thus the Siren maneuvered about, attacking and defending in tandem as she exchanged blade for blade against the enemy Wielder, who seemingly became more and more enthralled with her as she fought. More lightning flashed and lanced after her, as well as swept about in wave form, but Lorelei remained stalwart, dodging and deflecting around each burst while also counterattacking with both her blades, her energy shots, and more. Shou also was forced to dodge and deflect, but this was far from dissuading to him. He became increasingly aroused when the object of his lust, blood-based and otherwise, put up such a hardened resistance. At first, anyway.

Raising both of Furfur's blades and then slamming them on the floor, Shou unleashed twin lines of lightning, which ran across the ground and struck one of the opposite subsections. Lorelei winced, wondering just how many treasures had been destroyed with that attack. She lunged right and launched another line of violet rain against the Sanxing. The deviant warrior employed a series of acrobatic maneuvers to evade the deadly drops. The psion charged after him and executed two psionically empowered kicks, which Shou barely dodged, then followed up with a dance-like spin slash with her own blades. The Sanxing ducked, pivoted off a door, and unleashed dual lighting flashes, one after the other, then, seemingly to mirror her attack, executed a line of yellow lightning-infused kicks of his own. Lorelei focused on maneuvering around the initial set and then telekinetically grasped onto Shou's leg in the process of a decapitation strike, momentarily freezing him in place. Using

197

that same power, she launched back into the sidewall, the impact causing the vault to tremor around them, right before reextending psi blades and surging forward to impale and finish. Wounded, bleeding, and bruised from the attack, Shou otherwise appeared in full form, leaping up and away before either of the amethyst, star-shaped blades could pierce him.

Once again ignoring the deviant's crazed and enthused lines of thought, especially at the sight of his own blood, Lorelei spun around and fired another barrage of violet shots, followed by twin bursts of violet lightning. Continuing to dodge and deflect, Shou countered with yellow lightning, ensuring that his opponent needed to defend. The space all but suffused with the respective conflicting energies and rapidly deteriorating structures.

——————————————— ———————————————

With great and rapid force, the deluge fell around Kaguya as she moved with fluidic grace, evading every drop as she had the first time. Unhindered, Meng Lu the Sanxing hurled a water-like energy stream after her, which Kaguya also lunged up and around. Brandishing her ninjato, the kunoichi then retaliated with a kunai at her opponent's face, but Lu easily banked out of the way, flinging two more somewhat smaller waves for Kaguya to dodge. A pair of thrown shurikens, although deflected, bought the Flint raider just enough space for her to close in, her ninjato intersecting with Crocell's piandao form. Their weapons clashed, and the fight continued, with blue liquid energy attacks by Lu, efficiently evaded by Kaguya, while countering with her throwing blades. Unfortunately, none of the blades, nor her ninjato, managed to so much as graze the enemy Wielder.

"*Still* so lacking, *gōng zhǔ*," the Sanxing jeered as he dodged or deflected Kaguya's attacks, each of which would have been a precise, terminal strike otherwise. Even so, the Dragon Princess continued her offensive, producing a kunai and lunging at Lu's heart in such a way that it would have bypassed his ribcage and struck the organ within. Sneering, the Wielder power leaped away just before impact. Another blue energy wave filled the area, forcing Kaguya to recede as well. She launched another shuriken at Lu for good measure. Still midleap, a simple barrier was enough to deflect the throwing star, thereby allowing the Sanxing to land safely. And yet, the kunoichi retained her relentlessness, dodging the next "rain-fall" attack as she moved in once more, hurling two more kunais and slashing at the Red Phoenix's throat. Again, however, Lu easily knocked the two throwing blades aside with Crocell, then flipped back to avoid decapitation.

All throughout did the kunoichi again feel that certain temptation reach out to her, emphasizing her plight. Her attacks were true, and her form perfected, but she needed more power, pure power to match if not overwhelm her opposition. Otherwise, she would remain impotent. It was available to her, especially now. All she need do was reach out and...

Forcing back the temptation and the voice of the originator, Kaguya focused on her drive, again exchanging blade strike for blade strike with her opponent. She did not need such power, she resolved as she forced herself on, targeting whatever vital area that was vulnerable to her ninjato or any of her throwing blades, knowing that one strike would be good enough to end the conflict. It did not matter if that strike killed instantly, as it would put her enemy in enough anguish for her to follow with the killing stroke, finishing him. All without needing any of that thrice-damned power.

They continued their bout, Lu all but laughing at her attacks while ensuring that she remained hard-pressed. Kaguya still felt that voice from within, imploring her, pulling at her, tempting her. Hurling three more shurikens after the Red Phoenix warrior, she forced it back into silence, focusing that much more on the kill. The one strike, no matter what attack she utilized to make it, that would be the deciding factor. Even as Lu continued to weave around, launching additional "rain" and "water" after the Dragon Princess, seemingly as impervious to her blade as ever.

Chapter XVI: Cacophony of the Damned

Blue Dragon umbra *Tsushima*
Penglai System

"Shields down to twenty percent!" the tactical officer warned as more beam cannon blasts slammed into the *Tsushima*'s bow. The TO responded just as promptly with a retaliatory torpedo barrage, sending a line of shielded projectiles into the ever-growing formation of Red Phoenix warships. Additional explosions increased the mounting debris field. Yet, as with those previous attacks from both the *Tsushima* and the *Sun*, this did little to force the enemy fleet away from taking further action. The effect it had on reducing their numbers was negligible at best. If anything, they were doing well just keeping the black and red warships from closing in.

Through the tremoring of additional blasts to his ship's shields, Kazama knew that they were fast running out of time, as well as shield power. The enemy fleet was now a virtual, semi-circular wall around the two umbras, with beams and projectiles coming in, near constantly, from essentially every angle. All while the two umbras remained all but fixed to their present positions above Penglai, having no choice but to absorb the fire as Kapta Barbarossa attempted to find some way to deploy the retrieval ship. Only then would they be able to get the proverbial *Yomi-no-kuni* out again.

If only we weren't chained like this, Kazama thought through the next barrage, attempting to find some means for the two umbras to move away from the planet and take the offensive against the enemy fleet, just as the Flints had done at Ephesus. Unfortunately, he knew that was impossible, as to move out of position would risk allowance of the enemy fleet to deploy raiders into Shandong, and Kazama knew that the strike team had enough problems at present. Again there was no doubt the Red Phoenix had anticipated their being there. Kazama did not know how they had figured it out, but they had known beforehand regardless and had set their trap both on the surface and in orbit. Thus their present predicament, which threatened to worsen upon any further misstep. The Dragon Prince did well to keep that in mind, especially as his ship was pummeled more and more.

"Target that starboard *Zhejiang*! She's making a run for the planet!" Kazama commanded. A moment later, another pair of torpedoes exited their tubes and streaked toward the designated battlecruiser. As close as the enemy warship was by that point, it took but a few seconds for the torpedoes to reach their target, pierce her shielding and armor, and then detonate. Due to the enemy's proximity, the explosion buffeted the *Tsushima* shields, which somehow alleviated the turmoil, at least within Kazama. Unlike their enemies, the *Tsushima* and the *Sun* were quite successful in sinking whatever ships they targeted. Again had the two umbras not been stationary, Kazama knew they would have sundered that fleet entirely, but that in itself would not have served their immediate purposes.

No, everything was tied to the strike team and their recovery. Kazama would be damned – or more likely scattered to the void – with the rest of his ship before he left them behind. Therefore, his ship remained firmly entrenched in its position above the planet, and the enemy fleet remained just as firmly set on destroying them all.

"Shields have failed!" the TO sounded again, right as the ship tremored even more violently from the next set of beam cannon shots.

Holding onto the grips of his chair, Kazama again resolved even if they couldn't get her shields back up, the *Tsushima* could, and would, still weather the storm before her. And if not, then she would certainly take as many Red Phoenix ships with her when the time came.

"Taihō, ute!" Kazama commanded, his ship's beam cannons aligning and firing in tandem. Several more enemy ships were rapidly damaged or destroyed, yet this did nothing to dissuade the Red Phoenix from further aggression.

Bayue Palace
Shandong, Penglai

Spinning Amdusias overhead, Fu smashed his polearm into the ground, generating another booming shockwave. Recognizing the maneuver, Alex reformed his barrier and deflected the bulk of the thunder-like force, then darted left, simultaneously launching a blazing whirlwind at his adversary; Fu spun his Devilblade horizontally, forming a vortex to disperse the fiery onslaught. Alex was unrelenting in his attacks, propelling a torrent of fire at Fu and then another that spun as it flew, keeping the Sanxing firmly on the defense, before finally putting on a speed boost and closing in from the enemy fighter's right. Another flame infused slash, this time it connected with the Red Phoenix's side; Fu, moving through the corresponding pain, swept Amdusias about to try and catch his attacker in motion. Laughing, Alex leaped out of reach, then power vaulted back to execute a second, even deeper slash that caught his opponent on the upper thigh. Fu roared his painful response.

"Tama de hundan!" Fu bellowed as he spawned another white shaft aimed at the Flint pirate's head. Taunting his adversary, Alex danced around the attack, responding with a scattershot of flaming hail. The Red

Phoenix fighter stood firm, erecting a protective shield around himself. But the miniscule fiery orbs exploded in tandem and concentrated proximity, easily overwhelming the protection and severely burning the Phoenician in multiple locations. More white waves followed from the increasingly enraged Sanxing. Yet, the younger Flint avoided them all, deflecting or maneuvering around each attack as vexatiously as he could possibly make such evasions. All the while inundating his opponent with more and more flame, very much adding injury to insult.

The Red Phoenix *chǔn lǚ* might have caught him off guard on Atalanta, but Alex now had him firmly dead to rights. Like Ivan Baranov before him, Lei Fu was a power fighter, befitting the size, shape, and attribute of his Devilblade. And while he certainly had a fair amount of speed and more than enough endurance as well, his attacks were open and wide, as though meant to fight two or three opponents at a time. Certainly an overwhelming style under the best of conditions, but when a single opponent such as one Alexander Flint narrowed down the Sanxing's movements to a predictable measure, it became all too easy to evade or defend against each and every attack, as well as counterattack at the optimum moment. Thus the younger son of the Golden Queen continued to run effective circles around his adversary, striking him at each and every turn while the Sanxing struggled to so much as land a single blow.

"Gàn nǐ lǎo mǔ!" Alex goaded, once more recalling the appropriate insult from a previous encounter. He sent another draft of flame washing over the Sanxing, whose attempts at deflection were insufficient to prevent injury. It wasn't enough to finish him, but Alex could see that Fu was waning. The responding wave of thunder that propelled from the spinning Amdusias was ill-formed and ineffectual; Alex simply shook his head and sneered as he power leaped up and over the attack. Midair, he launched a torrent of flame directly downward, but that one Fu was able to deflect as the younger Flint touched down on the opposite side. Couldn't land them all, apparently.

The Sanxing, seemingly revived, dashed forward, the bladed end of

Amdusias aglow as he attempted to impale Alex in the torso. The younger Flint easily banked around the attack, not even buffeted by the shockwave, spun and cleaved Fu across the right side with a fiery slash. Without hesitation, Alex reversed direction, twisted around, and hewed at the Phoenician with another flaming slice across the left. He repeated the actions, relentlessly lacerating his opponent from all sides. All the while, Fu struggled to stand, barely able to sweep his Devilblade about in a defensive movement.

"Ready to give up yet?" Alex mockingly questioned, smiling with flippant brightness into Fu's now thoroughly scorched and charred face. "Or are you dead set on ending up as *char siu*?"

The Sanxing bellowed at the insolence, forcing Alex back with a lunge of his Devilblade, then spinning Amdusias, he smashed the pommel end into the ground to generate additional thunder. Once more, Alex had little trouble shielding himself from the resulting boom.

"Pork roast it is then!" Alex almost sang as he returned to the attack, charging back against his opponent and clashing Forneus against Lei Fu's blade. The younger Flint's attacks escalated exponentially as he resolved to see at least one of their principal enemies dealt with then and there.

***

Darkness and fire raging between them, the scions continued their bout as Astaroth and Haborym resounded with each contact. Their combat had intensified radically since the onset as both fighters moved and shifted through that section of the palace, executing each attack and defense accordingly without any indication of pause or fatigue. It was quite the running battle, one that the rest of the Red Phoenix forces wisely chose to steer clear of, as the dual, conflicting powers of two master Devilblade Wielders effectively collided in full. How the black and dark red energies were not surging beyond the palace and well into the rest of Shandong proper none could understand.

Jon created another black hole to absorb the next oncoming dark crimson wave, then formed three more that returned the fire from three different vectors, one blaze after another, only for Shun to dodge each in turn, all the while receding back to gain some measurable perspective. The elder Flint pursued without pause, launching a surging black cyclone before leaping up, then following with a second from overhead. They spun and darted across the space with no apparent pattern. Shun deflected both in tandem before power-leaping away as his adversary landed, Astaroth's blade positioned to impale. The chosen heir of the Red Phoenix returned to the offensive with a fire wheel attack from Haborym, one that Jon would be unable to abate in time, thus forcing the elder Flint to open a black hole and move through. Without sound, another black hole opened behind Shun, and Jon charged out.

Single eye glaring down into Shun's cold and utterly implacable pair, Jon slashed at his opponent's neck, attempting to behead, only for the Red Phoenix warrior to parry the blow. Another burst of flame emerged, appearing as an all-encompassing fireball, but Jon evaded effortlessly. The two fighters then moved back into their melee, the impact of their Devilblades echoing across much of the Vermillion Palace. Further attacks, blocks, and maneuvers followed, yet again neither Jon nor Shun was able to break the other's defense or land a single wounding strike. By and large, it seemed that the two Pirate scions were equally matched, in their wills, the powers of their respective weapons, as well as their personal focus. Jon's toward ending Ching Shun's horrid existence, while Shun was determined to eradicate the insipient heir of a false dynasty.

Touching down a fair distance away from Shun, Jon focused Astaroth's darkness at ground level, generating a wide field that drew in the surrounding debris and fragments. A mere second later, the black field rescinded, and additional black holes formed around the area, expelling the now pulverized scraps at tremendous velocities and varied trajectories. Essentially being bombarded with solid "ammunition" launched at multiple times the speed of sound, Shun did not attempt to deflect them. He ran, jumped, spun, twisted, and power leaped to avoid the deadly projectiles, executing the necessary movements to keep from being struck yet doing well not to expend too much energy. Only when he found a break in the barrage did he retaliate. In a move quite similar to one of Alex's techniques, Ching Shun formed fireballs overhead and launched them all downward, the darkened flames appearing to Jon less like one of his brother's "meteor showers" and more like hellish rain. Jon simply disappeared into a black hole and reappeared on the other side of the courtyard and watched as the ground burst into flames and several buildings were obliterated outright. Locating his enemy, Shun again closed in to slash Haborym against Astaroth.

The two fighters glared into each other's eyes in that short moment, both projecting the ire they felt toward the other. Like their battle at hand, neither was able to overcome the other in this apparent contest; both their wrath and their disdain for the other effectively matched and contended. Their opposing wills to destroy and triumph, to stand proud as the other lay dead at their feet, more apparent than anything that could be put into words. The corresponding hatred vibrated hotly between the warriors.

And then they broke apart, Jon being the first to the draw, executing another snap black wave. Shun dodged, though he was nearly drawn into the void and infinite cold. He countered with a blast of flame, one bolt following another. Neither so much as grazed Jon, who power leaped away, with Shun giving chase. The bout, and the fury in between, growing in intensity with each passing second.

———————————————— ————————————————

She was fast running out of time, Lorelei knew, yet could only do so much in dodging the additional bursts of lightning while closing in against the opposing Sanxing. Shou gleamed as the psion drew in close and executed a three attack combo with her psi blades. Lunging back, he evaded the initial two slashes and then vaulted to the opposite end of the chamber to escape the full spin slash. As soon as he touched down, he charged again, hacking at Lorelei with both of Furfur's blades and then moving to strike from overhead. Lorelei dodged all attempts to attack, levitating as Shou slammed into the ground. His impact generated a yellow lightning-based shockwave; the White Siren readily formed a barrier to deflect. Glancing around, it was alarming how much more of the vault was damaged. Lorelei realized the Sanxing was not disinclined to burying them in the collapsing structure. If anything, the thought only made him further crazed.

Despite that, she remained on the defensive as Shou launched a direct stream of lightning at her, banking around it, then narrowly crouching and ascending over the following two sweeps. Only thereafter did she reextend her psi blades and charge, slashing again after the Sanxing, who was just as quick at parrying her slashes and counterattacking, as well as leaping back from the following energy barrage. As a result of the latter evasion, Shou ended up landing on the vault's circular wall again, specifically on one of the increasingly few subsection doors, from which he began to gather energy around himself. Telepathically picking up on his intended attack, Lorelei realized her opportunity and lowered herself back to the ground, amassing her own energy. The pair remained in their respective positions for some time, right before both launched forward in a direct clash. Or so it seemed.

Initially appearing that she would contend with his attack head-on, the psion made a slight alteration in her charge, moving a little more to the right. Upon realizing what was about to occur, Shou attempted to evade, but it was too late. As he and Lorelei closed the distance in a near-instant, the White Siren reextended her psi blades and slashed out at the precise moment of contact. And though she failed to dispatch the Sanxing entirely as she had intended, she still struck literal blood all the same as she tore past, with Shou's left arm, still holding onto its Furfur blade, wholly separated and flying well away from the main body.

Struck along the torso, minus an arm and gushing blood, Shou let out an anguished, utterly tormented cry upon falling to the floor. Somehow he managed not to dissipate his remaining Furfur blade to grasp onto the stump where his left appendage had been. His incapacity didn't deter him long, however, as the agony easily transitioned into fury. Enraged, he swept his right blade about and launched another lightning bolt after the psion that had maimed him. Frustrated upon realizing that the Sanxing was still willing to fight, which he still could despite his rather critical wounds, Lorelei deflected the wave, but she again kept in mind that her time was limited. Lowering her barrier, she changed tactics and rapidly ascended into the now emptied turboshaft, her focus toward reaching the surface.

"Jiàn nǚ rén!" Shou called after her, moving onto the turboshaft himself and power leaping upward, intent on giving chase. Rather than a verbal or telepathic response, the psion's reprisal came in the form of another violet energy barrage, which rained down the narrow shaft in a concentrated stream of bolt fire. Obviously unable to dodge, it was all Shou could do to hastily form a barrier as the blasts struck him head-on, effectively sending him back to the ground from whence he came. The barrage ricocheted around the vault demolishing the structure until finally expending all of its energy, entombing the now unconscious Sanxing. Furfur disappeared from his right arm.

Admittedly, Lorelei would have loved to finish him then and there, but once again, time was critical if the whole of the strike team was to return to the *Sun* and get as far from Penglai as physically possible. Thus she continued her ascent, drawing toward the surface as fast as she was able.

"Nothing but ash," Alex repeated with glaring finality as he again took a moment to regard his handiwork, specifically the blaze before him that was once Lei Fu. It had taken a bit more effort than he had wanted, but the Sanxing was now firmly defeated, his impromptu cremation taking place before the younger Flint for all of Penglai to witness. In the end, the better man truly won.

Drawn of energy as he was, Alex could not help but take a moment to revel in the satisfaction. He didn't know if Jon had finished Shun yet, or if any of the other Sanxing had been dispatched by Lorelei and Kaguya, but with this one removed, there was little doubt that the rest would follow along all too shortly. They may not have obtained the Fengguan – that Alex had a gut feeling toward – but at least the night wasn't a total loss. No doubt Lady Ching would be enraged at the loss of one of her elite warriors.

Assured the battle was over, Alex turned aside and prepared to power leap toward his brother's location. Technically he could have remained and picked up the inactive Amdusias, which no doubt would revert to its stone form, but it was more imperative, assuming Ching Shun remained in the land of the living, he move to assist his brother. Between the death of one Sanxing and the hopefully soon demise of Lady Ching's eldest, the Red Phoenix would still have no choice but...

"Pretender's son..."

Alex halted as he heard the virulent hiss emerge from the still ongoing immolation. Cold sweeping over him despite the inferno, Alex did not know when or how he turned toward the blaze. He only comprehended what he now saw therein.

"Pretender's son...!"

Alex could only gape as he watched, realizing all too well what had happened and was still happening. Within the center of the fire, what should have been the immolated corpse of Lei Fu rose up and stood once more. Its eyes firmly aglow in white as corresponding energy lines pulsated across his form. All while the blaze shifted from its original crimson to that very same white.

"PRETENDER'S SON!!!!" the outcry erupted into an even greater thunderclap, one that resounded across the entirety of the palace and struck Alex head-on, nearly knocking him down. Outlying flames dissipating as Amdusias' guandao reformed in the charred puppet's hand, the possessed remains of Lei Fu now surged at monstrous speed after the younger Flint. It lunged upward, blade extended high to strike. Alex raised Forneus in turn.

Chapter XVII: Moonrise

Bayue Palace
Shandong, Penglai

It didn't take long, or much, for Kaguya to realize what had just occurred. As the rapid bursts of thunder echoed across the palace grounds, the kunoichi felt a dissonant resonance across the same span. A resonance that she had felt once before in particular, causing her blood to run cold. Indeed, only one thing, and one thing alone, could have happened to the one named Lei Fu.

"Zhen daomei!" Lu, apparently feeling much the same, cursed as he glared toward the source's direction. "I should have known that idiot would end up as such!"

Neither the curse nor the following expletives reached Kaguya, however. In that brief yet all too lingering moment, the Dragon Princess felt something else enter her comprehension, that of a woman, drenched in blood as blue energy pulsated about her form, an ornate and equally bloody blade in her hand. Her eyes, infused with energy, shifting toward and projecting supernatural vehemence.

Galvanized by that image, Kaguya found herself moving again, entering into a dead run before realizing it. She might not have had all the facts, but she knew that Alex had fought that particular Sanxing on Atalanta and that it was all too likely he was fighting it once more. She could only hope, desperately hope, that she made it before...

"Where do you think you're going, *meimei!?*" Lu called as he power leaped in front of her, unleashing another blue blast from Crocell that Kaguya was forced to dodge. "That has no bearing on our fight!"

So arrogant and focused on continuing their now increasingly superfluous battle, the Red Phoenix warrior failed to detect a critical change in the Dragon Princess' demeanor, as well as the newly emerged ferocity that all but shone from her eyes as her unwitting adversary pressed his attack.

The sonic boom struck head-on, shattering his barrier and flinging Alex through the air; it felt as though he had been hit with the full force of a hurricane. Shaking his head, he reoriented himself as he landed on his feet. He had little time to recover as Fu, or at least the incinerated ruin that Amdusias had taken possession of, was immediately upon him, its guandao raised for the hammer blow. Alex parried that, feeling as though he were blocking a meteor, and repelled the blade before executing another fiery slash along Fu's side. The aberration barely noticed the injury. Instead, it twisted around and, using the momentum to swing its polearm, generated another sonic boom that flung Alex into a nearby ceremonial gong, destroying the construct. The clanging of the gong combined with the monstrosity striking the ground with its weapon again created a cacophony of booming explosions that reverberated throughout the pavilion around them. The sound was deafening and disorienting.

"PRETENDER'S SON!" the possessed man's bellows combined with the ongoing racket. The intense hatred toward the children of

Morgana Flint being the very thing that had allowed Fu's Devilblade to slip through its Wielder's mental and physical defenses and take possession.

"PRETENDER'S SON! PRETENDER'S SON!" It continued to rant as it swung its guandao about and charged upon the younger Flint to strike again.

Knowing that deflection was next to impossible, Alex concentrated on dodging, leaping back as Amdusias struck the ground, the impact generating a large crater. Utilizing the pressure wave spawned by the strike as thrust to enhance his power leap, the younger Flint flew through the air and away from the reach of the creature. Creating a fireball while still in midair, Alex shot the blazing comet at high speed at the monster's head; it swatted the flames away as if to rid itself of a pesky gnat. Bellowing, it then hurled an even bigger glowing white wave that almost filled the space. Alex was forced to leap behind a large mound of rubble, again only narrowly evading the attack. Undeterred, the Sanxing aberration continued to generate random energy waves that crashed and rebounded around the grounds, destroying all in their path.

Alex, surrounded by a protective barrier, silently made his way around and through the massive piles of rubble, slowly closing in on his adversary from the rear. The monstrosity seemed intent on destroying everything in the vicinity, assuming the "Pretender's Son" would be caught in the demolition. Only once the effigy's barrage ended was Alex able to reengage and attack, causing a fire pillar to erupt around Fu, engulfing him entirely. Once more, however, the inferno had no effect as Amdusias generated another thunderclap, dissipating the flames and allowing its possessed Wielder to surge after his foe once more. This time Alex could not dodge and so barely parried the guandao's bifurcating slash.

The Red Devil held that blade back for a time, but eventually, it overpowered him, all but flinging him across the entirety of the palace pavilion. Fortunately, that gave Alex some room to maneuver. Upon landing, he evaded the next attack and then the one after, then generated more high-speed bolts of fire and concentrated bursts of flaming hail that inundated his enemy. But whatever landed on Fu was simply ignored and dispelled, the possessed man barely noticing. All the while thunder bursts and other empowered attacks continued without relent, with Alex managing to stay ahead of the majority of them. But he knew that he could not keep it up forever.

"PRETENDER'S SON!!" the possessed Fu continued to wail, generating yet another sonic boom. The ricocheting energy came at Alex from all sides. He knew he could not dodge every wave and erected a barrier to stave off the majority of the force. Again it shattered, and again the *mildly* weakened force struck Alex head-on. This time the younger Flint barely comprehended being lifted into the air and sent flying back, just as he also barely registered landing on his back repeatedly like a skipped rock, his movements stopped when he slammed into a destroyed gate. How he got up again, he didn't know; the pain he felt across his body was excruciating. Not that he had time to dwell on it, however, as Fu was again upon him, Amdusias raised in another hammer strike.

"PRETENDER'S SON!!!" it roared as it dropped Amdusias' blade, once more hitting only ground as Alex managed to jump away at the right moment. Unfortunately, this too generated thunder, which buffeted the younger Flint as he sailed through the air, causing him to land on his side and roll several times across the increasingly broken ground before returning to his feet. Once more, Alex knew he was expending too much energy, especially as he felt the damage accumulating across his body, but he drew a blank on how he could win this one. Yet winning was his only choice, as he dared not allow his enemy to remain when the retrieval ship arrived. And he certainly didn't want Fu to end up moving beyond the palace grounds, into Shandong itself.

Thus as he raised Forneus, he prepared himself as the possessed Lei

Fu charged headlong, roaring as it again brought Amdusias about to strike with booming force.

————————— —————————

Additional fire rained and sizzled as Jon continued to run, evading the flames before leaping up and simultaneously creating a black hole to absorb one particular raindrop. Rather than break it down as he had previously, Jon compacted and concentrated the energy as much as possible while still in midair. Upon landing, he stretched his left hand up to form a much smaller black hole, which extruded the flame as a dark red laser, sweeping it twice across the field, once across the ground, and then into the air. Anything it struck was immediately burnt to ash. Shun dodged the first sweep and performed a midair jump to evade the second as well. As he touched down, Jon charged out of a black hole, bringing Astaroth against Haborym for what had to be the several hundredth time that night. Both Wielders attacking and parrying as they had before; their efforts intensified as seconds passed, the drive to end the other and be done with it growing with each strike.

Abruptly, they separated, as Jon had opened a black vortex at Shun's feet. With the soles of his feet burning from the intense cold, Shun vaulted back, launching two simultaneous fire wheel attacks, both spinning out and then intersecting upon their target. Jon vaulted to the right as they converged, exploding upon impact. The resultant shockwave altered his trajectory, but the elder Flint remained strong, responding in turn by sending out three more vertical black waves, forcing Shun to dodge the first two and then power leap away from the third. Jon then reached out with his left hand, Astaroth's energy gathering around the palm. Suddenly caught in a gravity well, Shun was drawn straight at his opponent, Astaroth already raised for the killing stroke. Yet Shun remained just as quick, raising Haborym up to intercept the obsidian blade, concentrating energy into his own weapon to knock it and its Wielder aside. Jon landed once along the ground before bouncing back to his feet, feeling as though he had just been hit by an oversized sledgehammer.

Shun, determined not to let the elder Flint recover, moved quickly, striking from overhead. Jon swung Astaroth to parry and hold back Haborym; the force of the impact resonated through both Wielders. Jon held onto his defense as Shun applied more and more pressure, intent on breaking through Astaroth's solidified form and striking the Wielder underneath. Both warriors concentrated on their weapon's energy, both increased their exerted force, yet both were again evenly matched for that all too brief span. Yet as both warriors knew, one would eventually give out in such a contest.

And then Shun felt a certain shift in the air. He broke contact and hurdled away as a barrage of violet energy took shape and rained down from above, buffeting his escape. Exhaling and smirking slightly, Jon briefly watched as Lorelei moved into the fight, psi blades extended and already trading blows with the Red Phoenix. The White Siren's strikes were as rapid as they were hardened, but Shun managed to evade and parry them regardless, his honed reflexes and skill matching the Siren's assault. Yet Lorelei remained stalwart, keeping her new opponent firmly on the defense as she drove him back several meters, only being forced to evade upon the latter launching a point-blank fire wave. Jon, now reenergized, moved in the psion's place, again striking Astaroth against the dark red blade. Not to be left out, Lorelei circled, generating a series of violet bolts around the Red Phoenix warrior, which converged upon Shun, simultaneously encompassing him and forcing him to power leap even further back.

Landing a fair distance away, Lady Ching's eldest and heir apparent visibly glowered as the Black Angel and the White Siren resurged, side by side, both assuming respective fighting poses. Such posturing alone made Shun realize that he was now in a losing battle, even more so when the pair moved upon him again, Astaroth and psi blades both poised to kill. And yet the Red Phoenix warrior stood firm, meeting both Flint Pirates straight on, trading their empowered blows with his own.

With more power than one would have associated with its smoldered form, Fu lifted Alex up by the neck, grinning maddeningly as the younger Flint struggled against its grasp. Such was the power behind the lift that Alex was forced to dissipate Forneus so that he could bring his right hand against the Sanxing's wrist, holding on as he attempted to pull the fingers away with his left. It was all in vain, however, as the possessed one's grip was ironclad, the appendages not even budging a centimeter. Fu gradually tightened his hold, watching as the object of his undead ire struggled more and more.

Abruptly Fu's fingers splayed open, allowing Alex to fall back to the ground, a surprised outcry eliciting from Fu as he lurched forward. As he vaulted away, Alex saw, firmly embedded in the back of the warrior's head, a highly familiar shaped throwing blade, one that was soon complemented by two more into Fu's back and side. In his resurgent fury, Fu swung Amdusias about, forming and launching another great white torrent that swept the grounds. Undeterred, Kaguya leaped and bounded over the flow, landing upon a tall fragment of a decimated statuesque fountain. She launched a shuriken directly into the Sanxing's face, taking out its left eye but not striking deep enough to reach the brain. Not that it mattered, Kaguya knew, as it was the Devilblade keeping the burned man alive and active now, even as the remnant became more and more annihilated.

Immediately taking advantage of the kunoichi's support, Alex formed and rained more fire, concentrated each ball onto and around Fu, eliciting additional damage to the possessed's form. Amdusias might have kept its Wielder alive, Alex saw, but as apparent by the burned form, the opposing Devilblade was *not* regenerating it. Kaguya noted such as well as she ran, following up Alex's attack with another pair of kunai, striking and therefore whittling down the body even further. Both warriors kept that momentum, both attacking one after the other or at the same time, chipping further and further at the hulk. All too aware that Amdusias could not keep the corpse reanimated and moving forever.

Yet all through the attacks, Lei Fu's wrath at the "pretender's son" remained paramount, the possessed man bellowing and generating a great white shockwave that obliterated all within reach. Alex quickly threw up a barrier around both he and Kaguya, yet they were still knocked back simultaneously, though the kunoichi was the only one that landed on her feet. Not that it mattered much as Fu apparently chose to dispatch her first, moving upon her with his guandao raised high. Fortunately, Kaguya, knowing better than to take such a blow head-on, dodged and rolled to the side, launching another kunai that struck the burned man in the torso, and then another, and then another as she continued to dodge the follow-on white waves. By that point, Alex had regained strength and directed a blast of fire at the Red Phoenix, immolating much more of Fu's back, causing the burned monstrosity to nearly topple over.

Sensing the opening, Kaguya brandished her ninjato and lunged forward, set on cleaving a deep cut along the possessed man's left side, intent on slicing away the left arm. It would not finish him, she knew, but it would elicit more damage, possibly enough that she and Alex could both finish it in one or two more attacks. Unfortunately, the burned aberration, seemingly foreseeing the attack, rapidly spun his guandao about and swatted the kunoichi away with its poled end. The force strong enough to cause Kaguya to sail well into the distance before her body bounced two or three times across the ground, eventually rolling to a stop. The kunoichi did not rise back up. Snarling loudly, Fu flew into the air, intent on finishing her, Amdusias's bladed end poised to impale.

He never reached her. Alex leaped up and intercepted, effectively tackling the possessed man off his flight vector and sending him and the younger Flint alongside into yet another decimated section of the palace. Coming to their feet, the immolated man was the first to attack, thrusting his blade to impale, only for Alex to deflect with Forneous and evade injury. Yet before the redhaired pirate could form another attack, Fu struck the ground with his fist, generating a thunderclap which knocked Alex onto his back, flinging him several meters away and into a massive rubble pile. Dazed, Alex coughed and tasted blood. His vision blackened, yet he still maintained conscious-ness and managed to make it to his feet to meet the next oncoming attack. Just as the Amdusias driven Fu surged forward, intent on utterly obliterating the "Pretender's son".

Veering around the violet lightning, Shun once more attempted to close in on Lorelei, only for the psion to dance away before Haborym could reach her. In her place, Jon charged in from the right, forcing Shun to parry his attack and then counter with a fiery slash. Jon instantly pivoted, ducking beneath the blade while reaching out with his left hand and launching a line of black needles. Again, Shun formed a barrier to deflect, then countered once more with a vertical fire wave, one that left a trail of dark flame as it sped across the ground. Only then did Jon leap back, giving Lorelei an opening to swoop in and attack, which in turn caused Shun to dodge. The Siren followed up with another line of amethyst bolts, which Jon supple-mented with a series of black vortices rising up from the ground.

Barely managing to keep ahead of both attacks, maneuvering around the vortices while dodging the amethyst bolts, Shun knew that he could not continue the battle. Jonathan Flint had been a difficult enough opponent on his own, but together with the White Siren, such difficulties were greatly multiplied, and that was before one brought up the perfect coordination the two shared. Indeed, Shou should have dealt with the Siren, yet going by his own lack of support for his superior, it was a fair estimation that the Sanxing had been defeated. Just as it was a fair estimation that Lu had suffered a similar fate, while the abundance of thunder blasts in the distance confirmed Fu's present state.

Feeling his ire again rise above his control level, Shun grit his teeth as he leaped and maneuvered around additional attacks from the pair, both Jon and Lorelei now closing in at once and attacking at melee level. Through sheer speed and form did Lady Ching's eldest manage to avoid taking too much damage from either, but he still sustained damage from both Astaroth and those damned psi blades, with cuts and slashes appearing at different points of his body. No, he could not fight them both, Shun understood, nor could he separate them as they were now. Thus, as much as it galled him, especially after all that had occurred that night, he was left with only one option.

Taking Fu's example, Shun spun Haborym about and then, with great force, slammed its dark red blade into the ground, generating a fiery cyclone that rose up and encompassed him. Lest they be drawn into the vortex, both Jon and Lorelei receded back, an action they were forced to repeat as additional cyclones formed from the center and extended out toward either, winding and twisting through the air as they attempted to draw in the two pirates. Even so, both the pirate captain and the psion kept ahead of the tendrils, dodging and maneu-vering each time one or more came upon them, as well as eliciting barriers and other such techniques to redirect. Jon attempted to absorb and concentrate one of the cyclones but realized it was too much for him as he was now, both the present battle and his prior activities effectively draining him to his reserves. Sensing his difficulty, Lorelei moved to his side and erected a spherical barrier around them both that the tendrils were unable to pierce.

Shielded within the epicenter, Jon, knowing what their opponent was about to do, drew as much of his remaining energy as he could into Astaroth and then executed the largest black wave attack he had mustered that evening. Sweeping across the ground as a great black tsunami, the wave absorbed and dispelled the tendrils as it closed in on the main cyclone, eventually engulfing that as well. It then converged onto its target, forming into an even larger black, fiery sphere. Upon dropping the barrier, Lorelei expanded upon the attack, charging and launching twin bursts of violet lightning into the void, the energy shifting and churning as one with the flames and darkness.

The sphere soon dissipated; the spot where Shun had once stood was clear of all matter, only a great opening within that part of the palace remained. However, as both pirates saw, there was no inactive Haborym at the bottom of the space. They realized that Shun had evaded them and so lived to fight them another day.

Slowly, Kaguya regained consciousness; her head and vision blurred but clearing rapidly. Through her distorted hearing, she detected the distinct bellows, thunder blasts, and blazing of fire in the distance, indicating that Alex was still alive and fighting the possessed Meng Fu. That was enough for the kunoichi to force herself up; retaking her ninjato, she prepared to reenter the battle. Yet, whether through her fatigue or another force altogether, she felt her legs give out, causing her to nearly tumble back down. Fortunately, she was able to mitigate the fall by sinking to a kneeling position, though this did little to assuage her.

As she listened and watched through hazed eyes, Kaguya knew Alex was barely holding on and couldn't continue for much longer. The possessed man was just too powerful, too overwhelming in force, not unlike his Devilblade's attribute. And though the younger Flint was doing well in continuing the fight, even damaging the immolated apparition further, it remained apparent to the ninja and any others that may have borne witness that Alexander Flint would not survive. All the while, the berserk, possessed form of Lei Fu showed no sign of slowing down.

Again Kaguya attempted to rise back up, again she attempted to move to Alex's side and support him. And again, she fell to her knee, straining just to keep conscious, let alone upright. As much as she was willing, Fuma Kaguya knew she would be no good to Alex as she was now. Not that she was much good to him before, damn her.

For the first time in her life, Kaguya knew that she was wholly outmatched; even Ivan Baranov, as empowered as he had been

221

through Nyx, had not been so strong and overwhelming. She knew what possession entailed. The whole, seemingly infinite power of the Devilblade was focused on the Wielder, driving him or her into unrelenting fury and keeping them there, even as their physical forms deteriorated from both any oncoming attacks as well as from that same overwhelming power. Eventually, Fu's body, assuming Fu was still alive at all, would fail him and deteriorate entirely. Still, until that point, Amdusias would keep him vitalized and fighting, even after Alex was finished. And it would do so for days on end until either the killing stroke was made or the last of Lei Fu was indeed burned away.

Days, Kaguya felt herself remarking on. Alex barely had minutes, much less days. And what about the vast number of innocents within Shandong? What would happen to them once Fu breached the palace and entered the city proper? Or the rest of Penglai?

Once more she tried to rise, and once more she fell back onto her knee. Her breath now heavy, Kaguya felt the first of what would undoubtedly be infinite tears that night. She knew what she had to do, the only thing she could do to save Alex and the rest of the planet. This time there was no critical point, no vital area in her target that she could strike and end him straight away. This time she needed power, overwhelming power of her own. Enough to completely destroy Lei Fu in a single stroke, then and there.

She heard it again. Only now, it was not a simple temptation or even a siren call, but a warning that time was fast running out. If she intended to save the younger Flint's life, she needed to act, here and now. She needed to cross that threshold, from which there would be no return. And, ultimately, no forgiveness.

For only a brief moment did she hesitate, only for her ears to pick up on Alex's outcry as he was again struck by a thunderclap. Then, much as she had been, Alex was flung some distance away, from which he attempted to rise back up the moment he stopped sliding. Only he was unable to, now being stuck on his own knee. All the while, the burned specter, knowing that the kill was imminent, charged head-long, Amdusias poised to cleave the younger Flint's head down the middle.

Only then did Kaguya find herself racing to her feet. Racing back into battle.

——————————— ———————————

Damn, Alex managed to think through the blurredness as he watched Lei Fu's form surge straight upon him, seemingly in slow motion. He knew he should have raised Forneus up to defend against the oncoming attack, but his body would not respond to him, his arm barely managing to lift a centimeter or two from its present position. Strained and broken, the younger Flint attempted again to move, somehow and some way, regardless, even as Fu rushed and leaped up into the air. Amdusias' blade positioned to split him into complete halves.

So blurred was Alex's vision still that he barely registered a familiar form coming in front of him, raising her own blade up to parry. Much to his, as well as the possessed Fu's surprise, Kaguya remained firm, even as Amdusias dropped down upon her ninjato. What should have been a great shattering force only erupted in a blaring metallic clang as metal withstood metal, the ninja sword holding the guandao back entirely from reaching its original target. From that, Kaguya rose up and knocked the polearm aside, then moving in a blur, she slashed at the possessed man's torso. It was then, also for the first time that night, Fu suddenly vaulted back from the attack instead of otherwise ignoring it. The possessed Wielder landing several meters away, his remaining right eye, still infused with his blade's energy, stared out in apparent perplexity.

Rather than follow up with another attack straight away, Kaguya turned only once to look down at Alex. If the younger Flint didn't know any better through his obscured vision, he could have sworn he saw a tear run down the kunoichi's face. And then she faced forward once more, bringing her ninjato up for all to see.

"Moon that gleams over the sky," Kaguya began, her voice now firm and resonant. *"Light that shines across the horizon."*

With those words, a highly indicative mark took form upon the ninja-to's *habaki*. The unmistakable form of a Sigil, alight in luminescent blue.

Only then did Alex and Fu realize what was truly happening, the possessed Sanxing again rushing to attack. Yet he never reached his target; a great aura of light enveloped the kunoichi, and Alex behind her, preventing the intended strike as well as throwing the possessed man back an even greater distance.

"The power that chains the seas. And eclipses all within reach," Kaguya, whose own eyes were now aglow, continued the invocation. *"I call upon thee to sweep my enemies from the earth. To wipe them away from this universe."*

Kaguya felt Alex behind her, looking on in great and visible astonishment. This time, however, she did not turn to him, instead concentrating on her task. There was no turning away now or ever again. The tears that streamed in abundance down her face emphasized such.

"All while the stars and planets quell before your splendor." And then, at long last, Kaguya called out. *"By this rite, I summon thee, Kimaris!!"*

Once more did Fu surge toward the kunoichi, only for he and Alex alongside to be enveloped in that great expanding light. A light so apparent, so powerful, that it could be seen from all within, and without, the palace.

Chapter XVIII: Ultimatum

Bayue Palace
Shandong, Penglai
Twelve Hours Later

The destruction was as abundant as she thought it would be. Though Bayue Palace remained largely intact – structurally for the most part anyway – the scars of battle were quite clear, alongside the many destroyed buildings and edifices across the complex. Considering that the enemy force was composed of previously two, now *three*, Devilblade Wielders and one of the most powerful psions on record, Lady Ching supposed it could have been much worse than it had ended up. Even so, it would be quite some time before Bayue would be useable as a residence again. That caused her more than a bit of ire, especially as she again considered the *who* behind such destruction.

This, more than the seven destroyed basins and installations, confirmed to her once and for all that she had underestimated the Flints. While it had been one thing for them to strike the Red Phoenix in space, in which the power of the *Black Sun* and that still unknown Blue Dragon ship were all but unchallenged, it had been another thing entirely to infiltrate *her* residence to steal one of *her* clan's most coveted treasures. It terrified her even more that they very well would have succeeded if events had played out differently. Fortunately, Shun and the Sanxing had fended them off, at least to the extent that they had been unable to obtain the Feng-guan, but the facts and evidence still remained. What would have happened had their incursion not been foreseen?

The sudden collapse of another structure – a guard barracks if she was not mistaken – only emphasized that last question, as well as the totality of the Flints' actions. Signaling her bodyguards to stand down, Lady Ching gazed upon the latest ruin and the resultant dust cloud with solemn definitiveness, seeing much of her clan's future within that rubble. No, despite all their success up to the present, the Flints could never truly destroy the Red Phoenix, any more than they could destroy the other clans. However, what they could do, and were very close to accomplishing, was emphasize perceived weakness; that the "mighty" Red Phoenix could be laid low by only one ship and crew, their Blue Dragon supporters over-looked all too easily. It would undoubtedly galvanize innumerable enemies of the Red Phoenix, as well as cause her fellow Lords to view her far less prominently. Such precedent was inherently dangerous, especially when one considered the abundant dissatis-faction toward her Ladyship as of late. There would only be further rebellions like in Qingdao.

Fortunately, while the Flints had come dangerously close to accom-plishing their objective and had destroyed much through that process, they had failed in the end. The Fengguan remained secure, and there was no way the Flints could ever return to Penglai now. Though it had all come at great cost, up to and including the rather numerous ships that the *Sun* and her fellow umbra had destroyed upon their breaking out of the system, the Red Phoenix's infallibility, as well as Lady Ching's, were secure for the time being. As was the Flint Pirates' collective death warrant.

Indeed, Lady Ching understood all too well; she and her followers had gravely underestimated the Flints. Now she knew it would not be enough to "simply" destroy the pretender's children, nor the White Siren or the Dragon Princess by themselves. No, the entirety of the Flint name had to be put to the fire, such that none would ever dare to take it up again. That meant the entirety of the Flint Pirates had to be destroyed and destroyed so ruthlessly that the whole of the galaxy would shake from their obliteration. Only then would the name of Morganna Flint – the mere thought of which caused Ching's lips to curl back into a great sneer – be truly forgotten.

And she could do it too, Ching knew, for she now possessed the advantage. The Flints may have escaped her grasp at Penglai, but they had not done so without suffering their own damage. And while the arcane technologies that the *Sun*, and possibly the Blue Dragon ship, possessed would undoubtedly mitigate such damage, Ching had a feeling that it would still take time for them to do so. As a result, the Red Phoenix could not be in a better position to crush all of them, to hunt them down and finish what had begun on Atalanta. Especially as Ching herself still had many tools at her disposal to do so, up to and including one, in particular, she never thought she would use.

Reassured, the Lady of the Red Phoenix exhaled an airy breath. This so-called war with the Flints had cost her much in resources and manpower, including one of the Sanxing now. No doubt her enemies already saw the Red Phoenix and her as weak and impotent, while her actions had spurned her fellow Lords. It would take years, perhaps decades, for her clan to recover from it all, as well as to rebuild the image of eminence and indomitableness it had originally held.

Yet, in the end, she would still win. She would accomplish what Fuma had failed to do long ago and stand atop that pretender's corpse, undefeated and thereafter uncontested. That alone would necessitate the loss, the sacrifice. That alone would validate all that she had done into the present.

With that in mind, she turned away and marched back toward the front gate, her bodyguards following along. The hunt would begin anew once she returned to Siyue. And this time, there would be no salvation whatsoever.

Flint Pirates umbra *Black Sun* Deep Space

"I won't say this is the worst state we've ever been in, but it's certainly a close contender," Braun reported as the gathered briefing room attendees, Kazama once more being among them, looked upon a schematic of the *Black Sun*'s present state. It was as far from unblemished as anyone could remember. "The Moebius System is still online and addressing the damage as we speak, but it will still be days, perhaps weeks, before the ship returns to optimum levels. Certain systems, up to and including the cloak, are going to be offline for the foreseeable future."

"Weapons?" Jon questioned as he observed the large number of red marks across the display, already feeling his gut clench at what he was about to hear.

"Seventy-two percent remain operational. Moebius will bring that up to seventy-five in two to three days," Braun followed on assuredly. "That being said, shields remain at only fifty-six percent power, and it will take that much more time to build them back up to full again."

"In other words, we won't be fighting the Red Armada wholesale any time soon," Davis surmised, leaning his right arm on the glass-topped table. "So much for a third Ephesus, I suppose…"

"Unfortunately, that's far from assured, especially with our cloak out of commission," Barbarossa thought out loud, then turning to Kazama. "What's the *Tsushima*'s status?"

"More or less the same, including the loss of our own cloak," Kazama held back a sigh at his ship's condition. "She can, and will, still fight, but as you said, Kapta, we're in no shape for large-scale fleet action."

"Which doesn't leave us many options admittedly," Barbarossa responded, clasping his hands together as he frowned. "Especially as it will only be a matter of time now."

A swell of cold soon spread across the table; the attendees all understood. They had just stormed the Red Phoenix's capital, infiltrated the main residence of the Lady, and nearly made off with one of her clan's most iconic treasures. There was little doubt that Lady Ching would soon – if she hadn't already – direct the entirety of her fleet to hunt them down and finish them for good, and without their cloaks, it would only be a matter of time, as the Leo said. A matter of time before they were effectively cornered and dealt with.

Frowning, Jon also looked toward Kazama, though on an entirely different subject matter. Namely, what he and Lorelei had seen, with the rest of the city of Shandong apparently, just before the retrieval ship had arrived.

"Moving away from that particular subject matter for the moment," Jon began evenly, not bothering to hide his dissatisfaction at that revelation. "I would like to hear your explanation on her behalf."

Lorelei could not help but shiver as she felt that familiar coldness emanate from her Captain. Not just because Alex was presently in sickbay, nor even because Kaguya was not in attendance. No, this was the coldness she had felt before when he had confronted her following the Black Moon, when he had questioned her as to why she had not used her own power until the present. And so she felt it again, as Captain Flint gazed with inquisition toward Captain Fuma, all but verbally demanding to know why Fuma Kaguya had not used her own Devilblade until now. Especially as they had fought so many battles past, many of whom the outcomes would have undoubtedly been much different otherwise.

He would understand all too soon, Lorelei knew. As did Kazama, who merely closed his eyes as he began to answer.

"Kimaris..." he started evenly, visibly remembering. "...was our mother's blade."

A much greater cold swell ran over the table, one that even over-rode Jon's prior indignation like a greater wind converging on a lesser. If the opposite captain's words didn't indicate all of it, then the tone of his voice certainly did.

"No," Anna breathed in horror, a feeling that was matched by all around the table. There could have only been one explanation and one explanation alone.

Jon closed his eye, the first vestiges of regret already taking root. He had only met Lady Fuma Kaede once in his lifetime, but he remembered her as a beautiful, regal woman that evenly matched her husband in strength and majesty. Just as he also recalled how her swordsmanship, her mastery of the blade, was actually the better of the pair.

"How?"

"I don't know, Jon," Kazama breathed as he visibly struggled to force back the memories, the trauma he still suffered from that fateful night. "Goddamn it, I don't know!" He pounded his fist on the table to vent some of his pain. "Nor does anyone else. When Kimaris...overwhelmed her defenses, she came at Kaguya and me... Father had to..."

It took another minute for the Dragon Prince to recompose himself, from which he spoke evenly again. "Kaguya took ownership of Kimaris thereafter. She vowed that, so long as she lived, it would not find another Wielder."

The elder brother then emphasized as he finished. "A vow she made before Father, in our mother's name."

Jon bowed his head in understanding and regret. He felt Lorelei's hand slip into his under the table, which he grasped in gratitude.

"I'm sorry," Jon offered, allowing his remorse to show through for once. "I didn't..."

Kazama held up his hand. "There was no way you could have known," he replied in his own understanding. "It happened around the same time as Ephesus, so you and Alex were otherwise preoccupied."

"To say the least," Jon responded back, still retaining solemnity. For all that he knew and understood, even he could not fathom what Kaguya was going through now, locked away in her quarters as she had been since their return. It wasn't right. None of it was right.

Unfortunately, however, as had been long elicited, such was the least of their concerns. Which Davis reemphasized but a moment later.

"I'm sorry to hear all that," the helmsman stated respectfully. "But unless our next play is another ground action, our predicament otherwise..."

Jon decided that was as good a time as any. "Actually, that is our next course of action," he said, re-earning the table's attention. "In a way."

None of them liked the sound of his tone.

"May I ask what you are talking about, Captain?" Barbarossa

inquired with respectfulness, and underlying demand.

Jon nodded. "Before we set out for Penglai, I recorded a message in anticipation of this particular outcome," he answered simply enough. "Assuming Alex was able to place it within the Red Phoenix's central network, that message will soon be broadcast through the whole of the clan."

"Really?" Davis let out, now very unsure what to think. "And what message would this be?"

Jon glanced toward Kazama again. Which was more than enough for the captain of the *Tsushima* to realize his cohort's intent, much to his horror.

"What have you done?" Kazama breathed in open dread. Much like how he alluded to his mother's fate, so too did Jon do the same with his message's contents.

"The only remaining tactic I had," Jon responded, not about to back down now. "The same tactic my own mother utilized so long ago."

"And it only worked because her opponent was a man of honor!" Kazama contested, his disturbance paramount. "Ching is nothing of the sort!"

"She'll have no choice but to follow through regardless," Jon stated emphatically. "Especially if she wants to preserve her clan's image…"

"She'll send everything she has after us, Jon!" Kazama yet protested.

"She's doing that now, Kazama!" Jon responded. "At least we will have something of a chance at Gaochang."

"Forgive the interruption, Captains," Davis spoke up again, effectively for the rest of the table. "But what in the fifth circle are you all talking about!?"

Both Captains took a breath as Jon nodded for Kazama to answer.

"In the final month of the War of the Dragons," the prince began anew. "Lady Flint made an ultimatum to my father."

Barely noticed by the rest of the table, both Kaiser and Apache lit up with recognition.

"Gold Face help us..." the doctor proclaimed while the security officer's own apprehension was such that Gran, who no doubt now learned it herself, took her lover's hand.

"The War of the Dragons had been wrought for nearly a full year by that point and was close to escalating," Jon followed up for the others' benefit. "There were even claims that the other clans were about to take sides."

"Thus to mitigate the destruction and bring a quick, decisive end to the war, Lady Flint made an all too certain challenge," Kazama followed, frown reemerging and deepening. "The same challenge that Captain Flint is about to make."

With that, Jon tapped his keypad, causing the main monitor to flicker into a different screen. The same one that all realized was being broadcast throughout Red Phoenix space in the present time.

Siyue Palace
Zhengzhou, Penglai

"Zuì àomàn de húndàn," Ching murmured as she realized what was happening, and what was about to happen. Before her and the rest of her court, the overriding signal gradually took shape, projecting the image of her primary adversary for all to see and bear witness toward. Both there within Siyue Palace and throughout the rest of her clan's space.

"Denizens of the Red Phoenix Clan," the image boomed with the voice of legion. **"I am Jonathan Flint, Captain of the *Black Sun*, Leader of the Flint Pirates and Heir Apparent to the Gold**

Dragon Clan. I come before you now so that you may witness this challenge I make to your Lady and her house.

"By now, you may have heard that my crew and I have struck Penglai, the very heart of your clan, and before that seven other bases throughout Red Phoenix space. Such has been the result of an all too recent blood feud between ourselves and your clan. A war of aggression begun by Lady Ching herself, who, alongside her eldest and chosen heir Ching Shun, seeks to annihilate myself and my brother Alexander, as well as any and all who would follow or support us. All so the very name of Morganna Flint, and all that it entails, will vanish from this realm forevermore.

"As callous and unprovoked as your Lady's actions toward us have been, I do not speak this message out of mere condemnation nor to invoke the worthiness and righteousness of my cause. Instead, I reach out to your Lady in open invitation so that we may end this conflict amicably and with as little further bloodshed as permitted. The very same invitation my mother made long ago in order to end another war, whose own name and legacy echo well into the present."

With that, the captain's single eye narrowed in such a way that it seemed to glare directly upon Ching herself.

"I challenge you, Ching Shih, Lady of the Red Phoenix, to send your champion to meet me upon Gaochang IV," the projection declared. "In the Valley of the Dragons."

Both within Siyue and without, more than one witness let out an audible gasp.

"Through this final battle, we shall determine the ultimate victor of this war, as well as prevent any additional destruction," the projection ultimately resolved. "Once more as my mother, and her most worthy opponent, did long ago in that very place."

Again did that single eye narrow, this time in disdain.

"If you have any semblance of regard to the safety and standing of your clan, you will do well to accept this challenge. Though you have long demonstrated to retain no honor toward your name, you, as the leader of your clan, yet remain responsible for its well-being and the well-being of those within. Consider this alongside what we have inflicted upon your realm, as well as what we are capable of inflicting, should it become necessary."

Such words seemingly filled the air, once more within Zhengzhou and without.

"At the time of this message, we will have long set course for the Gaochang System, in which I estimate we will arrive in two weeks. That is how long you have to prepare your champion, as well as any who would follow him, for this battle. And while I have little doubt you feel tempted to have the Red Armada meet us in Shun's place, I repeat we have already wrought much upon your clan since the beginning, and we would wreak that much more to the end. I again implore you, if only for the sake of your citizenry, to keep this well in mind. As well as the aftermath that such destruction would bring unto you and your clan's prestige.

"Make no mistake Lady Ching. I find you derisive and contemptible, entirely unworthy of the title and rulership that you presently hold. Even so, neither my crew nor I wish for this war's continuance any more than we wish for additional lives to be sacrificed. It is for such reasons that this challenge is made, and though I do not foresee your answer at the time of this recording, I do hope it shall be of your son meeting me at Gaochang. Just as I also hope that this will indeed be our last battle, as again set in the manner and the spirit of my mother and my teacher."

Then, seemingly, at last, the projection reached its conclusion.

"For all else, may the best man win," it declared before terminating.

Chapter XIX: Dum Spiro Spero

Flint Pirates umbra *Black Sun*
Arcspace

"Kaguya?" Jon called over the intercom, already knowing that there would be no reply. When none indeed came, he entered in his captain's override; the door slid open and allowed him inside. He found Fuma Kaguya huddled on her bed as though to keep the outside light from reaching her.

"I wish to be alone," Kaguya murmured as the door closed, leaving Jon inside her chambers.

"I won't be long," Jon replied softly, taking immediate note of the kunoichi's posture and the brokenness of her voice. "I just wanted to see how you were doing."

Again no response came, resulting in a rather disturbing silence in the room. For the life of him, the elder Flint could not remember ever seeing Fuma Kaguya so shattered, both on the exterior and within. Not even when she had been so shaken by the events at Kurzis, which he did well not to bring to mind.

"May I see it?" Jon asked as he extended his hand.

Again Kaguya did not verbally reply but otherwise obliged as Kimaris took form in Jon's grip, allowing the captain to study it closely. Compared to its original unadorned form, the sword might as well had been an entirely different weapon, one forged and articulated by the finest artisans in the Blue Dragon. Jon couldn't help but marvel at it despite everything.

Though little different in its shape and functionality as a ninjato, there were many alterations to emphasize its status as a true Devilblade. The first and most obvious was its blue-tinted blade, which even in the darkness shone with a spectral, otherworldly brilliance. The once square-shaped, unmarked *tsuba* (handguard) was now gold and circular, engraved with two entwining dragons, both locked in an invisible, encompassing chase. The *tsuka* (hilt) also possessed dark blue weaving instead of the original black, alongside an equally golden *kashira* (pommel). All while the blade's sigil remained branded on either side of the *habaki*.

"Beautiful, isn't it?" Kaguya, at last, spoke up, her voice somewhat muffled as her head remained placed against her knees. "A far cry from the form I've used for so long."

That caused the kunoichi to laugh derisively. "If only it were confined to such."

Allowing the blade to dematerialize from his hand, Jon again looked upon the ninja in understanding. In spite of popular belief, Devilblades were not truly what they were defined as; the manifested blade was simply a control mechanism to focus and direct seemingly infinite power. Instead, the weapon's true form was that of an energy field that enfolded the Wielder within and without. Energy of the utmost purity that transcended flesh, metal, and all forms of physical matter, while remaining restricted to its host Wielder in disposition and subservience, indeed as an actual devil would be bound to the will of its summoner.

And just as the devil would behave toward its self-appointed "master", the "blade" was always watching over its Wielder. And waiting.

"I can feel it, Jon," Kaguya went on, at last turning her tear-afflicted eyes upon her captain. "I can feel it around me, within me. Seemingly docile, and yet…"

The ninja visibly shuddered with her words and what she felt. "Waiting for just one opening."

"Yes," Jon confirmed, understanding all too well how Kaguya felt. "Such is the nature of these weapons, if that is what they truly are."

Kaguya nodded, appreciative of the understanding. "It will one day take me," she spoke with inevitability. "It took my mother, who many claimed to have mastered it. It will take me as well."

"No, it won't," Jon responded firmly in objection. "You're not your mother, Kaguya. So long as…"

"Yes, so long as I retain my resolve, it will remain at bay. But how long will that last, Jon?" Kaguya could only question as tears flowed down her cheeks in remembrance and trepidation. "How long can any of us hold out against these…these *akuma*?"

"Forevermore," Jon affirmed. "No matter how much it takes, from *any* of us."

The captain went further. "I don't know what caused your mother's possession, but again you are not her, Kaguya," he reassured. "You will not suffer her fate."

"I want to believe that, Jon," Kaguya whispered, her eyes gleaming with fear and desperation. "I want to believe that, more than anything. And yet…"

Trembling once more, it took a long moment for Kaguya to bring herself back under control. "Please *oniisan*, allow me some time," she implored as she turned away. "We still have much before Gaochang."

Again Jon could only nod in understanding, both toward the request and how Kaguya had learned of everything despite her isolation, and so turned back to the door.

"Take care, *imouto-chan*," the Captain solemnly bid farewell before making his way out, allowing Kaguya the time she requested. Time to deal with the devil she now held without and within.

Blue Dragon umbra *Tsushima*
Arcspace

This must be how they felt before Ephesus, Kazama remarked to Izuna before taking another sip from his sake cup. Secluded as they both were in their private mess, the Blue Dragon captain allowed his discomfort to show. *I'm no stranger to battle Izuna, you know that most of all. But...*

Yes, it is something of a new experience, isn't it? the opposite psion frowned as she felt the myriad of emotions and turmoil between the two ships. Not even the fact they were both in arcspace inhibited her from such. In fact, their traveling several times the speed of light seemed to enhance the reception in some areas. *As many "final" battles as we've fought before, my love, I don't think we've had one with such overwhelming odds and uncertainties. And most definitely none with our backs so firmly against the wall.*

Indeed, Kazama concluded, unable to remember having fought any such battles in the past. But then, his circumstances had been vastly different from Jon and Alex's, and now Kaguya's, otherwise remaining within the Blue Dragon and not having embarked on some mysterious yet epic venture. *I don't suppose you're going to tell me if our side wins or not.*

That earned a small laugh from Izuna. *I might act as, and perhaps even* be *a diviner on some level Kazama, but I was never able to foretell the future,* she explained, as though her husband needed to be reminded, drinking from her own sake cup now. *And even if I could, you would simply yell something cliché like 'the future can be changed!' and charge off regardless.*

Heh, Kazama laughed a little as well. *Have I ever mentioned how fortunate I am to have you as my wife?*

Not as much as I'd like, Izuna smirked back, all too sweetly. *If it were my way, you would be worshipping me as Amaterasu incarnate.*

That earned more of a laugh from the pair before they settled back with a simultaneous sigh. A brief silence prevailed before Kazama "spoke" again.

I still don't know how Jon can do this, the Dragon Prince confessed. *To not only gamble against so much with so little but also to do so with his ship and crew...*

Such is part and partial to any captaincy, my love, Izuna assured. *Sometimes you have to gamble, even against odds such as these.*

I know, or at least I thought I knew, Kazama again admitted, still frowning at the idea. The Flints had already put so much on the line since Atalanta – since Ephesus, in fact – and now it was almost all or nothing from Kazama's perspective. It actually terrified the Blue Dragon heir on some level just how close Jonathan and the rest were pushing it.

Izuna easily picked up the feelings and uncertainty; she reached out and brushed her hand against her husband's cheek, emphasizing her touch with the usage of some of her power.

Jon knows what he's doing, Izuna again assured. *They all know what they're doing.*

Hearing that, Kazama looked up. A small vestige of hope having now emerged as he "heard". *Do you think the day will actually be won?*

Izuna shrugged. *As I said, I'm no foreteller,* she once more admitted. *But I believe Jon has more going for him and his ship and crew than what's apparent.*

She then turned serious. *Not that we won't be fighting as well when the time comes,* she spoke with grave certainty.

Of course, Kazama agreed as he refilled his sake cup, then took a long sip. There was little doubt that Shun would not be the only thing Ching would be sending to Gaochang IV. Nor that the battle would be confined to the planet's surface. *I only wish I knew what we will face.*

As do I, Izuna added with melancholy, her eyes now looking into the distance. Foretelling was one power that, for the life of her, she wished she held. Especially as she continued to feel Gaochang draw closer and closer.

Flint Pirates umbra *Black Sun* Arcspace

She was cold, cold enough to shiver, despite the relative warmth of the blanket now wrapped around her as well as the moderate temperature level of her quarters. For a moment Kaguya wondered if this was yet another effect of her awakening her Devilblade but ultimately decided Kimaris had no direct impact on her core temperature. Rather, it was the shame and the terror she felt that caused her to be devoid of heat, to feel as she did now, alongside everything else that was happening to her.

The thoughts, the memories that ran through her consciousness helped even less. There were two lines specifically, both playing through her simultaneously. The first one was obvious; that of her mother under the throes of her possession, charging after she and Kazama as they fled in horror, only for their father to intervene and deflect what may very well have been the killing strike. The great and terrible battle that erupted between their father and mother until their father, at last, struck their mother down, ending both her plight and the threat she represented. Her mother's body disseminating in traditional fashion, the inactive, stone-like formed Kimaris appearing in its place.

The second was far more recent but just as ominous. Alex, wounded and bleeding, fighting valiantly against the possessed Sanxing. Her own intervention, marked by her summoning her blade as her mother had once done, followed by her own great and terrible battle in Alex's place. Though it had been a trying fight, her increased control over herself and her weapon, coupled with the extensive critical wounds Alex had inflicted up to that point, eventually resulted in her supposed victory. All followed by the realization of her broken oath – her setting herself onto the same path as her late mother – and the breakdown and tears that commenced after that.

Both sets of memories resonated through her, each a separate event yet somehow melding together as one. As though to emphasize how much she had truly damned herself. How she had gone against all that she had vowed, had assured herself of, in that one moment of decision. Although she had saved *him* through such sacrifice, which otherwise would have, should have, made all the difference to her. And yet...

Abruptly she looked up, feeling a new presence enter her mind. *What do you want, psion?* she demanded almost angrily.

Nothing, in particular, Lorelei responded in her own nonchalant manner. *Your thoughts and despair have been so rampant I would likely feel them from the other side of the galaxy. So I thought I would have a closer look to see if you were truly as "damned" as you believe yourself to be.*

Kaguya did not have to actually "hear" that voice to pick up the sardonic tone behind it. Lorelei was so deep in her mind now that they might as well have been sitting back to back in the physical world.

Have your laugh then and be done with it, the ninja internally snarled in derision. *I'm not in the mood to suffer your audacity.*

Melodic laughter soon followed. *The one who would break her vow, made upon her mother's grave speaks to me of audacity? My what an*

243

ironic universe we live in.

Anger began to boil within Kaguya, only for Lorelei to telepathically dispel the tension. *I mean no insult, nor am I here to laugh at you, Kaguya. I only wanted to make sure you were alright, at least enough that you may yet recover.*

And? Kaguya demanded. Underneath her ire, she wanted to know herself.

...I believe you will, Lorelei admitted. *Whatever effect Kimaris has over you, it is by your own hand that you are broken now, not its.*

You don't think I know that!? Kaguya snapped before reeling herself back in again. *It's as you said, Lorelei-san, I violated my most sacred oath. Damning in itself, but the fact that I've brought a literal* akuma *onto myself through the process...*

An akuma *that, once you regain yourself, you will have absolute control over,* Lorelei pointed out. *I agree with the Captain on that much. You will not suffer the same fate as your mother.*

How would you know!? Kaguya demanded back, this time unable to constrain herself.

A slight pause ensued, with Lorelei physically closing her eyes from the other side. *Because I know what it's like to fear and despise your own power,* she admitted, *to the point that you would never use it if you had the choice.*

Blinking as she picked up on a strange sense of melancholy from the Siren, Kaguya could not help but wonder in that brief moment.

In the end, however, it is not such power that truly matters, Lorelei stated firmly. *It is how we would wield such power and for* whom.

Deliberately did Lorelei emphasize that last word, with images of Alexander Flint accompanying. Though she wanted to resist that particular siren call, Kaguya again could not help but feel some of the terror drain away as she saw *his* face. That ever radiant face...

You are not damned Kaguya. And you will recover from this yet, Lorelei assured, telekinetically rubbing Kaguya's shoulders in comfort. *You are strong, capable, and more importantly, you have the most essential reason in the world not to succumb... love. So long as that remains, the devil you have invoked will have no power over you.*

As the images of Alex drifted back into her subconscious, the kunoichi looked down again. This time in somberness.

I wish I could believe that, she admitted, right as the image of her possessed mother became a fixture again in her thoughts. Hadn't she held every reason not to succumb? If so...

There's no need for you to believe me because it remains the truth, Lorelei still assured regardless. *You will understand in due time.*

With that, the telepathic link severed as the psion's presence withdrew from her mind, again leaving Kaguya to the darkness and all that lurked therein.

───────────── ─────────────

Letting out a tired yawn, Apache continued to gaze over his still incapacitated patient, his old but still very capable eyes looking out for any sign of lingering ailment. Though well on his way to a full recovery, with his broken bones since mended and his interior and exterior wounds since addressed, Alex had still greatly overextended himself during this last battle. He was not quite ready to be released from Apache's care, or so the healer felt. Not surprising given all that had happened, though it still irritated on some level that the younger brother had pushed and broken himself to such an extent. What was it with these two and their habit of throwing themselves deep into the fray...or the fray throwing itself deeply onto them?

And I used to think their mother was troublesome enough, Apache thought, sighing this time as he shook his head. It must have been some hereditary genetic flaw, the Aquilan felt. After all, no sane-minded sentient would ever attempt half the things that...

"Kaguya…" the murmur escaped Alex's lips in a light wisp, seemingly floating out and upward upon utterance, complimented by the younger Flint's right-hand fingers flexing, as well as the arm itself shifting somewhat.

Again did Apache sigh, this time in understanding. Even now, in his strained unconsciousness, young Alex was still trying to reach her.

As I said, troublesome, the healer thought as he stretched his talon over the hand, holding it for just a moment. Indeed, no sane-minded sentient would ever attempt half the things Alex and his brother had done in their short lifetimes. And yet, the Aquilan knew, that's what made the Flints so special. As much as it still gave him such a ridiculous workload, of course.

Chapter XX: The Valley of the Dragons

Valley of the Dragons
Gaochang IV
Eleven Days Later

It was a desolate wasteland, that much could be said. Situated deep within Red Phoenix space, yet fittingly distant from any of the settled worlds therein, the fourth planet of the Gaochang System was little more than a vast, arid desert whose surface was exclusively that of sand and rock. Broken, rocky terrain extended throughout the sphere, as did jagged, seemingly impassible mountainscapes. Crevasses and ravines also ran across in random lines and directions, many of which held depths that could not be seen. All complimented by the occasional storm of dust and debris, which swelled and swept along at specific points and at specific times, causing further desolation to the already vapid surface. Bleak and inhospitable to the greatest extent, Gaochang IV's only saving grace seemed to be that it held a breathable, otherwise livable atmosphere, something that its four other brethren did not possess. And yet, even with that overall vibrant description, Jon felt the valley he now stood before remained well unto itself.

Though forwardly little different from the rest of the planet, there was something sacred, something ethereal about the Valley of the Dragons, the battleground in which his mother and Lord Fuma fought their epic battle to end their war. It certainly stood out compared to the rest of the planet, namely as it possessed the scars of battle throughout its scape, which were further emphasized by the wandering shadows cast from the equally wandering clouds above. More than that, however, this land was a piece of history in which a great event that forever changed the universe took place. Where the foundations of the Gold Dragon and his mother's legend were firmly laid, with all the galaxy witnessing.

Yes, Jon had heard that part of his mother's story many times throughout his life. How she and Lord Fuma fought for three straight hours, their mastery over their particular blades such that the powers they utilized against one another forever altered the valley, all while the denizens of their respective clans watched and waited for the inevitable victor. That victor would be Morganna Flint, of course, who would end up criticality wounding the Blue Dragon Lord, such that the onlookers held their collective breath when it appeared the Lady of the Gold Dragon would indeed finish him. Only, as Jon grinned upon recalling, his mother didn't, instead offering her hand in place of a killing stroke, which Lord Fuma, for whatever pride he may have felt, still took. Thus the war was concluded in *status quo ante bellum*, in which the Gold Dragon would be formally recognized as the fifth Pirate Clan and a signatory in the Treat of Libertalia, while the Blue Dragon would remain its own sovereign entity. A conclusion that in itself would serve as the foundation for the seemingly adversarial yet much deeper relationship between the two young, aspiring Clan Lords.

And so the eldest son of Morganna stood there, taking in the entirety of the sight. Where much of everything had begun, whose legacy was still embraced by him and Alex, as well as so many others. Up to and including the one who stood by the elder Flint now.

"To think this is where it took place," Kazama observed as he laid eyes on the valley that marked his own family's history, in a not so different direction from Jon's. "Where one era ended, and another began."

"Indeed," Jon responded, eye narrowing as another cloud passed overhead, enveloping the two heirs in shadow for a time. "And so it shall be for us as well."

Kazama nodded in agreement, knowing that this would be his and the Blue Dragon's fight as much as the Flint Pirates'. Though it was still not "official" that the Blue Dragon was taking part in this war, if it were remembered as such, there would be a time in the future where Fuma Kazama and the *Tsushima*'s participation would be known and remarked upon. Thus to be triumphant would further cement his own right to succeed his father as Lord of the Blue Dragon. While defeat...

"I'm sorry," Jon suddenly spoke, inadvertently snapping his friend out of his thoughts. "I wanted to tell you at the beginning, but if I had..."

"I would have tried to stop you," Kazama surmised before ultimately shrugging. "Think no more of it. What's done is effectively done, Jon, and we would have had to fight a final battle eventually."

The Dragon Prince grinned at the notion. "In all honesty, I take great honor in our journey ending here."

"As do I," Jon agreed, indeed feeling much the same.

And then Kazama frowned as another thought came to mind. "That being said, you know I cannot join you down here, no matter how much I wish otherwise."

"I know," Jon concluded, also feeling some remorse. As much as the

Dragon Prince had been an active participant in the conflict with the Red Phoenix, the fact remained that the challenge had been made by the leader of the Flint Pirates exclusively. Thus the battle, this part of it at least, would be fought by those in black and gold exclusively.

Of course, it was a sure bet Shun would bring the remaining two Sanxing with him. Normally Jon would have had Lorelei supplement he and Alex, who had since fully recovered, but the Captain had a dark and imposing feeling that he would need her more aboard the *Sun* to face whatever else Ching would throw at them. And both he and Kazama would be fools to believe one such as Ching Shih would not capitalize on the opportunity.

Thus there was one, and only one, that Jon would choose to join the Flint brothers. And unlike his brother, she had yet to fully recover.

"Should I try?" Kazama mildly suggested.

"You would fare no better," Jon answered, shaking his head. "No, only he can reach her now."

"As you say, Captain," Kazama acknowledged, emphasizing that, as much as Kaguya was his sister, she still wore the Flint colors, which meant she was Jon's responsibility. And it was as Jon said, only *he* could pull her back from the brink when all others failed.

Thus the two captains, the children of those who had entered this realm long ago, stood upon the land in continued reverence. Both taking solemn dignity in their knowledge that they would soon fight a similar battle. A battle that, as with the one long past for their fore-bearers, would determine both of their futures.

Flint Pirates umbra *Black Sun*
Gaochang System

"Once more unto the breach, dear friends," Anna raised her glass with her comrades before all took to their respective drinks. This wasn't the first time each of them had a "last" drink before the big upcoming battle, though it was the first where they had it with one another. The operations officer wondered if this would become a tradition, considering how many times they've indeed moved upon the breach. "And all wealth and glory to all of us when it's over."

"Amen, sister," Cheney proclaimed, raising his coffee – one of the two non-alcoholic beverages at the table – to her. "Not to mention vacation time that *doesn't* end abruptly."

Anna nodded in concurrence, as did the others. "Any ideas where we'll end up after this one?" she asked her fellows. "Because I doubt we're welcome back on Atalanta."

"Somewhere lowkey would be my guess," Gran translated for Kaiser, who took a swig from his prune juice before continuing. "An out of the way settlement, where the *Sun* can hideout as she regenerates."

"In other words, somewhere that's *not* on any starmap," Davis surmised, frowning somewhat at the idea. "Can't say I like that."

"Why? Because you'd have to settle for a down to Terra colonial girl?" Cheney inquired before shifting back to Boss. "Present company excluded, of course."

Boss merely sniffed in mock derision. "Canberra is hardly some out of the way colony," she retorted before sipping her whiskey.

"So long as she has all of her teeth and no webbed feet, no, that's not the issue," Davis spoke up to answer the raider's question. "I've just gotten so used to living the high life, I can't say I want to go back to hiding in 'out of the way' settlements on the fringes of space."

"None of us do, Davis," Anna assured. "But, unfortunately, this isn't going to be like with Baranov and Tartarus, where everything is smoothed over at the end."

"I know," Davis sighed, almost downing his rum over the despondency. "We've hacked off a Pirate Clan. And if and when the Captain and the others pull through today, we'll have killed the up and coming lord to said clan."

"Exactly. Tensions are going to linger for some time," Anna responded, though she frowned at the idea as well. "And, as mentioned, there will be the regeneration period for the *Sun*, which could take months depending on how much damage we incur in the next beating."

"What about the Blue Dragon?" Gran questioned. "Couldn't we just remain there like we did following Ephesus?"

Boss shook her head. "Too risky for Lord Fuma and us. We don't know how the other clans would take to the Blue Dragon providing safe harbor after a stunt like this."

"And it would make us an enticing target as well," Braun added, his puffy features folded into a glower. "No doubt Lady Ching will intend vengeance for her eldest's untimely demise."

"Or seek to take the *Sun* for herself, as could the White Tiger and Black Tortoise," Davis sighed again, frustration apparent. "No, as warm and fluffy as I feel over it, our course is truly set after this one."

"Well into the wild black yonder apparently," Apache spelled out with his own grimace, recalling some of the places he had spent his own "quality time" when on the run. Though he doubted they were in such bad shape that Jon would place them in such squalor, the fact remained that they were not headed anywhere with a beachside this time around.

"Of course, that's something we can all worry about *after* we're done killing the Phoenix whelp and his fellow hatchlings."

The table occupants all let out a simultaneous "heh" over that one. Indeed, that was the only thing none of them were going to contest. Whatever they were sure to face while the main battle took place on the surface, they all knew, one way or the other, they would win the day. Just as they had done in much harder previous "last" battles.

"Amen, Doc," Cheney again raised his mug in acknowledgment – an act that was soon mirrored by the rest of the table – before taking another hardy drink.

———————————   ———————————

With the door to the main cabin shifting open, Alex found his brother behind his desk with two tankards and a datapad in front of him. More or less the standard scene whenever he met Jon like this, yet the younger Flint still couldn't help but feel something was amiss as he entered and took his usual seat. Smiling, he and Jon clinked tankards and took their respective sips of Old Caribbean. Again, all standard, all normal, present circumstances notwithstanding.

"I trust you're completely healed?" Jon inquired as he put down his tankard.

"That I am, brother," Alex confirmed, setting down his own drink and cracking his neck to emphasize. "Ready and willing to kick Shun's *pìgu* back to Penglai."

"Heh," Jon stated, unable to stifle a grin. That line alone told him his brother was ready for the fight ahead. "Don't ever change Alex."

Alex smirked. "You know me, Bro," he responded brightly, shrugging his shoulders. "I'm everyone's favorite Red Devil."

"Indeed," Jon agreed, knowing how true that really was. Especially for the one in particular.

Taking another sip of rum, Alex nodded toward the datapad on the desk. "What's that?"

Instead of responding, Jon merely slid the pad over to Alex. He turned the pad to face him and saw that it held four numbers in a line, obviously a passcode.

"The access to Kaguya's quarters," Jon stated as he took another sip from his tankard.

Hearing that, Alex's smug demeanor turned to one of hesitance, his gut clenching accordingly. "And..." he inquired, staring at his brother. "What do you intend for me to do with this?"

Jon exhaled. "Go to her."

"Jon..." Alex's voice was no longer jovial but laced with an emerging offense.

"I'm sorry, Alex," the elder brother interrupted. "I respected the course you and Kaguya chose for yourselves. In fact, I found it admirable that you both took it slowly."

Alex started to respond, but Jon prevailed.

"Unfortunately, we're out of time," Jon affirmed, in a tone that showed he would take no argument. "She's hurting Alex, and you're the only one that can help her."

Alex sniffed. "Help her," he repeated, shaking his head. Though he understood where his brother was coming from, he still felt it was wrong on many levels. "Why can't Lorelei fight alongside us?"

"Because she'll be needed here when the time comes," Jon declared. "And unless she actually did kill that other Sanxing, we will be facing three high-level Wielders simultaneously. Or more precisely, I will be facing Shun, and you will be facing *two* high-level Wielders simultaneously."

Again Alex understood but still could not come to terms with what his brother was even suggesting.

"Besides, this isn't just about the battle," Jon stated as he rose from his chair and walked around his desk, Alex rising up to meet him. "As I said, she's hurting Alex, and she's been hurting for a long time. She is confused and afraid."

"Yeah..." Alex was forced to admit, having heard the story from Apache just before, alongside the rest of the events at hand. He never knew what had happened to her mother, and though he had seen Kaguya's anguish firsthand upon her awakening her blade, he hadn't understood the meaning behind it until now. "But still…"

"She chose you, Alex," Jon emphasized. "Over the Blue Dragon, over her family, over her honor, she chose *you*."

The elder brother elaborated that point even further. "In that moment of decision, she broke the vow she made to her father, on her mother's grave no less. All for your salvation."

Alex opened his mouth to try and argue, but Jon would not hear it. "You're the only one who can help her, as you've always done."

"But…I'm to blame for this!' Alex growled as he ran his hands through his hair. "She wouldn't be facing this now if I hadn't…"

"*Nugas agis*, Alex. It was inevitable." Jon argued. "At some point, she would have had to face the same decision."

Jon shook his head. "Unfortunately, it is now, and we don't have time to let her get used to the situation."

Alex tried to argue still, only to know that it was futile. He could not imagine how much pain and torment Kaguya was in now, but he knew it was as his elder said. The decision was inescapable, and he was the only one she would let help her.

Jon reached out and grasped his brother's shoulders. "This is a direct order from your Captain," he stated with all the authority he could project to the one before him. "Go to her now, reach her, bring her back, for her sake and yours."

His eye narrowed as he then commanded. "And don't come out until it's time."

Breathing deep, Alex still felt a heavy weight upon him, both from Jon's hands upon his shoulders and his self-imposed guilt.

"Do you understand my order, First Officer?" Jon inquired, retaining his projected authority.

A short moment passed between the two brothers before Alex turned and downed the rest of his tankard in one swig. Upon his placing it back on the desk, he nodded in acquiescence to his brother.

"Yes," Alex acknowledged. "I understand, Captain. But my methods remain my own."

Jon nodded in, both in acknowledgment as well as gratitude. "You have three days," he stated, recalling his ultimatum to Lady Ching.

Again taking a breath, Alex said nothing more, could say nothing more. Instead, he merely nodded in turn to his brother and his captain before exiting.

———————————— ————————————

It's strangely scenic, Lorelei admitted as she, or at least her psionic projection as her actual body remained aboard the *Sun*, "stood" on a stone outgrowth at the center of the valley, with Izuna's avatar standing on another nearby. With their respective powers, both psions could see the entirety of the valley in the physical sense.

Not what one would expect from such a desolate realm.

The exterior only factors so much upon settings such as this, Izuna added on, taking in the scope of their apparent surroundings. *Rather, it is the history that defines it most.*

Yes, Lorelei agreed, imagining the great, epic battle that had been fought here previously. She wondered how much of the valley had been transformed with such great powers, as well as the contesting wills of the Gold and Blue Dragon Lords. Just as she also wondered how much more would be altered from the battle that would soon take place.

Truly strange how much history repeats itself, no matter the time, place, or culture.

Izuna chuckled at the reference. *It seems to be a universal constant, doesn't it?*

Very much so, Lorelei responded, considering. *To have the children fight upon the very same field as their parents...*

Such can be said about any war, past or present, Izuna remarked, considering as well.

I suppose, though not many are as apparent as this advent, Lorelei sighed. *It's a shame that you and I won't be able to join them.*

Unfortunately, Izuna emphasized. Any other time the two psions would have been there, standing in their respective colors in the face of adversity. Unfortunately, they could not do so now, especially against a dishonorable cur as Ching Shih.

I don't suppose you have any idea what we will be facing ourselves.

No more than you do, Lorelei admitted, bringing her hand under her chin in thought. *As damaged as our ships are, we still took down a fair amount at Penglai, so I doubt Ching will risk any more of the Red Armada against us.*

That doesn't leave many other possibilities, Izuna surmised trying to come up with another idea.

Perhaps a nuclear attack? Lorelei quired.

Mass destructive weapons are banned among the clans by the Treaty of Libertalia, Izuna responded. *And even then, they wouldn't do any good against our defenses.*

True, Lorelei agreed, ultimately shrugging as no other ideas came to mind. *Whatever it is, it will obviously take into account the combined power of both ships, and as damaged as they are...*

We're going to have a true battle on our own hands, yes, Izuna finished, her expression now grim. *Perhaps they will have the better end of the deal after all.*

Perhaps, Lorelei repeated, again looking out over the arid, scarred valley.

The strain that Alex felt throughout his entire body grew as he approached her doorway. It appeared innocuous enough, but he could sense something else lay within. For a long moment, he stood there, trying to will himself forward to violate her privacy, to reach his hand out to the keypad, let alone open the door.

The memories of recent events flooded his thoughts. The image of Kaguya standing in front of him, blocking the killing stroke, fighting and ultimately triumphing over that possessed aberration, her mastery of her blade, her mother's blade, apparent even though she had only just awoken it. Only for that triumph to shatter as Kaguya well and truly realized what she had done. First, she had frantically attempted to cast the blade aside, only for it to reform in her hand each and every time she threw it away. And then she tried to break it on her knee, over and over, only for it to remain unbending to her attempts.

Most damning of all, however, was, in her sheer distress, when she turned the blade upon herself; a time in which Alex, in his own desperation to reach her, could not recall feeling or seeing anything but her despair as she knelt there, about to plunge the Devilblade into her stomach. Only then did the blade disappear from her grasp, refusing to take the life of its Wielder.

Understanding the futility of her actions, she broke down entirely, wailing loudly and openly as though she had committed the worst possible sin, which he now understood in her own eyes she had. All the while, he had tried to crawl her, to reach her, but eventually blacked out from his wounds. Even now, he could still hear her sobbing, feel her agony…

Eyes snapping open, he didn't realize he had closed them, Alex reached out and tapped the code into the keypad. The door shifted, allowing him entry.

"Kaguya?" he called out softly, turning in a slow circle as he scanned the interior of the quarters for her location. A movement in the shadows caught his attention. "Kaguya?"

Having just exited from her apparent bath or shower, Kaguya stood in shocked silence, a towel wrapped around her torso. And only just.

"Alex?" Kaguya breathed, stunned, eyes wide and unsure of the unexpected entry.

The younger Flint abruptly turned back around. *"Sumimasen!"* he blurted almost randomly, discretion automatically dictating his actions.

A long silence prevailed as both remained firmly where they stood, the sound of their breathing all that could be heard. The tension, as well as the heat, apparent between them.

"Did..." the princess found her voice. "Did Jon send you here?"

"He..." Alex paused before he answered, gathering his words. "He informed me of your... dilemma...."

He took another moment to breathe before following up. "I'm here, Kaguya," he assured as he dared turn back around. "I'm here for you and you alone."

Nodding at that answer, as though it were all she required, Kaguya slowly walked toward him. Hesitancy and confusion remained in her eyes, the agony brought on by her decision apparent in her demeanor. Heart pounding in his chest, Alex remained unmoving as she stopped in front of him and stared up into his eyes. She said nothing but silently reached out, took his hand, and slowly placed it over her heart, her hand covering his. He felt her heartbeat, heard her breathing, as well as the deliberateness of her drawing in his scent.

"Kaguya..." Alex began, only for her to tighten her hold slightly, imploring him to remain silent. He complied.

"Do you...remember Tanabata?" she questioned, her tone mellow yet intense as she spoke. "When we returned from Ephesus?"

Looking into her eyes, he nodded.

"You told me that...when the time came I..." she almost trailed off.

"...I would make the right decision."

Indeed, Alex remembered his words that night. *"I don't know what the future holds for us either... What I do know, however, is that, if such a time does come... you will make the right decision."* The uncertainty, the sheer dread Kaguya had felt toward her father's not yet spoken but potential command. To eliminate the Flint brothers and the threat they possibly posed to the Blue Dragon.

"Yes," Alex confirmed.

"Then please...tell me..." she implored him, almost desperately. "Did I... Did I make the right decision?"

Slowly Alex exhaled as he considered his answer. He could feel her heartbeat accelerate, her breathing stilted. Only now did he realize how much Kaguya hurt, how much she was *broken*. His heart ached for her and what, through fate and his own shortcomings, she had been forced to do.

Once more in understanding, he reached out and pulled her to him. As unsure as she remained, he felt her bury her head into his shoulder, again deliberately taking in his scent as she settled against him. For another long moment, they remained there, in that shared embrace, before Alex finally responded to her question.

"I cannot answer that, Kaguya," he confessed, softly kissing the top of her head. "It is not my place."

Feeling her stiffen in despair, Alex gently stroked her back as he continued.

"However, through my belief in you, I entrusted my life to you at Tanabata. Claimed you as the blade that protects, regardless of your original purpose."

Feeling more and more power enter him from his own words, Alex went on. "From that time onward, you have done exactly that. You have protected this ship, its crew, and its captain well, regardless of the risks and oppositions. Yet only now, through your protection of me, did you truly have to make the ultimate sacrifice."

Knowing that she was listening intently now, Alex prevailed.

"For that sacrifice, for that hardship, this life…" he willed himself to say the words. "This life you saved in its greatest time of need… *It's yours.*"

Kaguya leaned back from his shoulder and stared up into his reddish-brown eyes. Already the first vestiges of tears began to well as she understood the full meaning of those two simple words.

"My life, my love, is yours, Kaguya," Alex emphasized, reaching to stroke an errant tear as it ran down her cheek. "And will remain so to the end."

Additional tears began to spill from those blue eyes. Enough that Kaguya sniffled, crying as she looked back down and buried her head back into his shoulder.

"Do with them, with me, as you will," Alex whispered, holding her tight as he kissed her, softly and tenderly, as though to ensure that she heard him. "As you want."

They stood, holding each other, drawing comfort in the moment. Alex waited as Kaguya cried and contemplated his words.

"As I want…" Kaguya repeated slowly, her crying subsiding some-what as she did. She raised her head and gazed at him once more. The hesitancy and confusion that had earlier been in her eyes gradu-ally replaced with resolve and desire.

Her hands retracted from his chest. She stepped back and, without breaking eye contact, grasped the edges of her towel.

"As I want…"

The towel slowly slid down her body, her gorgeous body, and pooled at her feet.

Alex's mouth went dry, his heart skipping a beat as he stood and stared, his own clothing receding. She was every fantasy and need to him...

Slowly and deliberately, Kaguya stepped forward as he reached for her, wrapping his arms around her and holding her close. Feeling her breasts touch and press against his bare chest, the princess let out a gasp, the rapid beating of his own heart now upon her as well. She took comfort in the feel of his strength enfolding her, his hands stroking her as he placed kisses on her face and neck, his warmth infusing every part of her form.

Assurance, and along with it, joy, bloomed within her, encompassing the whole of her being as a spreading fire. She had indeed made the right decision. *He* was above all. Her oath, her family, her clan, all things she held dear and sacred, all secondary to him and him alone. Her choice to save Alexander Flint's life had been right, regardless of the cost.

For it was by that choice, that single decision, that they were set. The younger children of once great enemies united, standing against the universe as one. Now and forever.

Thus did she again draw his lips to hers, any remaining reluctance vanishing between them, immediately supplanted by need and urgency. Such was how the three days, *their* three days, before the fated battle, began.

Chapter XXI: Quo Fata Ferunt

Red Phoenix *Yunnan*-class battleship *Zhang He*
Arcspace
Three Days Later

There was a stillness in the air of his quarters. Not a coldness of temperature within that localized atmosphere, but a motionlessness that was somehow out of place, even for him. Shun could not quite identify the source, even as he remained seated, eyes closed and at as much ease as he ever allowed himself, but it was most certainly there, and it held a deathly quality, as though to mark the destination at which the *Zhang He* would soon arrive. Where everything would be decided at last.

After a moment or two of contemplation, Shun wondered if the sensation was not outside but rather *within*. If it was, he still couldn't identify the source, and it certainly didn't dissuade him from the oncoming battle, but it still made him uncertain. This would be the third time in which he would combat Jonathan Flint, and though he had most certainly triumphed in the first, he could not deny that he was not as assured as he had once been. Instead of the certain victory that he knew would have taken place on Atalanta, he did not foresee what would occur on Gaochang in that damned valley. It galled him to even contemplate such a possibility that his adversary may be the triumphant one instead of him. It shouldn't have even registered with him; he should have looked upon the Valley of the Dragons as the Flint family graveyard, in which the last remnant of Morganna Flint's legend was put to eternal rest. Not too long ago, he would have seen it precisely as thus, but now…

As he delved further and further within, a certain memory reentered his consciousness. That all too particular communique he had received from the throneworld just before the Flints had infiltrated Penglai. At first, he had assumed it had been from his Lady but quickly realized this was not the case at all. Rather, it had come from Lao Tzu, her chief advisor and in certain ways diviner, who had served the household for generations upon generations. Shun had never met the man and had only heard of him in whispering, particularly from his Lady, so he was rather taken back to have received a line of communication from him. Yet, for whatever astonishment he may have felt toward such an audience, it was the words that followed that truly disconcerted him. As much as Shun would ever allow himself to admit.

"You now stand upon a great precipice, young master," the "SOUND ONLY" communique window spoke with all the air of wisdom and understanding. "In which you shall make a most critical decision."

"Do not waste my time, old man," Shun responded with his own air of impatience. "My Lady may see value in your mystic ways, but I do not. State what you will, or leave me be."

"As you wish," Lao Tzu responded without any indication of offense. "I advise you to abandon your pursuit of the Flints, for such will only assure your death."

Shun raised an eyebrow, strangely intrigued in spite of the context. It was as he said, he did not put much weight in Lao Tzu's fortune teller ways, no matter how long the would-be shaman had served the Red Phoenix Lord's house. Yet, underneath that, the clan heir felt there was something more despite.

"And how would this be?"

Though he could not see the old man's face, Shun knew that it had taken on a sagely smile.

"The 'how' is unimportant young master. At least compared to the inevitability of the outcome itself."

Before Shun could respond, Lao Tzu went on. "Once again, you now stand upon a great precipice. One in which, by the choice you make, shall your fate be determined."

Despite his dubiousness, Shun decided to allow the shaman to have his say. "Go on."

"The choice is simple: you may adhere to my warning and abandon your pursuit, or you may not," Lao Tzu explained. "If you make the first choice, the Flints will be unopposed and all too soon victorious. Their next triumph will be so great as to force our Lady into concession, while our clan will suffer great dishonor in the days following..."

Shun actually laughed at this. "All because of a choice you advised me to make."

"Indeed," Lao Tzu once more replied in understanding. "Yet such an outcome can be mitigated and in time recovered from."

Shun quickly noticed the darkness that had entered Lao Tzu's tone, even through the comm line.

"If you choose to ignore my warning and continue your pursuit," Lao Tzu went on. "You will ensure the Flints remain opposed and deny them their victory, but only temporarily."

Again Shun raised his eyebrow.

"For, in the end, they will be even more triumphant, as our Lady will suffer a defeat she will never recover from and our clan forever stricken..."

It was then Shun felt a strange sensation. As though, despite the sheer distance between his present position and Penglai, the old man had fixed his eyes upon him.

"With your death at Jonathan Flint's hands," Lao Tzu concluded, his voice and words holding a grave finality that actually made Shun feel cold. "Choose wisely, young master."

If anything, Shun only felt affronted by such an assertion. He... lose...to the pretender's son? And much more be killed by him? Such audacity on the part of this pretentious old man! How could such a thing even be conceived for he, a warrior with no equal and the heir to the greatest of dynasties? It should have been the other way around! It should have been he that stood triumphant with Jonathan Flint's inactive Devilblade held firmly in his hand! How could one as respected and adhered to by his Lady even proclaim such fèihuà!?

And yet, as much as he wanted to tear into Lao Tzu for such offense, such insult, Shun found himself holding his tongue. As much as he tried to deny it, he felt a strange weight, a strange power, to the old man's warning. That, precisely as had been stated, he really was now upon a precipice, in which he faced the choice of either turning away or continuing to his fall. Either he allow the Flints' their victory, or he deny them for a time, yet still...

Shun sniffed contemptuously at the thought of it. Once more, he was not his Lady, his mother. He did not put any weight into the words of a soothsayer, no matter how venerated.

"I have listened to your warning, Lao Tzu," Shun spoke with as much respect as he could project through his veiled disdain. "And I have chosen not to heed it."

Again Shun could not see the sage's face, yet he somehow knew that

Lao Tzu nodded from his side.

"Very well," the seer responded. If there was any regret in Lao Tzu's tone, Shun did not detect it. And yet, the old man was not quite done. "In five days, the Flints will be upon Penglai, with the intent of infiltrating Bayue and appropriating the Fengguan. They will attempt their heist upon the night of the fifth day."

This time, Shun blinked in unconcealed surprise. Though a part of him wanted to question Lao Tzu upon this knowledge, he again felt that same weight and power to his words. That it would indeed be thus.

"I suggest you prepare accordingly, young master," Lao Tzu finished, the communique terminating then and there.

In the end, it had been precisely as the old man had said. The Flints had been on Penglai, and they had attempted to make off with the Fengguan. And, as much as it still galled him, all Shun had been able to do was deny them their victory. As opposed to completing his own task and ending them all.

Yes, that was where the stillness lay, Shun came to realize; the sensation one felt upon marching toward their death. Had Lao Tzu indeed been correct to that extent? Was that what he was doing, what he would soon face in the Valley of the Dragons? The more Shun attempted to assuage himself that he did not believe a single word of it, the more he felt himself give way. That he was now well beyond the precipice and now well within his fall. He was just unable to sense it presently...

"Bridge to Master Shun," the *Zhang He* officer called out over the intercom. "We are now on final approach to the Gaochang System."

Eyes opening, Shun tapped his wristcom. "On my way," he responded, standing up and making his way out of his quarters.

Once more, ultimately, the old man's words were naught to him. Regardless of what the soothsayer believed, it would be Ching Shun that would be victorious that day, and it would be Jonathan Flint's corpse that would be left at the bottom of that valley. All while the rest of the Flint band, and the Blue Dragons for that matter, would be scattered to the vacuum of space. Shun would see to all of it, regardless of what fate supposedly held for him.

Flint Pirates umbra *Black Sun*
Gaochang System

"Red Phoenix battleship now entering the system," the tactical operator reported right as the warship in question exited arcspace and then positioned herself before the *Sun* and the nearby *Tsushima*. "She is hailing."

"Onscreen," Barbarossa commanded. A vidwindow of a stern-faced man in black and red soon appeared.

"I am Ching Shun," the man announced up front. "I am here to answer Jonathan Flint's challenge on my Lady's behalf."

Exhaling through his nostrils, Barbarossa took a moment to size up his captain's opposite number. He was certainly imposing, his profile retaining coldness that surpassed open space seemingly, yet Barbarossa still detected a fair amount of pride, as well as ire, underneath that dispassionate visage. Well, no matter, the Kapta supposed. The Red Phoenix cubling was not his to deal with.

"Captain Flint and his secondaries are already on the surface," Barbarossa responded respectfully. "My Captain forwards his *anticipation* toward meeting you there."

If there was any emotional response on Shun's part to that proclamation, Barbarossa did not see it.

"Very well," the Red Phoenix heir answered. "My ship will remain in orbit to witness."

"As will we," Barbarossa concurred, earning an acknowledging nod from the other side of the screen. It then disconnected abruptly.

Again the Kapta found himself inhaling and exhaling through his nostrils. "All stations, remain on alert for additional contacts. Red Phoenix or otherwise."

The rest of the bridge crew would do just that, Barbarossa knew. Despite how compliant the other side was presently, none of them expected Ching Shun to be their only opposition that day. Atalanta and Penglai were still very recent events after all, while Lady Ching's disdain for all things black and gold remained very much apparent.

That kept well in mind, Barbarossa's eyes narrowed as he watched the Red Phoenix shuttle gradually exit the launch bay of its mother-ship. From which it then proceeded in a long, steady descent to *terra firma* below.

Valley of the Dragons
Gaochang IV

The wind swept across the landscape as the three Flint Pirates watched their equally numbered contenders walk toward them, great-coat tails flapping, dust clouds kicked up by their footfalls. Jon, Alex, and Kaguya all waited patiently, yet still remaining observant, as Shun, Lu and Shou, continued toward them. None of the Flints showed any emotion toward the opposition fighters. As for the Red Phoenix, Shun remained detached while both Sanxing all but gleamed toward their respective opponents. Lu visibly relished settling the score with Kaguya while Shou seemed to savor a bout with one of the Flint brothers. Even so, the two subordinates remained in lockstep with their master, the trio stopping a few meters away from the Flints. The baneful gaze of Shun's dark brown eyes matching the one in Jon's singular blue.

For a short while, the two sides stood their respective grounds, saying nothing nor provoking any kind of aggression. All while the wind continued to sweep, the Gaochang sun slowly descending toward the horizon.

"On behalf of our Lady and the Red Phoenix Clan," Shun spoke with utmost formality. "We answer your challenge, Flint Pirates, and now stand before you upon this hallowed ground."

Jon wanted to espouse a 'heh' upon that proclamation but resisted, wondering just how much Shun considered the ground he now stood on to be hallowed.

"On our own behalf, yet in the memory of our Lady and the Gold Dragon Clan, we accept your answer," Jon responded with matching formality. "Let this battle, as it takes place upon this most sacred land, bring swift and final resolution to our strife."

With that, the respective clan heirs formed their Devilblades, soon followed by their fellows. Each blade was now familiar to all combatants, though Furfur, clearly due to its Wielder only having his right arm, now took the form of an ornately colored liuyedao.

Once more, silence encompassed the two groups; they held their blades and fighting forms in anticipation, watching and waiting for the inevitable first move. For a brief period, it seemed to all six that they would remain there for some time yet, as it appeared none of them wished to attack.

And then, without word or warning, both Jon and Shun charged as one, meeting each other in the middle as the great 'clang' of their obsidian and carmine blades rang across the whole of the valley. So too did Alex and Kaguya follow with their own blades against Shou and Lu, eliciting two more such clashes that swept through the scape as metallic thunder. So began the final battle.

Flint Pirates umbra *Black Sun*
Gaochang System

Well, that didn't take long, Barbarossa thought the moment the tactical operator brought up the oncoming contact, which would enter the system in a manner of minutes. And then, a feeling of peculiarity dawned upon the Leo.

"Just one contact you said?"

"Indeed, sir, only one," the tactical operator reported, sounding as perplexed as the Kapta and the rest of the bridge. They had all been expecting Ching to throw something at them while the battle continued on the surface, but only one ship? As opposed to another battlefleet?

Lowering the command scope, Barbarossa decided to take a look himself. It really was one contact incoming from arc, though it had yet to be formally identified. Rather strange, Barbarossa thought. What could...?

"Evade! Hard to port!" Lorelei yelled in urgent warning. Without waiting for Barbarossa's word, Davis did precisely that, banking the *Sun* in an accelerated left turn as the *Tsushima* went the opposite vector. Only a few seconds later, all hell truly broke loose.

Reverting just off of planetary orbit, the newcomer fired its opening barrage as soon as it re-entered normal space. Within bare seconds, a virtual wall of beam fire extended through the area where the two umbras had once been and where the Red Phoenix battleship had remained. The latter was instantly destroyed, its shields unable to withstand the intensity of the fire. Though the umbras continued untouched, both crews came face to face with a true monster. A ship of unmatched power that seldom appeared in the galaxy at large, whose very name instilled fear and alarm upon any who heard it.

"A dreadnought," Barbarossa gaped as the *Sun*'s sensors locked onto the veritable juggernaut before them, adorned in black and red with the Red Phoenix seal proudly displayed throughout her hull. Now he understood why Lady Ching had sent only one ship after them.

Over one kilometer in length and bristling with weaponry, the dreadnought, which was close enough to be identified as the *Guangdong*, easily dwarfed the two umbras in size and projected power. Such power was further emphasized as it fired another barrage with its bow weapons, one whose beam cannon shots were complimented with massive numbers of missiles and torpedoes. Again the two umbras, taking advantage of their much smaller size and still functional mobility, evaded the oncoming fire and returned it with their own weapons. Silently, both crews watched in horror as the *Guangdong*'s shields repelled the attacks like a metal plate to thrown pebbles. Not even their torpedoes were able to pierce the behemoth's defenses.

"How in the Seventh Circle did the Red Phoenix procure that thing!?" Anna gasped amid their evasion.

Though such inquiry was not part of their immediate concerns, Barbarossa understood why Anna was taken back. Only the Thirteen Galactic Powers were known to hold dreadnoughts, and each only had one, which more or less served as the flagship of their respective fleets. The gargantuan vessels naturally drew much in the way of energy and resources, making them otherwise unfeasible for lesser nations to wield. Thus, the Pirate Clans had universally shifted focus to more practical ship types. As the operations officer had said, how could the Red Phoenix procure such a ship?

However, such ambivalence meant nothing now, especially as the *Guangdong* once more fired her main guns. Davis remained focused, bringing the *Sun* into a starboard turn and climb that effectively moved her up and over the oncoming cannon blasts while also doing well to keep her ahead of said cannons. Even so, Barbarossa knew the helmsman would not keep them out of the line forever, and as damaged as the *Sun* remained…

"All ahead full!" he called out, now centering his energy toward sinking that ugly, oversized beast and living to tell the tale afterward. "Weapons, fire at will!"

Valley of the Dragons
Gaochang IV

Their ferocity unchecked and the power of their Devilblades blazing in full form, Jon and Shun launched down the valley, the ringing of their blades marking each time they intersected along with the corresponding bursts of darkness and fire. In the middle of these attacks, both Wielders launch simultaneous energy waves, the black and red converging into the other with a tremendous reverberation and effectively canceling each out.

Jon immediately formed dual spinning black wheels of absolute zero temperature that flew at his opponent; Shun was forced to leap left and dodge the lethal cold. Large sections of the surroundings disappeared with a crackling sound into the black voids before they dissipated. Jon then formed and moved through a black hole, reemerging to charge Shun head-on, but the warrior, anticipating the foray, jumped and ascended upward, launching rapid fireballs out as he climbed. Dissuaded from his attack, the elder Flint leaped back. Shun spun midair and pursued, launching downward in a swooping motion, seemingly to strike at his opponent with Haborym straight on. Jon dodged the blow, but Haborym's resulting impact with the ground generated a fiery ring that expanded outward. Jon could not evade. He made a black hole to absorb the fire and create an opening. Sneering, Shun power leaped back just as multiple small black holes opened around his previous position, expelling the fire in directed bursts, obliterating the area. Undaunted, the two clan heirs vaulted towards each other, meeting in the open air above the decimated landscape, exchanging blow for blow as they soared across the terrain.

Farther down the valley, Alex and Kaguya battled with the remaining two Sanxing. As Lu and Shou moved against them, generating characteristic liquid and lightning-based energy waves, the two Wielders raised their respective barriers, deflecting each attack. Without pause, they responded. Alex unleashed a vertical fire wave as Kaguya created a lateral, crescent-shaped blue wave that coalesced and sped across the ground; the Sanxing took to dodging rather than deflecting. As he vaulted to the top of a large rock crag, Shou generated a series of overhead lightning strikes that converged on the Flint Pirates. Both warriors vaulted away, only to be forced into further evasion as Lu added his own "rain shower" to the attack, effectively generating a cloudless storm. Neither the lightning nor the drops so much as grazed either of the attacking Flint Wielders.

Alex responded by firing a scattershot of fireballs from his left hand, and Kaguya manifested three kunai, launching them at high speed as well, the fire and the energy infused throwing blades forcing the Sanxing back. The two warriors in black and gold charged their enemies, again bringing their respective Devilblades against their adversary's, Alex battling Shou as Kaguya clashed against Lu. All the while, not too far in the distance, Jon and Shun again reached ground level, Astaroth and Haborym continuing to strike in rapid succession.

As had occurred many years ago, the fighting would indeed bring a final, irrevocable conclusion to the present war. However, whereas the fated duel between Morganna Flint and Fuma Kotaro was said to have lasted a "mere" three hours, there was no such foreseeable time-span in the present battle between the Flints and the Red Phoenix, as all six Wielders brought more and more of their individual skills and powers against one another.

It had only just started, so would it end when the victors stood atop the inactive, reverted Devilblades of the other. Such a conclusion seemed distant as the harsh clangs of manifested metal, the myriad impacts of energy attacks, the corresponding explosions of rock and earth, and the howling battle cries of the Wielders echoed throughout the valley. All while, well within the background, the sun continued to set into the horizon...

Chapter XXII: Clash of the Heavenly Beasts

Red Phoenix dreadnought *Guangdong* Gaochang System

Wretched umbras, Captain Qin Guofeng thought as he watched the two ships in question continue their evasive maneuvers, keeping ahead of his mighty warship's main batteries but only just. If anything, the captain of the most powerful vessel within the Red Armada should have been insulted for his ship, which had been designed to engage entire battlefleets, to be relegated down to exterminating such lowly vermin. Wounded vermin at that, as neither the *Sun* nor her Blue Dragon comrade seemed inclined to cloak, instead attempting to engage the *Guangdong* in a more traditionally open manner. Either way, Qin still felt vexed over the whole advent to the point of noticeable irritation; again, he and the *Guangdong* deserved much better than this. Even so, as his orders came straight from Lady Ching, he had little choice in the matter. At least he could avenge his clan's losses at Taishan and elsewhere, up to and including the attack

275

on Bayue of all places. That would amount to some measure of glory, he assured himself.

"Main cannons fire!"

Again did *Guangdong*'s immense guns aim and fire, and again did the *Sun* and the Blue Dragon ship move into evasion, neatly circumventing – but still only just – the beams without so much as taking a shield graze. Qin only glowered at the pair. Vermin they may have been, but the fact was they were much smaller as well as faster than his dreadnought. Though they could not – would not – escape him, the fact remained that they could move around the *Guangdong*'s firepower the way insects could scurry around a bootheel and were doing so rather efficiently. Not that Qin was overly surprised, nor when the Blue Dragon umbra, whose name still escaped him and everyone else, much to his compounding irritation, dove all too neatly underneath a converging missile attack, its phalanx intercepting the projectiles as they flew overhead. The *Sun* was helmed by the Lady Killer, whose piloting skills were of the highest renown, and the Blue Dragon ship would naturally have her own master helmsman. And as damaged as either vessel was, their arc engines remained otherwise fully functional, which meant it would take some time and effort yet before even one was blown across the stars. Much to Qin and his crew's exasperation, of course.

Once again, the captain of the mightiest ship in the Red Phoenix's muster could only take solace. Though this battle was far from the trial by fire he had hoped to bring her into, the fact remained both enemy ships were responsible for eight direct attacks against his clan, and one way or the other, they had to be destroyed. If that meant having to utilize the proverbial hammer that was his ship to smash these two particular ants, then Qin would follow his Lady's command accordingly. Far too many lesser ships had already fallen to the umbras anyway, so he supposed there was wisdom in sending his dreadnought against them. He just hoped that he would be done with them before Master Shun was finished with his own set of vermin.

"Torpedo launch from the *Sun!* Two incoming!" the tactical operator reported in warning as two projectiles fired from the designated
umbra's bow. Qin only sniffed contemptuously as he watched the
high-powered weapons surge into his vessel's immense portside,
only to detonate almost unnoticeably against her shields. For whatever enhancements that Maximilian Braun may have made to those
weapons, they were still outmatched by his ship's defenses. Much as
the sting of a hornet or the bite of a snake was upon a rhinoceros.

Resist all you want, hàichóng, *for, in the end, you will burn before
me all the same,* Qin thought with a subtle yet quite vengeful smile,
watching as the two umbras struggled on.

Though it would take more time and effort than he would have liked,
the fact – nay, the *truth* – was that the battle had been decided the
moment the *Guangdong* had first appeared. The two lesser ships
could dodge and evade, as well as fight back on some level, all they
wanted, but eventually, they would succumb to him and his ship, no
matter who was at the helm or who was in command. Elusive the ants
they may be, but so long as the hammer remained and the hand that
wielded it was unblemished, it would eventually fall. And the impact
thereafter would be as undeniable as it would be spectacular.

Valley of the Dragons
Gaochang IV

More fire rained across the field, forcing Jon to recede as he dodged
and evaded each descending flame. Shun persisted, refusing his
opponent time to possibly generate a black hole and absorb the fire.
As he converged on Jon's position, he again raised Haborym for an
overhead strike. Jon skirted by power leaping to the left and sweeping
Astaroth about to generate a downward black wave, which Shun
was just able to raise a barrier to dispel, retaliating with a vertical
flaming barrage that sped toward the Flint captain. Pausing, Jon
reached out and formed a black hole, absorbing the flames. Shun

cursed to himself before leaping away, the elder Flint pursuing this time around. Black holes opened all around the Red Phoenix warrior, and flames shot at him from all directions, including directly under his feet. As he danced about avoiding the absolute cold of the black and dispersing the fire, he was unable to divine Jon's approach until he heard the hiss of his blade slicing through the air. Parring with Haborym at the last second, he blocked the killing stroke. Obsidian and carmine blades again slammed together in repetition as both Wielders charged against the other from different vectors, otherwise unable to overcome the other's resilience.

Landing some distance away from their latest clash, Jon again swept his Devilblade about, generating no less than five black swells that surged across the valley floor, splaying out as they extended toward his opponent's position. Naturally, Shun evaded, ascending up and over the multi-attack, then launching himself downward after the elder Flint. Jon reacted instantly, raising Astaroth to deflect, only for Shun to flip up and over the moment Haborym made contact, landing directly behind Jon. Pivoting, he swept his blade in a bifurcating motion, only for Jon to vault to the right before the fiery edge could so much as graze his torso. Midflight, Jon opened and moved into a black hole, which closed immediately, thwarting Shun's attempt to chase after. Another black hole opened behind the Red Phoenix warrior, discharging Shun's prior attack and forcing him to power leap away again. Once more, he cursed, remembering that skill from Atalanta all too well.

Fortunately, or unfortunately, for Shun, Jon was not interested in antagonizing him so much as killing him straight on. Generating another black hole off to his opponent's right, Jon emerged once more, initiating a black wave that would have engulfed Shun in his entirety had the opposite scion not been anticipating the move. Shun sent off a counterwave that effectively split the attack down the middle, then charged to meet his opponent head-on again. More clangs erupted between the black and red blades, some of the executed attacks further enhanced with their respective blade's powers, but again neither Jon nor Shun were able to land anything more than minor blows upon the other. And then Jon jumped away, a set of circling black blades suddenly appearing around Shun, which moved with him as he attempted to follow. Realizing all too well what was about to happen, Shun was forced to yet again abandon his attack, effectively double jumping to evade the blades as they converged in an instant. More black blades formed overhead as he landed, raining down almost simultaneously upon their Wielder's command.

Even so, the heir of the Red Phoenix Clan was far from finished. As soon as he was clear, he pooled Haborym's power around him, spawning a series of flaming whirlwinds – seemingly plagiarizing his opponent's attack –complimented by fiery hail that swept across the ground. Such was the overwhelming nature of the combined attack that Jon had to alternate between dodging the cyclones as well as generating black holes to absorb as much of the hail as he could while still moving, doing well to keep ahead of all of it. He made sure not to let any of the flames reach him; the pirate captain felt his opponent's fire had somehow intensified, such that he dared not let any of it so much as touch his clothing, lest it immolate him instantly.

Shun continued his onslaught, launching a follow-up attack in the form of a fiery beam that he swept from one end of the valley to the other as he would swing his sword. Rocks and outcroppings were pulverized upon contact as the ambient temperature climbed rapidly. Jon disappeared under the beam, descending into a black hole. Reappearing at the top of a distant cliff, he literally returned the fire, utilizing Shun's hail, once again expelling the flaming pellets from black holes that manifested around the Red Phoenix warrior. Only then was Shun forced to abandon the offensive and evade, with Jon moving against him soon after.

Thus the fire and darkness clashed incessantly, both Wielders again entering melee range and bringing their physical blades against the other, only for each attack to be repelled or evaded as before.

As determined as they were to finish off the other then and there, Jon and Shun both remained in full form, attacking, deflecting, and evading in near systematic fashion as they fought. Their sordid dance compounding the previous damages to the valley, but not yet afflicting the other. It would remain just so for much time yet seemingly, as the heirs to the Gold Dragon and the Red Phoenix battled against the other with full, unrelenting force.

———————————————————

Raising Forneus up to parry, Alex easily deflected Dian Shou's intended strike, knocking the Sanxing warrior back. Though his adversary was one-armed, the younger Flint was not about to take any chances with an opposing Wielder – especially one that had kept up with Lorelei to some extent – and so pressed the attack, executing three successive fire shots as Shou cut into a rightward dash. Remaining as evasive as ever, the Sanxing dodged all three waves before slashing his own blade about, sending a series of lightning pillars at the younger Flint, who zigzagged around two or three before leaping up and over. Wisely, Shou chose to leap back the moment Alex landed, striking the ground with Forneus, the impact triggering a full one hundred eighty degree fire wave that encompassed all over a fair distance, yet still diminished before it could reach its intended target. The moment it did, the Red Phoenix attempted to charge headlong, but Alex was faster and clashed Forneus directly against Furfur while keeping Shou firmly on the defensive. Additional clashes of metal, as well as fire and lightning, quickly followed.

"You're not the one I wanted," Shou glowered with real disappointment, all the while attempting to force his opponent into submission. "And worse, you're far less of a challenge than she was."

"The feeling's mutual sparkles," Alex smirked, an all too certain gleam coming into his eyes as his adversary actually recoiled from the unforeseen slight. "I wanted to fight someone with *two* arms."

Letting out an affronted bellow, Shou generated additional bursts of lightning from above, forcing Alex to recede before any of them could touch him. The force of each strike was enough to crater deep into the valley floor, as well as generate sonic booms upon impact, though compared to the unlamented Lei Fu's usage of Amdusias, the latter blasts were barely noticeable to Alex. Still, he wanted to end this as fast as he could and counterattacked by generating a fire pillar under Shou's feet, forcing the Sanxing to power leap away. Alex augmented the assault with no less than three additional pillars, each igniting the moment his opponent's feet touched dirtside again. When Shou landed on an unstable rock-strewn escarpment, Alex charged. Shou naturally raised Furfur up to defend, but Alex, knowing that the Sanxing had only recently lost his left arm, moved against his enemy's left side, Forneus aglow with fiery energy as he attacked. Unfortunately, the blade didn't connect as Shou yet remained fast enough to dodge, but the intense heat from Forneus' proximity combined with his unsteady footing was more than enough to throw the Sanxing off. He fell backward and tumbled down the incline. Alex twisted around and launched a fire wave, which the Sanxing just managed to deflect with a timely swipe from Furfur as he regained his balance.

"Sǐ pì yǎn!" Shou bellowed at his attacker as he fired a concentrated lance of his Devilblade's energy. Yellow lightning arced across Furfur's length. "I'll spike your head on my blade!"

"One-armed and *short-bladed* as well," Alex taunted as he dodged the energy bolt, grinning with patronizing delight while crimson fire emanated across Forneus. "Far be it for me to face a man with *two* crippling handicaps, but have at me stumpy!"

Unable to restrain his fury, Shou flew at the younger Flint once more; Alex leaped into the air to meet the Sanxing directly. Through their next line of slashes, evasion, and parries, Alex again emphasized the Red Phoenix's missing limb, attacking randomly yet all too deliberately against Shou's left flank at any given opportunity, driving the proverbial knife that much deeper into his opponent. Again, Alex wanted to end him as quickly as possible, without forcing him to the point of Possession, of course. He knew from Lorelei's description that this particular Sanxing was more unstable than the others, more prone to emotional retaliation. All it would take was to bring him to the precise edge, the same edge he had brought Ivan Baranov and Lei Fu toward not too long ago, and then make that little push.

Until that point, however, the Red Devil held his own, attacking with Forneus' physical blade and fire against his adversary's blade and lightning. All the while moving about the valley in rapid motion, Shou's infuriated visage remaining as constant a force throughout as Alex's impish and all too aggravating smile.

Energy "raindrops" falling across the field as they both ran, Kaguya weaved around each one in graceful succession as Lu concentrated his attack, attempting to snuff out the kunoichi at the onset. Upon sighting her next opening, the ninja countered with an iridescent crescent wave, which Lu chose not to attempt deflection against and instead dodged altogether. Much like the shuriken and kunai, the latter which Kaguya was quick to manifest and launch after Lu, Kimaris' energy attacks were swift and far more powerful than its Wielder's "basic" ninjutsu. Relentless, the Dragon Princess formed five glistening hoops of light, launching them as one upon Lu, who was again forced to power leap away. They impacted and cratered the ground where he had been. Responding fast, the Sanxing fired a water wave at the Flint pirate, only for Kaguya to power slash, once again in the form of a crescent moon, and cancel out the attack. Blue eyes glaring, promising pain and death, she charged after the Saxing.

The two blades quickly clashed, their Wielders glowering at each other as they remained locked together for a few more moments. With a surge of energy, both separated and then attacked again, slashing their respective Devilblades about with speed and precision, both attempting to strike and potentially slay the other with but a single stroke. Unfortunately, they were just as adept at defending against their opposite, alternating between deflection and evasion as they kept up the sheer momentum. And then, once more, Kimaris and Crocell connected, their blades aglow in their respective tones of blue, their Wielders glaring into the other's eyes, bringing about the full force of their physical strength and willpower to overcome their adversary.

"Know your place, *jìnǔ*," Lu snarled into Kaguya's face as he increased Crocell's pressure against her blade. "Or be swept aside."

Despite his great application of strength, the kunoichi firmly held her ground with enough force that the Sanxing actually felt himself on the verge of being overcome.

"The Sea controls the Rain," Kaguya declared with even more ferocity, drawing further upon Kimaris' power for her next attack. "And the Moon controls the Sea."

With that declaration, the kunoichi triggered a point-blank light wave that threw the Sanxing back a large distance. Kaguya then capital-ized on the strike by launching an even larger crescent wave that Lu was again forced to dodge. Incensed at the Flint *chòu biǎozi*, the Red Phoenix initiated further raindrops to fall from above; the ninja again danced around each droplet as she closed in. Another "water" breaker flew at her, alongside additional rainfalls, but she continued to disperse each energy attack as she advanced upon her opponent.

And of course, Kaguya couldn't help but muse as she caught sight of her partner with her peripheral vision; he was still fighting his own Sanxing in the background. Though Alex remained as stalemated against Dian Shou as she was against Meng Lu, the Red Phoenix fighter now retreating as flaming meteors fell from above, the Dragon Princess still could not help but grin to herself as she saw the younger Flint fight. *The Moon draws its light from the Sun.*

Feeling reassured with that knowledge, the kunoichi continued her attack, generating four energy indued kunai in her left hand and launching them out, the blades all flying at great speed and a perfect splayed trajectory. Lu moved to evade again, only for one of the blades to graze his left arm, making him feel like he had just dodged a beam cannon blast. Kaguya rapidly formed an oversized, energy-composed shuriken, which she threw after the Sanxing as well, nearly splitting him at waist level. Actually growling at the ninja's constant attacks, Lu generated and fired off a series of waterspouts, which arrayed outward before converging upon Kaguya, forming a veritable tornado. The assault was insufficient to slow Kaguya down; she power leaped well out of range before contact could be made, right before firing off a vertical crescent wave that cut deep into the ground as it extended across the terrain.

Blue Dragon umbra *Tsushima*
Gaochang System

Damned monster! Kazama managed to think amid *Tsushima*'s present maneuver, which narrowly brought the ship around the *Guangdong*'s next beam cannon barrage. His tactical officer responded just as quickly, firing the umbra's main cannons, which held a similar yield to the *Sun*'s. Yet these were just as easily repelled by the giant's impenetrable shielding, the beams almost *splattering* against the invisible barriers. All the while, her main guns turned to track the *Tsushima* once more, firing as soon as they achieved target lock.

Not for the first time since the battle began did Kazama wonder just how the Red Phoenix could have built such a juggernaut of a ship. No, the Treaty of Libertalia did not forbid the development of dreadnoughts between the clans, but it still must have taken much of the Red Phoenix's resources to just establish the production facilities, let alone construct the ship itself. He could not imagine what had driven Lady Ching, or the late Lord Ching Heung, to have such a thing made, especially when those same resources and efforts could have gone into another battlefleet. Just as he had difficulty understanding how the Red Phoenix had kept the *Guangdong*'s existence secret for so long, eluding even the Blue Dragon's intelligence network.

Not that such inquiries truly mattered in the present, however, not nearly as much as how Kazama and his allies intended to finish the thing off. Fortunately, as damaged as she remained with her partner, the *Tsushima* stayed well in the fight, moving into an ascent while launching torpedoes from all six of her tubes. Though the torpedoes were no more effective in piercing the *Guangdong*'s shields than the *Tsushima*'s previous attacks, it allowed the umbra some maneuvering room, namely to move up and over the massive dreadnought, taking her out of range of her enemy's main cannons for a few moments. Unfortunately, there were still her phalanx, which, while unable to break through the *Tsushima*'s shields, as drained as they were, still took a fair-sized chunk out of them as she completed her hurdle. Now directly off the *Guangdong*'s starboard, the umbra's rear cannons both fired as one. Their beams had as little effect as their bow counterparts.

Simultaneously, the *Black Sun* moved to assist, firing a torpedo barrage upon the *Guangdong*'s port quarter, ensuring that the dreadnought's weapons were not wholly focused upon one ship. Shun was grateful to Kapta Barbarossa for that, especially as he knew the synchronization and the superior mobility of the two umbras were what was keeping the *Guangdon* from destroying them. It wasn't much, and it certainly wouldn't keep them ahead of the juggernaut for very long, but it kept them alive all the same. As long as that remained so, he and/or Barbarossa would figure out a way to kill it.

"All tubes reloaded," the TO quickly reported.

"Ute!" Kazama called out before lowering his command scope to watch the next six torpedoes exit their tubes and lance out against the dreadnought, slamming against her shields in only a few moments. Again the damage was negligible, but Kazama gazed over the recorded data anyway. Somehow and some way this big, ungainly *kuso yarō* of a starship had a chink in her armor, and he was going to

find it. Just as he knew Barbarossa was looking for that same chink from the *Sun*, even as the two umbras continued to speed and evade around each of the dreadnought's cannon fire.

Even so, the question remained with Kazama and those around him, just how much longer could they last?

Chapter XXIII: Blazing Cascade

Valley of the Dragons
Gaochang IV

The sun had set well below the horizon now, altering the sky as night moved in place of day. This had little bearing on either of the two warriors, however, as both Jon and Shun retained their momentum, the respective powers of the blades remaining in the forefront. In fact, their battle had only intensified with neither Wielder showing any sign of slowing their pace, much less capitulating to the other, their individual expressions, both fierce and sanguinary, actively seeking to finish the other then and there. To end all that had started at Atalanta, the memories of which, as well as Penglai, remained foremost between them.

Swinging Astaroth about and stabbing its obsidian blade into the ground, Jon formed a series of black pillars that erupted from the soil surrounding Shun, driving him to abandon his offensive. He receded with a power leap but not before he was struck with the forward edge of one pillar, the hem of his sleeve immediately obliterated by the cold black void. The elder Flint gave chase, flying through the air as he hurled another energy attack in the form of a dark churning squall, which blew after the Red Phoenix warrior. Turning in flight, Shun rapidly spun Haborym generating a flaming vortex that sucked the squall inside and eradicated the danger. Continuing his offensive, the Wielder created a lateral fire wave that effectively split the terrain as it rushed across the valley, its flames rising high enough into the air to potentially strike the elder Flint as he completed his descent. Jon, however, reacted quickly, twisting right and altering his flight path to evade the inferno. He landed a short distance away. Immediately, Shun rushed him again, Haborym positioned to impale; undaunted, Jon raised Astaroth. Once again, Astaroth collided with Haborym in a thunderous knell, the pangs of metal striking metal, with fire and darkness blazing throughout the valley adding further to the desolation.

During that momentary clash, Jon and Shun both glared deeply into the other's eye. Through his own ire, Jon saw that Shun no longer contained his emotions, his fury and vehemence blazing with a similar intensity as his Devilblade. The elder Flint took some measure of triumph in that, having at last broken his opponent's composure, to such an extent that Shun had yet to even realize it. Not that Jon really cared if he did or not, as he drew further power from Astaroth and flung his opponent back into the relative distance, then followed up with another black wave. Shun dodged, turned, and counterattacked with additional fireballs, which rained with ethereal force around the Flint Pirate as he eluded the flames.

Further fire bursts also erupted from the ground, extending upward each time Jon touched down from power leaping, compelling him to move farther than he had intended. During one such attack, Jon spread his left hand out and formed a small black hole, which drew the dark flames into its swirling maw as he moved to another part of the valley. Glowering deeply when he saw it, Shun was forced to leap away as a secondary black hole formed over him, the flames falling downward in a thick column that burned deep into the valley's surface. Had he not moved at the precise moment, Shun had little doubt he would have been completely incinerated.

So concentrated was he on that single attack that Shun failed to notice Jon moving again, the elder Flint having already slipped through another black hole while a second took form at Shun's right. The Red Phoenix caught sight of the oncoming attack and attempted to escape, but he was far too late to avoid it entirely at that point. Emerging from the dark vortex with great speed, Jon launched straight at his adversary, slashing a deep cut on Shun's right flank as he shot by. Again Jon felt a surge of triumph as he touched the ground and leaped away again, having, at last, drawn blood.

Incensed by the wound, Shun twisted around and launched off successive fire waves, each larger and faster than the previous. Jon evaded all of them with consecutive maneuvers right before abruptly vanishing upon the last wave actually hitting. Realizing all too quickly that had been a doppelganger, Shun power leaped upward, just the actual Jonathan Flint moved in from directly behind, slashed, and caught Shun on the left ankle. The elder Flint then vaulted away as Shun launched another fire wave at his location, one that Jon couldn't help but feel was hastily generated, the entire ground becoming engulfed in flames with the impact. The heat was so extreme and sheering that Jon felt it even as he stood on a small cliff in the relative distance.

Once more did Shun pursue the *Sun's* captain, Haborym striking headlong against Astaroth as both Wielders entered into a running battle. Fire and darkness erupting and dissipating near systematically, the heirs of the Gold Dragon and the Red Phoenix maintained their bout as they charged through the battleground. The momentum, and the intensity, only rising as both Wielders gradually moved more and more toward the inevitable conclusion.

Red Phoenix dreadnought *Guangdong*
Gaochang System

"Damn it all," Qin cursed under his breath as the Blue Dragon ship evaded the next barrage from the *Guangdong*'s main cannons, right before responding with her own guns. The counterattack was no more effective against the *Guangdong*'s shields than those previous, but it was still irritating that he had yet to truly hit either of his two targets, let alone stamp them out entirely. It was all becoming increasingly frustrating, and Qin was not a man that took to being frustrated.

"Come about! All missile batteries, fire!"

With that, the whole of space seemingly exploded with fire as the dreadnought's missile tubes launched as one, sending multitudes of guided projectiles out from her immense broadsides. Immediately, the missiles locked onto their targets and moved in, with the *Sun* and her counterpart's phalanx igniting upon the warheads' approach, throwing out point-defense beam fire to intercept. Again Qin cursed to himself as he watched the two ships shoot down the missiles as well as maneuver, both to keep ahead of the projectiles as well as unmask their gun emplacements against them. Soon enough, space was alight with fire once again, this time with the amassed detonations of the missile barrage as the two umbras continued all but entirely unblemished.

Will nothing squash these zázhǒng *insects!?* Qin thought with rising anger as the last of the detonations died down, and the enemy ships retaliated with their own dual torpedo shots. No, he *still* wasn't worried about them actually damaging his ship at some point, but the fact remained this was presently a perfect standoff. The umbras couldn't hurt the *Guangdong*, yet they were too small and elusive for the dreadnought's heavier weaponry, while their own defenses were resilient enough to withstand her missiles and phalanx. And though Qin knew it was taking much in the way of energy for either ship to keep ahead of his, such that they could never hope to with-stand him forever, it was still borderline infuriating that his great dreadnought had yet to even critically damage them. And the more time it took for the *Guangdong* to destroy her targets, the more Qin knew he would hear of it from Lady Ching upon their return to Penglai.

"Bow cannons, target the *Black Sun*! Fire!" Qin called out again, seeing that the *Black Sun* was attempting to maneuver close in once more. With the designated turrets swiveling and angling toward the oncoming umbra, the *Guangdong*'s main batteries roared yet again, sending immensely sized beam fire streaking across space. It should have been an inescapable kill, against any other ship it would have been, but the *Sun* maneuvered around the fire all the same, shifting to starboard the way a man would have sidestepped an oncoming charge. Worse, Qin realized that in his concentration against the *Sun*, the Blue Dragon ship had slipped around to the *Guangdong*'s stern and launched another pair of torpedoes, both aligned perfectly with the dreadnought's arc engine. Again her shields remained unyielding, but Qin was under no illusions toward what would have occurred had they not been.

No, Qin corrected himself, the fact was *his* ship and crew couldn't keep this up forever. As much as he believed in either, he could not risk the passage of time against this enemy, an enemy that was clearly probing his ship for any viable weak point. Not that he expected either the Beast King or whoever was commanding the Blue Dragon ship to find any, but at the same time...

It is the sting of the smallest insect that causes the most pain, Qin recalled that proverb from the annals of his Clan's history, having been first spoken by an anonymous philosopher, who went onto describe the sting of an Ancient Terran bumblebee as compared to the equally ancient bullet ant. Indeed, that was what he was facing here, he knew. Though the *Guangdong* was a thick-hided beast, her shields and armor all but impregnable, he knew a bypassing sting from either of these insects would be crippling all the same. Thus he had to stomp them flat as quickly as possible before either found a suitable soft spot.

"Fighter status?"

"Fighters may deploy at any time," his first officer announced when prompted.

"Send them out!" Qin commanded straight away, watching as the black and red smallcraft launched out moments later.

The fighters wouldn't accomplish too much, he knew, but at the very least, they would hinder the umbras on some level. And though the *Guangdong* also carried a bomber contingent, Qin did well to know that such would be easy pickings for said enemy fighters and that, as best shown at Ephesus, the *Sun* (at least) could weather through multiple torpedo shots even without her shields. Besides, the Red Phoenix captain didn't want to play his entire hand at once.

My bootheel will find you yet, Qin thought derisively as his fighters advanced against the two enemy ships, who were now launching their own smallcraft to match. A great dogfight ensued thereafter, the Flint and Blue Dragon fighters contending with their Red Phoenix counterparts as their respective motherships continued to do the same.

Valley of the Dragons
Gaochang IV

More lightning bursts lanced down around him, forcing Alex to increase his evasiveness as he weaved through the barrage. More and more, the younger Flint was beginning to see why Lorelei had had so much trouble against this particular Sanxing; it was like trying to fight an actual thunderstorm, in which all of the lightning was directed straight at his person. Not that Alex hadn't fought individuals that used some lightning manifestations before, but Dian Shou was clearly in a league, as well as a mental sphere, of his own, much to Alex's rather mounting aggravation. It also helped less that he was a particularly speedy bastard; when Alex formed and launched another barrage of fireballs, the Red Phoenix warrior leaped away well before the first had ever impacted, then retaliated with more lightning, both from above and laterally. Eventually, Alex was forced to power leap to prevent injury in which he moved straight after his opponent, Forneus soon clashing against Furfur.

"Not a bad light show," Alex gleamed as he drove his blade against Shou's, who visibly struggled to hold back Forneus. The younger Flint took note of this as well. Obviously, his opponent was not used to fighting with one blade, much less one arm. "Are you available for theme parks?"

"Insolent bastard!" Shou barked as he put more power into his single blade and threw Alex back, then retaliated again with another lightning wave. Rather than raise a barrier, Alex simply swiped the lightning aside with a deft parry, sending it back to its originator, but then was forced to recede even further as a barrage of lightning struck around him.

"Ah, don't be like that!" Alex continued to call out as he maneuvered around the increasingly assorted attacks, making a show of "batting away" the lightning bolts, only countering occasionally with fire waves, pillars and cyclones. Though he knew he wouldn't be able to take out Shou in such a long-range duel, his usual banter and insolence were having a noticeable effect. Which it always did, much to Alex's pride in retaining his touch.

"Think of the children! How much joy you'd...!"

"Zhùkǒu!" Shou snarled again, his aggravation that much more apparent, alongside the intensity of his attacks, which Alex

continued to rather blatantly dodge and deflect. Further infuriated, as a result, Shou slashed Furfur about and drove after the younger Flint, raising his blade overhead to cleave Alex apart. The younger Flint evaded this as well, the lighting infused blade simply splitting and scorching the ground.

"I'll scatter your ashes around this valley, pretender's son!"

"Yeah, yeah, yeah," Alex laughed all the more as he hurled a smaller, more concentrated stream of fire that would have bifurcated Shou at the waistline had the latter not leaped over it. The wave "merely" slammed into a nearby outcropping, obliterating the whole structure, while Alex lunged upward to clash Forneus once more against his opponent's sword.

"Big words from a one-armed lightning bug!" Alex sneered once more, pushing the Sanxing that much further toward the awaited edge. He wasn't there yet, but the younger Flint knew he was gaining ground and quite fast. "Your friend Fu might not have been much, but he had both to *handle* himself with!"

Again Shou let a bellow, alongside corresponding lightning that cut deeply across and around the field. So fast were those attacks that Alex again had to focus on dodging as well as deflecting, raising barriers at key moments to avoid being struck. In the midst of the wanton bursts, the Sanxing surged forward again, an elongated, lightning-based energy blade extended from Furfur. He slashed after the younger Flint repeatedly, only for Alex to evade the larger portion of the attack. Unfortunately, just enough managed to reach him, inflicting a small cut on his shoulder instead of nearly cutting away his right arm had Alex not corrected his movement in time. The Red Devil gritted his teeth at the sharp and intense pang, feeling as though an entire ship's worth of electricity had shot through his body in an instant before abruptly canceling out.

That would not be enough to slow him down, Alex knew, as he

formed and generated a flare attack, blinding Shou in that brief moment. The younger Flint then executed a fiery slash that would have killed the Sanxing then and there. Still, Shou was fast enough to withdraw again, power leaping into the distance while firing another xanthic lance after his enemy. Fortunately, the attack was poorly aimed, enough that Alex hadn't really needed to dodge, thereby allowing the concentrated lightning to bore itself into another valley edifice, which exploded instantly after contact. Meanwhile, the younger son of Morganna Flint pursued his opponent. The latter was just able to clear away his blindness as the Red Devil came upon him once more, a further enflamed Forneus slashing at neck level, only for Shou to quickly intercept with Furfur.

"Pardon the expression, but look on the bright side," Alex chimed again, this time with more viciousness as he forced pressure on his opponent. "When I'm done here, lefty won't be the only thing you'll be without!"

"I can say the same to you," Shou snarled as he held his ground. "Your brother, that psion woman... I'll lay out the entirety of your crew beside your *thoroughly* incinerated corpse!"

"Just you try sparky," Alex taunted, right as Shou forced Forneus away and counterslashed, only for Alex to deflect that attack as well. Thus did the melee resume, with that much more fire and lightning between the two Wielders.

Gaochang System

Well, this one's a little different, Boss thought as her eyes fell upon the *Guangdong* in all of her one kilometer plus glory, just behind her oncoming fighter contingent. In lieu of the usual battlefleet, she and her fellow Corsairs and Buccaneers were up against one ship. A very big, very mean ship that effectively stood in for said battlefleet, alongside the multitudes of smallcraft that she had carried with her. The latter already converging upon the Corsairs and Shidens, those armed with missiles fired straight away before closing to vulcan range. The Flint and Blue Dragon fighters returned fire in earnest as the two sides merged and then scattered, breaking apart into smaller actions in but a few seconds. All while in the relative background, their motherships continued to trade fire, or more specifically, the *Sun* and *Tsushima* continued to dodge as the *Guangdong* continued to shrug off everything that was thrown at it.

Knowing better than to even think about making a run on the dreadnought, Boss did only what she could do at the moment and found a target among the swarm, which turned out to be one of the Jians. The angular fighter was fast and nimble as she had seen firsthand at Taishan, but that was hardly a hindrance to the Blue Comet, who immediately fell upon the Red Phoenix craft with great and terrible vengeance. A single burst was all it took to pierce its shielding and obliterate it straight away, in turn causing its wingman to shift out and attempt to evade her. She quickly struck him down as well without so much as skipping a beat, at which point her sensors picked up another pair of Jians moving upon her in turn, their beam fire smashing against her shields before she maneuvered out of the line. Flipping about, she gunned down one of the oncoming light fighters and then turned to pursue the second. However, before she could line up her reticle, another line of heavier beam fire slammed against her shields, forcing her to abandon the pursuit.

"Asshole!" Boss cursed as she shifted targets toward the Dao that had fixed itself on her tail, barrel rolling to evade. Though she was quite used to fighting superior numbers, she didn't account for how concentrated the *Guangdong*'s contingent would be upon her and her cohorts, especially when they weren't occupied with escorting bombers or otherwise dealing with outlying targets. As a result, Boss had to take care not to get overwhelmed and banked right as the Dao pursued, firing more shots in her direction but otherwise hitting nothing except open space. Eventually, she found a clearing that allowed her to pull an Immelmann, looping up and flipping toward the opposite vector; only in the vacuum Boss was able to "tilt" her Corsair down as the Dao moved to pass, firing her vulcans as soon as they crossed and striking the Red Phoenix fighter from overhead. She wasn't able to see it explode entirely as she completed her pass, but the Dao was certainly trailing fire as it disappeared from her optics. And so the ace continued on.

Naturally, it wasn't long before more fighters, in this case three of the rather unusually designed Qiangs, found her and attacked. Compared to the light Jian and the heavy Dao, the Qiang could have been considered a medium fighter, which Boss found strangely resembling the ancient Shinden aerospace fighter from Terra's Second World War. Not that it had any real bearing on the present, however, as Boss again maneuvered her Corsair out of their firing line, restarting the chase. She executed a snap cobra and gunned down one of the three. The remaining two pursued entirely non-dissuaded.

Though she kept well ahead of the two Qiangs, Boss still had some difficulty maneuvering due to the sheer volume of enemy fighters around her, with many of the outlying Red Phoenix craft taking potshots at her as she moved past, if not attempting to pursue. That in itself emphasized the direness of this battle, the necessity toward a quick conclusion, as there was no way the forty-eight Corsairs and Shidens that composed her contingent, as well as the *Tsushima's*, would last against the literal hundreds of fightercraft from the *Guangdong*. Yes, her Corsairs had their Braun-given enhancements, which the Shidens seemed to replicate on some level, but that only meant so much in a contest of endurance, more so against a force that outnumbered them multiple times over.

Again, she could not concentrate on that in the current setting; instead, she focused on killing whatever enemy fell into her crosshairs. Thus when the opening presented itself, she came about in a left bank and swooped in, annihilating both Qiangs in a single pass, then moved on to additional targets.

Valley of the Dragons
Gaochang IV

The "rain", and corresponding blue waves, were nearly constant now as Kaguya dogged her target, Kimaris remaining materialized in her right hand while a larger bladed kunai formed in her left. Knowing how lethal she was at close-range, even *before* she had awakened her blade, it was obvious to the kunoichi that Meng Lu was attempting to keep back as much as possible, thus the present torrent that she was effectively wading her way through to reach him. Not that it would slow her down, however, as she abruptly hurled her kunai out. It cleaved its way through an oncoming water-like energy wave in the process, only for Lu to dash right to evade injury. Infused with its originator Devilblade's power, the throwing dagger ended up flying into a nearby ridge, destroying the entire elevation upon impact.

Kaguya continued to maneuver into melee range, Kimaris brought down to strike. Lu parried with Crocell as both Wielders effectively moved through the still falling "rain", slashing and parrying in that brief contact while also launching more liquid and crescent waves against the other. Kaguya raised her hand up and created her own set of rain, in this case, light beams, but Lu skirted these as well. He receded, and the ninja pursued.

Indeed, the Sanxing was attempting to keep his distance, much to the kunoichi's inner bemusement, especially upon recalling their previous two bouts and hubris therein. The strain was apparent across Meng Lu's form, even if he was trying to remain composed, which Kaguya relished. It wasn't so fun now that she was fighting on equal terms.

Still, that didn't mean she wanted to draw out this fight any more than necessary, an outcome that could very well occur given the Sanxing's newfound vigilance against her. So she continued to attack, launching three more lateral crescent waves that scarred the ground as they flowed, which Lu was forced to pivot and dodge left. She augmented the strike with another trio of manifested enhanced shurikens, thrown out in a splayed pattern. Only rather than continuing on as their target evaded, the three throwing stars detonated in midair, eliciting shockwaves that struck the Red Phoenix dead on, momentarily hindering Lu's hearing and sight. That inhibiting was enough for Kaguya to draw in again, her blade prepared to bifurcate Lu diagonally from left shoulder to right hip. The Sanxing refused to relent, immediately parrying the stroke while generating a more concentrated burst of "rain", which forced Kaguya away as it pummeled into the ground, cratering the area. A following blue wave elicited additional distance. However, the ninja retaliated with a wide horizontal crescent slash that swept across the field, nearly dividing Lu from his lower half in the process.

"Sǐ!" Lu bellowed, calling out for his opponent's death as he gathered energy and charged, appearing as a surging torrent as he drove at Kaguya again. For the first three charges, Kaguya evaded, acrobatically maneuvering around each and every assault. Upon the fourth, she raised Kimaris at the last second and generated a barrier, allowing Lu to run straight into it. Despite the sheer force of the impact, the barrier held against the Sanxing's assailment, allowing Kaguya to power slash at her enemy's torso. Another timely withdrawal kept Lu's body whole, but now he had a wide, bleeding gash across his chest coupled with burns and charred clothes. Unrelenting, Kaguya pursued, dodging another blue wave as she persisted, Kimaris and Crocell soon meeting each other again.

Further emphasizing the shift in this third battle, the Sanxing offered no banter as he held his ground, defending against the Dragon Princess's attacks and countering in kind while Kaguya kept up the offensive. Through the continuous strikes, maneuvers, and parrying, Kaguya found another semblance upon her opponent's form: fear. He feared her now, feared what would occur if her blade indeed reached him again. And the more he attempted to force back that emotion as he continued to fight her, the more it encompassed him, affected him, turning Meng Lu into a dreadful, desperate man. One akin to a snake staring into a dragon's maw.

Kaguya knew that would be his undoing, the very vulnerability she needed to exploit to end this battle, and him with it. Thus she kept up the pressure, even as he again leaped away and launched a more hastily generated blue wave. A lateral crescent wave was enough to cancel out the strike, thereby allowing Kaguya to chase after the Sanxing, who hurled additional attacks against her as she charged. Both Wielder and Devilblade wanting, seeking their enemy's blood as they closed in.

Flint Pirates umbra *Black Sun*
Gaochang System

"We're hit!" the tactical operator called out in warning as one of the *Guangdong's* main cannon blasts, at last, struck its target. "Shields down to twenty-one percent!"

Again that day did Barbarossa curse. It was bad enough that their shield power had already been diminished from Penglai, but if one shot had been sufficient to cause that sheer loss, the Leo would do well not to allow a second strike.

"Redirect all available power to shields! I want them back up as much as possible!" he ordered as he lowered the command scope, once more searching for any kind of weakness in the dreadnought's form, or at least an indication that his ship's attacks were having any kind of effect. Just as before, however, he found none; the *Guangdong*'s shields remained in place, and her hull entirely unblemished from all strikes. All the while, he and Captain Fuma were doing everything they could just to keep from getting hit, but as emphasized in that last instance, Barbarossa knew that would only last for so much longer.

Is there really nothing we can do!? he raged in his own mind, probing, trying to find something, anything that could be exploited. Unfortunately, he still found nothing. The *Guangdong* would have been difficult enough to fight if the *Sun* had been in full form, but as afflicted as she was now, the dreadnought was nigh impossible for them. Such that, had this been any other battle, Barbarossa would have had no choice but to withdraw then and there. *Nothing at all!?*

You're doing fine, Barbarossa, another voice entered his mind, reassuring both in words and in projected feelings. *Just stay ahead of it like you've been doing.*

"Hearing" that, Barbarossa glanced over to Lorelei's station, where he immediately noticed that the psion was now deep in concentration. At that, Barbarossa realized a certain key fact about his enemy. For all the *Guangdong*'s power and capabilities, she did not appear to be equipped with a Psi Disruptor.

With that realization, Barbarossa smiled a fanged grin as he nodded to the former thief. *It will be done,* he "thought" as he raised the command scope.

"Send to *Tsushima*," the Kapta stated to Gran. "Tell Captain Fuma to break off his attack and concentrate on evasion. *Until* the given signal."

More than one head turned upon this as they could only wonder what that signal was, but Gran followed the command regardless. Just as Barbarossa mirrored it for the *Sun* as well, the tactical operator abandoning his next intended barrage as Davis put more power into the helm, doing well keeping the *Guangdong* from hitting them again.

All the while Lorelei, and Izuna aboard the *Tsushima*, both focused on their shared task. Diving deeply into the given space and matter before them, seeking out that first point of convergence.

Chapter XXIV: Audacity of Dragons

Red Phoenix dreadnought *Guangdong*
Gaochang System

There was an Ancient Terran adage that was recalled as they delved through the various and seemingly infinite mechanisms of their target: the more one overthought the plumbing, the easier it was to stuff up the drain. Though neither of them could say that their target was overengineered in that area, after all, neither of them had a medium to compare it to, the fact remained it was a machine of immense size, which meant that it had more in the way of moving parts and systems to keep it active. And any of these moving parts and mechanisms could be exploited in such ways as to "clog the drain", as it were. It was merely a question of finding the ideal parts and going from there.

Fortunately, as one of the two happened to have been a thief in a not so distant lifetime, it wasn't too hard to identify the more vital parts of the whole, as well as what parts aligned with what system. Once they found the ideal striking point, the pair immediately set to work, akin to a couple of "gremlins" – themselves of Ancient Terran myth, particularly centered around the First Age's Second World War – that worked endlessly to sabotage machines from the inside out. It was hardly an ideal comparison for either of them, for gremlins, outside more vistoonish dispositions that either had come across in one form or the other, were said to be hideous, nightmarish creatures, whereas both preferred to think of themselves as the far, *far* opposite of such. That aside, neither could deny that, as they sifted through the internal parts and modules, they were doing much the same as a pair of utterly mischievous, if far more visually appealing, gremlins. Breaking and ruining the machine from the inside in such ways that it took the "mere" sabotaging of one part or another to cause the whole to eventually fail.

As pressed for time as they were, however, and given the aforementioned immense size of the machine in question, both women knew they had to work fast and that they had to strike at one system first in order to change events on the outside. Fortunately, it wasn't hard for them to designate and isolate that particular system, again using the former thief's expertise combined with her actually considerable knowledge in engineering, and then move to exploit. And though it took more than a few minutes to make the necessary "alterations", the pair's efforts eventually bore fruit as the last module was broken. From that, the intended chain reaction began as, one after another, parts and mechanisms began to fail in multiple areas, causing the entire system to fail with it. All in such a way that, while it had taken them a rather great amount of time to go about their labor, it took but a few moments for the failure to complete itself over the whole.

All while the machine's occupants remained blissfully unaware until the very last...

———————————— ————————————

"Sir, our shields are dropping!" the tactical officer called out in newfound urgency, causing the whole of the bridge to look up in sudden alarm.

"Raise them!" Qin ordered, feeling an equally sudden coldness begin to spread over him. Already he suspected what had just occurred was not through accident.

After a few moments of struggle, the TO shook his head. "I can't! System failure!" he responded in near panic.

Which was precisely when one of the umbras' launched torpedoes struck the *Guangdong's* port side, detonating with great thunder and causing the ship to nearly pitch. Though the *Guangdong* was too large to be damaged that badly by a single torpedo, the effect, as well as the subsequent quaking, was more than enough for the crew to realize. As were the beam and projectile shots that followed.

"Evasive maneuvers!" Qin commanded, glaring upon the two enemy ships with newfound loathing. They had to be the source. He didn't know how, or what, they did, but one or both of those ships had caused his shields to fail. Goddamned insects.

"Get those shields back online!"

"I'm trying, sir!" the tactical officer responded, visibly struggling with his station amidst the now repetitive quaking.

The *Guangdong* was still firing at her adversaries, but once again, the umbras' smaller size, speed, and maneuverability came into play, keeping either ship out of the dreadnought's sightline. In turn, the pair, not unlike predators sensing blood, pressed the attack with newfound relish, striking the *Guangdong* across her form with as much power and force as they could bring to bear upon her, such that fire continuously erupted across that black and red hull, even if the dreadnought otherwise weathered the damage and continued to fight.

All the while, unseen but still very much present within the mighty warship's internals, the "gremlins" went about further sabotage.

Valley of the Dragons
Gaochang IV

Fire and lightning again sparked and flew as the two Devilblades slammed together, both aglow in reflection of the Wielders' fervor. For a long moment, Alex held Forneus there against Furfur, forwardly appearing to struggle to maintain his ground against the increasingly infuriated Dian Shou, something that the Red Phoenix Wielder easily picked up on. Not that he was taken off guard by the Sanxing projecting more force through his blade as his ire heightened, Alex certainly had his power to contest. Through the struggle, the younger Flint recalled his previous fight on Penglai as well as the ultimate outcome with Lei Fu.

Only, it didn't affect him so much as it might have otherwise. Following that *very* brief moment of uncertainty, Alex remembered Kaguya's words. Words she spoke to him on the last night of their "confinement."

"Meddle not in the affairs of dragons, for you are crunchy and tasty with tonkatsu. *"*

"You're wavering, *zázhŏng*," Shou espoused, ending Alex's remembrance. The Saxing forced a vast amount of power into his single blade, sensing victory. Alex's bootheels slid against the dirt in an agonizing grind.

"Not as much as you think, sparkles," Alex responded back with another grin, increasing his strength through Forneus and ensuring the blades remained deadlocked. Then, without warning, Alex sent a power surge into the point of contact, reflecting the Red Phoenix's power back at him, causing a brilliant flash to erupt between the pair. Temporarily blind, only by sheer reflexes did Shou manage to evade the inevitable killing stroke, but not entirely. With a flame empowered slash, Alex elicited a deep, fiery cleave and corresponding burned flesh from scalp to chin across the right side of the Sanxing's head. A howling cry followed from the intensity of the strike.

Hearing that, Alex grinned in triumph, knowing that he had literally left a mark as the retaliatory lightning blasts took place. The thoroughly enraged Shou surged after Alex, swinging Furfur in a mighty arc. Just as Forneous clashed with the Saxing blade, Alex power leaped aside, effectively allowing the Sanxing to fall face down in the dirt. The resultant crash generated a massive upward column of lightning upon impact, actually forming a new, lunar-grade crater within the valley. While the shockwave struck the younger Flint midleap, Alex managed to maintain his velocity and launch one more fire wave for effect. With a snap sweep of his Devilblade, Shou raised a shield to protect against the attack then leaped to reengage, moving so fast that he was upon Alex within bare seconds. Once more did Forneus and Furfur converge, the resultant metallic clang even more powerful than the last.

"Now that's what I call extra crispy," Alex taunted, smiling broadly while staring into Shou's remaining functional left eye. The right was now wholly sealed behind a sheered, hairless eyelid. *And me without any* tonkatsu.

The Sanxing elicited an even greater bellow, generating a point-blank lightning wave that Alex effectively 'rode' back to ground level, having quickly developed a barrier to keep the attack from doing any damage. Landing on his feet as the attack dispelled, Alex kept his shield up as the Sanxing, who remained in midair, formed and generated additional waves and bursts of yellow lightning, each assault effectively pounding against Alex's barrier with rapid hammer-like force. Yet, even as he felt his boots dig further and further into the soil, Alex maintained his defense, his grip on Forneus almost pained as he kept the blade raised. Only when Shou launched himself straight down for the apparent finishing blow did Alex power lunge out of the way, though he was still buffeted by the shockwave that followed.

Yet again did Alex withstand the force; alighting on a large boulder, he utilized the momentum from the shockwave to propel himself off the surface and charge against Shou's right side. The Sanxing barely managed to raise his blade to parry the oncoming blow, only for Alex to lunge upward and over, landing on the Red Phoenix's opposite side. At that, the Flint brother momentarily dissipated his blade and spun, smashing his boot heel against the burned and bleeding side of Shou's face, once more eliciting an anguished cry. Several more punches and kicks followed, knocking the Sanxing back in pained dishevelment, from which Alex reformed Forneus and moved to execute an overhead hammer blow of his own. Only then was Shou able to defend himself, bringing Furfur up at the last moment to deflect the strike.

"Who's wavering now, *zhàzǐjī?*" Alex rejoined as he viciously loomed over the Sanxing, Forneus barely held back from splitting Shou into fiery halves.

"I will obliterate you *completely*, pretender's son!" Shou seethed through his strain and agony, once more generating a shockwave to fling Alex back and away from him. Again Alex landed in the distance, but rather than reform his barrier, he ran. And then suddenly, there were two Flints. No, three? Four?

Rapidly turning his head, Shou fought to focus his one good eye, which was the real pirate? Bursts of fire were shooting at him from all five 'Flints, ' making it impossible to identify the real warrior. Enraged, writhing with pain, the Saxing launched retaliatory lightning blasts at all five forms, from all angles, as well as additional wave and bolt attacks. The five Flint doppelgangers maneuvered around or deflected each strike, effectively dancing and laughing in belittlement as Shou focused more and more of his powers against them, his rage and frustration swiftly accelerating.

And then, just as suddenly, four of the forms dissipated as the real Alexander Flint returned to the air, hurling a massive fireball at the

Saxing. Shou quickly generated a barrier and leaped up to meet him. From that, blades slashed and rang as they both flew, Alex continuing to grin, if more forcibly this time, well into the Sanxing's charred, incensed visage. The fire and lightning exploding across the landscape.

———————————————————

Three more kunai impacted the ground around Lu, all exploding simultaneously and generating blue-tinted shockwaves that he was forced to evade. Even then, Kaguya refused to relent, charging and leaping straight after him, Devilblade raised to slash him across the left side. Still, the Sanxing was able to parry the blow at the right moment, as well as those that followed. Eventually, the two Wielders executed spontaneous power slashes, the resultant collision causing them to fly apart and land in distant areas. Of course, that didn't stop either of them; Kaguya raised her left hand up, generating seven overhead energy bursts that fell upon her opponent, their descent once more taking crescent-like form and forcing Lu to power leap back before he was annihilated in the collective impact. The Sanxing retaliated with his own overhead attack, an even greater "rainstorm". Kaguya immediately reentered a run and charged through the downpour.

The "rain" fell far more rapidly and with much greater power now, such that the craters they elicited in the ground around her were more akin to meteor impacts than anything else. Yet Kaguya moved and maneuvered through it all, appearing as a near blur while she evaded each and every drop, in turn, launching a spread of four shurikens at the Red Phoenix. Rather than dodge, Lu once more erected a barrier, the four spinning blades impacting and detonating as others had, effectively canceling both energies out. Almost immediately, Kaguya was upon him again, quickly entering a spin and executing a line of power slashes that the Sanxing didn't bother to attempt defending against. Instead, he lept away, just barely evading that particular attack, as several of the luminescent, crescent-like slashes nearly cleaved into him, one had been close enough that he felt its intensity against his skin.

"Will you kindly die already!?" Lu roared in augmented fury as he moved to strike, focusing liquid energy onto his blade and leaping high, Crocell poised to kill. Kaguya easily dodged the assault leaving Crocell to impact the ground, the resultant shockwave eliciting an even larger crater into the valley floor, pulverizing the surrounding boulders and generating rock slides, but failing to so much as graze the kunoichi.

"Qinglong jiàn nǚ rén!" Lu spat.

"Suzaku kusottare," Kaguya sneered in return, her voice and glare far more contemptuous.

She again executed a crescent wave, this one shorter ranged but larger and more powerful. Lu could not evade it fast enough. Responding quickly, the Sanxing formed another barrier, but it was ineffectual. His shield shattering almost instantaneously, the crescent buffeted over Lu, the force of the impact sending him flying back into a crashing heap in one of the newly formed craters. It didn't finish him, but the Sanxing had barely survived. Laying in the rubble at the bottom of the crater, he could tell at least 2 ribs were broken, if not shattered, blood erupted from his mouth and other wounds from the force of the impact, and breathing was labored. Despite such injuries, Lu forced himself to power leap away just as Kaguya landed in the crater. The Sanxing struck again while airborne sending energy breakers toward his adversary, but the kunoichi slashed her Devil-blade about, dispelling the responding blue waves and sending their remnants smashing into another outcropping. Undeterred, she pursued her opponent.

Teeth gritting around his blood-covered lips, Lu landed, pivoted, and charged back against the kunoichi, mimicking her previous spin attack and generating a virtual whirlpool of expanding "water" as he closed in. Kaguya was forced to leap left, launching an airborne crescent wave as she did, only for the wave to be completely dispelled as it smashed against the liquid-like energy. From that, Lu finished his spin with a larger, far more encompassing wave, which surged after the ninja as a virtual tsunami. Kaguya knew right away she could neither evade nor defend against the onslaught; hence, she launched a retaliatory crescent slash to open a tear through its center, giving her an escape path. It was close, with the wave converging down upon her much like an actual oceanic shift, but Kaguya passed through it regardless, emerging at the other side in but a split-second.

Swearing viciously under his breath, Lu moved again, Crocell positioned for an attack against her left flank. The Sanxing nearly wailed as his blade once more met Kimaris' dead on, Kaguya holding her ground despite the greater application of force. Deflecting and dodging Meng Lu's fervent and even more abundant attacks while countering at each given point, the Dragon Princess remained stalwart against the Red Phoenix's frenzied ire. The clashes of blade against blade, as well as the thundering of their respective powers, were cacophonic as ever, yet she remained unyielding.

Blue Dragon umbra *Tsushima*
Gaochang System

Kazama found himself grinning in sheer schadenfreude as he read the data on his command scope, which showed that an entire segment of the *Guangdong* had just lost power. The *Tsushima*'s tactical officer quickly took advantage of that status, firing a pair of torpedoes straight into the afflicted areas. Sure enough, the projectiles were entirely unhindered as they launched into the *Guangdong*'s hull, burying as deep as they could go before detonating and ripping much of that segment out of the dreadnought with fire and fury. Obviously, it would take more than that to sink the massive and still heavily armored warship, but the fact was damage had been done and was being done as the *Sun* added her own torpedoes and supplemental beam cannon shots into the attack. A great contrast to the prior stages of the battle, courtesy of one former shrine maiden and her songstress comrade.

Indeed, as the *Tsushima*'s guns joined in with her fellow umbra's, Kazama nodded in clear approval toward Izuna, who, despite being turned away and otherwise concentrating, smiled in responding gratitude. Again it would still take much out of them to sink the dreadnought, but now that they could actually wound and bludgeon her, Kazama knew they need only concentrate the attack. Thus as an additional number of the *Guangdong*'s internals flickered or went offline altogether from the psions' dual sabotaging, Kazama directed his ship to do precisely that. She closed in on the dreadnought starboard side and raked additional beam cannon and phalanx shots across another vulnerable area. Once more, the dreadnought's armor held against much of the barrage, but as the beams continued to plow into the hull, fire and flickering lights were soon depicted, alongside additional parts of the Red Phoenix ship being besieged. The *Sun* brought her own fire against the dreadnought's port, the effect of her attacks in composition with the sabotage causing the *Guangdong* to list slightly to starboard as her helm struggled to retain control.

Suddenly, his helmsman brought the ship into a narrow descent to evade the next round of the dreadnought's beam cannon fire. Watching the cannon blasts launch wide into open space, Kazama did well to keep in mind that, while they were wounding the monster, his ship and the *Sun* both remained damaged and weakened from before, their respective Moebius Systems still operating to mitigate said damage. That meant that he could not afford to take any unnecessary risks, much less go all out against the dreadnought.

"Missiles, fire!"

Eagerly his tactical officer responded to the command, launching a full barrage of missiles straight into the dreadnought. Once more, the massive warship's armor held against much of the collective force of the projectiles, but as the target area was now without phalanx coverage, the entirety of the swarm blasted against the Red Phoenix ship. Additional ruptures and fire soon ran across the *Guangdong*'s increasingly mangled hull, with any weapons emplacements and similar systems affected if not destroyed altogether. All the while within the hull, Kazama knew that the *Guangdong*'s damage control teams were all but gnashing themselves trying to address the increasingly mounting damage, only to again be outdone by his wife and Lorelei-*san* aboard the *Sun*. Again, they need only concentrate on the offensive…while doing well to keep away from the dreadnought's responding fire, of course.

The tactical officer added another broadside from the *Tsushima*'s main guns, furthering the damage to the enemy vessel and causing additional parts of her to darken or brighten with fire, if not simultaneously. The *Guangdong*, at least the functions that were still in operation, responded in great ire, firing cannon and phalanx shots after the Blue Dragon umbra. But the *Tsushima*'s helmsman remained at the top of the game, neatly bring the ship around her adversary's attempts to harm. In turn, Kazama watched as some of his and the *Sun*'s fighters also joined in the fun, breaking away from their dogfighting to fire their own mounted beam cannons into the enemy mothership. More death and destruction were wrought as a result.

We'll beat this thing yet, Kazama deliberately thought, such that his wife would pick up on that resolve as he lined out a set of targets through the command scope. Moments later, another group of torpedoes launched and spread about, striking each of the designated areas and eliciting further flame and ruin across that black and red hull.

Valley of the Dragons
Gaochang IV

The fury between them now was savage. As Jon and Shun clashed their blades together, the elder Flint saw his opponent's visage; it was a mask of pure rage. Smiling internally, Jon felt triumphant as Shun had been pushed thoroughly to the edge. While they continued to exchange respective slashes, deflections, and evasions, the formerly undemonstrative heir to the Red Phoenix forwent his previous self-control and focused the entirety of his will and power into destroying Jonathan Flint. Although Jon remained just as driven and resolute against the Red Phoenix warrior, he knew not to let his own rage consume him. He had made that mistake once and would not do it again. Especially as this battle was reaching the end.

Thus he watched as Shun lashed at his left arm, attempting to ensnare him in a fiery grip. Jon lunged back and countered with a narrowed black wave that forced Shun to dodge then respond quickly, launching additional fire bolts. Rather than absorb them as he had previously, Jon sidestepped right to evade then executed an elongated power slash that managed to graze his enemy's right flank. Shun hissed as he felt the absolute cold against his side, knowing that a small portion of his body had been drawn into that inescapable, annihilating void. Even so, he refused to slow down, forming a vertical fire wave that flew after Jon at supersonic speed, once more cleaving a burning wound into the ground as it moved. Jon dodged by vaulting to the top of a rocky ledge, though a part of the wave caught him in the left arm. The elder Flint grit his teeth as he felt pure agony from the resultant burn. He could still use his limb, but the damage was such that it would not be at its full proficiency for the remainder of the fight, which Jon again felt was fast drawing to an inevitable close.

Confident, Shun charged yet again and brought Haborym's carmine blade against Astaroth's obsidian. For a long moment, both Wielders held their blades immobilized against the other, their eyes projecting their complete derision and hate for the other. Abruptly, feinting a lunge to Shun's right side, Jon spun and ran full speed to his left while launching three more black waves, two horizontal and one vertical. Shun evaded the first two and then dispelled the third with a flaming wall. The ricocheting black voids consumed everything in their paths until they dissipated, with whole sections of the valley wall disappearing into the abyss.

The Red Phoenix struck back by producing another series of fireballs which he launched after the elder Flint in sequence. Without pause, Jon spun and generate a black vortex which drew in the fire. Seething with fury, Shun could only leap away again as a dark shadow formed under him, a set of black claws extending upward that would have otherwise ensnared him. Finishing his spin, Jon immediately raised his left arm, ignoring the strain, and triggered the next round of black holes to form, shooting the dark fire back at its originator. Shun sprinted, skirting and occasionally deflecting the falling flames while doing well to keep ahead of the Black Angel's onslaught.

Like Jon, Shun knew the battle was steadily moving to its close, and with all of his might and power, he, Ching Shun, the next Lord of the most powerful of the pirate clans, the undisputed pedigreed warrior to the *yáng lājī* captain he now battled, would be the victorious one standing at its end. Only then would his original mission, assuming that Lu and Shou finished their opponents as well, be completed, and the bastard pretender and her mongrel children forever vanquished, consumed by the undying, eternal flames of the Red Phoenix. Thus did his Lady decree, thus did Shun resolve to himself.

Reenergized with his heightened rage and superiority, the eldest son of the Lady of the Red Phoenix intercepted Astaroth with Haborym as Jon surged forward to slash at Shun's stomach. The resultant attacks and defenses intensified in speed and rancor as both Wielders brought about their remaining strength and powers against the other. Both dead set in ensuring that only one would leave that valley.

Chapter XXV: Fall to Ash

Red Phoenix dreadnought *Guangdong*
Gaochang System

This…this can't be happening! Qin almost vocally hollered as everything literally fell apart around him. More and more of his ship's systems were breaking down and failing, practically every minute now, while his crew both on the bridge and throughout the rest of the ship could only scramble to address the failures as they mounted. Even worse, simply identifying the origin of the breakdowns was proving to be an insurmountable task; literally, anything could have caused one system or another to stop operating, from a corrupted command code to a short-circuit to something as baseline as a mechanical part out of alignment. All the while, the *Black Sun* and her Blue Dragon compatriot took ruthless advantage, blasting the *Guangdong* with anything and everything they had.

"Helm is back online!" the helmsman reported as more beam cannon blasts from the *Sun* smashed into the *Guangdong*'s starboard side, causing her to list again. No sooner had the report been given did the helmsman struggle to realign the ship while whatever phalanx and missile emplacements still operated returned fire onto the enemy umbras. Naturally, the *Sun*, as still damaged as she remained from Penglai, veered off while knocking out the latter missiles with her own phalanx. Still, in her place, the Blue Dragon ship fired a pair of torpedoes straight into the *Guangdong*'s immense underbelly, blasting her midships. Surveying the damage report, Qin saw that he had lost another beam cannon and several more phalanx from the attack, causing him to visibly wince.

We're being taken apart, piece by piece, he realized as he scrambled to find some tactic or strategy to address the situation, yet nothing appeared viable. He knew this was all the Flints and/or the Blue Dragons' doing. Somehow and someway, they were sabotaging his ship from within, effectively forcing her into a crawl while they continued to rain hellfire upon the exterior. And even more damning, they were doing it in a way that Qin couldn't even figure out, let alone defend against! Just what kind of pact with the Devil – the actual Devil – had the Flints made for them to be able to do any of this!? And what could Qin, the captain of the most powerful ship in the Red Armada, do to stop them before they literally reduced said most powerful ship to a hopeless wreck!? It was all so maddening!

"Enemy fighter incoming! Brace!" the tactical officer shouted in warning as a Blue Dragon craft made a run at the bridge tower. Qin was just able to brace himself as the smallcraft fired her wing-mounted cannons, blasting even more holes into the bridge tower as she passed. By some miracle she managed not to hit the bridge, but the quacking and flickering lights and monitors indicated that damage had been done.

Qin cursed at the fighter as it completed its attack and dove back into the ongoing melee. Between the damages to her sensors and her phalanx, the *Guangdong* didn't even have proper point-defense anymore. The Flint and Blue Dragon fighters were flying in and out with sheer impunity. Again it was all so damn maddening!

"Report!"

"Hull integrity down to sixty-three percent!" the operations officer called out in warning, right as further beam cannon blasts struck the portside. Having since resumed her attack, the *Black Sun* charged back in, firing another barrage of torpedoes that struck the dreadnought head-on, causing her to tremor so much the bridge crew thought they felt their collective jaws rattle. All complemented by additional warnings in red across the monitors as further systems went offline.

"Now fifty-seven percent!"

Through the chaos and franticness, Qin again found himself glaring down upon the black and gold hull of his primary target as she closed in, her bow cannons firing in sequence to compliment her torpedoes. The damned hateful insect not only refused to be squashed under his bootheel but had viciously and repeatedly stung him throughout his attempts. The Red Phoenix captain felt his blood boil as she completed her next pass, moving in so close that her phalanx were able to add onto her cannons, raining further destruction upon the *Guangdong* as she traveled over her, well in front of the bridge tower. The Golden Roger that blazed over her own tower flashed across the main monitor as she passed. As he watched that sigil waved in front of him as if it had been upon an actual black flag, Qin felt his rage reach its peak.

"Focus all remaining weapons on that golden bitch!" he bellowed with as much thunder as the *Guangdong*'s main guns had been projecting. "Ignore all other enemies!"

Thus did the *Guangdong*'s main guns, phalanx, and missiles fire once again, this time all converging upon the *Sun* as she veered off. And though the umbra's defenses remained solid, with her shields and phalanx easily repelling the fire she could not fully evade, Qin knew, as his own ship turned to starboard to pursue, she would not last. One way or the other, he would see Lady Ching's wish fulfilled, even if it was the last thing he and his ship would do for their liege and clan.

Valley of the Dragons
Gaochang IV

Sliding back on her heels as she deflected the latest blue wave attack, Kaguya was forced to power leap away as additional "raindrops" fell from above. Meng Lu was on the full offensive now, launching an assortment of energy attacks as he moved against her, attempting to overwhelm the Dragon Princess before she could draw close again. Yet Kaguya remained just as evasive, flipping away the moment she landed, sweeping her own crescent slash out to dispel another blue wave before it could reach her, then running left to dodge the following rain and wave attacks. More and more of the valley was shattered and broken as each strike missed her, instead leaving their mark across the field, much to the Red Phoenix's increasing and ever frustrated rage.

"HOLD STILL, DAMN YOU!" Lu bellowed as his opponent continued to make light of his constant, rapid attacks. Not one succeeded in wounding her.

Finally, one raindrop fell and grazed Kaguya's left cheek, the force of its fall enough to draw blood from the resultant wound, but otherwise not hindering the kunoichi in the least. Such only infuriated and escalated Lu's indignant frenzy. He had to destroy her now, he knew; his injuries were sapping his energy. And he had to do it before she could close in or counterattack, given how much more powerful she had become since her Devilblade awakened. The Sanxing was not about to follow his comrade Lei Fu into oblivion.

Kaguya held similar thoughts to her opponent. She had to end this battle, and she had to do it straight away. Not simply because she could not keep going in this fight forever; somehow and some way she knew the other battles across the valley, as well as in orbit, were drawing to their close. Just as she knew, once again somehow and some way, Alex, Jon, and the rest of the Flint Pirates would be there to meet her when it was all indeed over.

Thus, as she landed in a clearing and reformed Kimaris, Kaguya tightened her grip on her mother's former Devilblade. The very devil that had served her mother faithfully, yet had turned upon her thereafter, would for the second time be used in full fury. Resolute as she dodged the next hastily launched blue wave and accompanying rainfall attack, the kunoichi gathered and focused her blade's vast and seemingly infinite energy upon it and herself. All the while silently hoping that, somewhere out in the universe, Fuma Kaede was watching her daughter as the latter took up her mother's spirit. And once again, invoked the legends that had been recited to her so long ago.

"Aozuki-ryuu..." Kaguya murmured before she went into her full-on charge, the gathered blue energy encompassing her empowered her to "streak" across the ground. All while her now fully crazed opponent could but watch in horror as she veered around each and every one of his attacks.

"Mangetsu no Mai!"

Upon that cry and all too abruptly, Kaguya seemed to "blur" out of the visible airspace. Such barely registered to Lu as she seemingly reappeared before him, rushing and sweeping Kimaris horizontally – ethereal blue energy once more trailing after – to slash the Sanxing across the mid-torso. From that, the ninja again "blurred" away, leaving but a stilled afterimage of her final pose that gradually dissolved, right as she again appeared at the Sanxing's right to repeat the attack. Seven times did Kaguya attack like this, rushing against the Sanxing from a new angle and slashing him before abruptly vanishing once more, the afterimage of her final stance lingering for just a few moments as she attacked again. All while

Lu remained helpless and vulnerable to each of the seven strikes, his body continuously struck with meteor-like force, more than enough to afflict him even if he remained physically composed throughout.

And then, moving in the direct opposite vector as her initial attack, Kaguya rushed and impaled the Sanxing straight through the back to the front to complete her eighth "phase". Sliding to a complete stop in her finishing pose, the kunoichi then slashed her Devil-blade about in an equally finishing gesture, triggering the accumulated energy that she had injected into Meng Lu's body to erupt, consuming the howling Sanxing in a field of blue light that encompassed that entire portion of the valley. For that great instant, a full moon, alight in pure, majestic blue, emerged upon the surface of Gaochang IV. Only to gradually diminish and fade back into the night but a few short moments later.

Fuma Kaguya turned around and allowed Kimaris to dissipate. Her worn but no less triumphant eyes falling upon the inactive Crocell remaining where the Red Phoenix warrior had once stood.

"Ancient Terran Proverb," Alex recited as he again gleamed into his adversary's seething eye, which was now thoroughly bloodshot, the skin around it deeply singed. "If you're going to have a roast, a chicken is *always* better than…"

Once more did Shou bellow as he flung Alex back with as much force as he could yet gather around Furfur, the lightning waves and strikes resuming just after. By now, the Sanxing barely resembled himself, even if one kept his missing left arm in mind. Much of his body was charred and burned through the younger Flint's continuous attacks, which repeatedly added injury to insult, while very few patches of intact skin and hair remained on his head. The pain was just as unbearable to Shou as he forced his body to continue moving and fighting, now lashing out with any lightning burst and bolt that he could manifest *without* giving in to the temptation of allowing possession. All the while, his opponent maintained his dance around the falling and lancing lightning, his movements as mocking as his words.

"I'LL ROAST YOU TO A CRISP!!!" Shou roared as he charged headlong, using his Devilblade's powers to enhance his speed so that he ran straight up to Alex and then power slashed, the resulting attack cleaving a relatively distant rock formation down the middle. Yet even this failed to wound Alex, who merely ducked underneath the slash, and then power leaped aside as the Red Phoenix – or red chicken in Alex's mind – spun his blade around and jammed it into the ground, causing additional lightning to generate and rise upward from all around.

"PRETENDER'S SON!!!"

I'm really getting tired of that, Alex thought with bland irritation as he maneuvered around the additional lightning blasts that illuminated much of the valley. Not that it really mattered to the younger Flint. In a few short moments, there wouldn't be anything left of this particular goon to bother him.

"This one's for you, Mom," Alex murmured as he allowed himself to solemnly recall his mother's visage. Well over three decades ago to the present day, he imagined how Morganna Flint felt as she fought her own battle against Fuma Kotaro in that very place. The fatigue and strain she endured, even as she continued to fight to the conclusion, refusing to relent to the Blue Dragon Lord's fury as she gradually strove toward her victory. Such was how Alex felt now, and it engendered much pride knowing that he was indeed following in his mother's footsteps.

Of course, Lord Fuma had been a most honorable opponent, most worthy of the Golden Queen's proffered hand. Whereas by sheer contrast, Dian Shou was far from any such thing, and as Alex again vaulted away from another vengeful blast of lightning, the younger

Flint was not about to offer the Sanxing that very same honor. Instead, he was going to finish the process that Lorelei had begun on Penglai and ensure there wasn't enough of the *zhàzijī* left to fill a petri dish.

Thus, deciding to take a page from Kaguya for his finisher, Alex focused Forneus' energy onto himself and built up toward his impending attack. Shou launched at him again, the burned remnant of a once-proud Red Phoenix warrior thoroughly intent on wounding the younger Flint in such a way that he would not get up again. That served Alex's purpose just fine, as the attack he had in mind would require him to strike his target head-on, which was so much easier to do when the little red chicky was moving straight at him rather than attempting to dodge or deflect. And so, feeling the full, unbridled force of his Devilblade upon him, Alex took his stance and waited for that precise moment of execution.

"Red Sun Style…" the younger son of Morganna Flint spoke, again following up in the image of the one woman who mattered to him most, hoping that he could emulate her character in this next step. *"Rising Inferno!"*

From that, Alex burst forward, vanishing in that split-second only to appear directly behind Shou, cleaving a blazing red slice along the Sanxing's left side, nearly dividing half of the upper torso from the lower. The Red Phoenix halted all movement. In that brief second, Shou questioned what had just happened.

Alex remained crouched right behind, Forneus outstretched to his right and ablaze; the attack was far from complete. Similar to the previous reverse lightning strikes, the ground under Shou's feet suddenly turned red with intense heat and flame, right before brilliant red light ascended upward in a luminous pillar of fire. Incinerated, the Sanxing's cries died out as the tower reached well up into the sky, seemingly into space, making it appear, for that brief moment, that dawn had reached the Valley of the Dragons once more.

Then the moment ended, and the pillar receded and diminished. Upon that scorched circle that yet retained some amount of lingering flame, Furfur, once more stone-like and dormant, sat by innocuously. Not even ashes remaining in its former Wielder's place.

"Toasty!" Alex mockingly chimed in the precise manner of a visgame he and Jon used to play as children. Superfluous perhaps, and not quite in the majestically graceful styling that Kaguya favored, but it was fitting regardless. For Alexander Flint would always be Alexander Flint. No more, no less.

Gaochang System

Her target reticle shifting red, Boss pulled down on the trigger, activating her vulcans to fire upon the Jian fighter that had fallen into her crosshairs. The Red Phoenix craft, one more among the dozen or so that she had taken out in that battle alone, almost immediately crumpled and fragmented under her barrage, the Blue Comet flying through the debris without so much as a second glance. There were still plenty of enemy fighters out there, though, between the Corsairs and the Shidens, they were fast dwindling in numbers. The Red Phoenix apparently didn't invest too much in pilot training, it seemed.

Not that the things they did invest in were any more effective, Boss noticed as she stole a glance toward the *Guangdong*. She didn't know what Lorelei and Izuna-*san* were doing specifically, but they were obviously having a field day of sorts in their tampering, such that it seemed like the "mighty" dreadnought was just barely able to function, let alone continue fighting. More and more, the *Black Sun* and the *Tsushima* took great advantage of this status, both umbras firing in complete synergy on either side of her, while Boss' pilots and their Blue Dragon comrades also continued their strafing runs, adding to the destruction. It was almost outright bullying by that point, but then, by her reasoning, the Red Phoenix bastards had it coming like they did with many other things.

Veering around another set of enemy fighters, Boss decided to make her own run against the giant and so gunned her three sub-arc engines into full drive as she launched after the dreadnought. Strangely the enemy's remaining phalanx emplacements did not realign upon her approach, while the *Guangdong*'s other weapons remained entirely on track against the *Sun*. Not that it would have mattered much, of course, given how much of a hobby it was for Boss to weave in and out of a capital ship's anti-air fire zone, but it was a rather strange feeling to mount her attack run without so much as a missile being shot after her. Even so, she closed in regardless and triggered her beam cannons, blasting a long, fiery line into the *Guangdong*'s starboard side. Several more weapons emplacements and other equipment went up flames as she passed and then angled straight toward the bridge tower.

Glaring deeply at the edifice and imagining the crew within bracing as she approached, the ace wasted little time, firing another line into the structure. As immense as her target was, however, Boss kept her fire focused onto a particular point, where she at least suspected the most damage would occur. Whatever she managed to accomplish through that tactic, it at least blacked out the exterior lighting, not to mention elicited more flames. She passed by then placed another couple shots into the stern, taking out the beam cannon turrets placed there in the process, before being forced back into contention with the fightercraft as two more Jians and a Qiang closed in on her. Thus Boss moved off and back into the dogfight, leaving the *Guangdong* to wantonly shudder behind her.

Red Phoenix dreadnought *Guangdong* Gaochang System

It was over, Qin understood as he dazedly felt the blood trickle down his forehead, the world around him blurry and on fire. Through his fading comprehension, he just managed to depict his bridge in near-complete ruin, with the main monitor and control consoles flickering to stay active. Agonizing cries and groans came from those crewmen that had managed to survive the last attack, many more laying dead at their stations. All the while, additional alerts and warnings continued to sound in the background as the damage, both within and without, mounted. Indeed, as the captain managed to keep himself from blacking out, he knew that he and his ship were done. Neither one of them would leave Gaochang, at least on the mortal plane.

And yet, through his haze, Qin's eyes still managed to lock upon the flickering image of that hateful *Sun*, which was again attacking at the *Guangdong*'s starboard while the Blue Dragon ship attacked from port. As hurt and lightheaded as he was, the Red Phoenix captain still felt the flames of ire within toward that insipient umbra and her disdainful crew.

How dare they do this to him, to his ship. How dare they go against the natural order in the name of a false queen. How dare they disgrace his clan, the true, rightful dynasty, as opposed to their own falsehood! How dare they…!

"Ni tama de tianxia suoyou de ren dou gaisi…!" Qin snarled as he willed himself to move, forcing down his pain and weariness as he made his way toward the helm. Shifting aside the bloodied and burned corpse of his former helmsman, Qin took his seat and, using what inner faculties remained to him, managed to put the dread-nought onto a pursuit course after the *Sun*. His ship was sluggish in her turn, far more than usual, and there wasn't enough power to the arc engine to make her move fast, much less into full-on ramming speed. Despite that, Qin still had one tactic to employ as the *Sun* once again centered upon his flickering main monitor, her beam cannons still firing as the *Guangdong* completed her turn. Qin need only get his ship close enough to her for it to take effect.

With that in mind, Qin inputted his captain override into the helm, causing a projected keypad to emerge. After entering the next code sequence, the timer soon appeared upon the main monitor. The red, boldened letters therein counting down as the *Guangdong* drove onward against her much-hated foe.

Valley of the Dragons
Gaochang IV

Espousing an uncharacteristic battle cry as he wrought his latest blaze, Shun pressed the attack, forcing Jon to recede somewhat to evade the sweeping flames. However, the elder Flint was not about to move into the defensive again and so charged, bringing Astaroth up and against its counterpart in another great collision, the whole of the valley seemingly quaking from the impact as well as the contesting wills of the two Wielders. Once more, both glared hatefully, spitefully into the other's eye, right before breaking the deadlock and moving into full melee, slashing, parrying, and maneuvering with even greater speed and intensity than they had previously. Strain and exhaustion welling upon both, the scions of the Gold Dragon and the Red Phoenix Clans attacked and defended in full force regardless, knowing that they were fast approaching the much awaited, much wanted finish. A finish that would, at last, see one standing above the other.

Without pause, Jon reached out with his left hand once more, a black vortex forming upon his palm and drawing upon Shun via gravitational force. Not about to let his opponent gain a physical hold over him, Shun leaped back, temporarily diminished Haborym, and generated two fiery javelins in either hand, which he threw as one after his adversary. Not wanting to risk attempting to draw them in, lest they turn out to be too powerful to contain, Jon vaulted back again, allowing the two enflamed polearms to smash into the ground. Sure enough, the resultant dual explosions were great, their combined shockwave alone knocking the air out of Jon as he landed on the edge of a newly formed crater.

Shun moved upon him again. A timely black hole formed at Jon's feet, allowing him to "fall" away from Shun's forward strike, which would have caught him on the left side, forcing Shun to reverse direction to prevent his falling into the deep pit.

Another black hole soon forming overhead, Jon completed his "fall" in reverse, descending upon Shun's position with Astaroth set to impale, only for the Red Phoenix to power leap to his right. Another dark fire wave quickly followed; Jon canceled it out with a corresponding black slash, from which the elder Flint pressed forward and brought Astaroth against the Red Phoenix scion once again. This time Shun chose not to reengage in close quarters, instead spawning a line of fiery cyclones, three of them in total that twisted about in near unpredictable patterns. Jon evaded them all the same, maneuvering around the first two and then launching a black wave into the third, drawing the flames into the void as he charged onward. Shun again power leaped upward, right as another black hole and burst of dark flame emerged where he had been standing, immediately altering his vector and barely escaping as an equally lethal black hole opened above him with bolts of fire raining down. Unrelenting, Jon launched after him, at last allowing for another clash of obsidian and carmine.

As had been throughout their fight, no words or banter were exchanged between the two fighters. There was no need, nor capability for such, as both were entirely focused on the other's destruction. Even so, as Jon glared down upon his adversary, he knew that in contrast to his mother's fight so long ago, there would be no quarter, no offering of mercy from either warrior. There would only be the totality of death.

The battle continuing in midflight, Shun again executed another power slash, hoping to inflame his opponent; Jon slipped past the flames and knocked away the strike with his own blade. The pair landed on the upper ledge of the valley, both charging against the other the exact moment their feet touched the ground. Further clashes of darkness and fire reflected on the valley wall as the two warriors ignored their respective strain and brought forth the final remainders of their wills and energies against the opposite. One way or another, the victor between them, both individually and the clans they represented, would be decided.

Flint Pirates umbra *Black Sun*
Gaochang System

"Son of a bitch!" Davis exclaimed as he watched the *Guangdong* loom closer and closer toward his ship's position, the reading of her arc reactor buildup just as much a fixture on the main monitor. Even before Barbarossa could order him to do so, the helmsman threw the *Sun* into a quick evasive dive to port, all the while the tactical operator fired every weapon emplacement available at the charging dreadnought. Yet as fast as the *Sun* was, Davis had a sinking feeling she was not going to make it clear, any more than her weapons would obliterate the *Guangdong* entirely before her self-destruction was complete. Already he felt his lifelong terror begin to well up at the prospect, such that he painfully focused on his station and his maneuvering to keep it at bay.

Indeed, Barbarossa thought but dared not say aloud as he watched the *Guangdong* move in, even charging through a torpedo barrage from the *Tsushima* to reach them. He fired another salvo of six torpedoes straight into the dreadnought's bow, the combined explosions ripping much of her forward hull away, yet failing to stop or so much as dissuade the dreadnought's charge. This could very well be it, Barbarossa acknowledged, unless the *Sun*'s shields – what little remained of them now – could somehow hold…

And then, suddenly, the reading on the *Guangdong*'s reactor buildup abruptly ceased, the levels dropping instantly. Before anyone on the bridge could so much as blink in their collective shock, they all witnessed the dreadnought suddenly falter in its course, going into a drift as newer, more powerful explosions rippled across her hull. For his part, Davis wasn't so distracted by the action that he failed to turn the *Sun* about and speed away lest they get caught regardless, though even he didn't understand what was happening. Whatever it was, fire quickly erupted across the entirety of the *Guangdong*, effectively consuming the stricken dreadnought from bow to stern, right before an all-encompassing explosion erupted, but not to such an extent as to take the *Sun* with her.

"A funny thing about arc engines," Lorelei suddenly commented, drawing all eyes to her in astonishment. Though clearly exhausted, the psion grinned victoriously regardless. "Even in emergency shut-down, all that accumulated energy has to go somewhere."

It was only then that Barbarossa blinked and let out a roaring laugh as he and the rest of the smiling bridge crew realized the source of their salvation. Upon the arc reactor's abrupt termination and forced power drain, the two psions had rerouted the energy within, trans-mitting it throughout the ship, generating a massive, unsustainable buildup throughout the remaining equipment. When added onto the dreadnought's diminished hull integrity, the *Guangdong*'s fate had been effectively sealed. Destroyed by two extraordinary women of extraordinary power working as one.

"The Red Phoenix commander is signaling," Gran reported. "He and the remaining fighters are standing down."

"Heh," Barbarossa laughed a little bit more, this time in bitter irony. Apparently, this would not be the fight to the death that he had origi-nally suspected. "Respond that their surrender is accepted, and order our fighters to disengage as well."

Valley of the Dragons
Gaochang IV

The violence now insurmountable and the darkness and fire ever-constant between them, the two pirate heirs fought relentlessly,

their battle now a series of metallic clangs and thunderous erup-
tions. The sheer fighting and even the wounds inflicted were barely
comprehended and registered, while no further elaborate evasion
or movement attempts were made. They stayed in that part of the
valley now, their blades and corresponding powers slashing and
flickering between them as they concentrated on the attack. Their
intent to end the other narrowed to a piercing focal point, such that
nothing else could reach their conscious.

Yet, as fast as they were undoubtedly moving, it felt all too
agonizingly slow for Jon, who forced his exhausted, drained body
to keep fighting to overpower his opponent. Through his own rage
and will to destroy Shun, the elder Flint kept himself grounded,
refusing to give in to the same madness that now clearly consumed
Ching Shun, who had to be but a few steps away from possession.
A strange calm in an otherwise turbulent storm enveloped Jonathan; he remained well within it and acted accordingly, ensuring
that his attacks, as driven by fury as they were skill, stayed
focused and well executed. His afflictions all but entirely ignored
as he repeatedly brought Astaroth against Haborym, darkness
against fire.

It was through this calm, this focus, that Jon, at last, found his
opening. Though it lasted but an instant, such that the pirate
captain would never recall it again, it was just enough for him to
act. As Shun executed another flame-infused slash to behead, Jon
maneuvered Astaroth about to deflect the blade and knock it aside,
the force and power behind the intended attack actually causing
Haborym to miss widely. It would have otherwise taken an equal
instant for Shun to realign his blade and continue onward, but Jon
was faster and again more focused, twisting Astaroth about and
seizing upon his enemy's sudden vulnerability.

Before either of them could realize it, Astaroth plunged deep into
Shun's torso, the obsidian blade piercing out the Red Phoenix's back.

Gasping openly at the sudden influx of pain, as well as gagging on the blood that spurted through his constrained lips, Shun managed to swing Haborym in a final downward strike, which would have otherwise cleaved his opponent through the head. However, Jon's left hand easily reached out and grasped the glowing crimson blade, the darkness around the Flint captain's appendage ensuring that the fire did not reach the flesh therein. The pair remained standing in their lingering yet increasingly futile contest, Shun struggling to wound his enemy one final time, only for Jon to hold him at bay. All as blood fell from the Red Phoenix's mouth and torso to the soil below, the red staining deeply against the desolate brown.

"Pretender's...son...!" Shun hissed with as much hatred, as much loathing as he could project in that instance, all the while refusing to accept his fate, his defeat to the last. Yet the more he struggled against Jonathan Flint, the more his strength drained away with his blood, his body turning cold and feeble around him. It took all his remaining energy to keep Haborym manifested and against his enemy's left hand, still attempting to reach the elder Flint's body. Jon could all but feel the sheer animus transmitted through the physical contact, his opponent set toward remaining vengeful and abhorring to the end.

And to the end Jon would bring him, with his own hatred – once again the memory of Atalanta and the innocents therein playing through his mind – projected. The very last visage Ching Shun would see.

"True gold fears not the fire," Jon coldly recited the most ancient proverb, right before building up and focusing his Devilblade's power.

Within that epicenter did the darkness emerge and expand, far more vivid and seemingly hungrier than the night around it, such that it seemed an entire quarter of Gaochang IV became enraptured within the void. It swirled, pulsed, and sundered as it grew, drawing all within its maw until even the light of the distant stars themselves were seemingly blanked out with only an ethereal, shriek-like howl emerging from the void as it augmented, devouring the very air into its depths.

And then, not long after reaching its apparent terminus, the darkness receded and faded back, allowing light to enter into that section of the valley once again. A light that shone well upon Jonathan Flint as he stood there, Astaroth vanishing as his single eye stared down at the inactive, stone-formed Haborym. A light that well preceded the dawn that was to come.

Chapter XXVI: Aut Vincere Aut Mori

Siyue Palace
Zhengzhou, Penglai

It was with a minor sense of irony, and a major sense of victoriousness, that Jon found himself marching through the grounds of an *alternate* residence of the Red Phoenix rulership. Following his two Palace Guard escorts, the pirate captain eventually entered the main citadel and moved down the center hall. All throughout, Jon could feel the ire and disdain that the guards and the other personnel projected toward him, but this had no bearing on his mood. The war, however it would be remembered from then on, was over, and the Flint Pirates had been triumphant. Nothing the Red Phoenix could do to him or even try to do to him now would change that.

Thus the eldest son of Morganna Flint came to a set of ornate red, black, and gold-lined doors, which together depicted a great *fenghuang* taking flight before the multitudes and select edifices. Upon one of the flanking guardsmen entering the appropriate keycode to the side, the doors opened inward, allowing Jon to proceed with his escort.

Surveying the area, the pirate captain beheld the magnificent throne room of the Red Phoenix, which was even more majestic, if somewhat overly ornate, than the other parts of the palace he had traveled through. Adorned in lavish red and gold while being furnished with magnificent tapestries and imagery, the chamber was the ideal seat for any aspiring Red Phoenix Lord that would sit upon the Vermillion Throne. However, Jon was far less impressed with the Lady that sat there now, scowling down upon him as he came forward.

For a long moment, Jon stared up at the baneful Lady Ching, who said not a word as she glared down upon him in hatred and condemnation. Jon could easily detect the weariness and unwilling defeat upon her expression, the reluctance to admit that her champion, and by proxy her clan, had been beaten. Beaten by the children of the one she and those around her had labeled a pretender, a false queen. Oh, how Jon would have paid anything to savor that moment for a while, but given the tension that permeated throughout the setting, he chose instead to move things along.

"Lady of the Red Phoenix Clan," Jon began with great formality, addressing Ching's title if not Ching herself. "I come before you as he who stands triumphant over adversity."

With that, Jon kneeled down and swept his right hand, the four inert Devilblades lined out in front of him. "Before you are the Devilblades Furfur, Crocell, Amdusias and Haborym," even without looking up, Jon knew Lady Ching had just flinched at that last one. "Their Wielders, the most elite warriors of your clan, vanquished, and the blades themselves since returned to dormancy."

With that, Jon swept his hand back, the four blades vanished once again. "Thusly do I declare victory against the Red Phoenix Clan and any and all who would wear its colors or bear its mark," he stated with utmost affirmation as he stood. "And through such victory, I state the following terms."

Lady Ching clenched her teeth with visible ire, while for a brief moment, energy began to gather around her. Before anything could come about, however, the energy quickly diminished, and Jon went further regardless.

"Henceforth, you will abandon your wanton and unprovoked aggression against we who bear the mark and lineage of Morganna Flint," Jon declared, feeling the tension quicken that much more, though he felt it diminish somewhat as he continued. "No tribute will be given nor taken, nor will any form of property or treasure from the Red Phoenix be claimed. Our prize shall be the cessation of this blood feud and our proceeding as we have from here on."

Despite that, Lady Ching visibly seethed. If anything, she was more infuriated now toward the pretender's son. For she knew that the former terms, the refusal to take any prize, was not designed for her benefit, but rather the Red Phoenix's beyond her. For the upstart to cling to his deranged notion that he possessed any form of honor…

"Following that, you will go before the other Lords and give your consent to their allowing us to go our way," Jon stated additionally. It was likely superfluous at that point, as it was a sure bet Lord Pargo and Lady Levasseur had since taken his side over this entire conflict, but it didn't hurt to cover his bases. "Just as you will recognize the Flint Pirates, the rightful heirs to the Gold Dragon Clan, as *de facto* beneficiaries to the Treaty of Libertalia."

That alone caused Ching to rise up from her throne, her eyes wide with furious indignation toward what she saw as the upstart's sheer audacity. Even the outlying palace guardsmen, as well as the Hongwu agents in the less visible corners of the throne room, visibly quelled toward their Lady's ire.

"Unless warranted or welcomed, the Clans will leave the Flint Pirates to their own affairs," Jon once again proclaimed without any allowance for debate. "We will continue on into the galaxy, upon whatever course that the one true God, and He alone, has set for us."

"You ingrate!" Ching bellowed, deliberately using the common

language instead of her clan's native tongue. All so that the bastard son could understand the depths of her rage. Such was emphasized again as energy swelled around her, and this time did not diminish so quickly.

Even so, Jon remained undeterred. "These terms are non-negotiable, and as the one in defeat, you are obligated to adhere to them," the elder Flint asserted in a more subdued warning, which, given its levelness and his standing, carried far more weight compared to Ching's barely controlled fury. "Any breach will result in the continuance of hostilities between our two parties, as well as probable incursions from the Blue Dragon, White Tiger, and Black Tortoise."

Though she still seethed, Lady Ching managed to rein herself in enough to sit back onto her throne, curtly nodding toward the elder Flint in understanding. Like it or not, she had lost. Damning as it was, she was in no position to strike down the bastard whelp, verbally or physically, much less renew the tensions between the Red Phoenix and its three counterparts. Just as she also knew Lord Pargo and Lady Levasseur were more likely to stand alongside Lord Fuma this time around.

"With such given and established between us, my business is hereby concluded," Jon nodded, bowing formally as he would in the Blue Dragon, once again toward the Lordship of the Red Phoenix and not so much the one who held that title now. "Good fortune to your clan."

With that, Jon turned around and moved to follow the guards out of the palace. Upon Lady Ching slamming her fist upon the arm of her throne, however, the elder Flint stopped in his tracks.

"Don't think any of this is over, pretender's son!" Lady Ching bellowed in continuance of her indignation and fury. "You may have won this war, but I assure you, the Red Phoenix will rise from its ashes yet!"

Jon did well not to wince at that exclamation but otherwise allowed Ching to continue.

"It does not matter where your God leads you or where you may hide!" Ching roared outright now. "In the end, I will cleanse this very galaxy of your filthy name and all that it…"

338

"Were you truly so afraid of her?"

Like a blade against cloth, the question effectively slashed through the air and caused Ching to falter in her words. Only then did Jon turn around to face her, this time with a different brand of understanding in his eye.

"Did you truly fear my mother so much?"

Contrasted to her previous diatribe, Ching could not find the words to respond. She could only look taken back while visibly attempting to rein in her emotions as Jon faced her dead on. Once more, with the knowledge and understanding that his words hit home.

In the face of her uncertainty, Jon allowed himself to laugh, coldly and lightly. "Come now, it's so obvious. This entire conflict, your whole vendetta, was based around *fear*," he said, taking note of the guards suddenly drawing close to him, their hands tightening around their weapons. "You feared Morganna Flint, and now you fear we who claim her legacy. The Gold Dragon reborn..."

"Baí pí zhū!" one of the guards called out as they both raised their weapons, only to stop short upon the sudden emanation of darkness from Jon. Once he saw the guards lower their weapons and take several steps back – perhaps a little bit more than they needed to for ceremony – Jon allowed Astaroth's power to recede.

"How you feel toward my mother, my family, or myself is of no importance whatsoever," Jon continued, this time in a final warning. "All that matters is that you adhere to the terms presented and stay out of our way from here on."

Unmoving, Jon glared deeply into Lady Ching's eyes, forcing her due to pride to maintain eye contact. Indeed, now that he looked into Ching's eyes, he saw much fear within them. Fear toward a woman that had been better than her in life, such that her name and deeds easily eclipsed Ching's, even in death. Fear toward one who could not be so easily comprehended and so was considered a viable threat. Fear toward a woman of valor, who had built her kingdom and dynasty in but a single generation, with so many other accomplishments therein.

Fear toward *true* greatness, something that Ching and her ilk could never emulate, much less contest. For once again, true gold need not fear the fire, even that which may consume a phoenix.

"Comply with the terms. Otherwise, you will be reduced to ash once again," Jon stated with all the cold derision that he could bring forth. "And this time, you will not rise."

Turning, Jon, quickly joined by his escorts, proceeded past the double doors and exited the Vermillion throne room; the double doors closed audibly. Within seconds, Lady Ching's outcry thundered through the palace. The pirate captain allowed himself to smirk at last.

Black Pirates umbra *Black Sun*
Penglai System

With the local star ahead of them, peering up and over the horizon of Penglai, the *Black Sun* and the *Tsushima* moved out of orbit and gradually made their way from the Red Phoenix capital world. A symbolic scene for the crews of either umbra, for such was indeed the dawn that they had all awaited. A dawn that marked the very end of the war that had been so dreaded and yet had ended in belated victory. A dawn that marked the beginning of a new chapter for either ship and crew; for the *Sun*'s next voyage, as well as the *Tsushima*'s. A dawn that marked the endless possibilities of the coming day.

"And so it is here that we part ways," Jon spoke to Kazama, who sat upon his own bridge with Izuna by his side. "On behalf of the Flint Pirates, you, your crew, and your clan have our thanks, Captain Fuma."

"It was our honor, Captain Flint," Kazama nodded to his opposite number, which he saw as indeed one step closer to regaining his clan and that which was left by the Golden Queen. "On behalf of the Blue Dragon and its Lord, we wish you and your own ship and crew well."

Jon nodded in gratitude. "Be sure to forward my thanks and regards to your father."

"I will do just that," Kazama promised. His eyes then turned toward his sister, who now stood beside Alex's station. *"Ja ne, imouto-chan."*

"Ja ne, oniisama," Kaguya responded back with a nod and then a bow. One of honor due as opposed to formality.

Nodding in acceptance, Kazama then looked toward Alex. "Keep taking care of her," he spoke simply yet in clear acknowledgment.

His hand enfolded with Kaguya's, Alex smiled. "I will."

More unnoticed by the Dragon Prince's side, Izuna also projected her own farewell to her counterpart. *Safe journeys to you as well, Lorelei*-san, the Blue Dragon psion spoke telepathically. *And may we indeed meet once more.*

We will Izuna-san, *one way or another,* Lorelei also assured, projecting belief along with her words. *Take care until then.*

The farewells given and received, the vidwindow then disengaged. The *Tsushima* veered away and moved into the distance, entering arc thereafter.

Settling back in his chair, Jon decided it was time for them to get underway as well. Though their destination was far less ideal than Atalanta had been, it remained out there all the same, and the *Sun* would reach it. And it wasn't like the Outer Rim did not contain its own set of thrills and ventures, the good as well as the bad.

"Helm, take us about," Jon commanded as he and the rest of the bridge crew prepared themselves. Whatever would come would come. "Arc Five."

With that, the *Sun* entered arcspace, leaving Penglai, and the Red Phoenix Clan, well within her wake.

Three hours had passed since the departure from Penglai, and Kaguya once again found herself before the stars, albeit in the *Sun*'s observation deck, studying Kimaris. This was the first time she had done so since the conflict with the Red Phoenix ended. She thought back to the time before she had fully awakened her Devilblade and the corresponding escalation in the battles she had been facing. Kraft, the Baranovs, and now Ching Shun and the Sanxing, each form of opposition was arguably direr and more powerful than the last, such that Kaguya had feared that she would be unable to fight. She was skilled, even against those of supernatural power, but without her own power to match theirs, she feared she would become impotent.

Well, Kaguya thought as she stared down at her fully awakened blade, she had that power now, *her* power. She had hated it, at least in the beginning, for what it had done to her mother before her, but in the end, it remained her sword and her power regardless. And through it, she had not only saved the man who mattered most to her, but she had fought beside him and their elder against an unworthy yet dangerous foe. She could not discount such a thing any more than she could discount another event that had occurred so long ago. One that she had forgotten with the passage of time, at least until…

"Shame there's no moon this time," Alex sighed as he came up behind her, sliding his arms around her waist. As focused as she had been on her Devilblade, Kaguya had still been otherwise aware of the entry, and especially the *who* that had interrupted her personal reflections. She was a ninja, after all.

"It really is a beautiful blade."

"Yes," Kaguya concurred, also wishing there was a moon before them then. Kimaris seemed to gleam within such light.

Alex was quick to notice how Kaguya now looked upon her blade. Far from her previous apprehension, she seemed to marvel at its strange majesty, its beauty.

"Have you come to terms with it?"

"More or less," she admitted, allowing the blade to vanish once more as she lowered her arm. "A part of me still wants to hate it for what it did to my mother, how it took her away from Kazama and me, but..."

She frowned as she recalled the event in question. "Kimaris saved my life once," she spoke, causing Alex to glance down in interest. "Not long after I had taken guardianship of it, in fact."

"Oh?" Alex questioned, clearly intrigued.

The kunoichi nodded. "On one particular mission, I had ended up detected and surrounded," she explained. "Already wounded and exhausted of weapons and strength, it was all I could do to go down fighting."

Leaning back against Alex, she sniffed slightly as she remembered more and more details. "I didn't even have it on my person at the time, yet it reached out to me all the same," she continued, knowing Alex would understand what she meant. "But instead of tempting me with its power, it questioned me and my refusal to awaken it, even to survive."

She smiled somewhat. "Even in the face of death, I refused to give in to it, the blade that had turned against its previous master. And my response was heartily conveyed."

Her smile emboldened a little more as she elaborated. "Yet instead of leaving me to that death," Kaguya said, now recalling the event in full fruition. "It had seemingly chosen to honor my resolve."

Alex nodded, indeed understanding. "So that's why," he murmured softly, having wondered up to now why Kimaris had been in the form of a ninjato rather than as a fully inactive stone. "It partially awakened itself."

"As well as granted me the barest fraction of its power," Kaguya admitted, flickering a kunai into her hand to emphasize. That also explained a certain mystery Alex, as well as Jon and others, had long wondered about. "Through that interference, I not only survived but completed my mission."

She then flicked the kunai back from whence it came. "Strange, isn't it? The same sword that betrayed and led Fuma Kaede to her death came to save her daughter from a similar end."

"Not so strange," Alex stated, much to Kaguya's internal surprise. "As blasphemous as this may sound, Devilblades work in their own mysterious ways."

He turned Kaguya in his arms and then smiled as he looked into her eyes, that same warm, radiant smile that had long enamored Kaguya.

"And even then," Alex continued as he reached to take her face in his hands. "I'm glad it did what it did, no matter its aims."

Smiling in turn, Kaguya closed her eyes in comfort while slowly moving her head to kiss Alex's palm. Then she stepped forward and wrapped her arms around his waist.

"We still have a long way to go," Alex murmured as he pulled her close. "And chances are the battles we fight will escalate even further."

"Yes," Kaguya agreed. Yet, as loved as she felt now, such a possibility did not bother her so much.

"But even so," Alex spoke, kissing her head. "We shall remain one against all of it, Kaguya."

He then smiled that much more as he leaned down, kissing her on the cheek before whispering. *"Tsuneni."*

"Hai," she whispered in return, feeling very much like her namesake. The princess of the moon, enraptured by the light of the sun. *"Tsuneni."* She rose onto her toes and kissed him, deeply, slowly, and with as much love as she could impart.

Thus, they remained there, with the stars, moving onward toward whatever lay ahead. Whatever it was...they would face it together.

Epilogue: Premonitions

Siyue Palace
Zhengzhou, Penglai

Slowly the sun of Penglai rose over the distant horizon, marking the beginning of a new day for the planet's inhabitants. A truly magnificent sunrise, Lady Ching found herself marveling, something she had not bothered to observe in a long, long time. Yet as much as she had been unable to sleep in the last twelve hours – conveniently since that unwanted meeting with Jonathan Flint – she now took the opportunity, no matter how impromptu, to watch as the darkness of night receded toward the light of day. A most poetic transition, as it emphasized the same for herself and the Red Phoenix.

New beginnings were all that she could appreciate now, in the face of her complete, undeniable defeat. Her eldest and intended heir dead, her forces laid to waste, and her clan humiliated; it had indeed been her total defeat. And as much as she had blustered, to her disgrace in hindsight, that she would see the Flints all dead, she knew that she could neither pursue nor persecute them any further without provoking the other clans and their lords. Thus, Ching Shih was now well within the league of Raphael Drake and so many others, overcome and humbled by the children of that insipient Golden Queen. Who even now, nearly two decades since her demise, continued to haunt the Lady of the Red Phoenix, especially in her sleep.

As worn and weary as she was, however, the Lady of the Red Phoenix remained aware of her surroundings. As such, upon her detection of the newcomer – one of the very last people she wanted to see now – she visibly frowned in derision.

"I believe I said I wanted to remain alone."

"You did," the newcomer acknowledged as he moved to stand by her, the light of the coming day shining upon him much differently than it did his liege. "And I have elected to ignore that command."

Ching sniffed in contempt but otherwise said nothing. Like it or not, she relied too much on Lao Tzu to spurn him, even in moments such as these.

"I suppose you're here to laugh at me?"

Lao Tzu merely smiled and shook his head. "I believe you have suffered enough laughter, real or imaginary," he responded. "Instead, I will merely remind you of a certain warning I made to you, in this very place not too long ago…"

"Yes, yes," Ching reneged from physically waving her chief advisor off. "You told me that pursuing the Flints would not end well for the Red Phoenix or me. That we would suffer a grave defeat."

"One that you would not recover from," Lao Tzu confirmed. "Indeed, my Lady, this loss is truly insurmountable."

Ching somehow managed not to gnash her teeth, as though she had to be reminded of Shun's death. Granted, she still had other children to eventually take her place on the throne, but she could not deny that Shun had been the most capable of all of them. And almost as dire, she had lost four of her clan's most powerful weapons, as well as its elite warrior cadre.

"For what it's worth, I had given a similar warning to Shun before events had taken place," Lao Tzu went on, flashing that enigmatic smile that Ching had long detested. She wondered if he did that deliberately to irritate her further. "It seems, however, that my warnings are even less adhered to by this next generation."

Ching once more sniffed in contention. Perhaps not outright laughter, but she knew when her face was being rubbed in the defeat.

"Just what is it about them?" she found herself questioning. "What is so special about them to have God, Fate, the very Galaxy itself work so diligently on their behalf?"

Sagely did Lao Tzu shake his head again. "I'm afraid such wisdom and knowledge eludes even me," he admitted. "All I can say is that they have their own role to play in events to come. A role that only they, as well as *she*, may fulfill."

Only then did Ching turn ever so slightly to regard her advisor, the very man that had served innumerable Red Phoenix Lords well into the present. As the sun rose more and more, she indeed saw that its light shone upon him far differently than her. As though it took on an ethereal quality upon reaching his pale white skin and amethyst eyes.

"Be most prepared, my Lady," Lao Tzu proclaimed as he gazed out over the ever-rising sun. "For in this new day and those further beyond, much is still yet to come, to reach fruition."

Once more did he smile enigmatically. Only this time, Ching could not help but detect a trace of apprehension behind that smile.

"And when such things indeed come to pass," Lao Tzu went on regardless. "I fear this galaxy, all that we know and hold dear, will be changed. Forever."

www.ingramcontent.com/pod-product-compliance
Lightning Source LLC
Chambersburg PA
CBHW031102030726
47496CB00002BA/348